Maeven:
Book 2
Dragon Agent

by
Margaret Gregory

Cover designed by msgdragon
Cover Image Credits: © Can Stock Photo Inc. / fmarsicano
Cover Image Credits: © Can Stock Photo Inc. / amelislam

TYMOREAN TRUST SERIES:
Book 1 - Power Rising
Book 2 - Great Ones
Book 3 - The Return to Earth
Book 4 – Earth Mission
Book 5 – Alien Contact
Book 6 - Invasion

ATAPI SORCERESS SERIES:
Prequel – Korvu: The Beginning
Book 1- The Wild One
Book 2 – Atapi Sorceress

Maeven - Dragon Thief

THE THIRD GENERATION SERIES:
Book 1 - Wanda: From Bad to Worse
Book 2 - Wanda: Choosing Crime
Wanda – Early Days (anthology) Book 1 and 2
Book 3 – Wanda: Risking Life to Live
Book 4 – Erin: The Forcing of Wisdom
Book 5 – Wanda: A New Life Part 1 – Hidden Secrets
Book 6 – Wanda: A New Life Part 2 – First Mission
Book 7 – Wanda: Full Circle
Book 8 and 9 – Erin: The Call
Book 10 - Royal Favour
Book 11 - The Serpent's Shadow

For permission requests, address the request to the author c/o
Permissions,
TAT Indie Publishing
PO Box 2728
Rowville, Victoria, 3178
www.tatindiepublishing.com.au

Table of Contents:

CHAPTER 1

Eight years before the birth of the new dragon mage .

"There! That's the man!"

Gamman Mogray looked up and saw the mayor and a well-dressed man looking his way. Another man, a local, was pointing at him. Around his own neck, his bone talisman was hot enough to burn his skin. Carefully replacing his chisel and hammer into his apron pouch, he put the log he was carving down and turned as if going for a drink.

"Get him!"

Gamman abruptly sped up to a run, and ducked between two of the stone and wood houses. He had no idea why they were chasing him, but he never ignored the danger warning of his talisman. He gripped it now and chanted an incantation as he ran for the bridge across the river. He hoped they would not think he'd go that way or he might get half way across and find nothing under his feet. Maybe he'd make it before they fetched the wizard. Just in case, he muttered the words of a binding spell and set it on the bridge. He felt a jolt as it settled – he had just been in time.

As he reached the far side, a ball of brilliant light lit up the area. It hovered above him. Now they knew where he was and being invisible was only slightly helpful. He recalled the magic from the binding spell and used the returning magical energy to attract the roots of trees to come to the surface behind him.

He was aware of, but too panicked to gloat, that the bridge had indeed vanished, ditching several of his pursuers. The tree roots were working to trip more. However, once within the trees, he had to slow, and the light was betraying his position. He touched the talisman again and sent a warning – hoping his wife would sense something was very wrong. It wasn't the first time they had been forced to flee, and once again it was obvious they couldn't stay. He did regret not being able to collect the payment for the four stools he had been commissioned to make.

Gamman moved back out of the trees. He could run faster along the clearer river bank and he remembered the lagoon he passed coming to and from the town. Going there was a risk, because there was another river crossing there, but if he could dive under the water, the ball of light would follow and be quenched. They would still know which way he had gone, but without the magical tell-tale, he could cut away from the river and get to his camp.

Shayla Mogray felt a sudden surge of alarm and grabbed the neck of her herb bag and ran back to the wagon. Her son, Deltian, might only have been four years old but he shared her alarm and followed. His dog at his heels.

Once there, Shayla told her son, "Pack a change of clothes and a blanket." She went to do the same for herself and her husband, then gathered the rest of her herbs and a sack of food. There wasn't much of that and wouldn't be if Gamman had not been paid.

The glow in the sky, seeming to be coming their way, caused her to drag the packs and her son to the cover of a downed tree. Then she ran to fetch their wagon beasts from the clearing where they were staked to graze. She was leading them back when Gamman arrived, soaking wet and puffing hard.

"We have to leave," he managed to say.

"I've packed a few things. Do you have your tools?"

"Yes. Get up on Old Chaser with Deltian. I'll ride Brownie. You will have to manage the small packs. I'll take the two big ones. Get going, back along the way we came here. I'll catch up."

Moving Brownie close to their living wagon, Gamman touched its wooden sides and chanted a spell to hide it. Then he urged the beast to trot after its yokemate. His mind was still full of the need to flee, but he had no idea why. Images of the well-dressed man kept intruding. His clothing had been much better than what the mayor was wearing. With a shock, he realised that the man must have been one of the King's high lords. Why had the man wanted him?

Gamman caught up to his wife, and when she turned to glance his way, he saw her expressionless face.

"What did you do?" she called back over her shoulder.

He moved his horse closer to hers. "Nothing that I know of."

Now she looked at him, trying read his soul.

"Truly, I wasn't using magic. I don't need it to carve. Someone pointed me out to some King's lord and a gang of townsfolk began to chase me."

"There must have been a reason. Perhaps because you ran off? He might have wanted to give you a commission."

Gamman thought back over the four weeks he had been going into that town. He'd worked during the day, socialised a bit as he usually did – citing his skills and seeking commissions. The only odd thing was that bridge…

"You know that bridge I told you about. How it had an interesting design, but I didn't think it would hold any weight?"

"You fixed it up, you said."

"I know. But what if the wizard made it like that on purpose?"

"Why?"

"I don't know. But I didn't do anything that time it fell down. It had to have been magicked."

Shayla recalled the incident. She had been in town herself that day. Deltian had started to run to it but had slipped when she called him back. He'd been just on the nearest part of it, and when she stepped on to help him, had felt it beginning to fall. She had grabbed her son and run.

"But you fixed it up," she insisted again.

"And made it stronger," Gamman agreed. "I didn't think that anyone was around when it happened."

Shayla looked ahead again. "I did hear some odd things when I was in town for the market. There were a lot of guards around. When I commented on it, I was told they were there to keep the town safe. I didn't ask 'safe from what?' but I later heard talk about brigands. Do you think they were bad in this area?"

"I haven't heard about any raids," Gamman admitted. "But, maybe the bridge is a defence against them. Maybe someone did see what I had done and thought me a spy for the raiders."

"Maybe they just don't like wizards," Shayla sighed.

"No, it can't be that. I'm not very much of a wizard. I can only do very simple spells. Mostly I'm just good with my hands and with growing things."

Deltian, still hanging on to his mother, felt their worry, although he was too young to understand the cause. He just kept checking that his dog was keeping up.

The overwhelming fear had come again, waking the fleeing family. Shayla had disobeyed her husband and only gone to hide. Now she was crouched behind some bushes, an arm around Deltian, who was holding onto his dog. Somehow, the raggedy guards from the town had caught up to them. If Gamman hadn't called a couple of them by name, she would have thought they were brigands. Once again, they'd had little enough warning.

Old Chaser was tied to a tree, well off the road and a short way back. The two of them should have kept going, but she had wanted to help her husband – until she had seen the overwhelming number of men.

Gamman was giving a good accounting of himself, using fists and feet, but all he was doing was buying time. It ran out. The King's Lord, the well-dressed man that her husband had described, rode up on a dark brown stallion.

Shayla felt the hair on her neck prickling. Magic was at work. With a series of quick hand gestures, the Lord caused all the fighters to become like statues. His companion then dismounted and walked between the stationary figures to her husband. Thinking her husband was about to be killed, Shayla prayed desperately to the dragon god she'd only heard about and bit her fingers to prevent herself crying out.

The man only felt at Gamman's neck, and found the talisman that dangled from a braided leather strap. For an instant, she thought the talisman had caught a ray of sunlight, but that made no sense. It wasn't shiny, or smooth, just some type of bone, or stone, with runes etched on it. Why would that lord want it? It was just an old heirloom that Gamman had inherited from his father. It didn't even look valuable.

All it ever seemed to do was grow hot when there was danger – just as her own was doing now. She had inherited hers from her mother.

With more gestures, the Lord demanded the talisman be brought to him. When he took it, he studied it and smiled.

"What do you wish done with him, Master?"

"Immobilise him. You do know how to neutralise a wizard?"

"Yes, m'lord."

"Then bring him back to Mayor Potter's dungeon. I can find out everything he knows about this when he is there."

The servant went to his saddlebag and his master did something so Gamman could talk.

"Where did you steal this from, wretch?" the lord demanded.

"It's mine! My Pa gave it to me, just like his Pa did to him."

"It belongs to the King of Thulor!"

"No! It's mine!"

"We will discuss this back in town, wretch. Now, where is your lovely wife and your brat?"

Gamman refused to answer, but another gesture somehow forced him to speak. "They've gone on ahead."

"You will call me, Master!"

"Master," Gamman echoed.

The lord gestured again, and the rest of the rabble was able to move. Gamman had been bound and hooded and was being held by the lord's companion now the paralysis spell had been removed.

"Go after the woman. They can't have got far if their mount is as ancient as this one."

Shayla wanted to cry out again, for she could see the man behind her husband draw a knife and reverse it to knock him on the head. Gamman slumped to the ground. With little concern, her husband was dragged to Brownie, and slung over his saddle. The loose end of the rope he'd been bound with was thrown under the horse and used to tie him on.

Watching silently, Deltian felt tears running down his face as Brownie, with the unconscious body of his Da, was led out of sight. His mother waited until all the men had gone before going in the same direction to retrieve Old Chaser. She spoke to him, explaining what she intended.

"We have to cut through the forest. They sent that man ahead to look for us, and if we go back to that village, they will take us like they did your Da. We haven't done anything wrong. They'd make out we were thieves or something."

"Why Mama?"

Shayla looked down at her son. "Your Da had something that lord wanted. He thinks he can just take it. By saying that amulet belongs to the King, no one will question things. They could kill your father even, because everyone knows the King hates thieves."

Deltian wanted to cry more, but he thought his Da would want him to be strong, and look after his mother. "What about the wagon, Mama?"

She just shook her head. He realised on his own that they needed two horses to pull it.

"Del, we just have to keep going. I have friends down south. If your Da gets free, he will look for us there. On foot, or with Old Chaser, we will be less noticeable than with a wagon."

So that was what they did, leaving the trail and making their own path. Old Chaser pushed through the underbrush, trampling it and leaving it flat in his wake, and Shayla, Deltian and his dog coming along after.

They soon ran out of food, but Shayla knew plants and as they travelled, gathered the edible ones, along with nuts and berries and wild root vegetables. Several times, Deltian managed to catch river fish using his Da's precious line and hook. Every time though, the loss of his father's presence was as distressing as ever. He missed watching as his father turned rough logs of wood into new shapes with his skilled hands. He missed the little magics his father could do to make their life a little easier. Now, they had to use flint and steel to light a fire, and if the wood was wet they ate raw plants. They had to risk drinking water that might not be pure, and not being able to keep warm with a small spell to trap warmth in the wagon. Hunting too, Gamman had a spell to give them luck catching hoppers. His dog had to hunt his own food, but sometimes he brought them an extra hopper. One day though, his dog had not come back.

In the first town that Shayla felt it was safe to enter, she took some of her hand made clay jars filled with creams she had made. With the coins she made selling them, she brought bread, honey and milk. Some she used to get better crafted clay jars, and wax to seal them. "I can charge more if they look expensive," she had explained to Del.

They dared not stay in the town, for as strangers, they would be too easy to find. They did stop a few days when they found a cave near a stream. Shayla washed their clothes, and warmed enough water in a metal pot, for a basic sponge wash. While they were there, she also took time to make more of her creams and potions, the particular ones depending what plants she had foraged.

She had got into the habit of talking to Del, as she had shortened his name, but like he was an adult. So while she worked, she told him about the plants, let him learn what they looked like, mentioned their properties – both good and bad – and how to make them into a useable form. In spite of his young age, he remembered and learnt.

CHAPTER 2 - Del

Time progressed for Del, without him counting the days, but two years had passed. The friends his mother had sought in the south had moved away and, though they waited in that town for a time, she had not felt safe there. She had taken to the trails again, staying out of sight unless visiting towns to sell her creams.

Del was nearly seven, and he had grown strong from all the walking and carrying. He never complained, and did all he could for his mother. She always seemed tired and, even when she smiled, there were deep worry lines on her face. She was thinner than she used to be too, eating very little, while telling him to eat more as he was still growing. They had long ago sold Old Chaser, to get money for food.

He had been washing at the stream when he had heard her scream. Even after dressing as fast as he could, and running back to their camp, he'd been too late. He found his mother unconscious, battered and bleeding. Remembering what she did when he was hurt, he used some of their boiled water and an old rag to wash her face and the other exposed wounds. She roused and saw him. Her hand went to her neck.

"Take my amulet, my brave one. It helps to heal, but it needs to be worn."

Hoping that he could use it to help her, he untied it from her neck and put it around his own. He didn't know how to use it, so he just placed it against her cool skin and wished really hard that she would get better.

She smiled at him and raised one hand to touch his face. Then her eyes closed and her hand dropped. Next morning, she hadn't woken. He was on his own.

Del did not want to leave his mother, but he was afraid that whoever had hurt her would return. So, he dragged her further under the overhanging rock where they had been sleeping, all the while crying and telling her how sorry he was. He considered himself strong and didn't even wonder that her body weighed so little that he had no trouble moving it. He covered her with one of their thin blankets and weighted the edges with hand sized rocks, hoping to deter scavengers. Then he went to collect the few possessions they still had and as many of the pots of creams as had escaped the feet of her attackers.

With everything he had found packed in a sack, he retraced the path back to the last village. While part of him wanted to go on alone, he knew he was still ignorant of many things. He couldn't defend himself, except by running. He might think himself strong, but he was far from being a man. He had no money to get things he couldn't scrounge for himself. And most difficult of all, was knowing that winter was coming and the plants and animals would become scarcer and he would need somewhere warm to stay. Until then, when there was two of them, they helped each other stay warm. Once they had stayed in a remote deserted hut for most of the winter, but the next winter they had nearly frozen to death.

After three days of knocking on doors, looking for work in exchange for a place to sleep and food, and only getting laughed at, he wanted to give up. They all saw a boy, small for the age he claimed and sickly looking. They all said, "Be gone, boy, or I'll have the guards on ye."

He was getting desperate when a man coming out of the tavern grabbed him by the arm.

"Where's you Ma and Pa, boy?"

He said his Ma was dead and he didn't know about his father.

"Too bad, boy. Ye look hungry, are ye?"

Even though his mother's talisman seemed very hot, and the man was unkempt and his rotten teeth disgusted him, he was ravenous. So he nodded.

"Come on boy, I'll give you a feed, and I might just know someone who could use a pair of strong hands."

The food was more than he'd had at one time since he had been alone with his mother. The warmth in the tavern, along with a full belly and the small amount of ale, made him sleepy. He didn't recall falling asleep and had no idea where he was when he woke, or even how he had got there.

Del learnt very quickly that his new position was as a drudge for a company of uncouth ruffians. As time went on, he learnt that his thin straw pallet was in the tent of the group's leader, one Calgin.

Calgin frequently cuffed him for perceived sins or lapses, but he also provided some protection from the others who leered at him, or grabbed him in the dark so they could grope him all over. That these men were brigands, preying on travellers, soon became obvious. They never took him when they went raiding, just left him tied up at the camp. When he realised what they were, he grew cold, wondering if one of these men had beaten his mother so badly that she had died. The thought of running away occurred to him, but it was in the midst of winter, when even these men had lean rations. However, with them he had some protection, a safer place to sleep, warmth from the huge fires they favoured, the scraps from their meals. The work was hard and thankless but they gave him what the villagers had denied him.

When he had first arrived, his little pack of herbs would have been tossed aside and trampled as worthless except that he had told Calgin that his Ma had been a healer and the herbs helped with headaches, fevers and rashes. He'd stopped himself before saying that some could make a grown man sleep.

"Then you can be our healer too, boy!" Calgin had decided, and as such he told his men, "Hands off." Not all of the men obeyed however.

When the rabble had stolen ale or wine and drunk themselves senseless, they demanded relief for the morning hangover headache. It improved Del's day to mix the headache herb with the sleep herb, and a touch of what his mother called sweat root, to his potion. The men took his brew, cursed at the bitter taste, and stumbled back to where they slept.

Del hadn't tried to use the amulet to heal, until he wanted to help the girl. The bandits had taken turns with her, keeping her gagged and tied to prevent her escaping or being heard. Calgin had been first, as usual. When they were all sated, they simply left her outside. All she could do was whimper.

He brought over a mug of the pain herb infusion and removed

the gag so she could drink. She hissed at him that she only wanted to die.

"I haven't anything to do that," Del had told her. If he had, several of the rabble would have been dust already. "But maybe I can heal you enough so you can run away. But drink this first."

He had untied her hands then, and steadied them so she could drink. Without his usual additions to it, the brew didn't taste bad.

"Okay. I haven't tried this before," Del admitted, "But my Ma once did this for my Da when he was hurt bad."

He tried it then, holding the amulet to her forehead and calling on the stone to heal her. It had worked, for in the residual firelight, he could see the girl looking at him in awe. Just before dawn, she was ready to depart, wearing a none too clean pair of trousers, and a jerkin discarded by two of her ravishers.

When the girl had been found to be missing, he was rightly blamed, although he loudly denied it. Vorman, an ambitious new-comer, had given him a thorough beating. He had hardly been able to crawl back to Calgin's tent and chew on some of the pain herb leaves. It had little effect on his pain, but enough to allow him the thought of trying to invoke the amulet to help him. The soothing cool breeze that seemed blow right through him brought near instant relief. He didn't let on that he was better so quickly, and the men didn't expect to see him any time soon. Calgin had looked in on him and heard only moans from the figure under the blanket on the pallet. He went out and Del heard him roaring at Vorman.

Since Calgin had cared enough about his recovery to bring him water and his usual food scraps, Del stayed cowering in the tent for two days, emerging only at night or when the men were away from camp, to relieve himself. When he did let the men see him emerge, he pretended continued soreness.

That rough kindness from Calgin meant a lot to Del. So, some weeks later, when Calgin stumbled into his tent bleeding profusely and weak from taking Vorman to a draw in a duel, he used the amulet to help him. If he had to choose between the two as leader, he preferred Calgin because he had never tried to feel over him. He had worked most of the night, stitching closed the worst slashes, and then trying to force them to heal. Calgin had to be able to fight

- for as sure as the sun rose, the younger Vorman would try again.

He had not thought that Calgin was aware of his efforts, but near morning, the chief's hand had grabbed his. "You doing some witching, boy? Are you a wizard?"

Del tried to pull free. "No, not me."

"I feel it, boy! What are you doing? Trying to kill me?"

"No! I didn't want you to die. I just know this bit of rock seems to help heal things. I don't know how, but it worked for my Ma too, but my Da couldn't use it."

"Well, boy, you just keep on doin' what yer doin'. I ain't ready to quit yet."

Calgin never mentioned the amulet and how it had helped him, but Vorman took one look at the recovered chief, recalled how a near dead girl had got away and had his own ideas.

The questions came the following week, after Calgin had been found with his throat cut. Vorman immediately claimed the leadership, and Del. When Del finally admitted how he had helped the former chief, the new leader made it clear that Del was only to heal people when he was directly ordered by him.

That wasn't hard to agree to. Del felt that every single one of the rabble deserved to suffer for their ill deeds. The rest of the new chief's orders were less pleasant. Vorman was one of the worst gropers, and after the first time he used his new drudge as a means to pleasure himself, Del tried to run away. He was soon caught, and beaten again. The next time he tried to escape, he realised that Vorman had got one of the rabble who was a hedge wizard, to put a spell on him so that he couldn't go far from the camp, or if they were travelling, from Vorman himself.

With escape not an option, Del gradually found ways to avoid the notice of the rabble, and Vorman as well. The new chief never realised that Del's herbal addition to his special drink was not just a tasty one, but a lust inhibitor. It made his deplorable situation easier to bear.

He never grew resigned to his situation and kept dreaming of being free. Then, two years later, the talisman stopped working, and Vorman had no more reason to protect him. He was only 12, weedy and ill-nourished.

CHAPTER 3 - Maeven

"Thwack!"

The clod of wet mud landed an inch from Maeven's eye. She glared at her young tormentor who was a dark haired lad, probably only nine or ten years old, in dark brown breeches and tunic. His feet, like all the village lads, were browned and bare. He began to look uneasy and decided to run off.

Maeven sighed in frustration. The pillory, which she was currently occupying, was a new addition to the isolated mountain village. The self-righteous men of the community here must have got even more parochial than four years ago when she had lived amongst them.

In the narrow-minded mode of thought of the elders, she was responsible for all the odd things that had been going missing from the scattered houses. They knew she had the skills of a thief and had been living nearby. It seemed those two facts were enough for them to blame her. They had hustled her to the pillory, immobilized her neck and wrists and told her they would consider her situation whilst she considered returning all the stolen things.

The elders had not even thanked her for saving one of the village children who had fallen into the stream just uphill from the village. Well, what could she expect? They had not thanked her for helping save them from the attentions of bandits four years ago, either.

Maeven wondered what they would say if she told them that she had not just returned here a month or two ago but had been living in a cave up the mountain for the past three years.

Three years of living in a dark cave with three dragons.

She had not envisioned that kind of life when she had run away from home. In fact, the austere little shacks the villagers lived in were more comfortable than the cave. However, the company of the dragon Mortmellor, her son Darknor and the baby dragon Petulor was preferable to that of almost all the villagers.

Too bad, she had not listened to Mortmellor's advice and not crossed the stream. The old, greying, female dragon did not like many humans and generally did not care what happened to them. However, she had reminded Maeven that the dragons' magic could not hide her beyond that stream.

Maeven risked being seen because she had not wanted Gillan to drown, even if his father was one of the narrowest minded idiots in the village.

She frowned as she spotted her little tormentor returning with friends, all with hands full of mud.

"Thwack!"

That one hit above her head and dripped onto her hair and down her neck.

"Splat!"

"Ouch," Maeven said involuntarily. "You hooligan! You aren't meant to put rocks in the mud!"

The boys looked startled. The woman had the same tone in her voice as their fathers' did when correcting them. All three boys dropped the rest of the mud and wiped the remains from their hands onto their homespun breeches. They stared at her and began to back away.

"Who told you that you could throw mud at me?" Maeven demanded.

"Da said you were a thief an' that's why you're there, an' you was being punished," the first boy said defiantly from some distance away. One of his friends, an older boy began to walk closer.

"Why don't your Da dirty his hands?" Maeven challenged. "Does he throw mud and stones at you to punish you?"

"Na, he gives him a sore rear!" the nearer boy smirked, implying his own Da never did that.

"Is that where your brains are, Josep?" another young voice challenged.

The speaker was no more than four years old with a mop of blond hair.

"She saved Gillan. I think your Da was mean, putting her here."

"Na, I saw Phineas bringing him back!" Josep argued.

"He'd be drowned if she hadn't dragged him outta the water," the blond boy yelled.

"Where were you, Wys? I'll tell Zeke you was up the hill again. He'll tan your hide!"

"I'll tell him you threw mud and rocks – I wish he'd tan your hide!"

It was almost as if Wys had caused Zeke to appear. A tall man with a short square cut beard strode into the cleared area.

"What are you boys doing here?" Zeke looked at all of them.

He glanced at Maeven in the wooden pillory, taking in the mud splotches and the mud on the hands and breeches of the three elder boys.

"Wystan, you are not to speak to this woman. Please go back home at once."

Maeven's eyes followed the little boy as he raced off obediently.

"Josep, Toma, Fenes – come with me," Zeke continued.

The boys followed Zeke, forcing one reluctant step after the other. Later, Maeven heard the sound of smacks on bare flesh and the weeping of three not so tough young toughs. She was not in the least sorry for the boys. She was, however, angry with their elders for assuming her guilt without proof and making her stand in the sun from mid-morning to mid-afternoon.

As the day progressed, no one else approached her. It was obvious the townsfolk were shunning her and frankly, she did not care. She knew they would not want her around, and for three years, they had been ignorant of her existence there. After saving Gillan, who had tripped and rolled into the stream, they could have simply told her to go away. They hadn't, and all she could do about her current situation was to draw on her supply of patience.

Sometime near evening, Maeven was watching the clouds building up beyond the hill when she became aware of something forcing the trees and undergrowth aside as it trudged down the hill. The creature came into view, large and silvery scaled in the sunlight still shining through the clouds.

"Mother, way are you standing there like that?"

Maeven looked at the child-dragon and said, calmly enough, "The people of the village think I am a thief. This is how they treat thieves."

"Shall I go and fight them?"

"Petulor, there is no need. They're not worth the effort and I can handle them. If they let me speak."

The child-dragon, already ten times Maeven's height, growled. "Humans are coming. I do not like them!"

"You don't have to like them, Petulor. They are basically good people – just a little rigid in their ways. Please move back and give them room."

Maeven recognized Phineas, Zeke, Titus and Lucas. The four men faced her. This was the second time they had confronted her since putting her there.

"Have you decided to tell the truth?" Phineas asked sternly.

"Goodman Phineas," Maeven said patiently. "I bear you no ill will. However, I fear you do not follow your own teachings. 'Be kind to all strangers, trust the word of your neighbour, value truth above all things and do not chastise the innocent.'"

It was hard to project an aura of righteousness with your neck restrained between two pieces of wood.

"You are no stranger to us and we know you are a thief. You do not deny it. You have on your wrist a symbol of blasphemy - the mark of evil magic. Where are the things that are missing from our homes?"

"I know nothing of such items," Maeven maintained patiently. "You accuse me without proof. If I had not felt compelled to help one of your children, you would still be in ignorance of my presence."

"And we would not know who was taking our special things – Goodwife Bertha's polished stones, Goodman Til's tiny model horse and plough ..." Lucas persisted.

The list of items contained little that was of value outside the community.

"What possible use would such things be to me?" Maeven asked reasonably. "For the past three years, I have been living in a cave, up near The Slide. I trap hoppers and wild mice for food and scavenge in the forest for wild, edible plants. My feet are my only means of travelling. I knew that I would not be welcome back among you, so I have not angered you with my presence. If I were to steal anything from you, it would be food. Are you missing any?"

The four men finally looked at her. Really looked. They realized her thinness and saw that the sharply defined bones in her face. Would they also realize that she was no longer the young vulnerable pregnant girl they remembered but a woman who had experienced horrors? Could they discern such subtle changes?

"We have sent a messenger to the Kings Own Guards, telling them that we have seen a symbol of evil here," Phineas told her.

"You will not be allowed to leave until they assure us that you are not an agent of evil. If you would consent to remove the object, we will allow you to stay in the village until the Kings Guards make a decision on your innocence."

Uh, huh! Maeven thought to herself. They now have doubts about me stealing from them, so they bring this up.

"Goodman Phineas, please don't approach the bracelet or try to touch it," Maeven warned urgently. "I do not wish ill luck to come to your community."

"Are you threatening us?" Phineas thundered.

Maeven sighed and drew a deep breath. They would not like her answer.

"No, Goodman Phineas. I am simply warning you of a fact. I have tried to remove the thing, but I cannot. I know, better than you, the nature of the evil it represents."

"If the object can't be taken off you, we will cut it off you!" Phineas decided.

Maeven paled as she realized that he meant.

He reached over his shoulder for the axe that he usually carried, since he was the community's woodcutter. His other hand grabbed her wrist behind the board.

A long tongue of flame appeared out of nowhere, it reached far enough to singe Phineas's black hair and beard and bathe his hands with intense heat. He dropped his axe and patted his hair and beard.

"Petulor, I told you to keep out of it!" Maeven said aloud.

The voice of the dragon was clear in the minds of the four men.

"He was going to hurt you, Dragon Mother."

"Petulor, they are simply trying to deal with things that are outside their experience." And they won't listen to outside advice, she added silently for the dragon's benefit.

"What... are you talking to?" Zeke asked, feigning calm but glancing in the direction from which the flame had come and seeming to notice the trail of fallen trees.

"Me!"

Petulor made herself visible to the four men. The sun, which had gone behind a cloud as Maeven had been talking to the men, appeared again to make Petulor turn from grey black to silver.

The men all took two steps backward, looking exactly as she

imagined they would if the deity they prayed to had appeared before them.

"You talk to dragons?" Phineas said, awed. He could not stop staring at Petulor.

Maeven permitted herself a grin. For all of their faith in their God, the old legends of Dragonkind still held them.

"It's a mixed blessing," Maeven said with emphasis, eying the dragon. "Petulor is young, but she is a dragon-mage."

"How can she bear to be near the thing you wear?" Titus asked with distaste.

"You have it wrong. While I am within Petulor's sphere of strength, those who would use it to try to find me, cannot. I usually do not venture down past the stream, for that reason. When she is in the cave, yonder, that is the limit of her protection. I only ventured further today to help Gillan."

With fingers that trembled, Phineas undid the locking clips on the wood and released Maeven.

"Please accept our apologies for our suspicions. One favoured by dragons cannot be evil."

Maeven stretched with relief. There was no way she would tell him that she could still be a thief and favoured by dragons.

"Petulor, you have made your point, thank you."

The dragon faded from view again.

Maeven had more than a little glee bubbling inside her now as she watched the grown men grovel. Zeke regained his composure first.

"I would be honoured if you would guest in my house."

"Thank you, but it would not be wise, it would be better if I returned to my cave home."

"Please reconsider, now that you are here, I need to talk to you."

Maeven sensed that something was worrying him.

"Perhaps I might ask to stay with Reyna," Maeven suggested instead.

"I will ask Goodwife Reyna to welcome you," Zeke promised and he strode off.

Maeven stared at the other three men.

"I accept your apologies. I still think kindly of you for taking me in when I was in trouble."

Maeven turned abruptly and began to walk in the direction of Reyna's shack - the one she had lived in four years ago. As she neared it, a woman, glowing with health, ran out and raced towards her.

"Ven! Ven!" Reyna hugged her with unfeigned affection.

"Goodwife Reyna," Maeven replied with a soft laugh. "Being married seems to agree with you."

"Gervain and I married a year ago," Reyna told her friend. "I'll be a mother in the spring."

"That's wonderful!" Maeven congratulated, thrilled for her friend.

"But what have you been doing, you are so thin!"

"Scrounging for my own food," Maeven said carelessly, as if it was no matter for concern.

"Oh, come inside, I want to hear about everything," Reyna insisted.

"Zeke needs to talk to me. May I invite him here after your meal?"

Reyna nodded and spoke to Zeke, "Bring Lorinda and those young rascals of yours, about sundown. We will have finished eating by then."

Zeke nodded in return and strode off leaving the two women alone.

"Gervain won't be back tonight. He's gone down to the trade town with a message from the Elders and we need some things for the baby." Reyna gently pulled her friend inside.

"I don't really want to meet Wystan yet. I haven't come to take him away."

"Ven, he's your son and an absolutely lovable, obedient child. Everyone likes him."

"But?" Maeven queried sensing a contradiction.

Reyna looked uncomfortable. "Just lately he's been different. Not exactly secretive, but choosing his own company, as often as not. And odd things have been happening around him."

"Like what?"

"Things moving without being touched, and when some of the older kids try to bully him they start to trip over their own feet and fall in a heap."

"I saw him earlier," Maeven admitted. "He told some boys off for throwing mud and stones at me. He wished out loud that they would get their hides tanned, and right then, Zeke came up, took the boys away..."

"And tanned their hides!" Reyna finished. "Yes, exactly what I meant."

Reyna suddenly realised what her friend had not said.

"Oh no, they didn't have you in the stocks did they?" She was angry for her friend's sake.

"Yes, they did. But I finally made them release me."

Reyna laughed, "You haven't lost your manipulative touch then?"

"Phineas even apologised." Maeven grinned and Reyna raised her eyebrows.

"How did you manage that? Phineas believes he's never wrong."

"Oh, I had some help from a young friend of mine."

"Who?"

"Um – a dragon."

CHAPTER 4 - Maeven

"A dragon!" Reyna echoed. "I wish you'd tell me who you really are. For the Lady's sake – how did you convince them you had a dragon?"

"I don't think you can really say I have a dragon. It is truer to say that she has me! People fascinate her, but some of them around here she doesn't like. At the moment, she is perched up the hill a bit keeping an eye on me. Would you like to meet her?"

"Meet a dragon?" Reyna squeaked. "She won't … eat me?"

"No, she's not quite so indiscriminate now."

Reyna eyed Maeven suspiciously, wondering if her friend was teasing her. However, if she wasn't, she really wanted to meet a dragon.

"Come with me."

Maeven took Reyna's hand and, together, they walked up the hill. There was no sign of a dragon but Maeven seemed to know where to go. They stopped in a clearing and Maeven spoke to the air.

"Petulor, this is my friend, Reyna."

Reyna could see a glow appearing and she suddenly realised that what she thought was a warm, smoky breeze blowing through her hair was the dragon's breath. She squeaked and jumped back two steps.

"*I like this human,*" Petulor said, her head gently rubbing Maeven's.

"I heard her!" Reyna said, surprised.

"*Of course, I wanted you to.*"

Petulor raised herself up to her full height.

Reyna looked up and up. "How did you and Maeven get to be friends?"

"*My mother named her Dragon Mother!*"

"Take that to be something like a nanny," was Maeven's wry comment. "And be thankful you aren't having a baby dragon. Petulor is only three years old."

"Oh, only three! Will she grow much more?"

"She is about a third of the size of the dragon who clutched her," Maeven estimated. "Though Thulor was ancient when I met her –

she may have shrunk a bit."

Reyna went very silent for a long moment. Then, daringly, she touched the dragon, patting her nose. Petulor blew on her hair again.

"Thank you for letting me meet you, Petulor. I have to go now."

"You are my friend now, too."

Maeven spoke silently to the dragon and Petulor faded from human sight, but not from Maeven's dragon sight. Then she ran to catch up with her friend who seemed suddenly distant.

"You wanted to know more about me," Maeven said quietly. "I value you as a friend, has that changed?"

"My mother never held with the new-fangled religion they practice here," Reyna said unexpectedly. "She was a priestess of Dragon Lore. I know that Thulor allied herself with the Royal family and powered protections for her realm. Why did she choose you to hatch her daughter?"

"Why a thief and ne'er do well?" Maeven clarified. "I don't know why, but I had the talents needed to get Thulor's egg back from the presence of her enemy."

"That wouldn't be enough! You would have to be a member of the Royal family. When Frederick hatched Thulor, he had already become a member of the King's family."

They had reached the shack when Reyna spoke again.

"I am so dense! I should have seen it. Ven. Maeven. You're Princess Maeven!"

"Up here I am simply Ven," Maeven stressed. "You would do well to forget that I have any other name."

"Then Wystan is..."

Maeven took Reyna's hand, gripped it firmly, and entered the shack. "...is Lorinda and Zeke's child."

"Why?"

"Were you aware of any unusual events just over three years ago?"

It was obvious by the thoughtful look on Reyna's face that she was recalling that time.

"At midsummer, the sun disappeared. No, it was there but it gave very little light. It felt like a major storm was brewing. Old Adelbart had us praying all night."

"If that was all you noticed, you were spared the worst," Maeven said softly going over to perch on the edge of Reyna's bed.

"Thulor's enemy knew she was dying and was trying to take the kingdom and stop the birth of her successor. It was a close thing. I had to get Petulor away. She was the one who brought me here, or rather to a cave up near the Slide. I have to try to protect her until she reaches full power but at the same time, she is protecting me. Without her magic, I am in danger and dangerous to those I am around."

Maeven fingered the bracelet on her wrist - a braid of three golden snakes with jewel eyes.

"This thing – is the enemy's tag; his way to find me. My family hurt the enemy badly, but he did not die and when he is strong enough he will be looking for Petulor and me. I don't want to endanger anyone, and especially not ..."

"No! I understand," Reyna said thoughtfully. "Your family will all be targets. I wish you could've told me all this before. Though why tell me now?"

"A lot of things have happened since then." Maeven's voice was very quiet. "I am no longer a scared, pregnant, seventeen year old disgraced Princess."

"Even so, don't think I've forgotten when I came here and my mother died. Scared, young, pregnant and being shunned by everyone you might have been, but you helped me. And don't think that I didn't work out that I and probably most of the townsfolk would probably be dead now if you hadn't manipulated the men and dared them to spy on the bandits."

Maeven looked away.

"I still sense that about you – it's how you hold yourself and how you speak."

"I see that I will have to watch myself if I want to blend in with commoners," Maeven thought aloud. "As to why tell you now, I just wanted someone here to know – just in case. Anyway, I want to hear about you and Gervain – I think he was eyeing me off at one time and he wasn't quite a man then."

Reyna accepted the change of subject and complied by telling her the town gossip over the past three years. She had a wicked sense of humour; learnt from listening to Maeven point out the idiosyncrasies of the townsfolk.

"After you left, the older boys kept coming to call," Reyna recalled. "They kept offering to help me and did things for me without being asked. Actually, anything they could do to impress me. It was very amusing, but it was obvious that they had only one thing on their minds."

"Gervain?"

"Oh, he was the randiest of the lot, but he made me laugh. He knew he was young and inexperienced but he didn't mind admitting it. We met secretly, and I knew with him, if I wanted him to stop, he would. We kept it up until he was old enough to marry me."

Maeven chuckled, the Elders would have been furious if they had found out.

"And..." Reyna turned serious. "He was the only one of them that didn't think the town well rid of you."

"You are a true friend, Reyna," Maeven told her softly.

CHAPTER 5 - Maeven

Ven had borrowed a dress from Reyna. Her own clothes were drying by the fire. They had been of tough material for hard wearing, but living in a rock cave, she'd needed to replace them every half year. Her current ones were tending towards threadbare, but would have to last until the traders came again. Then she would have to cut the new ones down to fit her and resew the seams and hems. Fortunately, the traders also carried a supply of strong needles and thread. The sewing that she had once detested at least helped to pass some time. Some of the excess fabric, and been turned into little pouches to protect and separate the herbs she had bought or found.

Her changed appearance had a positive effect on her guests. Lorinda, and more particularly Zeke, automatically began to treat her as they would a fellow townsperson and Wystan did not recognise her as the woman he had defended earlier. The twin toddlers did not care; hers was simply another skirt to hang on to.

"Twins! Lorinda, how marvellous!" Maeven exclaimed.

Zeke looked proud and Lorinda flushed with pleasure.

"And Wystan, almost a man already, how old are you now?"

"I am four, Mam," Wystan said, pleased to have this strange adult's attention.

"Your Da and Ma must be proud of you."

"I help Ma chase Zeni and Lort," he claimed.

"That would be a big help," Maeven grinned. "Why don't you ask Reyna if you and your little brother and sister can have a biscuit?"

Wystan's eyes lit up and he turned to Reyna, who took his hand and walked him over to her table.

"I didn't come to get him," Maeven said very softly, relieving the strained look in Lorinda's eyes. "You have been better parents to him than I could have been. I will have to take him one day, but until then, he is safer here."

Maeven stopped talking as Wystan returned.

"Ma, Reyna has some carrots that are ready to pull up. Can I help her please, before it gets too dark?"

Lorinda nodded and smiled gratefully at Reyna.

When he had gone, Maeven spoke.

"There was something worrying you," she asked Zeke.

Zeke glanced away, stared at the floor and then spoke. "There have been some odd incidents. Wystan seems to be at the centre of them. If I knew he was doing something, I could act. But the only explanation is that he is doing magic."

"And that's absurd!" Lorinda said with conviction.

"Unfortunately, it's very likely to be true," Maeven said, realising that she had to proceed carefully. "You are lucky, living up here. You can live in peace and serve your God. The concerns of the greater kingdom rarely affect you. However, no matter how much you choose to deny it – magic is a fact. The King has a Court Wizard and one of his daughters is a sorceress."

"What has this to do with Wystan?" Zeke asked uncertainly.

"I had the misfortune to be in a town when the Kings Own Guards set out to rescue some captured women and children. I decided that it wasn't a good place to be and left, but there was a wizard with the bandits and he tricked me and ... I couldn't go home. I honestly never considered that the child would be mage gifted or, from the little I knew of magic, that such a talent would appear in one so young. Tell me what has been happening."

"I found Wystan with some things that did not belong to him," Zeke began. "I asked him where he had got them and he insisted that he found them in the garden. Later there was a fuss because the owners found them missing. I asked him about them again and he still insisted that he had found them. Naturally, I was angry with him, thinking he was lying to me, though he never has before, and I made him take the things back to their owners. He did know where everything belonged, without asking. Anyway, he was punished and the matter was closed."

Then Lorinda commented, "A few times I have asked him to fetch things for me and he hadn't wanted to leave his game. He didn't complain, but when I turned around, the thing I wanted was right near me."

"Recently, more things have gone missing," Zeke admitted. "After each theft, I checked amongst Wystan's things but didn't find anything. So I have no proof, but I can't help wondering ..."

"Now he's tending to be secretive, preferring to play by himself…" Lorinda trailed off.

"I don't know what to do," Zeke hated to have to admit such a thing.

Maeven saw the unspoken plea. "I have no problems with the values you are trying to teach him, nor with the way you have raised him so far."

Maeven met their eyes. "If you would let him come to visit tomorrow, I'll try to get him to talk to me about these incidents. If he does, and he thinks he might be doing something, I will stress that what he is doing is unacceptable and he will be punished if he persists. He is only four, he might have no idea he is doing anything. He might simply be wishing."

"What if we frighten him or make him angry? What might he do?" Lorinda asked, turning pale.

"If you continue to let him know that you love him, even when you have had to correct him, I don't think he will do anything. I trust you to be fair."

"What should we do if we are sure he has used magic?" Zeke asked.

The very idea of magic was foreign to him and he did not want to admit to his fellow townsmen that his son might be a magician.

"As you have done. If he has something that is not his and someone else is missing it – act as if he took it, like before. If he's wished a job done – berate him for being lazy. If you can, and I know it will be hard, ignore the fact of 'magic' and concentrate on the results and act accordingly. Magic is a skill; the user needs to use that skill ethically. In this community, magic is not used. I will tell him that."

Zeke nodded thoughtfully, most of Maeven's advice was in accordance with his beliefs, except for the bit about magic – how could he accept that and then ignore it?

"I will have to give this problem some thought. When do you expect the King's own guards to arrive?"

"Two or three days."

"I will talk to the leader and see what I can arrange – there may be a way to restrain his magic. If, later, you can't manage Wystan, talk to Reyna, I'll give her a means to contact me."

"More magic," Zeke asked with a shudder.

"I'm no sorceress, but Reyna can go to Petulor who will be able to find me. No offence intended, but Petulor doesn't like the men here but she does like Reyna."

Lorinda began to ask who Petulor was but Zeke quelled her question.

The storm began in the darkest part of the night. Maeven woke, listened to the thunder rumbling and saw the glare of lightning through the cracks in the window shutters.

It wasn't that storms were unusual in the mountains, but Maeven felt that this one was "wrong". The feeling was nothing she could put a name to, but one she trusted with her life.

"Reyna?" she spoke quietly from the pallet on the floor.

"What?" came her friend's reply.

"I need to go out for a while, but I will be back after the storm passes."

"You're crazy! It'll be teeming soon," Reyna protested, coming fully awake.

Under the blanket, Maeven felt something moving around her wrist. Her stomach heaved but she controlled the impulse to be sick.

"No, I have to go. I'm not safe too far from Petulor. She's gone back to the cave. If I don't go – it might find me."

"It?" Reyna sounded scared.

"Something is looking for me," was all the explanation Maeven would give as she pulled on her tunic and breeches, then the long sleeved jerkin. She did not push the arm with the bracelet all the way through the sleeve. She hoped that the snakes of the bracelet could not see if they were covered.

"Must you go?" Reyna asked. The rain she had predicted had begun to fall in heavy drops. "Nothing will be moving about in this."

"Reyna, you will be safer if I go. It wants me, and I will not ignore the feeling I have now. I promise I will be back."

Maeven slipped quietly out of the shack, quickly becoming drenched but finding her way up the hill the nearest point of the creek without mishap. She knew the area well and could see her way, even in this moonless night. Her father had called this ability - dragon sight.

The rain continued to get heavier but that made Maeven feel

better. If her enemy, the Serpent, located her, it would not send its agents out into this weather. The snakes that could turn into human form hated water. It was unlikely that any of the Serpent's little messenger demons would fly in this weather either.

Maeven hurried as much as she could and finally crossed the creek. The edge of the rain was sharply defined in mid creek.

If she had wanted proof that the storm was unnatural – this was it. Normal storms were unaffected by Petulor's magic.

The bracelet became solid again but Maeven kept it hidden as she continued to climb. Petulor met her half way up and blew her warm breath over her human friend.

"The Serpent is getting stronger," Maeven told the dragon. "It is searching."

"*I can taste its magic in the air. Evil!*" Petulor admitted.

"Yes."

"*You must stay up here,*" Petulor rebuked.

"That would be the smartest move," Maeven admitted. "Though when did I ever choose smart?"

"*Why must you go back?*"

"I promised to talk to Zeke's older boy. I have to make him understand about his magic and the dangers of using it up here. Then, also, the King's Own Guards will be coming here – I need to get news from the palace."

"*The boy - is your child,*" Petulor stated intently.

"Yes."

Maeven could sense the dragon wondering why she was not looking after her own child. Finally, the dragon asked her that.

"When he was born it was too dangerous for me to have a child around," Maeven ignored the complexity of the situation back then. "It isn't much safer now. Besides, I can't raise a child in a cave with you."

"*Why not...?*"

Petulor may have received all of her Mother's knowledge of magic – but she still had to learn about people.

"Lorinda and Zeke can give him a steady, normal human relationship. I can't."

"*If he has magic, he should be here for you to teach too!*" Petulor insisted.

"I'm a thief, Petulor. I may steal spells to use but I don't know how to make them. I am certainly not teaching you about magic. You know everything your mother, Thulor, knew about that. As for the rest, Mortmellor has been teaching you all about being a dragon. I'm not sure that I am any more than a nursemaid, who might teach you a bit about people."

"*Maybe I can teach him about magic...*" Petulor suggested.

"Not yet, my young friend," Maeven spoke with real affection. "He might be a year older than you, but in human terms he's still a baby. I would prefer he doesn't use magic. The people below won't tolerate it, and it could attract those seeking me. Besides, I don't know how dragon magic or human magic works. I can't be sure if they are alike or not. Your mother powered what little magic ability I had. I haven't been able to do anything magical since she died and her residual power faded. It would be very useful to be able to make my stuff follow me invisibly again instead of having to stuff my pockets."

Petulor went off to consider what her human mentor had discussed. Maeven, who was relieved to end the conversation, stopped pacing and sat on some rocks where she could still look down on the town as well as watch the storm as it slowly moved away towards the border with Declanor. Later, she walked to where Petulor had curled up in a clearing and rested against her.

As morning drew close, Maeven stood up to return to Reyna's shack. Petulor raised her head.

"*Try some magic?*"

Maeven felt a familiar tingling in her body. She picked up a rock from the ground and whispered the words of a "follow" spell. When she dropped her hand, the rock stayed in the air. She walked two paces back; the rock followed her.

"Very good!" Maeven praised the dragon with a grin as she did a little dance with the rock as her partner.

Next, Maeven spoke the words of an invisibility spell on the rock and it disappeared. If Petulor could maintain the magic, the rock would still be with her later in the day.

"How did you do that? Let me do spells? I thought I would have to be wearing one of your mother's talismans."

"I know you," Petulor stated as if it were obvious.

"What about my father and sibs, and the wizard? They're all helping you to protect the kingdom. Their talismans have been impotent since Thulor died too."

Petulor rested her head on her fore legs and thought. *"Yes, I know how my mother did it. I feel them all now. I have sent a burst of my magic to each one. Now they should be like before and, if they want, they can draw on the energy in my mother's crypt."*

"Well, lucky them," Maeven commented mildly. She really hadn't considered what he father and sibs were doing since she had run out on them. For the past three years, she had been too busy merely surviving. Over time, she had gradually acquired some comforts from the nomadic traders. They camped not far from her cave, but Petulor's protection meant they never saw the entrance.

Before returning to Reyna's shack, Maeven decided to get a few things she had hidden in her cave. If she could again do spells, and keep useful items 'with' her but not in her pocket or a carry sack, then she wanted her knife, a pouch of dragon shells, and a few coins. She added a pouch of special gems as well.

The delicious smell of baking biscuits greeted Maeven on her return to Reyna's shack. Outside, the day had cleared to cloudless and sunny, but the ground had not yet dried out. Maeven shook the mud off her boots before entering.

"You should trade some of those biscuits for bits of the fancy work the other women do," Maeven said impishly, praising her friends cooking but teasing her about her lack of sewing skill. "What happened to the ones left from yesterday?"

Reyna gave Maeven a thoughtful look. "The jar was empty when I got up this morning."

"Were you hungry last night?"

"A little, but I only had two after you left - before I went back to bed. I didn't eat them all."

"Odd!" Maeven commented, meeting her friend's eyes.

"Yes," Reyna agreed, carefully saying nothing. Then she changed the subject.

"I kept you some porridge for breakfast. I thought you could use something warm in your belly."

Maeven had only just finished her hearty breakfast when there was a knocking at the door. Reyna opened the door and saw a stern looking Zeke with Wystan who was trying to wipe traces of tears away from his eyes.

Maeven took her dish to the washing tub and pretended to ignore the visitors.

"My son has something to say to you, Goodwife Reyna."

Zeke stared at Wystan as if expecting him to say something. The little boy opened his mouth to speak and then closed it again. Finally, Zeke explained.

"I found Wystan eating biscuits in his bed corner this morning. He said – he had wished he could have more of your biscuits and he had found them next to his bed. I have told him that it was wrong of him to take them. Wystan…"

"I am sorry for wanting them, Goodwife Reyna," Wystan's voice was almost too low to hear. "Da says I must do work for you to make up for having them."

Reyna nodded thoughtfully. "So that is where they went to…very well, I think there are a few tasks that a small, agile lad like you could do for me. I'll send him back after the noon meal."

Zeke took his leave.

"Well now," Reyna said thoughtfully, eyeing Wystan. "What should I get you to do first?"

Maeven interrupted casually. "I noticed that a couple of the shingles on the roof are loose. If he could show me what to do, we could fix them for you."

"Ah yes, the very thing," Reyna agreed. "I had a wet patch on the floor this morning after last night's rain. Gervain keeps promising to fix it but he is so busy at this time of the year. Though we do have a ladder you can use."

Wystan looked happier as he followed Reyna to get a hammer and some of the scarce metal nails. When he returned he finally had a good look at Maeven and recognised her. He seemed afraid to talk to her.

As he followed the two women outside, he finally had the courage to tug on her sleeve and ask, "Is my Da still punishing you? Is that why you gonna help me?"

Maeven grinned at the boy. "No, I sorted out things with the

Elders. I said about helping you because I have never fixed a roof before."

"I help Da all the time," Wystan said shyly.

"I am sure he must think himself lucky to have a good helper."

"Yeah, he says he is...are you really a thief?"

Maeven did not answer at once; instead, she lifted the ladder from the ground next to the wall of the shack before Reyna tried. She saw Wystan looking at her, waiting for an answer.

"I used to be," she answered as she carried the ladder to the other side of the shack.

"Da says stealing is wrong."

"It is, I suppose."

"Did you ever get caught?"

Maeven put the ladder against the edge of the roof before turning to answer Wystan's question.

"Only once, well, twice."

"What did they do to you? Did they tan your hide?" The boy's eyes were big and round.

"When the Elders here found out what I could do, they didn't dare tan my hide. I was ..." Maeven broke off before admitting she had been pregnant.

Reyna broke in. "They didn't dare because she had saved their hides. She pinched the weapons from some bandits so that the men here could deal with them fairly."

"The bandits didn't catch you?"

"No. I was a very good thief!"

"But you stole..."

"Yeah! The Elders had a problem with that. They tried to ignore me instead."

"What about the other time?"

Maeven drew a breath. "The other time, I was caught by the King's Own Guards. They put me in the King's dungeons."

Maeven climbed the ladder to the roof, aware that Reyna was interested in her story too. No doubt wondering why her father had done that.

"What was that like?" Wystan asked after he had scrambled agilely up after her.

"It was very dark, very uncomfortable and very unpleasant,"

Maeven summarised. "In fact, standing in the pillory was like a holiday in comparison."

Wystan shuddered. "Do you know why Phineas is there now?"

"I was able to convince the Elders of my innocence. They accused me because of that one past act, which as you realise was stealing, even though I was trying to help the community. I can only surmise that Phineas is trying to atone for accusing me unjustly. They know they must look elsewhere for their thief."

Wystan was looking thoughtful.

"Can you show me what to do?" Maeven asked.

The diversion was obviously welcome. As they began hammering nails into the wood shingles, it became apparent that Wystan was not concentrating on the job in hand.

After a while, Maeven put her hand over Wystan's and asked gently, "Is there something worrying you? I would be happy to help and you can be sure I won't be gossiping to the community about it. They are tolerating me, but Reyna is the only one here that is actually my friend. I have also travelled a bit and I have seen a lot of odd things."

Wystan considered her offer seriously for a while. Then his fears spilled out.

"They'll take me away, the guards will. Those...those things they accused you of taking ...I ...I have them. I didn't go and steal them, honest. I just wished I could have them and later found them with my stuff. But Da, he don't believe me. He made me take the other stuff back and he ...I couldn't sit down for days. I'm scared to tell him about the other stuff, and I'm scared to take it back."

"I understand your fears," Maeven said quietly. "What do you think has been happening?"

Wystan shook his head. "I thought they was given me."

"But they weren't..." Maeven stated thoughtfully, preparing to try to explain to this young child about magic. "I think you have a rare, often unappreciated talent. You can think of it like this – anyone can whittle rough images out of wood but only a talented carver can make them look real. Your talent is being able to make things happen, to wish for something and get it. Now, at first glance, that may seem like fun, but it's not, as you have already found out. You wished for something that you had seen and it's appeared. It didn't come out of nothing – it came from someone else's house. That does make it stealing, even though you didn't mean to."

Wystan turned pale.

"Now, what you should do with anything you still have or anything else that might appear – is to wish it back where it came from. Then, be very careful what you wish for."

Wystan nodded, looking relieved that Maeven had not insisted he take everything back in person.

"Is that what Da would have made me do?"

"Ah, not exactly. The effect, however, will be the same. Without the sore backside."

Wystan managed a small smile.

"And a piece of advice," Maeven added. "I would be very wary about wishing a job done, when you'd rather be playing. You need to remember that the people here don't like idlers any more than thieves. If they can't see you getting up and doing your chores, they will be angry with you."

"What good is a talent then?"

"Living up here – not much use at all," Maeven said bluntly. "The people here don't believe in magic."

"Does that make me bad?"

"Magic exists. It isn't evil, but some people do bad things with it. If you could be trained, there are useful things you could be taught to do – good things; but, again, you couldn't do them here."

"Could you teach me?"

Maeven smiled ruefully. "No, I'm not even a charm witch. I know some wizards and a sorceress or two but I don't know that they would be willing to live here. I will talk to the Guards when they come. If I can arrange something, you won't be able to tell anyone about your lessons. If I can't, you will have to try hard not to wish for things that aren't yours."

"If you can't find someone to teach me, will I have to go away?"

"Would you want to?"

"No, but I don't like it when Da punishes me."

"You aren't meant to. It's meant to remind you that what you did was wrong, so that you won't do it again."

That idea was a revelation to the child.

"Your Ma and Da love you," Maeven stressed. "They are trying to teach you the values that they live by and they are – decent – people."

Maeven would have liked to mention other points but the child had enough to think about.

"I wish you were my Ma. You know a lot and I can talk to you without you getting mad."

"Like I said – be careful what you wish for…"

Maeven turned her attention, and Wystan's, back to the repair of the roof.

CHAPTER 6 - Maeven

"Oh my!" Reyna said with an expression of a cat with a dish of cream. "If I wasn't already wed to Gervain...hmm."

Maeven looked in the direction of the arriving King's Own Guards and tried not to flinch. Heading the group was an impeccably dressed blond haired man with an exotic cast to his features. He was clean-shaven and incredibly handsome. Reyna was not the only married woman eyeing him.

"El Haba!" Maeven breathed involuntarily as she stood back behind the welcoming committee.

The past three years had not given her an answer to the way she felt about him. Just seeing him roused feelings that frightened her and even though he had chosen to swear an Oath of Fealty to her father, the King of Thulor, she still did not know whether she could trust him on a personal level.

The leader dismounted and handed the reins of his horse to his second in command. Three of the Elders, all scrubbed until their faces glowed and with hair neatly and identically trimmed, walked out in front of the gathered community to greet the Guardsmen.

Maeven glanced at the still mounted guards. They were all young and unfamiliar to her. Their faces were not as well schooled as the leader's. Two had faint smiles and the other three had looks of mild distaste.

Maeven walked forward, surprising Zeke who had been told to 'mind' her. She stood level with the three elders as they began to speak.

"Thank you for coming Guard Captain," Phineas greeted with no trace of deference.

"Your message was one of urgency, Elder."

"Yes, a woman amongst us wears a sign of evil," Phineas began.

"Elder Phineas, I am quite capable of speaking for myself." Maeven's voice carried clearly. The three Elders looked at her with distaste; their women were not meant to be so forward.

"Guard Second Namir, please listen to what these respected Elders have to say. I will speak with this woman. Zephan, Tellar, with me."

"Yes Captain Arlen," the Guard Second answered crisply. He competently steered the Elders away from the watching crowd even as his Captain followed the woman in another direction.

Maeven politely offered the Guards seats in Reyna's shack. The junior guards declined, and the Captain insisted that she sit down first.

"Captain Arlen," Maeven said thoughtfully. She saw a faint smile on the man's face.

"I believe you are already aware of the existence of this artefact, the item that has caused a great deal of concern to the Elders here."

"Indeed, my lady. Has it started to cause you problems?"

"It has begun to stir," Maeven told him carefully. "Two nights ago, I felt it seeking. The weather outside had become extremely unstable. It was not a natural storm."

"How can you be sure?" the man now calling himself Arlen asked intently.

"Normal storms are not affected by Dragon Magic. The one of which I speak, could not penetrate the protective shield around Petulor."

Arlen looked thoughtful.

"How is Petulor?"

"Growing."

Arlen nodded and asked, "And you, My Lady?"

Maeven shrugged, "Well enough."

One of the two young guards pushed away from the wall where he was standing.

"I know who you are, you're Pr--"

"I'm Ven!" Maeven said firmly, meeting the man's gaze and daring him to say anything else.

The man stared back, finally agreeing, "Ven."

The man was not stupid, none of the King's Own Guards were. He had quickly realised that her safety depended on anonymity.

"I have no idea what the Elders will say about me," Maeven admitted. "They don't like me, but I'm in good company. They don't have anything nice to say about the King either! Elder Phineas was prepared to cut my hand off to remove the serpent bracelet. Fortunately, Petulor took exception to the idea."

"It would not have helped," Arlen commented softly. "The snakes would have crawled until they reached you again and moved back to what was left of your arm.”

“Why am I not surprised?” Maeven muttered. “Do you know how I might remove it?”

“Not with any degree of safety,” Arlen admitted with regret. “However, whilst the enemy is using it to track you, he is vulnerable to being tracked in turn.”

“Does the King’s Wizard have a spell to do that?”

“Wizard Roman, under advisement from ... other wizards... has a suggestion. Are your skills up to it?”

Maeven moved her hand so that it was between the Captain and herself. She made two pebbles appear in her hand. Arlen merely nodded.

“Tellar, go down to Namir and advise the village men that he is speaking with, that they have no need to fear danger from this piece of jewellery. Zephan, please wait outside.”

Arlen waited until his men had gone before speaking again.

First, he gave her the spell that might enable her to get a picture of the location of her enemy, the Serpent.

Then, “Have you been up here for three years?”

“Not in the village, but nearby. However, I will not be staying, and that leads me to a problem I need to discuss with you. Though first, can you tell me what things are like elsewhere?”

“After the Serpent fled, things were slowly returning to normal throughout the kingdom. Then, about a year ago, the darkness covered the land again. I do not notice it here as much as in the lowlands. With the darkness come blights that affect crops and people. The crops, well, barely one part in ten is edible – the rest is sickly at best, warped into grotesque forms at worst. A persistent new weed grows in the fields that have the edible crops. It is competing for growing space that the farmers need to grow food. The people fall ill with all kinds of exotic conditions – the healers are working with herb witches and the like to find cures or remedies. The Serpent has sent little demons adrift in Thulor and people who go outside at night often disappear. Bandit attacks are also becoming more frequent; we feel sure that Vatarik is controlling them.”

“Is the Serpent seeking you?” Maeven asked abruptly.

“I have no doubt that he wishes me dead,” Arlen admitted calmly enough. "However, his spies, the little messenger demons, cannot tell me apart from my brother's other agents."

"I can't say that the same is true for me," Maeven admitted. "How are my siblings?"

"They are well, last I heard. Your Father has sent them away from the Palace. He remains, with his Wizard and a handful of servants."

"How can he bear the hardship?" Maeven said snidely. Her Father liked his little comforts.

"He cares for his people," Arlen corrected her. "He had the others safely away before the enemy force laid siege to the palace. Men and strange night creatures have surrounded the palace for some months now. They are trying to turn the palace to rubble. It seems the Serpent wishes to break the kingdom before the new dragon comes into her power."

"Why were you in the trade village?"

"Your father thought it best if I were posted as far from my homeland as possible. He sent me here two years ago. I never expected to find you here."

"I bet my father did. How is Atlantis?"

"The Prince's Consort is in hiding with her husband."

Maeven chuckled with real mirth. "She swore she would never get married..."

"There was a battle of wills," Arlen commented dryly. "The lady consented when His Majesty pleaded that it was necessary for the good of the realm and beyond. He also made it plain that they must ensure the continuance of the Royal Line."

"And...?"

"I fear that it may not be possible," was the quiet statement. "Rhovert told me of the little snakes that were put on him and which bit him. They are dreft, and if they bit him where he said, he may be unable to engender an heir."

"Have you told Father that?"

"No."

"Why not?"

"His Majesty has seen a child and knows it will be King one day. I am hoping he is right and I am wrong. Your line must continue and I do not wish to make him lose his hope for the future – it is all that is keeping him from despair."

"I should tell him about our child, but something is keeping me from that. Once it was shame, but now ..."

"The child is safer if he is anonymous," Arlen stressed.

"Unfortunately, that may not be true much longer."

Maeven stared at the Guard Captain, still undecided about how she felt.

"Would it help if I said I was sorry for what I did to you?" Arlen said with difficulty. "I am not that man anymore."

"Perhaps not! You, no matter what you call yourself now, are still having an effect on me that scares me. And I know you no longer have a controlling spell on me."

"That is mutual, my lady, and simply looking at you rouses me to recklessness."

"Do you still consider me married to you?" Maeven asked.

"In Vatarik, you are indeed my wife."

"And here?

"Your father will not recognise it unless it is your choice."

"Hmm...Arlen, can you return here without being so obvious and eye-catching? I need to talk to you and now is not a good time."

"I will return in a day or two – if that will suit you?"

Maeven nodded and did not follow him when he left.

When he had gone, Maeven drew in a deep breath and let it out again. When that did not settle her inner agitation, she continued to take deep breaths. She was feeling almost back to normal when Reyna returned.

"What happened between the Guard Captain and you?" Reyna asked bluntly, staring at her friend.

"We talked."

"Other than that!"

"What do you mean?"

"That Guard Captain looked like he had a bad case of unfulfilled lust. And you look..."

Maeven blushed extremely red.

"What's wrong? He's handsome enough to tempt most of the matrons in the community. You aren't wedded...so why not?"

"I'm not interested in that ...not with him!"

"He's Wys' father!" Reyna suddenly realised. She already knew the circumstances of the boy's conception. "Tell me about it."

An hour later, Maeven finished telling her friend about her encounters with the foreign Prince-Wizard. She began with her flight from the bandit camp, when the wizard had tricked her and placed a controlling spell on her before raping her. Then she had told of each subsequent meeting with the man. There were many details she still kept to herself; she glossed over the time when she thought she was going to be hung by saying only, "He used magic and trickery to help me escape."

"He doesn't seem like that now," Reyna commented. "And surely, if there was any doubt, the King would not have accepted his pledge."

"I know that but I can't help remembering how I felt."

"Of course not!" Reyna agreed, recalling her own, similar experience.

She looked thoughtfully at her friend.

"You helped me get over my experience, Ven. Maybe I can help you now."

"How?"

Reyna seemed to squirm. "Had you ever... you know... like Gervain and me, before ..."

Maeven understood what she meant. "No and it wouldn't bother me if I still hadn't."

"You don't like men that way?"

"No."

"What about women, that way?"

"I never thought that was...what are you trying to say?"

"I think what helped me...well I was no virgin before those bandits had me. There'd been one boy and well...I told you my mother was a Dragon Priestess?"

Maeven nodded.

"Well, there are no Dragon Priests! Those chosen or called to be a Priestess live in secluded communities. And they only interact with men when they want a child. The rest of the time, they share themselves amongst the other women. The thing is, mother encouraged me to – I won't say love the other women, but I got used to the sensations of lust, amongst women. I can teach you to enjoy it and prove to you that you can love without losing control."

Maeven was still feeling the sensations she feared and did not know how to quell them. She trusted Reyna, but…"What would Gervain say about this?"

"He won't ever know. He doesn't know everything about me. We enjoy each other and I do not intend to seek a relationship with a woman, certainly not any of the ones here. This is something I want to do for you."

Reyna watched for her friend's reaction.

The thought of what her father would think crossed Maeven's mind, and was instantly dismissed. When had she let the knowledge of his disproval influence her choices?

"*Accept the gift, dragon mother,*" Petulor's voice came into her mind. "*The man has a talisman but you must learn to welcome him. You are safer when you are carrying a child of his. The Serpent's seekers are confused by the mixture.*"

In her mind, Maeven thought back, "*What do you know about these things? You're only three years old and not even mature yet!*"

"*I will be old enough to mate soon,*" Petulor thought back unperturbed. "*The fate of two kingdoms should not rest on only one child. I can make sure you are not interrupted.*"

"Please…" Maeven said quietly.

Reyna hugged her friend and began the lesson.

CHAPTER 7 - Maeven

In the two days since Arlen had left the village, Maeven had given a lot of thought to leaving the area as well. If the Serpent had begun looking for her again, she didn't want to draw him back near the village. Not that she cared particularly for most of the villagers, but because of her son and because the village lay over Exconidor's crypt.

When she had first come to the cave, and Ciabolo had chased her, he hadn't noticed the crypt and Petulor had hidden there. She had spoken to the ghost of Frederick, Exconidor's champion, who had promised to guard the young dragon. He had also said she would be safer here. It felt like that was no longer true.

Being able to talk to other people, even the parochial villagers, had reminded her she was human. The three years she had spent in the cave, struggling to survive, seemed like a boring waste of time. Though she had been able to watch over Wystan from a distance. Now knowing that he was developing into a wizard meant she had to act. The villagers would cast him out if they knew. Zeke may not be able to hide the knowledge forever. She had promised to find someone to train her son. But did she want Wystan sent off with strangers? She ought to go with him, as Lori and Zeke were unlikely to want to leave the village.

He may not be much safer if he went to the palace, where her father and his wizard were. Where else could he go? She hoped that Arlen, when he returned, had some ideas.

Mortmellor hissed and a dribble of flame erupted from her nostrils.

Maeven rose from the rock ledge in the cave where she often sat and walked towards the silhouette in the cave entrance.

Recognising Arlen, she spoke softly to Mortmellor in the ancient language she had learnt from the dragons.

"This man is my guest. He bears one of Thulor's amulets."

"Then Petulor needs to put her smell on him!" was the older dragon's disgruntled reply, as she retreated further into the cave.

"Ven," Arlen asked tentatively, he could not see in the darkness of the cave.

"I'm here," Maeven replied, coming to the entrance. "Come in. I have a lamp somewhere I can light, though I don't usually need it."

She took one of Arlen's hands and led him into the cave. Before she had a chance to look for the lamp or the tinder and flint, Arlen had created a small ball of light in the palm of his free had.

"Stupid of me to forget you were a wizard," Maeven said more to herself.

"Reyna told me I could find you here. There was something you wished to discuss with me?"

"Several things," Maeven said abruptly, to cover the confusion in her mind at the contrast between this polite man and the creature he was when she had first met him.

"How about we sit?"

Arlen pulled her over to a convenient rocky outcrop but made no other move. Maeven sat and pulled her hand free.

"I have been thinking about what you said about Rhovert, about perhaps he couldn't sire children. And I know neither of my sisters seem interested in marrying."

Maeven realised that she was fidgeting with her hands and betraying her agitation. She took a deep breath. "You said that Father would accept you as my husband, if I did – I have decided I will."

Arlen felt his heart begin to beat faster; this was what he had always wanted but he sensed unspoken conditions. "What ... made you decide?" he asked, careful not to betray his feelings.

"I'm not in love with you," she said bluntly. "But it would be expedient. It would make our son legitimate and I want to get pregnant again. If it's by you, those seeking me are confused."

Somehow, Arlen doubted that these were her only reasons. Before he could comment, a strange female voice came into his head.

"I told her the fate of two kingdoms should not rest on a single child."

Arlen felt the hairs on his body stand up. He stood and looked around – there was strong magic there.

Maeven reached out to him and took his hand, the one without the glow.

"It's Dragon Magic you can sense, Petulor is growing in power and you are still not attuned to it.”

Arlen sat back slowly but stiffened again as he saw a silver glow brightening in front of him and a head, ten times bigger than his own, wafted warm sweet smelling breath in his face.

“Two kingdoms,” he forced himself to say as calmly as possible.

“Your brother still has no heir,” Petulor thought at him.

Arlen, once known as Prince El Haba of Vatarik, did not smother his snort of amusement.

“How do you know that?” he asked.

Petulor just wafted her breath at him again.

“Will you stop playing inscrutable know-it-all, dragon-brat!” Maeven snapped at Petulor.

“I am sending my power through the talismans, like my mother did. I can see and hear what each wearer is doing. I heard a report being given to the King.”

“I thought she just powered protections for us,” Maeven said in surprise. “Apart from my little spells of course.”

Petulor did not reply. Instead, she sent a wisp of power through the talisman that Arlen wore and another into Maeven’s mind. For the next half hour, they were not aware of anything but each other. Neither knew or cared that Petulor watched and learnt and meddled a little. When they were again ready to turn their attention outwards, it was towards each other in a silent exchange of understanding; the realisation that something had changed between them.

Maeven silently hugged the man who had managed to make her lose her intended control so thoroughly. She felt him relax and hug her back, gently, in contrast to the wild passion they had shared. Tears leaked from her eyes as she realised that she had found something that she had not realised that she had yearned for. She had found someone who accepted her unconditionally; someone who gave her the close human contact she had missed since her mother died. Even her Father, for reasons of his own, had never hugged her except for one short moment. And she mentally thanked Reyna for opening her eyes so she could accept this gift, from this man.

“You are My Lady,” Arlen said very softly. “From the moment I saw you...”

He accepted Maeven’s tighter embrace as her acceptance of his claim. He would not press her to speak her thoughts aloud. He did not want to spoil the moment.

"You can't stay here," Maeven finally spoke aloud, as she pulled herself free. "Together we make too tempting a target."

Arlen began to rise, knowing her words were true. The Serpent hated them both for defying him and his brother both feared and hated him.

"There's something I want you to do," Maeven continued, as she picked up her discarded clothing. "It's important. We have to go down to the village; you have to meet someone and you will see what I mean."

"I'm intrigued..." Arlen admitted, hoping for more detail but it was not forthcoming.

He dressed carefully. He had not come back to the village in his Guard livery, but dressed as a traveller. A minor illusion had ensured that no one recognised him from his visit two days previously.

They had almost reached the little stream when they heard the screech of an animal; a black feline came into their view. It was proceeding now in a stalking crouch.

Maeven led Arlen on a diverging course, waiting to see what the creature was hunting.

She was moving so quietly, so stealthily, that the cat had not noticed her approach. Arlen appreciated her courage and the ease with which she had materialised a large hunting knife into her hand. Arlen had his sword, his magic and the experience of having hunted these cats himself.

It was soon apparent what the cat's prey was and Wystan, who had wondered far from his home, was playing with the river pebbles and oblivious to his danger.

"No!" Maeven roared, alerting the boy and startling the cat into looking at her.

When the cat realised that its quarry was getting away it began to bound after it.

Arlen was only moments behind Maeven but he could see that they would not reach the boy in time. He drew his sword as he ran but it was slowing him down.

Wystan tripped on a tree root, landing heavily. The cat, quickly closing the distance to the boy, gathered itself to spring onto its victim.

Before Arlen could chant a spell to kill the creature, a flash of brilliance stunned it and it fell awkwardly, trapping the boy beneath it.

Maeven reached it moments later and used her knife to kill the beast; at least she hoped she had. It was bigger than her normal prey of hoppers. Arlen automatically checked that it would not be able to spring up at them and helped Maeven to lift the heavy carcass of the trapped and howling boy. Wystan accepted Maeven's arms as comfort but continued to sob hysterically.

The events had been witnessed from below. A group of men alerted by the noise and armed with farming implements were running up the hill. Zeke was leading them, his eyes on his son. Wystan pulled free of Maeven and Zeke swept him up into his strong arms.

"Thank you for saving him," Zeke said, sincerely.

Maeven merely nodded and bent to pick up her knife. Phineas stopped in front of her and glared. His antipathy was apparent. Then his eyes caught a movement on the wrist that held the knife and he grabbed her by that arm. "Look, this thing of evil is alive."

Maeven had not noticed that the metallic snakes were writhing. The jewel eyes in the tiny darting heads were looking everywhere, glowing a bright green.

Arlen sheathed his sword, placed a hand on the snakes, and whispered an incantation. The snakes hissed and bit him but their efforts had no effect. Instead the snakes tightened convulsively, went limp then solid.

"You are a wizard!" Phineas accused Arlen, his face betraying his distaste. "We do not allow practitioners of magic here. You will leave at once, blasphemer."

"And if this beast had a mate?" Maeven suggested, recovering quickly from the snakes' manifestation. "Are you prepared to kill it before it kills one of you?"

Phineas paled, he had killed smaller predators – foxes and wolves – but never anything so large and so fast. The boy would have been dead if the magician had not stunned the creature. Then he recalled that this woman, this thief, had the courage to run at the beast and to approach it and ensure it was dead. It was not a womanly action.

Maeven read his thoughts in the look on his face; her patience snapped. "You hypocrite, Phineas Adelbartson. You have to find faults with everyone. At least one man here is sincere enough to say 'thank you' without stopping to count the points the other person owes him. You're a great one for being neighbourly and helping and preaching..."

Maeven turned and stalked back towards Arlen but stopped suddenly, feeling the itch of magic and realising that Petulor was nowhere around.

"Petulor?" she called mentally, but received no answer.

She turned in a slow circle and saw that Arlen was doing the same. The Elders were looking worried as if they also felt something.

"Take the boy away!" Phineas told Zeke.

"No! Stay in a group," Arlen commanded.

Something in his air of command caused them to obey even as they looked anew at the traveller.

"What is it?" Maeven asked Arlen as she drew closer to him.

"Something has targeted us here. When I tried to read what was seeking, it recognised me."

"A mistake!" Maeven said succinctly. "Can you deal with it?"

"It wants the boy. It felt the surge of power and assumed it was from him. It doesn't know about Petulor."

"We will just have to convince it we were tricking it." Maeven said with more calm that she felt. She knew the dragon had not stunned the cat.

A figure solidified in front of Zeke. It was man shaped but it moved with a sinuous glide.

"Give me the boy!" the creature hissed.

Zeke held Wystan tighter and the boy hid his face.

Maeven felt a tremor of recognition; beside her Arlen had stiffened.

"Well, well, well. If it isn't the little snake himself," she taunted, hands on her hips and the knife no longer visible.

The man thing spun around. "You!" it spat.

"In the flesh," she agreed as she eyed the creature. "I see you aren't really yourself – couldn't you find anyone stronger than a hedge wizard to take over?"

The creature raised a hand and sent a blast of energy at Maeven, but it bounced off a shield that Arlen had erected around the two of them. Arlen walked forward and the creature's attention switched to him.

The illusion of insignificant farmer was gone. Now he displayed the arrogance of one with power.

"I see my brother has more sense than I gave him credit for. So far he hasn't stooped to the level that our father reached."

The creature hissed angrily. "We will sssee!" it hissed as it swung around to make a grab for Wystan. It found that Maeven had stepped between him and the boy.

"How stupid can you be?" Maeven demanded, glaring at the creature. "The boy is little more than a baby! If he was going to be a mage, and in this town that is unlikely, we won't know for ten or more years. Arlen is a strong wizard, stronger than you are. You've been tricked."

"I don't trussst your tongue woman!"

"You wouldn't know the truth if it bit you!" Maeven retorted. "What use is the body of a baby to you?"

The creature swung its arm around again and stunned the Elders with a blast of power. It was too angry to be subtle. Wystan dropped from Zeke's arms, unharmed but whimpering.

"I will have it because you wisssh me not to."

Maeven felt a roar of anger in her mind. Something big flew over, knocking Arlen down.

Maeven ducked instinctively and plucked Wystan from the ground, even as the man-creature was knocked aside.

With Wystan in her arms, Maeven began to back away. Her thief's instincts were yelling at her to run but she knew better than to turn her back. The creature she faced changed its form in front of her eyes.

It became a giant serpent, towering over her. She stood her ground.

"Run!" she ordered Wystan, as she lowered him carefully to the ground. He needed no further urging.

Her knife appeared again in her hand but even as she slashed the air in front of her, the creature struck, contemptuous of her puny weapon. It grabbed her arm and sank its two fangs into it. Maeven felt the arm go numb, and saw the knife drop from her useless hand. She used her left hand, clenched into a fist to punch at its eyes and her foot to kick at its chest.

"Ssstupid creature," it hissed, taunting her. "I will have you!"

Her punches were having no effect at all but she kept twisting, kicking and punching.

Maeven could not argue with the creature's judgement of her, but she would not let him have her son.

"*Petulor, do something!*" she pleaded in her mind. "Arlen, where are you?" she said aloud.

A burst of flame licked about the serpent but it stopped inches from the creature's scales. A large stone dropped, appearing suddenly above the snake but it too did not injure the snake. Maeven saw that Petulor had not enough power yet to damage the creature.

"Petulor – get – my – son – away."

The ground shook as Petulor sent a blast of power at the snake. Maeven felt the force of it but the snake tightened its grip on her and she was not blasted free. Instead, Maeven felt the paralysis spreading and her legs collapsed beneath her, dragging the snakes head down.

Arlen stumbled to his feet, and then rushed the creature with sword in hand. He slashed at it, using all his might and imbuing the sword with his magic. It hissed angrily and dropped its victim to the ground before rising to its full height again. There was a purple bleeding gash on the side of its head but it appeared not to notice it.

Arlen was ready for it to strike and his sword slashed its eyes as he jumped back to avoid its bite. It hissed again, and moved its head around to try to sense what it could no longer see. Arlen dodged and continued to slash at the creature, causing more bleeding wounds. It began to writhe in agony and its tail flicked around sweeping him off his feet and part way down the hill.

Climbing painfully to his feet, Arlen saw Wystan crouched behind a tree and an angry dragon about to strike.

"Dragon! No! It is too strong. Get the boy away. Get him away!"

Petulor back winged and roared defiance as she landed in a clearing.

Arlen grabbed Wystan and ran to the dragon; hoisting him onto the dragon's back.

"Hold on to the dragon," he ordered the frightened child. "You'll be safe."

The snake was busy with its victim, swallowing it from its feet.

Arlen continued his attack, both magical and physical but the creature had renewed its protections and his slashes had little effect.

"Traitor, you will be next!" it hissed, ignoring his attacks as if they were a minor irritation.

Arlen saw the effort was wasted and dropped his sword and gripped Maeven's shoulders and pulled with all his strength. The snake's tail swept around once more, this time stunning him when he landed hard against a tree.

When he looked again, the serpent had gone – and Maeven had too. Lying on the ground was the golden bracelet that had been used to find her. He looked at with loathing and slumped on the ground in defeat. An unfamiliar sensation of grief filled him. Finally, Ven had accepted him and now she was gone. He had not even met his son.

"Fool!" he berated himself. He saw the boy in his mind, the blond hair, the olive skin – and suddenly knew why Ven had risked herself. The boy was their son. Arlen slowly pulled himself upright and recreated the illusion of harmless traveller. He had to decide what to do next. Without conscious volition he took the bracelet and placed a mage bond on it, rendering it harmless to him.

"Where is the woman?" Phineas demanded, drawing Arlen's attention. The three Elders were all waking from the effect of the magic blast.

"She is gone," Arlen said, watching the play of emotions on the man's face.

"Gone where?"

"Where is my son?" Zeke asked, looking around with real concern.

"Your son is with Petulor and safe. Ven would not let the creature take him."

"So where did the woman go?" Hartog demanded. "We don't want her back here!"

"The creature took Ven when he could not have the child."

"So the God's wheel of justice has turned. The sinner has been taken ..."

"You pious bastard!" Arlen dropped any pretence of civility. "That woman you deride has saved the life of two children from your community within a week. Innocent children! Should she have let them die and done nothing? What has she personally done to you?"

"She is a thief!" Hartog proclaimed and Phineas nodded his agreement.

"Oh, yes. What exactly did she steal from you?" Arlen asked pointedly.

The two men stared back at him.

"Or was it the weapons that she stole from the bandits so that you could get rid of them without bloodshed – the ones you later claimed were removed from them by your God!" Arlen accused, meeting the eyes of the men. "You make me sick – I know the type of men the bandits were, so well that I know you should be grateful that they never found you and your virtuous women. If nothing had been done about them they would have found you in time and I wouldn't be arguing with any of you now."

"We will not listen to such blasphemy!" Hartog said stonily.

"I am afraid that I do not share your faith in your God. Therefore, I will offer you a warning. You are not isolated from the rest of the world up here. You may not care what is happening elsewhere in the Kingdom of Thulor, but you should. Something evil is trying to take over this realm and if the likes of that creature succeed you will not escape its intentions forever, it might only delay it a while. When it chooses to act – who will help you then? I do not think even your God will be able to save you."

"She knew that creature," Zeke said without accusation.

"Yes, and you can all be thankful that it is only a shadow of its former self and that she kept its attention on her. It was a powerful force of evil when Ven bested it with only thieves' tricks, minor magic, and more courage than any of you would have had. At the height of its power it would have made you mindless slaves in a heartbeat and used your life energy to fuel its own power."

"That's totally evil!" Zeke said aghast.

"That's when it was being merciful. You can't imagine what it did to creatures it didn't like." Arlen could not prevent the shudder that shook him. He knew that only too well. "It hates her," he said quietly.

"If the creature has what it wanted then it won't come back!" Phineas stated.

"Won't it?" Arlen challenged.

"It wanted my boy!" Zeke challenged his fellow Elders.

"Her bastard," Hartog reminded the younger man. "Nothing disturbed our peace until she came!"

Zeke looked at his feet for a moment, as if calming himself. He spoke without looking at his fellows.

"I will escort the traveller to our border. Perhaps you both should go and reassure the community that all is well now."

"Thank you, brother Zeke."

Phineas and Hartog seemed eager to leave the company of the traveller.

Zeke said nothing until they were well gone. "Where would the dragon have taken my son?"

"I do not know," Arlen admitted, "but I will find him."

Zeke seemed to see through Arlen's illusion and sense his resolution to do just that.

For a moment, he pondered why a stranger would be so concerned about a boy he did not know.

"You are the boy's father," Zeke said softly.

Arlen merely nodded.

"He is a good child but he has magic. Ven said she would find someone to train him," Zeke continued softly. "As much as I love him – he should not come back here."

"I understand," Arlen said. "I will make sure that he does not forget the love you have for him and you may be sure he will be safe and loved."

"Thank you."

CHAPTER 8 - Rhovert and Atlantis

The afternoon sun was warm on the riders' backs, although the breeze near the top of the southern mountains was cool. The horses, sturdy mountain bred geldings with shaggy coats, were finding their own way up the steep and often rocky mountain trail.

A shadow passed over and Prince Rhovert of Thulor looked up at the cloudless sky and shivered suddenly. At the same moment, both horses began sniffing the air, and moving their heads around.

Rhovert drew his sword, and held it across his lap – ready for use. Atlantis, his consort, reached for a horse bow and moved her quiver closer to her hand. Both had travelled these mountains before and knew the types of predators that roamed the heights. The two legged ones were as dangerous as those with four paws. They proceeded at a cautious pace, looking ahead for possible ambush sites.

Atlantis had a sudden vision, stronger and more vivid than any she'd ever had before. "They've a huge canine. It will jump down on us at that large rock."

"How many men are there," Rhovert asked in a low voice, accepting the statement.

Atlantis let the warning vision play out. "Six. Three on each side, and they have a net."

She halted her horse to wait while Rhovert rifled through his saddlebag. He found a small, ball like object – one of a range of oddments his sister, the sorceress Finora, had made for him.

"They all look pretty starved," Atlantis added.

Neither she nor Rhovert were dressed like nobles, but to the rabble ahead, they would seem well off.

"Come on," Rhovert directed, and they spurred the horses to a pace resembling a normal oblivious pace.

"Stop," Atlantis said, just before the rock. Both reigned their horses to a halt.

In front of them, a net fell harmlessly, and when it reached the ground, a huge, brown canine leapt and not finding the expected prey, looked around. As it spotted the riders, Rhovert threw the ball he held. Its attention was instantly diverted. The ball smelt like fresh meat and bounced like it was alive. The dog's mouth caught it, its teeth puncturing the outer casing and liquid gushed out. It fell, unconscious.

The raiders raced into sight, screaming curses, then slowed when they realised that their quarry was neither terrified nor tangled in the net. Only for a moment, and they came on again. One fell with an arrow in his shoulder. Two more saw Atlantis nock another arrow into position and thought to confuse her by moving in two different directions. The one with his sword out seemed intent on watching for a moment when she was distracted, the other seemed to just be edging away.

Atlantis wasn't fooled, the immediate premonition that had to have come from her dragon talisman, showed her the second one straightening up and preparing to rush her. Instantly, she had her horse turning enough to send the notched arrow at him. The horse kept turning as she readied another arrow, and fired instinctively. The two anguished cries told her the arrows had flown truly.

Rhovert had his sword in hand, as two raiders ran at him. His mount pivoted, taking direction from its rider's legs. Starved looking these men might be, but they knew how to fight. Two attacked, the third stayed back, knowing he'd be in the way. However, they had not expected their targets to avoid their trap, or to fight back so effectively. First one, then the other took a slash at the man on the horse. Rhovert parried the first, and blocked the second, twisting his blade. When the first attacked again, his face met the hilt of Rhovert's blade and he growled obscenities as he tried to pull his tormentor from his horse. His sight was blurred and he didn't see the foot coming at his chest. He was fast enough to scramble backwards, away from the feet of the horse.

When the third man began to rush forward, Rhovert bellowed, "Stop!"

The three men still able to fight, suddenly became statues. Atlantis eyed him.

"I didn't know you could do that." She was still watching the third man who was on her side.

"Your brother told me that anyone could do magic if they had the right potion, or in our case, one of the talismans -assuming that Petulor was sending power to them. When you just had that premonition, I hoped it would work."

"Then what do you plan to do with these?" Atlantis gestured at the angry looking statues.

Rhovert dismounted and stood face to face with one of his attackers. "Why did you attack us?"

That one made no attempt to answer. Rhovert studied each of the others in turn. Finally, the one with the arrow in his shoulder and still able to move, staggered to his feet. "We just wanted food, Sir, or some coins to buy some."

"Why didn't you ask?" Rhovert challenged.

The man in front of him spat in his face, and began a torrent of curses.

"Enough!" Rhovert commanded. "If you are too lazy to hunt for yourselves or train that dog to hunt for you, and prefer to rob travellers, you are no better than brigands. The King has placed a bounty on all brigands – dead or alive."

The warning was not lost on any of the men. The third swordsman and the one with the arrow in his shoulder, began to inch backwards.

The one facing Rhovert shouted, "I will personally kill any of you who think to run off. This lousy merc needs magic to be good. I bet he's too much of a coward to fight me one on one."

Rhovert laughed at him. "So speaks the man who needed two others to help him fight me."

The man's eyes narrowed and his face tightened. He was probably feeling the 'Stop' command wearing off.

"I am prepared to give you all a chance to go off quietly and leave us alone," Rhovert proposed. "If, as you say, you are all starving, I will give you the three hoppers we caught earlier, and our last few copper bits."

The man spat again. "You've got more than that we can take. We've not seen a woman for months, and such a pretty boy merc like you is even looking inviting. What's you reckon, men?"

Rhovert turned his heard slightly, caught Atlantis's look and nodded slightly. There would not be a third chance for these men.

Movement by the man in front of him was the only warning Rhovert had of the next attack. He saw the knife came up in the man's left hand as he yelled, "Horus! Attack!"

Rhovert gripped the man's left wrist and kneed him in the groin. The man's head came forward as he doubled over in pain, and then it collided with the hilt of his victim's sword. The man went down and the next man to come back at him went down with a deep slice in his side.

The dog, still groggy from the drugged ball, teetered over to Atlantis, who put one hand out to pat him. The raider who thought to trick her before, tried to rush her, only to end with an arrow in his chest.

The dog licked her hand when she reached out to pat it again. She glanced up as Rhovert challenged the one remaining uninjured raider.

"So, this is how low you have stooped, Jerint Hardacre. How did you manage to escape the Serpent and still have half a mind?"

The man stared and licked lips suddenly gone dry. "I..."

Atlantis moved up beside her consort, studied the man and then said, "Because he hasn't. Once you swear to the Serpent, you are his until death. The question should be, why is he down here near Declanor, when his master is sending his spies and raiders down over the north border?"

"Indeed," Rhovert agreed. "Jerint? Talk and I might let you live."

"Prince Rhovert, Sir, I didn't know what I was agreeing to. Makes me sick now, knowing."

"Why were you lot down here?"

"We was to stop people crossing the border."

"How many groups are there?"

"There's..."

Abruptly, the man seemed unable to talk, and clawed at his throat as if being strangled.

With a sharp curse, Atlantis drew a knife and thrust it between the man's fingers, and into his neck. A high pitched scream, too high for a human throat, punished her ears. It only lasted a second.

"What..." Rhovert began to ask, but when the man fell, limp and dead, he saw the knife had gone through something red-brown and ugly, before continuing into the man. "We had better check the others. Father mentioned little demons."

Atlantis needed no prompting. The vile little creatures would go to find a new host if not killed before their original host's body cooled. The other men she checked had none of the parasitic creatures, and the leader of the group was the only other with one and Rhovert dispatched that, and its host.

When he looked over the scene, he saw that the two raiders that had still been alive had killed themselves rather than face the fate of brigands when caught.

"We will drag this lot off the trail," Rhovert decided. He was more than glad that his consort was not one of the delicate court ladies. The need to kill sickened him. "When we get to the border guard station, they can arrange to get them and identify the rest of them."

"What about the dog?"

"They trained it to attack. I don't know if it is safe to keep him."

The dog came up to Atlantis and pressed its body against her leg. Its head came to her waist.

"Sit, Horus," she told it gently and it obeyed her. She went to help Rhovert with the bodies, glancing at it every now and then. It watched her, ignoring the two horses that had taken the opportunity to wander over to nibble the nearest patches of tufty grass.

"What did you do to it?" Rhovert asked as he headed for the horses. The dog was still following Atlantis with its eyes.

"More like what did you do? What was in that ball?"

"Just something to knock out wild predators," Rhovert shrugged. "Finora might have added some magic to the herbal tincture."

"What say we head off and see if it follows?" Atlantis suggested.

"Well, release it from your order or it will starve to death right there," Rhovert suggested. "Heck, if it follows, it does, but it had better be able to catch its own food."

He found some grass to wipe the blood off his sword, enough so he could sheathe it. He ignored the remonstrations of his past weapons teachers and promised he would clean it properly as soon as they came to a stream or rivulet.

CHAPTER 9 – Maeven

The serpent shape flickered and settled into a man shaped figure and a smaller, slighter shape at its feet. The other two humans in the chamber were unaware they had an avid voyeur. The paunchy wizard ogled them as he fondled himself. Seeing the activity had elevated the sense of satiation that was a reward from his true master. As the sensation peaked and ebbed, he heard a voice in his mind.

"Iss the woman alive?"

He leant down, felt for a pulse in the woman's neck and not feeling one there, used his foot to tip her on her side. The motion caused an eruption as the woman vomited. Even though he was now sure she was alive, he fastidiously checked the woman's neck again. This time he felt something.

The feeling of arousal was rising again and the wizard knew it was leaking from the demon that controlled him. Some of the demon's thoughts were also leaking, he knew from them that the sight of the woman was rousing ecstatic thoughts of revenge and torture. The demon was very pleased with the success of the raid, even though he had failed to capture the wizard child. The wizard anticipated his other reward, being able to siphon off power from the demon that he could transfer to his personal power artefacts for use at a later time.

"Carry the woman to the king," the wizard heard now. The demon's power was already feeding into him, making him feel more powerful than the king. The demon had a powerful mind, but he needed a human to merge with to be able to move freely in the human world.

The wizard put a smirk on his face. He enjoyed the perks of being the mouthpiece for the demon. He got to give orders to his childhood friend – the bossy, arrogant prince who had enjoyed lording it over him. Now, the self-proclaimed King of Vatarik had to take orders from him.

Breathing through his mouth, so he didn't have to smell the woman, he lifted her without particular care, and walked to within an arm's length of the king's opulent four poster bed. Still he went unnoticed, and he ogled the completely nude, voluptuous concubine who considered herself queen of Vatarik. He felt his own manhood rousing again as the king performed with the woman – smacking her hard as he thrust unmercifully. The woman screamed and began to writhe as her own crescendo came. The king collapsed on her and only then noticed the watcher.

"Wedek, I'll have you whipped. Who let you in?"

"Tut tut, your kingship," Wedek chastised. "Our master did."

King El Rasho rolled off his woman and stood up, reaching for a scarlet lounging robe to cover himself. He stepped away from the bed as if the woman was of no further interest. The woman, still in the throes of extreme arousal, didn't care if the wizard was ogling her.

"So, what trash did you bring with you," El Rasho drawled. He hid the annoyance he felt at being interrupted by the hedge wizard. He could never be certain when the Serpent, Ciabolo was ascendant in the man.

"The master sends you a present," Wedek said in his own voice.

"Another female?" El Rasho said silkily, he stared into the wizard's eyes and enjoyed seeing the man take a step back in fear. He ignored the female as he dominated the wizard who began to tremble, recalling the punishments the king had given him when he was angry.

"A ssspecial female, your highnesss," Ciabolo's sibilant voice came from Wedek's throat. The wizard's eyes had gone from brown to orange in an instant.

El Rasho stopped his sly leering at the wizard. He grew instantly wary now that Ciabolo was dominant, not Wedek.

"Have you desscided yet, human," Ciabolo increased his presence by altering the appearance of his wizard bearer. He looked now to have purple tattoos all over his uncovered arms.

"Have you recovered fully?" El Rasho countered, allowing his concubine to approach and fondle him as he spoke.

Ciabolo did not answer the question.

"I am not a wizard; I cannot help you regain your power," El Rasho continued.

"There iss room for only one Emperor," Ciabolo snarled. "If you want to be ssseen to be Emperor, you will join with me now."

El Rasho felt the demon's power trying to force his mind, amplified through the little incubus demon nestled into the base of his throat. The temptation to be able to control some of that power, as his father had, was difficult to resist.

"Ciabolo!" El Rasho managed to say, "You cannot afford to be impatient. I cannot commit myself to you until I have engendered an heir."

"Then look to my gift, human. Your brother proved hiss manhood by getting thiss one with child."

"My brother is a traitor," El Rasho snarled, finally looking at the unconscious female. Then, he didn't try to control his expression as recognition dawned.

The smile that distorted Wedek's face was a reflection of his own.

Ciabolo said, "I will give you one human year to get an heir, and then you will join with me."

"Yes, yes," El Rasho agreed without considering what he was saying.

His eyes were glittering with spite and his mind was full of the dreadful things he could do to this woman. "Put her down over there," he told the wizard, pointing to the stone ledge around the fountain in his suite. He pushed his concubine aside and followed the wizard and his burden. His nose noted a smell about her and he wrinkled his nose with revulsion. The woman would have to be cleaned up before he went near her.

"Jillicen!" he called to his concubine who had donned a wispy gown. She hurriedly turned her scowl to a seductive smile.

"Clean this woman up." He caught sight of the returning scowl.

"I'm twice the woman that bitch is."

"The master wishes it, and you will enjoy watching, won't you my dear."

Jillicen only then recognised the woman who had been her mistress for a time in Thulor. "And my reward?" She smiled in anticipation.

"After I have done my master's bidding on this rack of bones. I will do what you want of me to forget her."

Jillicen's smile returned and she went off imperiously to summon servants to prepare a bath in the king's suite. A glare from El Rasho sent Wedek hurrying from the royal suite, but he had the smirk back on his face.

Maeven woke slowly. The air around her was warm and sweetly scented. A faint breeze moved air across her skin and she realised that she was completely undressed. It didn't seem to matter, she was relaxed, loathe to move.

The roof over her was unfamiliar, yet reminiscent of somewhere she had been before. Her mind wondered, idly, *Where am I?* No answer came.

"She's awake now," a voice announced.

That voice! She knew it. Spiteful, covetous, oily. The face that leant over to look at her was one out of her worst nightmares. Not only did it herald history repeating itself, but painful vengeance because she had escaped from the man once before. The face had a finger width black moustache and a pointed black beard – not blond like his brother who had raped her first, but with whom she now had a connection. She wanted to scream, but it was like her throat was still paralysed.

"Oh, don't worry, I am not about to hurt you," the oily voice of the man told her. "No, not until I know you can feel pain. I intend to punish you for tricking me, and escaping when I had laid claim to you. Now I learn that you let my brother prove his manhood. I am so glad that you destroyed the proof."

The face moved its focus so the eyes looked her up and down. "Really, you are too scrawny for my taste. Boring too, no doubt. If you could be inventive, like my queen here, then you might actually enjoy my punishment."

Maeven found her memories returning, and the woman glaring at her took a name, Jilli, and a role as her maid for a few days. Then the things she had heard about the woman returned, and El Rasho's words took on meaning.

He went on, "Since my master wishes me to get you pregnant, I intend to make it pleasant for me, for as long as it takes."

A shiver went through her. He was going to hurt her, and in doing so, get roused by her pain. He was sick.

"The healer tells me that the venom will wear off by this evening. I'll be back then. In the meantime, I'm letting you have company. I don't want you trying to escape. If you did, you'd deserve what you get. A well whipped wench is so very satisfying."

If she could have looked away, she would have. The laughter

of the self-proclaimed king and his ambitious concubine, brought on nausea that did not go away when they left the chamber, and it worsened with each new visitor. They were guards, clad in black uniforms of loose fitting cloth, bound at wrists, waist and ankles. It was clear that they had permission to molest her, touch her in any way they wanted, but mercifully, not go any further.

As the day progressed, she found more movement possible, but still not enough to help herself. It just gave her visitors more ways to make her feel soiled.

The arrival of silent black clad servants, and the departure of the latest tormentors, was not a relief. Yes, they washed her once more, brushed her hair, anointed her with scented oils, prepared her for the attentions of a king, but it was impersonal, and without interacting with her. They slipped away as soon as El Rasho and Jilli returned.

Memories of a past time were vivid in her mind, and she told herself that she had survived then, and could again. She would not scream, that would only excite him further. She would endure, but already the voices in her head were sounding like panicked birds.

El Rasho grabbed her by the carefully arranged hair, and dragged her up from the pallet where the servants had left her. It looked opulent, but felt like it was filled with rough-hewn stones.

"What first, my queen," El Rasho turned his head to his concubine.

"Let me tell her how much I loved serving her."

"Do that," he allowed, focusing again on his victim.

A short moment later, Maeven felt herself being hit by something wide and flexible, that stung wherever it touched.

"Look at me," El Rasho demanded, as Maeven closed her eyes to focus on dulling the pain. "How do you like our little warm up?"

"She can keep it up. Then when it is your turn, I won't feel anything," Maeven told him, adding, "I didn't realise this was so arousing."

El Rasho gestured sharply and Jilli stopped. He threw Maeven back down on the pallet and began. He had no intention of being gentle, or considerate. This was worse than the first time she had been taken unwilling. This man's brother had been the first, but he had roused her before taking her. She had been hurt and humiliated but it had been gentle compared to this.

This was a man's revenge on one who had outsmarted him. It was revenge on his brother who had taken something he had wanted. This was revenge on a kingdom that still resisted him and an act of defiance towards the creature that wanted to be his master.

Maeven endured, sure of one thing; El Rasho would want her alive. He would want to humiliate her in a hundred ways. This pain would stop.

She had no excess flesh on her so his grip on her arms was bruising. His teeth drew blood from her breasts and her head ached from being bounced on the hard pallet. Soon this bout of revenge would exhaust itself and El Rasho would turn to the voluptuous Jilli, who was already writhing with lust, aroused by seeing pain inflicted on one she detested. Finally, the welcome blackness enveloped her.

When he saw his victim was no longer conscious, King El Rasho continued to bring himself to a crescendo of sensation, and then briefly rested on the bony contours of the scrawny Princess of Thulor.

Finally he withdrew, hoping he would not need to repeat the act too often before the wench quickened with his child. It wasn't that he didn't enjoy hurting her and humiliating her - it was that he preferred his women well fleshed and willing to go to extremes to please him. Like his current favourite, Jillicen.

Then there were other ways to break the foreign Princess and he would enjoy them too.

CHAPTER 10 - Rhovert and Atlantis

The ambush had left Rhovert very wary as they continued on their way towards the border. He wondered if it had been the chance encounter it had seemed, or if the enemy knew he was trying to reach Declanor. Too bad Jerint Hardacre had been unable to tell him much before the controlling demon had acted. More to the point, had the little demon managed to contact its master?

He continued on, looking around as he rode and watching the birds for signs of other travellers. He hoped the dog would warn of anyone close by. It was trotting on the far side of Atlantis as if she had raised it from a pup.

"Did you bewitch that dog?" Rhovert asked to pass the time.

"Not that I'm aware," Atlantis told him. "Though Roman has always been good with animals. I never thought I was, since most of the large critters I've faced have wanted to have a piece of me. Whatever your sister put in that ball, must have done something."

"Well, let's hope it stays friendly."

"I think if we treat it right, it will. And it might give us warning of trouble."

"We will see," Rhovert compromised. "From here to the guard post should be fairly safe, but if the enemy is trying to stop people going over the border, there may be more groups of bandits around."

"I wonder why he doesn't want Thulor to get help from Declanor? They don't have a big army or lots of wizards."

Rhovert shrugged. "If Arlen is at the guard post when we get there, I'll see what he thinks. Either way, I will ask that the information gets back to father. At least I have done that much. Up until today, I've felt like I have been running away, or sent away. I preferred things when I was moving about the kingdom and reporting back to Father."

"The King has other means to find out what is happening in his realm," Atlantis, the Prince's Consort reminded him. "And you are the logical person to be his envoy to Declanor. I just wish he would let me look for Ven!"

"My sister is good at surviving," Rhovert said, though with a trace of doubt. "I think he knows that she is alive and well. But I still feel I am doing nothing to fight the Serpent. Even three years ago, it was mainly you girls that defeated him."

"Us girls!" Atlantis said thoughtfully. "Ciabolo's mistake – he underestimated us. I think he has underestimated you too. Most of the court nobles think you're useless – thanks to your play-acting at court functions. You should be thankful – if he thought you a threat, I think he would be giving you more of his attention."

"You may be right, but what makes you think I'm that important?"

"Apart from being your Father's heir, you mean? I don't know. Something about your father's insistence that we produce an heir – it seems to be an obsession with him. It makes me think that he considers the continuation of the Royal Line is as important as the defence of his kingdom."

"It might be worth considering, though he certainly hasn't confided any such notion to me," Rhovert said mildly, omitting to repeat what they both knew – that the King seldom explained himself to anyone.

They continued on, mostly in silence. Until Rhovert noticed a shadow passing over again and checked the sky once more. There were still no clouds. He shivered, hoping there was not another ambush ahead. Then he heard the dog begin to growl, deep in its throat, and his horse began to prance uneasily and not want to keep going forward. He eased his horse to a stop and Atlantis pulled hers up next to him. They exchanged looks.

"Trouble?" Rhovert quizzed Atlantis.

"I don't know. I haven't had another vision, and my amulet is cool."

Rhovert reached up to touch his own, just as a warm smoky breeze began to blow into their faces. It was odd, because until then, the breeze had been cool and gusting from behind.

"Benbow boy, what's wrong," Rhovert spoke to his horse, respecting the animal's instincts. He looked around carefully but saw nothing to raise his own suspicions until he looked along the trail ahead of him again and a silver glow almost dazzled him.

Rhovert looked up and up and saw the dragon's head lowering until the dragon's snout sniffled his hair. His horse was quivering with fright.

"King's Son – you must come!"

It took Rhovert a moment to recognise that the strange voice in his head was speaking the old language.

"Dragon mage – what is your name?" he answered in the same language.

"I am Petulor, daughter of Thulor. Please hurry; there is someone near who needs help."

Petulor sprang aloft, and dust flew into the air. She flew slowly, allowing them to follow her at a rate the horses could maintain.

"Maeven went off with Petulor; do you think it's her?" Atlantis asked as they spurred the horses to a trot on a smooth section of trail.

"I don't know," Rhovert admitted. "I just feel we have to hurry."

The wailing had a definite childlike quality.

"I want my Ma!"

Rhovert just had time to grab the reins of the other horse before Atlantis was off it and running toward the cave. He dismounted and found a place to tether the horses, ordered the dog to "guard", then followed at a run.

Atlantis remembered these caves from a previous visit but she did not have to go in very far. Just on the edge of where the sunlight reached was a heap on the floor and the source of the audible misery.

Without a second thought, she gathered the child into her arms and hugged him.

"You are safe now, little one," she repeated until the crying eased. Then she said, "Tell me what happened."

The story came out in disjointed pieces and it was a short while after he had finished speaking before his two listeners finished piecing the story into a logical sequence and the full import sank in.

"Dragon's Breath!" Rhovert swore. "This is all Maeven's mess! We will have to take him back to his foster parents; they will be worried sick about him. Petulor! Has that dragon got no sense?"

Rhovert strode back to the cave entrance and looked around but saw no trace of the dragon. He stomped back.

"I don't want to go back!" Wystan said defiantly from the protection of the Atlantis's arms.

"Why not?" Rhovert asked, still seeing the child as someone else's problem.

"I want Ven! She understands me! She don't treat me like a baby. She saved me from the snaky person!"

"But your parents love you!" Rhovert chided him, crouching down to be nearer eye level with him.

"The dragon said Ven was my Ma!"

Rhovert stopped himself from cursing again. That innocent little admission made the situation so much more complicated. He sat down on the rock floor and finally took a really good look at the boy.

"The snaky person swallowed her, but the dragon says she's still alive." Wystan's eyes had grown wide.

"So Ven has got herself into a bit of trouble again," Atlantis said casually, but the eyes meeting Rhovert's were full of worry. "And Petulor had the sense to bring him where we could care for him."

"And knowing Ven, she will be giving the snake indigestion!" Rhovert commented to hide his real thoughts.

Wystan gave a short laugh, and then quickly sobered up.

"I want to help my Ma."

"So do I," Atlantis agreed. "Though I have a very good idea of where they will have taken her and it is not a place for a young man with no fighting skills."

"I can blast anyone who tries to stop me, like I did that cat!" Wystan claimed, looking determined.

Rhovert looked to have had a second major revelation. He suddenly knew, without any possibility of doubt, who had sired the boy.

"I am willing to wager that my father doesn't know about this."

"I would not be too sure," Atlantis disagreed. "He keeps so much to himself. However, he might not know all. I had heard Ven say things, about that time she didn't want to discuss, but she'd said she'd..."

"Who is your father?" Wystan interrupted, aware that he was being talked about.

"Ven is my sister," Rhovert answered obliquely. If Maeven had not told the King about her child, he doubted that she had told anyone else either.

"Then you are my Uncle."

Rhovert smiled across at the boy. "Yes and my name is Rhovert and my wife, who is hugging you, is Atlantis."

The idea in his mind was shared by Atlantis, that the boy might be safer if he did not know he was heir to the Kingdom of Thulor after his Uncle.

"I'm kind of hungry," Rhovert said to change the subject. "What say we find enough wood to build a small fire in here and let Atlantis catch us some hoppers for tea?"

Wystan thought he was being teased. "Women don't catch hoppers!"

"This one does," Atlantis confirmed. "At least I do if we want to eat tonight."

Atlantis, along with the dog Horus, returned to find a small fire going, the horses tended and the bedding arranged on the far side of the fire. Then, whilst she prepared to cook the three hoppers, she listened to the seemingly endless questions Wystan was asking of his new uncle. It occurred to her that such an intelligent child was much better away from the restrictive life of that mountain village; particularly since he was also magic gifted.

After a while she gave the surprisingly patient Rhovert a break from answering questions by telling Wystan some harmless tales about his newly discovered Ma.

They were both glad of the break to eat their cooked hoppers and that Wystan fell asleep soon after he had finished his share.

"We could take him to Gisella," Atlantis suggested, referring to her sister-in-law. "She's back at home in Declanor and her brother is a minor wizard. He can at least start to train him; show him how to do things with only a trickle of power."

"It sounds like a feasible idea," Rhovert considered. "He'd be safer out of the kingdom. I will have to tell Father about him; though I would give much to see his face when he finds out!"

"Then simply send a coded message to tell him he has a grandson. The details can wait until we see him in person." Atlantis suggested and shared Rhovert's anticipatory grin.

"I can't believe that Maeven never even mentioned him to you," Rhovert confided in his wife. "The rest of us and Father, well, she wouldn't tell us for any one of a hundred little reasons, but you are her closest friend. However, it is probably just as well, because he hasn't been a target of the kingdom's enemies. I really like him, 'Lantis, he's gentle, intelligent, polite..."

"And have you considered that it will take some pressure off you and me?" Atlantis interrupted.

"Do you dislike your wifely duties so much?" Rhovert teased.

"No, but we have been trying, dutifully, for two years now and if I was going to conceive..." Atlantis could not bring herself to voice her doubts.

"He isn't in the direct line," Rhovert pointed out, reminding her of one of the King's arguments in getting them to wed.

"He has a crown shaped birthmark like you and Maeven!" Atlantis told him. "He told me it was like part of a wagon's wheel but it's the same as yours. What does that tell you?"

"He is indeed of dragon-blood and favoured by the dragons. Well, this complicates things too," Rhovert pointed out. "That is if we want to keep his existence secret. We will still have to pass through the guard post."

"Are they expecting you?" Atlantis asked.

"No. Father said to stay out of the public eye. What are you thinking?"

"Wystan and I could go ahead first, and you could follow – or we follow you."

"No, I won't risk that – even though I know how good you are."

"Well, we can say that we are escorting the boy to a relative in Declanor, which will be true. Though if anyone recognises you in your merc get up, I'd be surprised. How common a name is Rhovert anyway?"

"Not all that common."

"And, I am not so well known. Nor did your father announce that we were wedded. No one would expect you to have a son."

"When we get to the guard post, you take Wystan and see about getting supplies and I will talk to Arlen if he's there."

CHAPTER 11 - Maeven

Wherever she was, Maeven was glad of one thing – she was alone. The floor might be stone cobbles, and the only light from an unshuttered, high barred window, but she was blessedly alone. Her head was aching, and the rest of her body sore, but by herself she had a chance to see if she could draw on Petulor's magic from so far away.

Lying quietly, she tried to imagine the cool breeze she had come to associate with the dragon's magic, like the time she had been healed back in the dragon's crypt under the hill village. She felt it very faintly, but it was enough to dull her aches, and pains. With the headache easing, she was able to think. Could she get away?

Forcing herself to get up, she felt her way around the walls, to the door, and felt around that. She couldn't even find a keyhole. Not that finding one would help – she didn't have old Merlie's magical keys with her. They were still hidden back in her cave in the hills. So, her first priority would be to get them to put her somewhere else. Well, there was a way to do that – convince El Rasho that she liked it in his dungeon, because she would likely get ill and not be able to conceive. They hadn't given her any food yet, or she would have found it during her feel around. So that was another point. They didn't have mage bonds on her either. In that way this place was better than her father's dungeon. That had been the worst time of her life, so this was better. It still could be worse, this might have been somewhere down in the caverns under the lake. Some of Ciabolo's noisome creatures probably still lived there. She couldn't defend herself from them - she must have dropped her hunter's long knife when fighting Ciabolo's snake manifestation. She must remember that they didn't like water, though would Ciabolo need to manifest that way very often?

Her mind ran over the very short list of things she had magicked to follow her once Petulor had decided to power her little magics as her mother had. Item by item she recited the spell to reveal them, and then individually hid each one again. It meant that she still had some magic residue from Petulor. She might still be able to do an invisibility spell on herself, or bribe a servant, but she would have to hoard the magical residue for the right moment. Unless she could get more.

Suddenly, she berated herself. Yes, in the little pouch of gems she had made follow her, she had some fine powdered dragon shell. That was a powerful healing agent. She could swallow some to heal, or perhaps to get it to act like a potion to power a spell. She would need water, or some sort of drink to wash it down. It would be like swallowing sand, otherwise.

Feeling more confident, Maeven did another round of the dark cell. This time sliding her foot from side to side before each step, to check for things on the stones. She hoped her flimsy concubine robe had been thrown in with her, for at the moment she was still without any covering. This time, her hand touched the wall higher than it had the first time, and her hand touched an old rusty chain and memories of her father's dungeon returned.

"Just have to hope his foulness doesn't think of mage bonds," she thought to herself.

She was under the window when she heard a scraping noise, and something being pushed over the stones. A light showed where the sliding wooden panel was, but it was   too small to crawl through. She waited until the light had gone before moving that way. She crouched to feel what had been shoved in. A flat piece of wood, two pieces of flat, hard bread, a wedge of crumbling cheese that smelt bad, and a carved wood mug of water. She smelt that, and took a small mouthful to taste it. It seemed okay, but she didn't want it or the food to cause her to be sick, or have the flux. She had yet to find a privy hole if the area had one.

Her intention to ignore the off smelling cheese and the hard bread, didn't last. Her stomach began to growl and knot in hunger. She sat next to the tray, recalled a spell for purifying water and decided to add a pinch of dragon shell as well to be sure. While she had the pouch accessible, she decided to add a tiny bit to the cheese and a little on each piece of bread. It wouldn't hurt...

In fact, once she had forced the cheeses down, and softened the bread with a little water, and ate that – she was feeling much better. All her pains were gone and in the dark, no one could see her smile.

One of the black clad guards came for her a day or two later. It wasn't until they reached a better lit passage that she recognised him as one of her molesters on the day of her arrival. He was already doing it again, as he held her arm tight and forced her to walk. He didn't try to go any further, and Maeven wondered if he didn't dare. She wondered, What would happen if he did?

When they reached a servants only level, Maeven had decided to risk a small spell – one designed to raise lust in a man. Her escort gave a low growl, pressed her against the wall and used his free hand to start unbuckling his trousers. Just when he had his manhood exposed a voice roared, "What are you doing, Levester?"

Hiding her shaking, which was stifled laugher, with wide eyes and a fearful expression, she watched her escort's superior drag him aside and hit him hard enough to knock him out. With a snarl of his own, this man dragged her himself, until he reached a bathing room where he called for the servants. They had a bath ready for her, and again prepared her for her liaison with the king. Maeven's amusement faded, at this reminder of fresh pain to come.

As she tried to distance herself from El Rasho's soon to come attention, Maeven decided that she was better off than the soft ladies of her father's court, or those in the retinues of his Lords. They would have been catatonic by now. They would never have lived for years in a cave with minimum luxuries, and the need to find their own food. She had become hardened to that life. In some ways her current existence was a vast improvement. Just not all of it.

She had the use of servants and they were not treating her harshly, just doing as ordered in an efficient and thorough fashion. She had tried to get them to talk, but after a while, when they ignored her, she had seen the dead look in their eyes and gave up. They were either drugged, completely broken, or controlled by intense fear of magic. That might be her intended fate when El Rasho had finished with her, but she was determined not to let it happen.

Jilli came in just as the servant slaves had finished robing her in another of the see through diaphanous gowns that the wives of Vatarin Princes wore. She sniffed, and made a face.

"Seems that nothing can take the stench of the dungeon from you."

"Good," Maeven agreed with alacrity. "Means that the bastard that you prostitute yourself with, will lose interest in me faster."

"Unfortunately for you, he thinks he can get you pregnant."

"Yeah, more fool him."

"Why?"

Maeven just laughed, and that brought Jilli close enough to twist her fingers in the hair of the one she considered an interloper. "Just what do you mean, bitch?"

"Well, for one thing, you'll have to put up with him paying me a lot of attention."

"He'd much rather have me."

"Perhaps, but he will have to keep coupling with me until he gets me pregnant, if he can. Hasn't had any luck with any of his wives yet. And since he has me in the dungeon, in the dark, with very little food, and all the sicknesses I can catch down there, the chances of me getting pregnant is very, very small."

"Huh!" Jilli released her fingers, thinking on what Maeven had said. "But he intends to make you hurt!"

"Yeah...that gave the act some unexpected spice," Maeven hinted, although it was a complete lie. Jilli would probably believe it she decided, since it was true for her. "It will mean you keep getting second use out of him," she went on. "He won't be quite as lusty when it's your turn."

Jilli hid her reaction well, but Maeven saw the tightening of her lips and the narrowing of her eyes.

"Is he going to let you hit me again?" Maeven asked.

That didn't get her an answer. Jill just grabbed her arm and said, "Come on, he's waiting for you."

El Rasho quickly sensed Jilli's disgruntlement. Maeven didn't hear their low voiced conversation, but eventually she caught the words, "...this evening." After that, Jilli looked less sullen, but she didn't seem to be roused by watching her lover perform with another woman.

This time, it was as bad as before. Maeven finally pretended to black out again, so El Rasho would finish and leave her alone. As she expected, he called for Jilli and took her to his bed.

Thinking her hated rival was unconscious, Jilli didn't moderate her voice when she began to belittle El Rasho's performance or lack of it with her. She was jealous, but the king was not to be denied the reward he had promised himself. He knew exactly how to rouse his queen from the initial slaps to the eventual moans of pleasure.

After they had finished, still thinking she was oblivious, El Rasho began talking.

"You are my queen. Nothing I have to do to that scrawny wench comes close to what you do to me. You know why I have to do this."

"No, I don't! If you get a child from her, it will mean he'll want to take you over. Then you won't be able to do what you please. You'll be useless in bed. Wedek only gets off when he watches us."

"If I don't get a son, he'll throw me aside." El Rasho sounded petulant.

"Well, I don't care if you don't get her pregnant."

"Let's not argue about the royal wench. I have an unpleasant duty. One of my guards thought to take her himself. I will let you watch him being whipped and I will let you have him afterwards."

"You'd reward him?" Jilli asked.

"No, the reward is for you. Once you finish with him, I'll have him hung."

Maeven felt no remorse for the guard. He and the other who had "guarded" her on that first afternoon were beasts in human guise. They liked inflicting pain on others – including the servants who had no recourse to fight them off. The promise given to Jilli though, and her pleased response, made her feel ill. She'd had a reputation for seducing men back in Thulor, but this...was even more perverted.

Maeven was returned to the dungeon again, until El Rasho had her dragged out again to be made ready for him. The only difference this time was that Jilli was absent. She wondered at that, and dared to speak as El Rasho pounded into her.

"Jilli getting jealous, is she?"

"She has no reason to be, bitch."

"True, you're no great lover."

El Rasho paused for long enough to slap her hard. "And you might as well be a sheep."

"Good to know you aren't enjoying this. I'm getting to like it. If you can manage what your brother did, I'd be very surprised, but if you did, you could give Jilli the door. I don't think you do such a good job on her after you've had me."

It earned her another slap and a growl of, "You know nothing. A cup of Felianthe, and I am ready for anyone."

"Well, if you don't want Jilli to start preferring someone else, you'd better start using it."

Holding her down, El Rasho finally reached his climax, while she was still watching the exertion on his face.

"Took you long enough. I had my thrill ages ago."

El Rasho pulled himself free, and when he was on his feet, he grabbed her and dragged her up.

"I will break you yet," he promised. "Once I have what I want."

He abruptly kneed her in the stomach, and when she bent over, he began slapping her backside until it was deep red. When his anger abated, he threw her aside, and growled angrily when she pretended to be writhing with lust. It wasn't all pretend. She used a mind trick Reyna had taught her and as El Rasho yelled for his servants, she did allow herself the sensation that had been denied to her.

To her surprise, this time she was not taken back to the dungeon, but into a room full of women in the filmy gowns worn by the king's concubines. She had been redressed in one of those gowns, and this was, apparently the reason why. Twenty eight pairs of eyes greeted her. None were friendly. She was more competition for them, her harshly treated body an evident sign that she'd been with the king.

Maeven soon discovered that this pack of women detested foreigners. She wondered if Jilli had ever spent time amongst them. It might have been what roused the sentiment.

Having to deal with so many women was something she had never had to do before. When she had been younger, and her mother still alive, her mother's ladies had been a friendly twittering bunch. The current silent, malevolent regard was unnerving. When one did approach, and talk to her, coldly, she didn't understand more than a word or two.

"I'm sorry. I don't understand you," she said, staying where she was just inside the door. The speaker's face twisted into an ugly scowl. She gestured to a very young woman and called a name. "Inari."

The woman neared, but did not come close to the speaker. Maeven was pointed to, and the girl given an order. Only then did she come close, take Maeven's arm and urge her into the room, past the hostile stares, to a seat in the far corner of the room. It turned out that the girl had a smattering of the Thulan language, and her instruction to find out what she could about the newcomer.

Maeven kept her story simple, and made no mention of her rank. She merely said she'd been taken from Thulor because the king's brother had got her pregnant and the king's master wanted him to do the same. When her story was translated, more questions were asked. The women had gone very still when Inari translated the mention of the King's master, and to mutter amongst themselves when she mentioned the demon inhabiting the king's wizard.

Inari explained, awkwardly, "Demon bad. Thought it went with old king."

"It didn't. It wants the king. And it doesn't like me because I stole something from it," Maeven added, and from the way her listeners grew more wide eyed, they understood that she was not to be harmed.

Once they started to question her, it opened up a flood of questions from all the women. Maeven supposed it was because she was different, and their lives were monotonous, and seemingly purposeless – since Jilli had arrived, and more so now she had.

"Tell them, the last thing I want is to have anything to do with the king. Even less to give him what he wants," Maeven insisted.

There were expressions of disbelief as Inari translated. She told Maeven, "It be great honour to be king's wife and give him child."

"Not for me!" Maeven retorted. "If I give him a brat, he won't treat me any better. Probably throw me in his dungeon, or get rid of me."

Still they did not believe she was not interested in the prestige, and explaining why was proving difficult. She decided she needed to learn the local language. However, one thing did seem to get through to them. She wasn't like Jilli, wanting to lord it over them.

They simply exchanged looks with one another when Maeven suggested they could act like they hated her if they wanted to.

"Why?" Inari asked, bewildered.

"Because your king wants to humiliate me, make things horrid for me. If he thinks he is, I will be better off."

None of them understood, but were relieved that they only had to let her live amongst them. Inari was directed to teach the newcomer the language, and be her mentor with regards to the proper behaviour of a royal wife.

During the next two weeks, Maeven felt they had accepted her, even if they did not treat her like they did each other. Part of this was the language barrier. Except for Inari, none wanted to learn Thulan, or teach her Vatarin. Inari as the youngest, and newest amongst the group, was the lowest on the pecking order – excluding the newcomer.

An observer, had there been one, would see Maeven being treated as a pariah. However, when Jilli came to take her to the king, the hostility ramped up – partly because she was going in place of one of them, but mostly because they detested Jilli. The spiteful comments aimed at Maeven made Jilli smile, but when she had gone, the wives smiled at her stupidity.

When Maeven returned, worse for wear, the hostility switched off as soon as the door closed on them. Several more of the younger women, more recent arrivals who were like Inari, little more than teenagers, stopped being so keen to please the king.

While the women's quarters were better than the dungeons, they still did not provide an easy place to escape from. The door that led from there was well guarded at all times. If she wanted to leave, all the women would see her go, even if she could get past the guards. She did not want to get the women in trouble. Somehow, she would have to see if she could convince Jilli that she liked it there so much that being alone would be a dreadful penance. And she'd have to hope they didn't return her to the dungeon.

CHAPTER 12 - Rhovert and Atlantis

Wystan was happy to ride in front of his aunt as her horse and that of his uncle took to the mountain trails again. His experience of the previous day was still on his mind, and when he aired that worry, his new-found kin were able to reassure him. He liked having the big dog with them too. It liked him, and it was the biggest dog he had ever seen.

The new experience of being away from the village where he had grown up, also helped to distract him. When the horses pulled up at the border guard post, his eyes were as huge as saucers. The square was so much bigger than the one he was used to. It had more than ten buildings around it, instead of only four. The guardsman who moved out to greet them looked like the ones he had seen back at the village. He wasn't interested in them, as much as the savoury smell in the air was making his belly growl.

"Morning, travellers. Who do you be?"

"Berto," Rhovert growled in the deep surly voice his merc persona affected.

"Where you be travelling?"

"South. To drop the boy with relatives. Right now though, I want a word with your commander."

"Why is that, Berto?"

"Six bodies. Back down the track."

"Yes, Sir! This way. The Commander would appreciate your report."

Rhovert dismounted, and went to lift Wystan down. When Atlantis dismounted, without needing help, and strapped her sword belt on the youth who came over just stared.

The guard called over a young man to attend to the mountain horses.

"A light feed, leave the tack on. We won't be staying long," Berto directed. "And some water and feed for the dog."

Atlantis said quietly, "Stay with the horses, Horus." The dog seemed to understand because it trotted after the horses.

Berto followed the guard to the commander's office, but he didn't let on that he knew the way. He had seen the runner, unobtrusively sent to herald them.

Commander Harker was seated behind a desk covered in papers. He saw them enter and spoke without pre-amble. "I hear you saw some trouble on the way."

"Trouble, yes. But not the sort the bastards expected."

"Why don't you take a seat and tell me about it. And who this young man is."

Atlantis allowed Rhovert to move a chair into position for her, and Wystan climbed onto her lap. She provided the cover story and Harker nodded.

"This realm is no place for anyone right now. That's why I am in the guards. Lady, why don't you and the boy visit the canteen?"

Berto guffawed. "My partner here, tamed the great hound those bandits had. You afraid she'll do the same to you?"

"I was thinking of the boy," Harker managed to say convincingly, though his face had flushed.

"Berto! Leave the man alone. I'll see to the supplies."

Rhovert merely waved his hand in dismissal. He waited for the door to close before producing a wad of papers from inside his tunic.

When they were alone, Rhovert passed them across the desk. "Official reports from His Majesty, and my official papers."

Rhovert already knew of Harker's reputation as a competent and effective commander. "That's my real reason for travelling. I'm Prince Rhovert, envoy from King Westron to Declanor."

Harker, who had begun to scan read the papers, looked up and stared. The unexpected statement had startled him. This man, no, this mercenary, he had heard of but he was the complete opposite of his memory of the prince. Many thoughts went through his mind, but he merely said, "I'm here to help with your mission. Do I take it you wish to remain inconspicuous?"

Rhovert shrugged. "I don't plan to send up magic sparkles to announce myself. First though, we left six bodies down the track. One was Jerint Hardacre."

"Hardacre? The lord's son?"

"The very one. He had a little demon incubus, so had the leader of that group. Jerint managed to say that the enemy has many groups around here, I'd say all disguised as bandits, to stop anyone getting down into Declanor for help. Then the incubus killed him. You will need to send that info to the king."

"Incubi? Demons?" Harker's eyes had widened.

"Maybe they were Succubi, I didn't ask before killing them. Either way, they're nasty. Is Captain Arlen here? He knows about the things."

"No, the captain is away. Some business in the hills to the north of here."

Rhovert merely gave a terse nod. "You should try and identify the others of that band. Have you another wizard who could put a preservation spell on the bodies?"

"Let me attend to that now," Harker decided, standing up and moving to the door. He called for his aide, and the man arrived promptly.

"Have acting Captain Tomms come here."

Arlen's second in command arrived at a trot, and was directed into the room. Harker gave the orders, and Rhovert gave a precise description of the location of the dead men. Tomms left, and could be heard calling his troop.

"What other help can we be, Prince Rhovert?" Harker managed to hide his scepticism. "Do you wish an escort?"

"No. We can travel a lot faster as just a couple of travellers. An escort would be like having an arrow pointed at us. Maybe you could send a patrol ahead to check the route, and have another follow behind?"

"Done," Harker agreed. "Though even that may not guarantee a safe passage. You do have the youngster to consider."

"So far, my partner and I have avoided more of the bastards than we've met. The lady, as you mistakenly call her, is as deadly with a blade as the Princess Leanne."

Harker nodded. He had heard of that formidable royal. In his mind, the way this 'Prince Rhovert' spoke of the Princess, confirmed his thought that "Berto" the merc, was only pretending to be the real prince.

What he had read on the first page of the orders from King Westron had stated, "Please give all assistance to the bearer of these orders, Prince Rhovert of Thulor."

The wording sounded ambiguous, and there was still a little doubt in his mind. He told himself to act as if the man was the prince in disguise.

"Is there anything else that you can tell me of the tracks you used to come here?"

Rhovert answered that succinctly, and gave the sort of detail Harker needed. In turn, he quizzed the commander on the state of the trails between the post and the border. Finally, he asked, "Do you have some spare parchment or paper I could use to send a report back to his majesty?"

Once again the aide was summoned by a yell, and when the man arrived, Harker said, "I will send out a patrol immediately, and a rider to the border post. You can use my aide's office for your letter writing. Is the letter urgent?"

"No, it can go with the regular reports."

To his aide, he said, "Give Prince Rhovert any assistance he requires, and do be discreet about his presence here."

Rhovert grinned at the aide's surprised look as he stood up, "Thanks Commander."

Rhovert was aware of the frequent glances the aide sent his way, but kept his amusement to himself. The first chance that young man had, he would spread the word that the Commander's visitor was actually the Prince of Thulor. The word would spread until the older guards heard of it. The veterans on this post would know that the Prince had a reputation for being 'useless'.

The conflicting rumours would serve well to confuse the enemy, should they get to hear them. If more of the so-called bandit groups had traitors with them, like Jerint Hardacre, who had also seen him acting the fool at court occasions, they would be sure to think him a walking trap, and leave him alone. Real bandits, would be wary. Other raiders, disguised as bandits, may not.

"Would you like an ale, my lord?" the aide asked.

"Yes, a huge one," Rhovert agreed as he sealed the letter he had written for Arlen. In case it was seen, he put, "Hoi, Captain. Berto here. Found a dragon benighted boy on the trail. Related to that dungeon wench. Taking him to relatives of my swordswoman partner. The king does not need to know of my intended short deviation from orders. Will report on my return."

He folded, rolled and sealed that letter using his talisman to form a reverse etching in the white wax. He also put an anti-tampering spell on the letter. He was finding being able to do such simple magic quite useful. Now the letter to his father.

"Father, have reached southern-most trade town safely. Bandit groups particularly prevalent down here. Most are likely northern raiders in disguise. One had Thulan traitor with demon incubus. I feel I should inform you that you have a grandson. He will be placed in care of Lady Gisella for safety. Will write with results of meetings with your equal down south. Rhovert."

That letter was treated like the first, and given to the aide to be sent north with the regular correspondence. Then he strode out to find Atlantis.

He noticed their two mountain bred horses over by the blacksmith's forge, both had feed bags on. It was also obvious that Atlantis had already acquired the needed supplies. Horus was lying near the horses, but he twisted and sat up and looked over at him.

Rhovert followed his nose to the base canteen.

Atlantis carried some official documents from King Westron that authorised the guards to release supplies to her and Rhovert as his official envoys. She received raised brows from the quartermaster, more because she was a woman and dressed as a man than out of disbelief of the orders.

"You travelling with the prince then?"

"Yes," Atlantis confirmed. "Since I know the roads down this way, and I have a commission to deliver this young man to relatives in Declanor."

The man grunted, as if he had thoughts that were being kept prudently inside his head.

"Met the prince once, up at the palace."

"Oh, were you assigned there?"

"No, it was a celebration of some kind. I came with one of the lords. Lord Mellior."

"Well, I doubt I will be invited to a palace celebration," Atlantis claimed. "Not that there is a lot to celebrate these days." She mentally amended, each time I have been at a palace occasion, I was forced to go.

"Yon prince is lucky to have someone to tend to the details."

Atlantis laughed, "At least until just after the border, anyway."

When her saddlebags were full and she had a sack strapped to Rhovert's horse, she headed back to the food tent. Some of the off duty guards were there, and they merely nodded as she and Wystan found a seat and waited for the owner to take their order. She ordered for Rhovert as well, expecting him to join her soon.

While waiting, she overheard some of a low voiced conversation from a table behind her. She smiled faintly, for the men were speculating about who was impersonating the Prince. What had caught her attention had been, "If the Prince was as competent as that guy, I'd be less concerned about the fate of the kingdom."

It certainly hadn't taken long for the gossip to get around.

Nothing about Rhovert's current look was reminiscent of his languid foppish court attire or behaviour. He was currently bearded, his clothes were travel grimed, and his weapons had seen hard use and had never been fancy or decorated. Arlen and perhaps the base commander would know he was the real prince, but the general troops would be convinced that the King's envoy was only pretending to be the Prince – perhaps to lure out bandits. Word of the dead ones they'd left by the track had spread too and no one believed the real prince would have survived them.

Rhovert joined them after Wystan had finished a large meal of fried tubers. It was something he had never had before. He would probably doze off once they moved on.

"Well?" Atlantis quizzed him, as she pushed his cooled food towards him.

"They'll collect the offal we left behind, and try to identify them and pass on the message I had for father. Arlen wasn't there. He went off to that mountain village – probably relating to the events there."

"Well, I think I know what they were," Atlantis murmured. "Should we send word to him too?"

"I left a message. I worded it very carefully. If he visited your friend there, he might already know some of it. My message should reassure him about the boy."

Wystan was glancing from one to the other of his companions. He didn't know what they were talking about, but he sensed they were tense about something.

Rhovert grinned suddenly, as he realised Wystan was listening. "Oh, and we will have an escort once we cross the border. The commander is sending a rider a head to organise that."

"How is the road between here and the border?" Atlantis asked, wondering why they would have an escort, but deciding to ask once they were under way.

"It's been quiet," Rhovert told her, but the look in his eyes suggested he had more to say on that subject. "However, I will be keeping alert for trouble, as always. Have you got everything we need?"

"Yes, plus some extras for Wis. Extra clothing and blankets and washing stuff."

"Can you see about having the rest of this wrapped up for me to eat on the way, while I get the horses?"

Atlantis just shook her head. "Yes, of course."

Rhovert managed to fill Atlantis in on the rest of what he had heard while Wystan dozed in front of her.

"Harker said there has been an influx of bandit groups around here, and we are likely to meet some between here and the border. He plans to send a patrol out ahead of us, and another behind, but that still won't guarantee a trouble free trip. He believes they have a way to find out who is passing through. He doesn't think any of his men are passing information, but he plans to do a check for those little demons when Arlen returns. He was shocked when I told him about Jerint Hardacre."

"One thing in your favour, the general troops are convinced that you might be calling yourself Prince Rhovert, but you are really an imposter. I caught snippets of a variety of theories as to why you are pretending that."

"That's all very well, but someone who doesn't know anything about me, except my rank, may think I look like a prince should look."

"Dirty and scruffy?" Atlantis teased. "Needing a nursemaid?"

"Whatever! Maybe if the brigands think we are a trap on horseback they will leave us alone."

"I hope so," Atlantis said fervently. She glanced down at Horus for additional reassurance.

CHAPTER 13 - Rhovert and Atlantis

It was almost dusk when Horus's low growl gave them warning. Atlantis immediately suggested moving off the trail. Rhovert didn't try to quiz her. He just warned Wystan to stay very quiet. When he was sure the horses were hidden, he waited with them while Wystan clung to his leg. Atlantis went off to scout. He knew she was much better in the uncivilised lands than he was. She wasn't away very long.

"They are at the stopping place I told you of," she whispered. "But I think they are packing up and planning to move out under cover of darkness. I think we should stay here until they do, then go to another place I know of."

"What about staying here?" Rhovert asked.

"That rabble will likely have left scraps that will attract scavengers," Atlantis warned.

"Well, you showed me how to make a small shelter and your brother tried to teach me some protection spells that might now work. Might even work for you too if Petulor has begun to send power to the talismans. And I think having Horus with us will deter the scavengers from getting too close."

Atlantis considered, "Well, we have enough water for tonight and can get more in the morning. And no one will expect us to be here rather than in a regular stopping place. Only thing is that it will be getting cold tonight."

"We have that little brazier. It won't betray too much of a glow and will provide heat and let us have a warm breakfast."

"Alright, you two get a shelter set up. I'll just go and watch for the rabble to be gone. I want to know if they are likely to be ahead of us tomorrow."

She returned to the little camp when it was quite dark. Wystan was asleep and Rhovert had a tiny wizard light to guide her. It was one like her brother had made for her that just needed shaking to activate. In the Golddreamer family, there were two types of people – those with magic and those without. Her brother had got all the magic.

"I'm already to set the protection spell," Rhovert whispered. "I just want to do one extra thing. Finora gave me some stuff that smells like the musk of the big cats. It should be an additional deterrent to any night roaming creatures."

"Will it spook the mounts?"

"Not if they are within the protection, which they will be."

"Okay. You do that while I visit behind some bushes."

Later, as she and Rhovert were bundled either side of Wystan, under two layers of blankets, she reported, "They headed back the way we came. I heard some mutterings, but I can't say if they are after us specifically. If they are, they have no idea that we have come this far already. They might think that a king's envoy would have an entourage and travel with a portable palace. It might be a good idea to leave as early as we can."

"I don't think I will try to argue with you. You are my master out here."

The next morning, they left before dawn and had only travelled an hour when Horus again gave them warning. Once again they moved off the trail, and waited until the band of raiders had time to be well away —in the other direction.

The next time, a little before noon, Horus gave warning at the same time Rhovert saw raiders swarming down the side of a hill, almost on them. There had only been time to set Wystan down, order him to hide off the track, and order Horus to guard him. They then spurred their mountain horses as if trying to out run the rabble. They ran into more of them, with horses, and had a fight on their hands.

Rhovert had his sword out and at the same time, let out a howl that was somehow amplified over the clashing of steel. It was the hunting call of one of the mountain felines. The horses bucked and shied, unseating their riders and galloping off. Rhovert disabled three men before they had a chance to recover.

Atlantis had her sword out too, since there was no use using arrows for this close fighting. Her skill surprised the men who saw her only as a woman – a prize.

Of the twelve who had attacked them, half were out of the fight within moments, but the rest, now having a measure of these two grew more cautious and cunning. They had worked together for a long time and had tactics that had not yet failed them. Yet even these did not deliver up their victims.

They heard Atlantis calling to Rhovert, but figured she was scared and calling for help. In fact, her talisman was showing her how the group were moving and she was warning her consort, even as she was defending herself.

The fight lasted for half an hour, with the raiders never able to close on their targets, and recklessly tiring themselves with their belief in their superiority. One by one, they went down under the swords of the two still mounted on the sure footed horses. Those unable to roll out of the way, were trampled. The last two, took the option to flee.

Both Rhovert and Atlantis slumped with exhaustion, dismounted and went to give the other a hug of relief. It had only been that they could now call on Petulor's power, and use some useful protection spells, that had kept up their own stamina.

They still had a distasteful task to do before going to find Wystan, and that was to search the bodies. As usual, the men carried nothing to identify them. Some had coins, or small metal ingots in their pockets, but these were left. They also checked for the little controlling demons, and were relieved to find none.

"I wouldn't want Wystan to see this sight," Rhovert said. "Let's get them to one side of the track at least. We could cut branches to cover them a bit."

"Or, there was this spell Maeven learnt that could hide stuff. Make it look like whatever was behind it. It was similar to something my great grand sire discovered."

"Well, when you remember it, we'll try it. If it works, we can leave here quicker."

If it had not been for Horus guarding him, Wystan would have gone even further from the road. The sounds he was hearing from not too far away, frightened him. The clash of metal on metal was nothing like the rhythmic sound make by the blacksmith that visited the village. The rough voices yelling threats and curses promised only death and pain. He knew he was too little to fight them, but he feared being left alone in the middle of nowhere.

Oh, he'd heard arguments before, between men in the village, but they were never so loud, and the words were icily polite. If the disagreements could not be settled that way, they were settled by fist fight matches, watched by Phineas or another of the elders.

While he hid, trying to block the sounds from his ears, he wondered if his aunt and uncle could possibly survive all the men. He had never known that a woman could be as good with a blade as men. All the women he had seen were obedient to their husbands. And in the village, there were few weapons. He really wanted to help get rid of the bandits, but he remembered too, that he had to be careful what he wished for – if he didn't know how the wish would work. He thought of the panicked moment when he had blasted the cat creature, but he couldn't try to do that now, it might hit his new kinfolk. In the end, he just went close to Horus and put an arm around him, letting the subliminal growl distract him from the noise.

Finally the clashes got fewer and the loud threats had stopped. The silence was as frightening as the noise, for now he realised that the noise had meant his kin were still fighting. Now, he didn't know who had won. He began to inch towards the trail, but Horus growled louder, making him turn back and look. Wystan wondered if the dog was trying to talk to him.

He stayed where he was, down in a tiny gully, hidden under some scrubby bushes, and having a limited view of the trail. He watched, hoping to see Uncle Vert or Auntie Tis.

He heard sounds of someone running unsteadily, seeming to reel into the trees right at the edge of the trail, heard someone urging another on. They paused within his view, cursing each other and using words he'd never heard before to describe the two they'd been bested by. They were both splotched with blood, and had open gashes on their faces, chests and arms. The sight made Wystan feel sick. He'd seen one of the villagers looking that bad, although no one had realised he was around. Later, there had been a funeral, and Mancy's wife was crying.

His horrible memories were broken only when he heard his name being called. He crawled out of the bush and ran up to the trail to where Atlantis stood, and gripped her tightly around the waist. He felt the wet stickiness and realised the dark clothes she wore were soaked with blood. He pulled back and looked at her. She seemed alright.

"Rhovert and I are fine, Wys. The blood is not ours. Are you and Horus up to scouting for some horses that ran off?"

The chance to help with a familiar task took Wystan's mind of unpleasant things. "They didn't come this way, or I'd've heard them. Two people did though."

"Then we'll go the other way to look. Rhovert is just tidying up the trail so others can use it."

Wystan walked between her and Horus, and only realised he had reached the site of the fight when he saw the remains of reddish dirt on the trail. He looked around, eyes wide, but breathed easier when he saw Rhovert using a small shovel to move what looked like mud splats from the ground.

"We'll take Horus with us," Atlantis announced when she paused. "I don't think the horses will have gone far, since your cat call wasn't repeated. They will probably have found some grass to feed on."

"I'll catch you up," Rhovert promised. "If you find them, we can take them to the border guard post. I think we will try to move on as fast as we can, and eat on the go."

"I have never seen a knife so big!" Wystan said, wide eyed as Rhovert was cleaning his sword.

They were billeted in a small hut at the Declanese border station. It wasn't luxurious, but it was far better than sleeping under bushes.

Rhovert didn't look up as he said calmly. "It is a sword, Wys, not a knife."

"The Elders say swords are evil because they kill people."

"That is partly true," Rhovert said, carefully considering his reply. "Swords can be used to kill, but they are not evil by themselves."

"If you aren't going to kill someone, why wear one?"

"I don't go out looking for someone to kill; Atlantis doesn't either, and she is as good with a sword as I am. If we did, we would indeed be evil. I wear a sword so that I can defend innocents from evil men."

"Those men on the trail earlier, were they evil men?"

"They were desperate men," Rhovert said looking at Wystan. "They don't have a proper home, or work to earn them a living. They looked pretty lean, I wouldn't say starving, but they get what they want by stealing from travellers. It wouldn't have made any difference if I had offered them money, they wanted everything of ours. Once, they may have been decent men, but now...I was not prepared to let them kill me, my wife and you. I was not prepared to let them kill any others when they had used up all we had."

"Did you kill those men, Uncle 'Vert?" Wystan's directness was disconcerting.

"Yes, some of them. Two had the sense to flee." Rhovert looked away.

"Was I wrong to want to kill the cat?" Wystan asked, causing Rhovert to return his gaze.

Wystan had mentioned the incident, but not known the outcome. The details had come to the guard post, and Rhovert had heard them from the base commander. He had the advantage of knowing other things that he had not shared with Harker.

"When you blasted the cat, you were only trying to defend yourself," Atlantis told him gently. "You stunned the creature; others killed it. No one will blame you for that and had you been bigger, you could have fled before it re-awoke."

"Does it get easier each time you kill something?" Wystan asked.

"Not for me," Rhovert admitted.

He felt a little hand slip into his free one and he wondered what the sensitive little boy was picking up from him and how much he understood. His questions had not been those of a four-year-old.

CHAPTER 14 - Del

"Boy!" the bandit leader, Vorman, yelled.

It was a lusty roar from one dripping blood all over the ground.

Del felt himself grabbed and shoved towards the two men who had stumbled into camp. Shaking off the rough grip, he looked towards Vorman and cringed inwardly. He knew the lout was likely to be furious. He had returned on foot, without his horse and without any spoils. That augured ill for his 'boy' later. Still, Del knew he had no choice. He ducked into Vorman's tent, where his own thin pallet lay, and grabbed a flask of some strong local brew and his bag of medicines, and came out at a trot, heading for the swarthy dark haired brute.

Vorman dropped onto a log near the fire pit. "Fix this, boy!" he ordered brusquely.

Del examined the head wound. It wasn't too bad. Then he saw Vorman fiddling with his outer jacket, and pull his hand out covered in blood.

"Get those rags off and lie down," Del said, his tone surly. He didn't want to get any closer to Vorman than he had to. To be sure Vorman didn't try to grab him, to get the clothes off, Del dived into the nearest tent and grabbed a blanket. The wool reeked, but he didn't care. He just threw it on the ground, straightened it out flat, so Vorman could lie on it.

"You!" Del turned to the nearest of the other men, who were looking to see how bad their chief was. "Get that fire back going and heat some water."

The man so addressed snarled, and might have refused, if Vorman hadn't added his own threat.

Vorman had slipped off his blood soaked jerkin and finer but not cleaner linen undershirt and grabbed the flask of the latest batch of foul brew the rabble had liberated. Del let him have a hefty swig, then grabbed the flask off him. From his pouch, Del took out a metal plate, some of his prized metal needles, some thread and a mug. Into the latter, he poured some of the brew and put the needles and thread into soak.

Then he took out a wad of rags, ones he had washed, and dumped them into the water remaining in the bucket kept by the fire. One by one, he took them out to clean the blood from around each wound. One he packed into the shoulder slash to stem the blood still oozing from it. All the while, Del breathed through his mouth, trying to ignore the smell of sweat and gore. Would he ever get used to it?

He kept his hands busy while he waited for the water to boil. By rights he should have boiled the rags, but he had stopped bothering. And he should have left the needles and thread soak for longer, but again he didn't care. None of the rabble deserved his consideration. They soon got back to beating on him after he fixed their hurts. It was only at times like this that they appreciated him.

He wondered as he threaded the needles and made the most of his power over the men, how many others of the twelve who had gone out would still return later. Three horses had come back riderless. Whoever had attacked Vorman and the others, must have been skilled indeed to get that deep slash on Vorman, but Del was not going to ask.

"Hurry it up, Boy!" Vorman growled. "If I don't bleed to death, I'll freeze."

Del finished threading the last needle and shrugged. He tossed the flask of drink back at Vorman for him to have another swig.

"Keep still!" he ordered in return.

Before he began, he heard the water in the pot beginning to boil and stood up to toss in some herbs and some rag strips, then he returned to kneel where he could work on the slash.

His mother had taught him healing, but it had been his father who had shown him how to stitch up wounds. Both had stressed the need to keep the wounds clean. Del did what he could with his materials, but none of the men cared about personal cleanliness, and in truth, Del didn't particularly care if the wounds later went septic and the man later died. When that happened, he always pointed out that they hadn't done as he told them to.

Years ago, he'd been able to hold his amulet and use his free hand to touch the wound to heal it. Even these rustic bandits had been impressed by that magic. But for the past three years, he'd had to rely on his non-magical knowledge. He could still heal, but it was slower. If he hadn't had that he'd have been dead long since. He'd have been beaten to death for not miraculously healing the results of their many drunken fights.

Del was convinced that Vorman would want to get back in action well before the wound healed, and maybe he'd kill himself trying. So, taking a deep breath and flicking aside the disgusting dried rat's head that Vorman wore on a leather strip around his neck, he began the disgusting task of holding the flesh together with one hand and forcing the needle through the edges with the other. Vorman twitched and said nothing.

Del was reminded of something his father had said, "No sense, no feeling." Vorman just keep swigging the brew between stitches. Finally, the blood oozing from the slash slowed, and he could tie off the last of his neat stitches.

"You!" he told the bandit by the fire. "Bring the pot of hot water here."

Again the obedience was reluctant, and this time it came with a look that promised later reprisals.

"Any others need fixin?" Del asked, "B'sides Jolie?"

That got the other thinking. "There's three back addled."

Hit on the head, Del translated. They'd have headaches if their skulls were intact. Likely the other seven were goners. If they didn't get back before night fell, the others would fight over their stuff.

Using a stick, Del lifted out a length of hot linen, quickly rolling it into a long thick pad, and placed it over his stitches. The herbs infusing it would help stop infection. The hot rag didn't seem to worry Vorman, he was still busy swigging the brew using his hand on the uninjured side. Del quickly tied the bandage in place, and then put a second pad tied around the head wound. Vorman merely grunted.

"Don't use that arm for a week," Del told Vorman. "Get some of them others to lift you."

"Weak as a wench you are," Vorman growled. "You wash them clothes, boy, but right now, go get some gear from Toofools tent. He ain't coming back thanks to that damn fancy man and his wench. Unnatural she was."

Del's first concern was to rinse the needles and repack thread and unused rags into his pouch. He bundled the used rags together to be washed. Only then did he obey the last order, knowing he'd have to help Vorman get dressed so he wouldn't break the stitches. At least now he felt safer getting closer to Vorman. He'd swigged the whole skin of brew, into which he had added some herbs to help kill the pain, and to make him sleep.

Vorman shooed him away as soon as he had a shirt on, and Del was glad to take his stuff and the water bucket away. The bloody rags he tossed in the water pot and put over the fire.

"We'd better not be eating that tonight, boy," another bandit growled.

"Might be all ya get," Del countered. "Ain't no one brought back hoppers." They couldn't blame him for that, Del knew, so he ignored the scowls. He continued to let his rags boil until he thought they were ready to hang out to dry over some bushes. He emptied the water from the pot in the privy hole and took it and Vorman's clothes to the little stream. He rinsed the pot and filled it first, then rinsed as much of the blood from Vorman's clothes as he could. He didn't have soap.

As he worked, Del wished yet again that he could leave the gang of brigands. It had been eight years now, and he still couldn't. He had learnt the hard way not to try. Twice he had hidden when the band was going to move on. Both times, they searched until they found him, then beaten him for giving them trouble. They had some sort of mage leash on him, ever since that first time, and it still held even though the mage that put it on had died of a septic wound. Even when his own magic had fled. Back then though, he really had been too young to fend for himself. Now, if he could get free, he could.

Back in the camp proper, Del hung up the wrung out clothes in Vorman's tent. He didn't trust his own rabble not to steal off him. The chief was sitting by the fire pit and the rest of the rabble were standing around listening to him, occasionally one gave a gruff response. Del had his ears fully tuned, but he pretended not to be listening as he went about his other tasks. He'd put the refilled water pot back on the fire, figuring they would likely be having dried trail food stew.

Some of the rabble wanted to pack and leave, afraid of the demon swordsman and his demon wench. Del hid a smirk. Odds were they'd picked on a couple of off duty guards. Seven killed! Whoever they were, weren't slouches. Mostly Vorman and his rabble picked on travellers that were farmers or crafters, with little skill with weapons. Even so, Vorman was more than a match for most opponents. He had beaten down four attempts to oust him as leader so far.

"No!" Vorman roared over the babble. "We stay. Tomorrow we're gonna track that fancy man and the wench and teach them who the lord is around here."

"Them musta used magic," one bandit said aloud.

"Nuh!" Vorman shouted. "Magic ain't worked for years, has it Boy?"

"Huh!" Del feigned stupidity, but Vorman didn't repeat the question. He'd made his point. Enough of the remaining rabble recalled how the boy's amulet had used to heal and no longer did.

One of the hunters returned then with three hoppers that had been caught in his traps. That seemed like a better omen and the rabble wandered apart.

Del stayed to help the hunter skin and dissect the carcasses and put the meat and edible innards into the pot. One of the others added dried vegetables, roughly chopped, and Del added some of his herbs when few were looking. No one commented though, since his usual additions were tasty. None of them realised that some were also added to keep them quiet. That evening, he didn't want any of them deciding to take their frustrations out on him, in lieu of any available wench.

"Here, Boy!" Vorman called, and he gestured urgently. Hiding his reluctance, Del obeyed. Vorman's voice was already slurred, and him – drunk, frustrated and angry – was not a good mix. It was not the time to cross him.

As soon as he was close, Vorman's hand shot out and grabbed Del's wrist. In a low voice, Vorman demanded, "I want you to heal this faster, boy. Tomorrow, I'm going out after that bastard that did this to me."

"Can't," Del reminded him. "You gotta keep it still a week."

"Try your magic, boy! I reckon Joster was right. That fancy pants swordsman and the wench musta used magic." The voice was still low, since Vorman didn't want to appear weak.

"I'll try then, but don't blame me if it don't work none," Del warned.

Del took a deep breath and used his left hand to reach for his talisman – nothing. He kept trying to feel the cool breeze that was how he felt magic. Then he shook his hand free of the bandits grip, considering how he had done it before. He switched hands and held the talisman with his right and putting the left over the wound on the bandage. Still nothing. Then he touched the flesh beside the bandage – it was hot. His hand felt cool. He thought of the breeze, pictured it healing...

Vorman reached out and gripped his wrist to keep it over the wound. "It's working, boy!" he slurred.

At first, Del wasn't so sure, but when he peeped under the bandage, the red, ragged puckered skin was smoothing out and fading to pink. With a thrill of awe, Del continued to feed the breeze through his hand, while Vorman seemed to have passed out. He didn't intend to heal it completely, just enough so that he would not have to redo all the stitches again in the morning. He was also thinking of Vorman going to sleep for the night.

Almost as soon as he thought it, Vorman rose unsteadily. "You've earned your keep this day, Boy."

Del grinned, he would eat well that night. With fewer greedy mouths to feed, he'd get more than just scraps for his meal. He'd be able to skulk around the fire too, without fear of being beaten or molested. He reckoned the others would all be asleep before dark. With a faint smile, Del went to collect his rags and finish hiding his herbs and equipment back in an excavated hole under his thin pallet in Vorman's tent.

He lay awake that night and considered the day's events. Vorman was stupid, wanting to chase those who had bested him. But, Del didn't care enough to try to stop him. If he split the stitches, and bled to death, or that swordsman finished the job, then he'd be free to go off on his own. He hoped that Vorman might forget that his talisman had worked again, or believe that he'd used up the magic in it. The bandit chief coveted the ability, and Del had not forgotten how his father had been dragged away because he had one and was probably dead now, like his mother.

CHAPTER 15 - Arlen

Arlen put the parochial village with its obsequious elders out of his mind. He had enough to think on in wanting to get the woman he knew he loved, away from the entity that hated her.

He had no doubt that Ciabolo had taken her back to Vatarik by whatever magical means he had used to get to the village. He would probably give her to his brother to play with. Both would want to punish her for outwitting them. Then too, his brother had seen her first and laid claim to her, but El Rasho had not been clever enough.

Even to this day, Arlen could not explain what had caused his former self to go down near the river. Overwhelming lust, the moment he had seen the woman, had made him act like a beast. He hadn't known she was a Princess of Thulor, but when her identity was discovered, he had risen in Ciabolo's regard. His brother had been furious.

A lot of time had passed since then, and he wasn't the same person anymore. To anyone in Vatarik, he was a traitor. However, since swearing an oath of allegiance to Thulor, he had felt free.

And now, when he had finally come to an agreement with Maeven, the enemy had captured her. He had to go after her and for that, he had to convince King Westron.

On re-joining his troop of border guards at the trade town, he sought out Commander Harker.

"You've missed a lot of fun, Captain," Harker greeted him. "Just after you left, I sent your troop out to recover some dead brigands. A couple of travellers took them out. A merc calling himself Berto and his woman. He recognised one of the group, Jerint Hardacre, some young hothead from the court apparently. We are to try to identify the others. Got them under some kind of preservation spell in the old weapons shed."

"Two swords took out the group. How big was it – those bastards hunt in packs."

"There were six in that lot."

"That lot, Sir?"

"Well this Berto was headed south. Later, the pair of them took on a group twice the size – between here and the Declanese border."

Arlen recognised Prince Rhovert's merc nickname. "I've met Berto, and his woman."

"So I understand. He asked if you were here. They couldn't wait for you to return though. They had urgent business. Did a good job of confusing everyone."

"Did he give his business?"

"It was no secret. He told me he was the Prince, said the woman was his partner, and the kid was being taken down to Declanor to relatives."

"He said he was the prince?" Arlen asked for confirmation.

"Yes, as bold as anything. However, I've seen the Prince and he's a useless fop. I think the envoy is using the Prince's name under the King's orders."

"I expect you might be right," Arlen agreed. He knew better but was not minded to say so. Prince Rhovert was safer if people underestimated him. "You said he's gone on?"

"Yes. I sent a rider ahead to the border, and a scout party ahead and behind them. The rider was to return when they had passed the border."

"Have you sent word of these raids to the King?"

"Not yet. Thurston, your apprentice, has been keeping the preserving spell on the dead brigands from the first group. He says he has nothing to spare to send messages back to the palace."

"Well, I can see to that this evening. That's when the king's wizard is usually alert for messages. I can send the reports then, plus I have some matters to mention to him too."

"Oh, yes. Those hill folk. Did you sort them out?"

Arlen tried to keep his lips from curling in disgust, but from the Commander's grim smile, he had failed. "When I left them, they were satisfied that the cause of their concern would not return. The pompous hypocrites. They don't know when to leave well enough alone. The one thing that still concerns me was the fact that there was a large black feline prowling the area. I saw it. One of the townspeople managed to kill it. I thought those creatures were prevalent in the north. Not down here."

"No, we've had other reports. Sightings that we could never

follow up. Usually it is only one animal, seen alone, so we don't know if there was only the one or a pride of the things. The reports can be found in the archive."

"I'll have a look at those," Arlen decided. He wanted to ask more about the child Harker had mentioned in passing, but to do so would make the child seem more important. He hoped that his first thought was right, that Petulor had found Rhovert and left the child with him. Should he mention the child to the king? No…

Returning to the matters in hand, he told the commander, "I'll check on Thurston, and the bandits."

"And I will want a report on the hill folk from you as well," Harker directed.

Arlen nodded. He would give the full report based on the first visit, and an outline of the return visit. There were some things that the guards, and the king, didn't need to know. Some, of those other things he might mention in confidence to Roman, to pass on to the king.

He headed for the storage shed. He could make the stabilisation spell last without needing to fuel it with his personal energies. Thurston was talented, but he did not have a talisman, or a great deal of training.

His mind turned back to the events in the hill village. Maeven had agreed to ratify their marriage, make it valid in Thulor. He could tell the king that, but nothing would be done about it until the king heard it from Maeven herself. Wystan would still be a bastard and out of the succession.

Then his mind asked, "Did Rhovert know who the child was? If he knew Ven was his mother, had he guessed who the father was? What would he think when he found out?"

"Sir?"

Arlen turned to see Harker's aide.

"Sir, Guard Captain Arlen, a merc left this for you."

"Thanks." Arlen felt the spell on the roll, recognised the etching in the wax, and forced himself to put the letter in his pocket. He did not want to open that up until he was alone.

That evening, Arlen set up the magical message, but stayed back and let Thurston report to the face he saw in the floating bubble. He could hear the voice of Wizard Roman coming from it as he asked questions to clarify parts of the report. Only when Thurston had finished telling all the minutiae from the post, including the safe passage of the envoys to the border, and the two bandit groups they had encountered, did Arlen touch the bubble so that Roman would become aware of him.

"A further word, Roman. Two of the brigands in that first group had controlling incubi demons. Hardacre was one, and the other looks like a native of the north."

"I will let his majesty know. Was there more?" the disembodied voice asked.

"Yes." Arlen gestured a dismissal to Thurston and continued speaking after the younger man had gone. "I have spoken to the king's youngest daughter. She had been living these past years, quite unsuspected, in a cave above that village your sister spoke of."

"Is she well?" Roman asked.

"She was, well enough," Arlen said, then paused to consider his next words. He told of the events in the village, and the outcome after the cat incident. He made no mention of his private time with Maeven. "Petulor was not strong enough to weaken the Serpent's shields. Nor was I, even though the Serpent had only taken on the body of a minor hedge wizard."

"Where do you think he took her?" Roman asked.

"North of course. Where he can do as he wishes with her. I want to go after her."

"I will speak with the king and send his reply."

The message was ended from the palace end and the bubble popped. Arlen settled into the commander's chair to await the reply. He would not be interrupted until he left the Commander's office, not even by the Commander who was uncomfortable in the presence of magic.

The reply was not long in coming, for a new bubble appeared within five minutes of the other vanishing.

"You are to stay in the south," Roman said flatly. "Other arrangements will be made in the north. You are the best person to be on watch for the enemy's activities in the south."

"Very well," Arlen agreed, although it was not what he had wanted to hear. He would obey, for he had made an oath to King Westron.

Arlen ended the contact, but did not hurry from the office. He was guiltily aware of the things he had not mentioned, like his agreement with Maeven, and the opportunity he'd made to make her pregnant again. He wondered if he had. He hoped so, because then his brother would be outfoxed, again. He would be sure to try his manhood with her, to try and make her pregnant. If he thought he'd fathered a child on her, he'd be arrogantly sure of his right to the crown of Vatarik. He wouldn't dare risk the mother of that child...he wouldn't hurt her dangerously until the child was born alive. That meant they had time to rescue her. But would his brother keep her alive once he had a son, or if she only produced a girl?

Some resentment still lingered at being kept in exile in the south of Thulor, but his mind turned to the advantages. He was no coward, but was he ready to go against the Serpent, Ciabolo, and his brother? He hadn't managed too well in the encounter in the village.

Then there was the boy, his son! Who was even now on the way to a safe place in Declanor. By being in the south, he was closer to the child but he couldn't help Ven.

A voice in his head seemed to say, Ven tricked Ciabolo and his brother before, she is not completely defenceless. His son was more vulnerable. Perhaps, King Westron had unwittingly done him a favour.

Only then did he recall the letter in his pocket. Now, being alone, he took it out, neutralised the spell and unrolled the letter. Rhovert had been clever, making the message terse and cryptic, but he understood the message. They had found Wystan, Petulor had led him to the boy. He knew the child was Ven's and had not, and didn't intend, to mention the boy just yet. The only question Arlen had was, whether Rhovert realised he was the father. Was that mention of the dungeon-wench confirmation? The letter gave no indication of Rhovert's reaction.

CHAPTER 16 - Atlantis

Atlantis, with Wystan still travelling in front of her saddle, turned off the main trail onto one that led to the farmlands. While travelling from the border, they had met no trouble. Now, the escort stayed with Rhovert and he merely touched his hand to his forehead to wave her off. Neither needed long teary farewells at parting, each was used to being on their own. The Declanese guards who had accompanied them for the past two days, assumed that she was merely a chance traveller who had met with the king's envoy on the way.

Not unexpectedly, Horus had chosen to follow her and Wystan.

"Where are we going, Auntie Tis?"

"To the little town where I grew up," Atlantis told him.

"What's it like?"

"Well, there are lots of farms around it. So the land is wide open, with relatively few trees. The town itself isn't very big. The buildings there are mostly for trade, but some artisans live there, and there is a hostelry for travellers."

"Will you be staying?"

"No, Wys. I have to re-join Rhovert and head back to Thulor."

"Oh."

"I know all this is confusing, Wys, but I know you will like Gisella. She's my sister-in-law. She's also a herb witch and her brother is a bit of a wizard. Not a strong one, but he will be able to teach you a little bit about magic."

"Ven said she'd find me a teacher, but if she couldn't I had to hide my magic."

"Yes, the folk in that village of yours don't believe in it."

Atlantis decided that Maeven had been wise to have the boy fostered there. No one would expect a child there to have magic at all, let alone be as potentially powerful as Wys. If an unscrupulous wizard had sensed the boy's power, he would have grabbed the child to use for his own ends.

"But I used it on that cat," Wystan said. "Is that why I had to go away?"

"Did they tell you that?"

"No, I heard things."

"Well, I don't know what you heard, or even if you heard right. What matters now, is that you are better off away from there. And for you to learn that it's better not to go around blasting things, even if it was to save yourself. That much magic is too showy, and you'd soon burn yourself out. Krit Cornseeker, can to a great deal with only a trickle of magic."

"I wish I could stay with you, too."

"So do I, Wys. But while you are learning from Krit and Gisella, I'll be trying to help your ma."

"Will your folk teach me to fight with a sword?"

"Krit is a farmer, not a fighter. So I don't know. One of the other townsfolk might be willing, but usually the youngsters start that when they are a bit older."

Wystan straightened in front of her, no longer leaning back against her. It seemed, that now he had an idea of his immediate future, his anxiety had been assuaged. She hoped the effect would filter through to his dreams. Each night since he had been with them, he had woken at least once from nightmares of the cat attack, or of seeing Ven taken by Ciabolo's snake form.

Her own dreams had been troubled too. She was concerned for her friend, even though she knew Ven to be strong, resourceful and tricky. None of her dreams had the force of a premonition, like she had experienced just before the bandit attack, so she had to trust that Ven would survive and make trouble for the Serpent, Ciabolo.

Horus, who had trotted ahead and gone off the trail, came back with a hopper in his mouth. He let Atlantis take it and put it in her saddle bag, while Wystan held the reins of the horse. It was the third one he had delivered to her and she gave it a pat of thanks on its big shaggy head. Then it turned and trotted back along their trail, something its previous keepers must have taught it, along with helping to ambush travellers. The dog was so gentle now, that her horse had lost all fear of it.

Atlantis knew that having Horus trotting alongside the horse was sure to make her noticed and she was not wrong. As she approached her birth village, the farmers who had fields bordering the road contrived to be working near that boundary. Once they saw her, and recognised her, greetings and subtle remarks about the length of her absence, were called out.

She replied to each in her usual fashion.

"Haven't you seen a real dog before, Dalruth Furrowmaker?" That farmer had remarked on the size of Horus.

To another it was, "No, Athena Birdwatcher, I have not come home to stay. I'm just visiting, as usual."

For some reason, maybe the 'you can't see it' spell she'd tried, none of the townsfolk seemed to notice Wystan, or she would have had more pointed greetings to answer.

She was not surprised when Gisella came racing out of her brother's house to greet her. One of the child sized watchers would have been dispatched to alert her. But her sister-in-law stopped abruptly when her eyes settled on Wystan.

Atlantis reined in her horse, dismounted, helped Wystan down and went to give her sister-in-law an enthusiastic hug. Gisella returned it, before asking what was foremost on her mind.

"Is Roman well?"

"Last time I saw him he was," Atlantis assured her. "Doesn't he keep in touch?"

"Well, yes, but not often. What's happening in Thulor? Oh, and who is this? Where did you get that enormous dog?"

"Hey, can we go inside?" Atlantis laughed. "And can we get Krit to come in too? I need to talk to both of you."

Although Gisella sent a neighbour's child off to summon her brother, she and Atlantis had exhausted the subject of Roman and the state of things in Thulor before a tired Krit Cornseeker arrived. Wystan was sitting next to Horus, leaning against the dog as if he were a cushion.

"Heard you were back," Krit greeted her. "You staying?"

Atlantis shook her head, and Gisella glanced at the boy who had consumed a pile of her biscuits and seemed on the verge of sleep. Krit gave Atlantis the same sort of speculative look that his sister had. Gisella had yet to have her rampant curiosity satisfied. To speed things up, she fetched her brother a cool drink, while he went to clean up.

"Now, Atlantis," Gisella prodded. "Let's hear the real reason why you are here. Who is Wys?"

Atlantis allowed herself a faint smile. "You probably heard via Roman that the King made Rhovert and I get married, but he is not ours. We found him in a cave just across the border. The one where I went looking for dragon shells that time."

The faces of her two listeners lost their anticipatory grins and settled into merely interested.

"He lived in that hill village I told you about. However, this lad is gifted with magic."

"How did anyone in that village of old stuffed shirts dare to arrange that?" Gisella snorted.

"Well, they didn't. Wystan was being fostered there and, until recently, they didn't know about the magic."

Gisella looked to be thinking on the right track, but Krit growled, "If there is a roundabout way of saying something, trust you to take it! So who are his parents?"

From floor level, a small voice announced, "The dragon said Ven was my Ma and Atlantis is my Aunt."

Gisella's mouth dropped open, before she asked, "And who is the father?"

"A guard captain." She didn't intend to mention names, but Gisella nodded. She had still been at court when Maeven had returned as a captured thief. "One who is also a strong wizard."

That made Gisella gape like a fish again. It narrowed the possibilities to one and created many more questions.

Atlantis shook her head to forestall the asking of them. "He must have just been born when I first met Ven. And you'd be aware of the chancy situation then."

"Indeed," Krit agreed. "Ven was wise to have him fostered. But why is he no longer in the village?"

Atlantis sketched the information she'd gleaned from Wystan, and gestured for him to get up and join her.

"Ven promised to find a teacher for him. I'm told that learning the basics is the same, irrespective of the strength of the gift. I don't believe that his grandfather's place is suitable, as Roman is keeping busy with the plague of illnesses, crop disease and strange beasties. Rhovert and I felt that you and Gisella would be ideal to care for him and to teach him to use small magic effectively."

"He'd have to stay here? We'd foster him?" Gisella's eyes were full of joyful hope.

"If you are willing."

"Oh, yes! Yes! If Wystan is happy with that."

"I'd like to be with my Ma," Wystan admitted. "But she was taken by that snaky person. And Auntie Tis has to go back to Uncle Vert."

Gisella couched down and spoke to Wystan. "That is terrible, and I hope Atlantis can get her back. But I would be very happy to have you stay here. I could teach you what I know about healing magic and herbs. Krit can teach you other things – plant magic and simple spells."

"Can I learn to use a sword?"

Krit looked over and said, "You're a tad young, lad, but I will ask. Tavis Longblade is teaching a group of youngsters."

"And I can assure you, Wys, that Gisella cooks way better than I can," Atlantis told the boy.

"What about Horus?" Wystan asked.

The dog sat up, hearing his name.

"Where exactly did you come by such a handsome specimen of royal carriage hound?" Krit asked, as the dog wagged his tail vigorously.

"I could say confiscated from some bandits, but I think in truth, he chose us. I think he has adopted Wys as an honorary pup. He also knows how to catch hoppers, so he can help you keep your corn plants from being nibbled. Besides, I have never seen an animal you can't manage. However, if he decides to follow me, I won't be surprised."

While Krit went with Wystan to make friends with Horus, Atlantis drew Gisella into her kitchen.

"There's a lot I haven't said, Gis, and you can probably guess why. If people ask, he is an orphan from that Thulan hill village, with very minor magic. The reverse is true. He has a very powerful gift and it has already begun to manifest."

"I will simply say that you found him wandering," Gisella offered. "But he is the grandson of the king of Thulor!"

"Yes, but so far, Ven has managed to keep that fact from everyone except Rhovert, Arlen and myself, and now you."

"Do you mean that his majesty doesn't know?"

"No, and Wys doesn't know that his grandpa is a king either. He is safer if he is anonymous."

"But we are just low born peasants. Not even Thulan."

"He is only four," Atlantis pointed out, "Although he sounds older when he asks questions. He has a lot to learn about life, as well as magic, and I would like him to have peace to do it."

"I won't risk him," Gisella promised.

"I am totally sure of that. And in fact I will be envying you. I have come to love the boy, but I can't look after him. Rhovert and I have tasks to do for the king. And we are still trying for a true born heir, but we both have doubts that will ever happen. If we can't, Wys will be Rhovert's heir."

The full import of the request for her to foster Wystan showed in Gisella's expression. "And the King will trust me?"

"He has no reason not to," Atlantis assured her. "But for now, unless Roman mentions Wys first, don't say anything about him, okay? If he accidentally sees him when you are chatting via his bubble thing, he can just be a local lad you are fostering."

"I don't like keeping secrets from him."

"It's only until we get back and tell the king about him in person. Even then, as I said, I don't think he will object to you fostering him."

"Okay then, was there anything else?"

"Only that Wys has been having nightmares. You might be able to help him get over them."

Abruptly, Gisella took Atlantis into a tight embrace, which she returned with understanding. "You will be a great mother, Gis."

"And I will make a collection of herbs that might help you and Rhovert."

"Can't hurt, even though I think the serpent's little dreft creatures bit him."

Gisella pulled away. "Dreft?"

"Magic creatures, little snakes. Their poison can result in impotence."

"Is there anything in your grandfather's writings?"

"Not that I recall, but I will check when I can. The journals are with Roman, back in the palace in Thulor."

With a nod, Gisella wiped her watery eyes, and asked, "Will you be staying tonight?"

"If you will have me."

CHAPTER 17 - Rhovert

Rhovert's arrival in Declanor was first derided as a joke by the guards at the gates of King Sevin's palace. The effeminate reputation of the Prince of Thulor had preceded him, it seemed. However, his escorts produced the letter of authority from King Westron and the guards had to admit him. The escorts translated the instruction that the he was to wait for an escort from the king.

That was what he had expected, therefore he used the time waiting in the stable yard to look around. He had caught sight of a fleet footed lad racing off towards where he could see the upper levels of the Declanese palace. He didn't let on that he understood the local language and, as a result, heard odd snippets of gossip about himself. Some amused him.

His two escorts still hovered nearby. In the past two days since splitting off from Atlantis and Wystan, he had kept to his merc persona. This had quickly enabled those two to be comfortable around him and treat him like one of themselves. If they had doubts about whether he really was a prince, they kept them quiet.

Within a very short time, he was being ushered to a guest chamber to have a chance to wash off the travel dust, and take refreshments. The servant withdrew after telling him the King would see him as soon as he was ready. She knew some Thulan.

His saddlebags arrived while he was washing, and he was able to dress in a formal outfit, but nothing like his usual attire at his father's court. After a long drink of the cool cider provided, he summoned the servant. Now that he looked like a noble, the servant gave him a subtle second look and became more formal as she led him to the king.

King Sevin had just ended a session of his court and was still in his formal attire when Rhovert was announced at the door of his private sitting room. With him was wizard Indra, the court magician, who was a man of advanced years.

Rhovert bowed and greeted King Sevin with the precise degree of respect that their relative ranks demanded. He straightened and patiently endured the King's scrutiny.

"You look very like your father did when he and I last met."

Rhovert smiled. "My father insisted that I bring you his personal regards as well as the official greetings. He also warned me against playing games of chance with you."

This elicited a bark of laughter from the king and a deep frown from Wizard Indra. He spoke quietly to his king, but Rhovert heard enough to understand that the wizard still had reservations about the identity of the prince. Again, he was not surprised, nor dismayed.

"Wizard Indra," he greeted with a nod of respect. "I understand that you have met Wizard Roman Golddreamer, my father's court wizard?"

Indra's expression betrayed some surprise, but he merely admitted, "Yes, I have."

"Then, I have a present to you, from him. Do I have permission to present it?" Rhovert knew these two men were friends of Thulor, but in the current chancy times, they had to be cautious.

When he received a nod from the wizard, he produced a palm sized orb from his pocket, spoke a few words that Roman had taught him and made him memorise, and a light appeared within the globe.

Indra straightened in surprise. "I had not known that the King of Thulor, or yourself were mages."

"I'm not, really," Rhovert admitted candidly. "But I have discovered, as did my youngest sister, that the dragon will power small spells for us. It is like a non-mage using a magic potion to power spells."

As he spoke, he pulled out Thulor's talisman from around his neck. "I prefer to make use of a sword to avoid trouble, and in my view, what is more useful is that the dragon will send us energy when we need it, like during a fight."

"Ah, yes, like with bandits," King Sevin suggested.

Rhovert looked at the king to say, "Yes, your Majesty. There seems to be a plague of them just over on our side of the border." He then returned his attention to Indra.

"I was told that you can use this orb to contact Roman. Something about thinking into it and picturing him." Rhovert held it out and let the wizard examine it visually before taking it.

"That young lout has no doubt changed a lot since I knew him."

"Well, he's still a bit of a lout," Rhovert said. "Anyway, I had the impression that would not matter."

Indra murmured words in Declanese, and his eyes suddenly lit up. He snapped a sharp sentence and in response, Rhovert clearly heard, Roman's voice speaking in his native language.

"Hell's blazes, Master. Thirty years on and you can still make me jump."

The wizard positively beamed and all the remaining tension drained from him. As did that of the two guards who were at the door. Rhovert had confirmed his identity to the satisfaction of King and Wizard. He smiled as the king and wizard became intent on the orb, where now, King Westron was greeting his Declanese counterpart.

Rhovert waited respectfully as the two monarchs exchanged greetings and his father succinctly outlined the situation in Thulor, then passed authority to Rhovert, saying, "My son has the details of what I wish to have discussed."

Before the odd conversation finished, Westron asked to speak to his son. Rhovert moved closer to the orb. "I received your deliberately cryptic message. Do you wish to enlighten me further?"

"No father, I would prefer to do that in person, when I return."

"Then I expect you to return promptly when you have finished there."

Rhovert nodded, but made no promise. He let Indra extinguish the light in the orb, and handle it as if it were a fabulous piece of art. The king summoned a servant to take the outer layer of his finery, and then sat in a chair near the unlit fire on the hearth. He gestured for his guest and wizard to choose a seat as well.

"Even though my friendship with your father goes back longer than your life time, I will not strip my land of fighters and wizards," King Sevin said straightaway.

"I understand," Rhovert agreed. "Neither my father, nor myself, consider that an acceptable request. The favour he wishes me to ask of you is simply that you fortify your border with Thulor, and provide safe passage for those of Thulan blood wishing to travel here, or return from here, and the same for your people."

"Fortifying the border, given what your father told me, would be sound policy. However, have you thought of a way to be sure that only respectable travellers try to cross?"

Rhovert settled down, presenting ideas and a second strange object, and went on to negotiate some lesser matters. He added one of his own, that of providing a safe haven for important individuals.

CHAPTER 18 - Del

Vorman wrenched off the restrictive bandages and roared, "Boy! Get your skinny carcass over here! Right now!"

Del tried to ignore the call. He knew why the bandit chief was livid. He'd figured out that three days had passed since his injury. It hadn't just happened the day before. Through the gap in some bushes, he saw Vorman emerge from his tent and look around. Saw him scowl. The number of men in the camp was noticeably smaller since the seven deaths.

Vorman had made it clear he wanted to go after the fancy man that had skewered him, but now he had no hope of following the man's trail. Del knew he was going to get a beating, or worse, but the victory would still be his own. Besides, it was about time someone made Vorman suffer as he'd done to so many people. This time, Del had been told to go with the others to strip the dead ones of anything of value. He had seen the signs of a child with the pair of swords folk. Hopefully, he had helped that little one to have a better life than his own.

Something was pulling on him. Del twisted, expecting to see one of the other bandits trying to curry favour and drag him to Vorman. No one was there. The feeling intensified, and finally, very much against his own will, he found himself running towards Vorman. It had to be magic, Del realised, and he could do nothing about it. How was Vorman doing it? He wasn't a wizard. This wasn't like whatever it was that kept him in the camp unless ordered out...or was it?

As Del got close enough to smell Vorman's rancid body odour, he saw him drop his hand from the ugly shrunken rat's head amulet he wore. He reached out to grab, but Del ducked, just not low enough, for Vorman's good arm swept him up and lifted him by his waist and carried him back inside his tent. His other arm was already fiddling with the fastening of his trousers.

"You done me out of catching a woman, boy," Vorman snarled. "Now you gonna make up for that."

Del struggled harder, but he was no match for the bigger meatier older man, who threw him onto his rough mattress, and somehow held him there while he dropped his trousers and pulled off Del's own.

Afterwards, Del crawled back to his own thin mattress, his whole body throbbing from the beating and the other things Vorman had done to him. The bastard himself was now in the deep sleep of the satiated. It took more energy than he had to reach up to his neck to feel for his talisman. At the same moment that he realised it wasn't there, he blacked out.

An unknown length of time later, Del stirred. Every ache and bruise reawakened by a kick to his ribs. He barely understood Vorman's rantings, as he jerked around in the tent.

"What witchery are you doing, boy? This piece of rock is burning me."

There were sounds of scrabbling and something hit him in the face. More scrabbling, and Vorman was out of his tent, yelling at his followers.

It was quiet when Del finally woke, realising that his hurts were less intense, but not gone enough to make him want to move. He closed his eyes when he heard the sound of someone approaching the tent and moving the flap.

"You okay, boy?"

It wasn't Vorman. The gravelly voice was Nanti's. "Can I get you a drink, boy?"

Del tried to speak, but little sound came out. Nanti was one of the men who had managed to crawl back to camp, Vorman hadn't let him do more than basic wound dressing, for him. The sound of the man withdrawing was soon followed by his return. He entered the tent with a full mug of water.

"Here, boy. Let me help you sit a bit."

Del let him. In most ways the man was as bad as the rest of the rabble, but he'd never mistreated Del.

"Th...Thanks," Del managed as the first sips of water moistened his parched mouth and lips. He drank all that was in the mug. His mind began to work. If Nanti had dared to enter the chief's tent,

Vorman must be intending to be away for a long time, and Nanti wanted something.

"Don't know if ye's can, but you musta helped the chief, did ya? Did ya bit of rock work again?"

A nod was the only answer Del gave.

"Reckon you can help me and Issi and Oddum?"

"I don't have my..."

Nanti held up the triangular amulet and the dangling leather strap and chuckled. "This thing don't hurt me. Himself was spitting and cursing. I think he took yon stone but it burnt him something shocking. He has a real nasty welt on his throat."

Del reached for his talisman and the mere touch began the sensation of cooling through him, easing his aches.

"Thanks. Give me a bit. Then I'll see to helping."

"You're a good lad. You don't belong with the likes of us."

"Can't leave."

"Yeah. S'right. Anyways, when you can. Reckons we'll be pulling out soon. Heard say about lots of guard patrols."

"They know why?"

Nanti chuckled again. "Thinks I do. Himself chose the wrong gamey. Talk is the fancy swordsman was a King's envoy. If we lies low or scuttles, them guard patrols might take out those others."

The foreigners, Del knew he meant. Vorman had a hearty dislike of them and considered them fair prey. That was the only thing about which Del agreed with the chief bandit. Vorman called them soft. Quite a few of the band's horses had once belonged to foreigners. Their dead riders had been too clean, too well fed to be bandits.

Del eased himself into a less painful position. "Let me touch where you were wounded," he told Nanti. "I think this will help heal us both at the same time." The other was quick to agree. There was always the chance that Vorman would return sooner than expected.

He did. But not until Del had helped the other two men, who paid him with food they had stashed away. He wasted no time consuming it. He was ravenous.

When Del heard the sound of horses approaching the camp, and the soft whistle of all clear from the man on look out, he felt like he wanted to run and hide – if only his bruises and muscles would let him move. They had healed some, but he was still stiff. Instead he peeked out and watched the string of horses enter the camp.

However, something about Vorman's body language made him relax. He had long since learnt to judge Vorman's mood, and right now, he was sure that something had made him very pleased. And seeing four good horses led in gave part of the cause, and the five sacks thrown down into the centre of the camp by the men who had gone raiding with Vorman, gave the rest.

One of the sacks was picked up by Vorman and tossed at Oddum, who was designated cook while he healed up.

"Food stuff – cheese, flour, sugar, dried fruits," Vorman chortled. Everyone else murmured excitedly. "Herbs, boy!" Vorman tossed a small bag his way. "You'd know what use they be."

The largest bag contained clothes, boots, belts...all taken from the dead. Whoever wanted something better would fight over them. Del would wait to see what was left. By then he may have got over the sick feeling about wearing a dead man's clothes.

"And..." Vorman held up a bulging, obvious heavy pouch like a conjurer. "Gold, silver, copper and gems."

"Ahhh," came a concerted sigh.

Vorman usually kept half of such bounty, and shared the rest. This time he surprised Del by including him in the spoils. He must have forgotten his anger, Del decided. Probably, this raid may not have happened if he hadn't been kept in camp.

"You're back being useful, boy," Vorman said as he took his half the coin and gems to his tent. "And I got two new slaveys." He gave a quick glance towards two men still tied near one of the new horses.

Del followed his gaze and shivered. The looks they were giving Vorman could have cut tough leather. They had seen the division of the spoils and were barely restraining their anger. He studied their faces. They didn't look like all the other foreigners he'd seen, but they must have been with such a group, or Vorman wouldn't have kept them alive, or brought them to camp as prisoners. He wondered why they had been brought, but he wasn't going to ask. In his opinion, those two would scarper first chance they got.

Feigning more soreness that he still had, Del retreated to his corner of Vorman's tent and carefully dug a new hole under his pallet to hide the first coins he had ever had. Then, he spent the rest of the afternoon, watching the two men who were now tied to two trees. He kept within the tent, out of their sight, for their glares could still have curdled milk.

"Boy!"

"Yes?" Del crawled out of the tent, deciding to seem obedient and that he had forgotten how Vorman had treated him.

The chief's voice dropped to an unusual low. "Boy, you got any herb like that will make people spill their thoughts?"

"Huh?" The question was unexpected, but he considered for a bit, wondering what Vorman planned. "No, but I got some ferret bane. It's a poison, but having blue flower after it, will stop its effect." Del wondered if Vorman understood, and by his grin he did.

"What's that ferret stuff do?"

"Makes them think their heart's going funny," Del said. "A tiny bits good for people who are really hurt bad, a lot of it ain't."

"Well, boy, what say you take out two new recruits a drink, with some of your tasty herbs in, and see if they will talk to you?"

The men were thirsty, but suspicious too. To appease them, Del took a mouthful of the foul wine and managed to swallow it without spluttering. He wasn't worried by the tiny amount of the drug he had. Then he held it to the mouth of each man in turn so they could have six mouthfuls each. That would be enough to start giving them the effect of the poison, but even if they each had half the flask, it wouldn't kill them.

Del knew the men had noticed all the recent bruising on his face and exposed skin. They each growled a thank you, before one asked, "Can you loosen the ropes, boy?"

"Nah. Do that an' he'll kill me."

"We'll take you with us if we get free," the other suggested.

"Can't."

"Why not? That lout don't treat you right."

Del shrugged. "Tried, couldn't. Anyway, how you live out on your own?"

"We go back and join a different group. We don't have to hunt our own food. We get paid with supplies."

"Huh?" Del tried to sound dumb, hoping the man would explain. He did.

"Yeah, we get paid to annoy or get rid of uppity nobles and show the rustic yokels how the king is milking them dry with his taxes."

The talisman around Del's neck began to heat up. These men might be prisoners, but they were dangerous and traitors.

The other man spoke again. "Yon chief likes his riches, doesn't he?"

Del shrugged. "Sometimes he gotta buy food for us." Del had never known it to happen, but it was the reason Vorman claimed

Vorman called for him and as he turned to go he caught both men looking at each other.

Later, when both men were sweating and chilled, Vorman wandered over. Del had the blue flower antidote ready, and he took the flask with him as he sneaked around behind the men to listen. The chief had already quizzed Del about what the men had said, now he had questions he wanted answered.

The men had secrets, but they were feeling too ill to hold out. Vorman found out how bands like theirs had been organised, what they were being paid to do, but even with the claims of being paid in food, he was not interested. Their dead group leader had been just a lackey for someone else. He was interested in knowing who the real leader was, but these men only knew of the mayor in Ackbridge. In his eyes, the Mayor was another lackey, and probably wouldn't care what happened to these, since he had so many other groups to feed. The men had read Vorman right, he wanted power and wealth, not just food to survive.

One of the men finally admitted, "Reckon whoever's in this wants rid of the king."

Vorman growled his disbelief but called, "Give them another drink, boy!" He had a faint smile on his face.

"More of that vile brew, boy?" Del was challenged. "That last lot made us sick."

Del shrugged, "They's all drink it. So it must grow on you. But it's all I got."

"Rather have water," the other said.

"This lot has some flavourful herbs in it," Del told them. "Might make you feel better."

He got a searching look, before the men allowed him to put the flask to their lips.

After all his own band had eaten that night, Vorman again strode over to the prisoners. This time, as he spoke to them, he was fiddling with the dried rat's head neckpiece. Del watched from near the fire, not about to leave the warmth. He was surprised when Vorman cut the men loose, but moments before, he had felt a very uneasy feeling settle into his gut. The two men stumbled towards the fire, not surprising, since they'd been tied up for so long. And were probably starving too.

There was still a little of the evenings stew left in the pot, and that was after Del had had his fill for the first time he could remember. He found two of the unused bowls, and put them near the fire. The men saw what he did, went directly to them and the pot, helped themselves to the little remaining, and sat on the ground to eat.

Something about their behaviour seemed wrong, but Del couldn't decide what. They didn't seem as arrogant as before, but then they'd been tied up for hours. He had the feeling they'd try to leave first thing, but again, maybe the chance to eat something seemed a better idea. It was smart, they'd likely not find food elsewhere for a time. Well, if they left during the night, he didn't care, so long as they didn't kill him first.

That night, Del couldn't sleep. He crawled to the tent flap and watched the fire. The two former prisoners were still like two logs, having been told they could sleep there.

"What you a'feard of boy?" Vorman drawled from his pallet.

"I reckoned myself those two'd scarper," Del admitted.

Vorman chuckled. "Maybe I convinced them to stay."

"I thought they were jest yes men to the furriners," Del decided to say. "And thought t'selves better than us."

"Yeah, had that idea too," Vorman admitted. "But they know stuff I want to know. But if they want to try leaving, they won't rat on us."

Del stared out as he asked, "You magic 'em?"

"Why you say that?" Vorman hissed.

"Guessin'," Del said. "You dun something to me."

"Yeah well, you was a little tyke. You'd've died in days had you run off. Was for your own good."

"And them?" Del risked a glance at Vorman. The smirk on his face gave him shivers.

"It be good for them if they don't try." Vorman chuckled. "You get to bed, boy."

Over the next three days, five men stumbled into the camp. All were scruffy and had only enough energy to slump onto the ground and beg for a drink. Vorman had Del add herbs to the brew to make them sleep then had each one searched, but none had anything of value but their clothes. When each woke, they begged to be allowed to join the band of brigands.

While this partly inflamed Vorman's ego, he was also getting edgier. He went to the first of his new recruits, and demanded, "You know these walking dead?"

One said, "Seen a couple in Ackbridge, just before we left. Joker's group."

"Ackbridge, huh?" Vorman growled. "Well I don't want more of their rejects. I'm not some do good charity. How come you two got out with your wits?"

"We'd had a good hunt," one said.

"Did you now? Killed a few useless nobles did you?"

"Yeah."

"You had enough stash on you – reckon you didn't go there but kept the loot."

"We was told to go north."

"Was ye now? To kill more nobles?"

"If we met any."

"Expecting better picking were you?"

"Were to meet someone who needed good men."

"Well, maybe we'll just do that, hey?"

Del, just arriving with some wood for the fire, heard Vorman shooting questions at the other arrivals. The five who were just starting to speak sense after a couple of days of sounding addled.

"What happened to you. Why were you kicked out?"

"Master, it wasn't like that. We'd gone to the town, like we do regular, taking our stash and getting supplies. This time we was told there'd be a meeting. Something big was up. We were told to have a drink, on the mayor. At the tavern, me and my mates went in, but they just stopped and turned like a statue. Everyone in there was, 'cept the tavernman. He saw me and said I should get out and go, leave town. Place'd sure given me shivers, so I did."

"Yeah, master," a second said. "Dimsy and me found the same, got told to go right quick if we wanted to keep out wits intact to take off. Tavernman said the rest were demon fodder."

Vorman said nothing, although there were murmurings from the remainder of his original band. Talk of demons did that. Del noticed the subtle signs of Vorman fidgeting.

"You," Vorman nudged another of the newest five with his toe. "Did they try to stop you?"

That man looked like he'd been in a fight.

"Not then, master. They weren't looking for runaways. I got stopped by some guards. They were going to throw me in a dungeon. I played dumb farmer and said I'd been robbed. They let me go."

Del looked at Vorman, who was now rigid. There had been signs of a lot of guards, as well as bands like those these men had come from.

"This place ain't healthy no more," Vorman announced. "Everybody, pack your stuff. We're leaving tonight. Boy, you start putting stuff on my horse. You, Bugeyes, start packing my tent. Do as the boy tells ya."

The look the man just called Bugeyes gave Vorman, had more of the original hatred they'd had before Vorman had magicked him. Del decided he needed to be careful, and decided to be polite to the man. "Come on, this way."

Del didn't need telling that he was to keep Vorman's stash of coin and gems from being seen by these men. He also wanted his pack of herbs and healing stuff protected. He pretended not to hear Bugeyes, and the other named Asstail, talking. They thought they could make a run for themselves, taking some of Vorman's coin. He thought of warning them, but a voice in his head said, "No" and he recalled how his talisman had grown warm near them. It wasn't now, and hadn't since Vorman had magicked them. But if Vorman had used a potion to do it, it might wear off anytime, and they might kill him, after killing Vorman. Not that he'd mind if Vorman died, maybe he'd be free then, but...they didn't need his help.

Vorman's two captives had been unnaturally docile since he had cut them loose, now Del wondered if they had been foxing. They had packed everything as Del directed, and helped him tie everything onto his and Vorman's horse. Then one grabbed Del, stopping him calling out, and they had drawn knives and demanded he hand over the coin Vorman had stolen from them. Del's sudden fear had been picked up by the horses and they whinnied, drawing everyone's attention. In moments, they were surrounded by drawn swords and one cross bow.

"We'll kill the boy," Bugeyes threatened.

Del's mind went into a whirl. Would Vorman care if they killed him? Part of him recalled what Vorman liked to do to him, and thought he would. Then he was good for healing their hurts, surely he wouldn't want to lose that skill.

"Cowards," Vorman sneered. "You can have him if you like. He's not particularly useful. Can't fight worth squat."

The knife touched Del's neck and his mind kept blurting, "Don't let them kill me."

Something whizzed past the top of his head, Bugeyes hissed in pain and swore. Next thing he knew the man was throwing his knife away, cursing, something about wizards.

It had been Nanti who had loosed the arrow that had scraped Bugeye's cheek. Now he called out, "You want to leave little man, leave the lad and go. I'll give you to the count of five, or next time, I won't miss."

Del felt himself tossed aside, as the two men glanced at the men facing them, they saw the wisdom of leaving. He wasn't so sure it was wisdom, but they didn't know what he did. They'd not get beyond the edge of the camp – then they'd be told, "Too bad, you didn't take the advice." For himself to leave, Vorman had to give him an order. And just now, the Chief was mighty quiet.

The men left, looking back frequently to be sure the men weren't up close. When they reached the camp edge, an arbitrary line walked by the sentries, and without warning, the first turned into a human torch, screaming until Nanti finished him off. The other, was sent flying backwards, not burnt, but stunned by the blast of magic.

Vorman gave a satisfied grunt. "Toss him over the back of one of the packs and bring him along. He may still be useful. All of you, let's go before that bastard brings guards on us."

The night ride was not the first Del had experienced, but this time, he felt the unease of all the men around him. Killing the man didn't bother them, but the need for travelling quickly and silently, listening for night patrols of the guards had them all on edge. Not one of them would escape hanging if caught. Del realised any soldiers would probably assume he was as bad as the rest for staying with them. How could he prove he couldn't have left?

By morning, Del was so tired it was hard enough to stay in his saddle. Vorman led them to a hidden valley, just past a small town and allowed a break to water the horses and let them graze. He sent Nanti back to town for food, using some of the coin he'd kept. He wanted all to think them traders or legitimate travellers.

Del led his horse to the trickle stream Vorman had mentioned, and stopped to drink some water himself, and fill a small flask he carried. He thought he should check on Asstail, and see if he was awake enough to drink.

Oddum had hefted him to the ground and taken his horse to the stream. The man was moving feebly. His face was a mess, where the magic blast had sent searing heat at him. Del, put his little flask to his mouth, and helped him to take tiny sips. Then, he found a piece of cloth in his pocket, that he wet and use to dab the burns. While Vorman wasn't looking, he touched his amulet and gently placed a hand on the man's cheek. The breeze blew through him, and the worst of the burn began to heal.

The heavy hand that grabbed him by the neck, was unexpected.

"Boy, he don't need to have pretty looks. And I didn't say to help him, did I?"

"No, but you wanted him along. You could have dumped him. Figured he needed to be well enough for something."

"You reckon you know more than me, boy?"

"No. I was just trying to make sure he was useful."

"Well you just don't do unless I tell you, boy."

Del slunk away, glad that Vorman had too much else on his mind for punishing him. He could hope that he would forget about the incident.

When they were underway again, Del kept as far back from Vorman as the magical tether on him allowed. He let his horse follow all the others, while his mind mulled over his chances of getting away. At least Vorman had only beaten him for trying, but could the fate of Bugeyes be his fate?

That night, when they were camped close together in a tiny clearing, Del quickly fell asleep, but his dreams were full of vile images, of Vorman's rat's head coming alive.

Next day, as he rode, he considered his dream and a lot of scattered facts formed into a whole. Vorman had been touching that rat's head when he spoke to the two prisoners. The thing had made his own amulet so hot when Vorman had it, that it had burnt him. That had to mean the rat's head confined powerful dark magic. Lucky it hadn't overpowered his own talisman. Unlucky that the reverse hadn't happened. That vile thing must be providing the power for the spell that kept him tied to Vorman. If only he could be rid of it, without harm to himself. Then he might get free.

CHAPTER 19 - Roman and King Westron

"Your Majesty, you need to come - something odd is happening below." The servant, one of the few remaining at the palace, bowed as he spoke.

"Odd, Cencom?" King Westron replied mildly.

The King rose from his favourite chair, stiffly, and walked slowly to the window. "It looks quiet to me."

"Sire, out past the North gate - the army seems to be fighting itself."

Westron found himself to be curious and followed the servant to the stairs that led to a high tower. He climbed stiffly to the balcony of the watchtower and moved around to overlook the north gate.

The army from Vatarik was indeed acting oddly. Men were running around, some were suddenly thrown in the air, others dropped as if stepped on.

"Sire, you should not be up here," Wizard Roman chided. "I cannot be sure the shield will hold if they see you here and decide to make a concerted effort to get you."

"What do you make of this, Wizard," Westron asked, ignoring the rebuke.

As he spoke, three heads were separated from their bodies and flew through the air. It seemed also, that someone was firing fire arrows into the ranks of the enemy.

Roman Golddreamer reached for his talisman and incanted a spell. The King had, involuntarily copied the gesture - finding his talisman had, once again, a familiar chill.

The invisible cause of the carnage below became visible as a silver creature of legend or nightmare. Westron recognised it. "Dragon!" he called with his mind.

The silvery creature turned its head in the direction of the King, ceasing its killing frenzy.

A few brave soldiers tried to skewer the dragon but their swords did not touch even the scales of the dragon. The dragon roared a challenge and most of the soldiers dropped their weapons and ran.

"Father-King?" came an answering thought into Westron's mind.

The huge silver dragon launched herself into the air and flew towards the palace tower.

"Why are you risking yourself, Petulor?" Westron asked with mind and voice.

"They took Dragon-Mother!" The dragons mind voice was unyielding as she hovered at tower height.

King Westron saw in his mind the dragon's memory. He hid his feelings as his mind saw his youngest daughter being swallowed by a giant serpent. It was as Arlen had reported, and the snake had just vanished.

"Petulor, we need to talk. Please land in the courtyard below. I will join you."

Petulor blew her sweet breath over Westron, before spiralling down as directed.

King Westron walked steadily to the steps and preceded his servant and his wizard. His muscles ached from the exercise. The pall of darkness that was afflicting his Kingdom was giving him symptoms of advanced age.

Petulor landed neatly, coiling her tail and tucking her wings in close to her body. Her appearance had startled the servant who was fetching water from the well. She was staring nervously at the dragon and inching her way sideways back to the kitchen, the water forgotten.

King and Wizard arrived together, approaching the dragon without fear. Petulor snuffled each with her snout and blew more warm sweet air over both of them. She lowered her head to be at eye level to the king and waited.

"Petulor, you should not put yourself in such danger. There is only one of you, but there are many of my subjects who can fight in your stead."

"Father-King, I was not in danger - their weapons cannot harm me."

"Petulor, what if they had one of their powerful wizards with them down there? Are you strong enough yet to face the Serpent?"

The young dragon roared a challenge.

"If you could not save my daughter, you are still not yet strong enough to win against the serpent. And he, as Arlen reported, has only recovered enough power to subvert a hedge wizard."

Petulor lowered her head to the ground. "You are correct, Father-King."

"Brute force is not the answer," King Westron said gently. "Most of those soldiers below are simply unfortunate farmers who are controlled by the little demon allies of the serpent. That is why I do not fight them. It is the demons we need to kill, not the men. If the men die, the demons simply move to a new host, and it will be my subjects that become their victims. Subjects who would be made to commit treason."

"Father-King, what would you have me do?"

"Can you sense all the bearers of the talismans?"

"Yes, Father king. What power I can spare I share with you and them at need. Since the Dragon-Mother suggested it."

Westron nodded, feeling an inner relief that his older children had at least that much protection.

"I have not experienced any visions of the future since your birth," Westron commented thoughtfully. "Do you know how your mother managed that?"

"I have all of her knowledge. I will consider what she gave me. Do you wish me to give premonitions to the others as well?"

"Perhaps a warning of short term future dangers," Wizard Roman murmured.

He had been privy to the visions that had been given to the king and knew that only a strong man could deal with them. Those that must fight would only be distracted by too many possibilities.

Westron nodded in agreement to what his wizard had suggested.

"As my wizard advises, Petulor," he said thoughtfully, still considering the dragon's remark. "I was once able to get flashes of vision and sound from around the other bearers of the talismans."

"That can be done, Father-King."

Again, Westron nodded. "What else did your Mother do for us, Petulor?"

Petulor raised her head and tilted it to one side, a gesture so human-like that he had the sudden vision of Maeven as a child of five waiting for him to explain something to her.

"I must.... Consider." Petulor admitted. "She knew every dragon's length of her land - I have yet to renew all her links. The serpent's spells are tainting the land."

"Perhaps you should concentrate on repairing your links to this land of Thulor," King Westron suggested. "As you fly over, if you sense pockets of evil, or danger, you could pass the knowledge to me."

"Yes, Father- King."

"The sense of your presence might weaken the ability of the little demons to control the subjects of Thulor," Roman suggested quietly.

"You are indeed wise, Dragon-Wizard," Petulor said, bringing up a talon to scratch at her chest. Several silvery scales fell to the floor and turned black. Petulor blew them in the direction of the wizard.

"I cannot venture far out of the borders of Thulor," Petulor said unexpectedly. "If you could get these scales into the Serpent's kingdom - I will be able to funnel power to those who hold them. Or, if they are with an agent of the serpent, I might be able to learn things about them."

"You believe that my daughter is back in Vatarik?" Westron looked suddenly calculating. He knew that Arlen believed that too, but he had refused permission for the Guard Captain to go back there. "I have agents who would risk all to deliver them..."

"I would hope that the Dragon-Mother could be found ..."

"You cannot sense my daughter," Westron stated flatly.

A small dribble of flame escaped from Petulor's nostrils. "No!" Her tail thrashed, betraying her agitation. "I sense that she lives and all is not well."

Westron betrayed nothing of his thoughts. "Three scales, Petulor?"

Petulor's tail stilled. "Humans are so easily damaged," she said carefully. "Three chances to succeed, do you need more?"

"I hope not, Dragon-Mage," Westron sighed.

"Would it be rude of me to enquire if you will be preparing for your successor soon?" Roman Golddreamer asked unexpectedly. "His Majesty told me that your Mother laid your egg when she was very young."

Petulor ruffled her wings and looked skywards. "I am old enough to mate; I know what I must do to conceive a mage-dragon and how to protect it over the centuries. The Dragon-Mother has taught me much."

"I hope my daughter taught you how to outwit human thieves," King Westron commented dryly.

The dragon looked back at him. "Indeed, and advised me to ensure that it was not the direct line of decent of the Kings of Thulor who were given the secret of the egg's location."

It was the first time that Roman Golddreamer had seen his monarch look surprised. The look quickly turned speculative.

"A subsidiary line of descent," Westron concluded. "It would make sense ... an enemy would expect us to know. And when the time came for your successor to be born?"

"The egg will be returned to me!" Petulor stated with confidence. "I will go, but first, you must come with me to my birthplace. There is something I would show you."

Before either king or wizard could take a step towards the stairs down, they both saw the tower and the view blur, and felt a sensation of movement. The blur of colour changed to black, and as the movement stopped, the King felt his legs buckle, and Roman barely managed to stay erect. A silvery light began to disperse the blackness.

King Westron dragged himself erect with the help of his wizard. He tried to ignore the pain in his knees where he had landed heavily. The experience of being dragged through air and rock had been the most disconcerting experience in his life. He looked around the normally dark chamber beneath the palace dungeons - now lit by some kind of magic light.

"I must be getting old, Wizard," he muttered. "You look as if you enjoyed the journey down here."

"That was incredible, majesty," Roman admitted with eyes that shone in the magic light.

Petulor had taken them directly to where the desiccated remains of her mother, Thulor, lay.

"What can you see, Dragon-Wizard?" Petulor asked.

Roman looked around the cavern and then his eyes took on an unfocussed look as he repeated his scan.

"Magic is pooling here," he said finally.

"Yes," Petulor whispered to both men. "Dragon magic. Use it to protect my kingdom."

Roman bowed his head in respect of the dragon's wishes.

"Can any wizard use this?" he asked, expressing his concern.

"Only those with the blood of Thulor and the ability for magic," Petulor stressed in return.

Roman looked at the dragon. "I am from Declanor…"

"…with the blood of Thulor," Petulor repeated.

With his eyes closed, Roman stretched out his right hand to touch the 'pool' of magic. It felt like a cool breeze on his hand. His mind tested the shields he had about the castle, sensed a weakening where the army had been attacking earlier. The cool breeze blew through him and the shields strengthened. His eyes flew open. "I thank you for your trust, Dragon-Mage."

The dragon merely nodded.

King Westron felt the breeze flow through him and his knees stopped hurting. He stood taller, as the myriad aches and pains that had plagued him for three years faded to nothing.

"Father-King, the sickness within you is a reflection of the sickness in my kingdom. Basking in the magic of the pool can only remove that which is not natural."

"Can it cause the demons possessing those unfortunates outside to remove themselves?" Westron thought to ask.

Petulor did not answer at once. "I do not know. They are not natural to this world and they have arrived only recently, but they are natural creatures - summoned from their true place by magic, not created by it. I will learn what I can of them. It may be that you must search beyond the borders of my kingdom to find the gate through which they are summoned and seal it."

"How?" Westron demanded.

"I suggest, majesty, that if or when such a gate is found, we study it. The answer might be obvious. There must be something near the portal that attracts them."

"Very well, wizard, I will leave that problem in your hands. However, I would like to have one of those unfortunates from outside brought down here to see how the demon is affected. Petulor, I have been invigorated by your presence. I and my subjects are yours to command, however, I will go from here via the tunnel to the dungeons."

"You honour me, Father-King," Petulor blew her sweet breath over him and faded from view.

At her departure, the light in the cavern faded but Roman

Golddreamer made his own magic light to show them the way through the tunnels.

The King ignored the snarled comments from the occupants of several cells that he past as he strode back to the main section of the palace.

The five men and two women were murderers, and had used the poor conditions for their own benefit. They deserved no pity and were under sentence of death.

Instinct, rather than foretelling, had caused him to delay their execution. A time might come when killers such as these might be useful. If their loyalty to Thulor could be assured.

Back upstairs in his private chambers, King Westron summoned a servant, and while he waited for one, he took a quill and parchment from nearby and began to write. He had folded the paper over, when the man arrived.

"Send this message to Gwillard Ley," Westron ordered. "I need a scholar to research several matters. If he is willing, have him brought in by the east tunnel. Wizard Roman will ensure he is protected."

The servant bowed and departed.

"Is it your experience with dragons, that they are a secretive race?" Roman asked the king.

Westron had appointed Roman as his chief advisor and over the past three years had chosen to drop all formality between them, at least in private.

"They have had to be to survive. They have long been hunted. However, I only ever met Thulor on that one occasion."

Roman recalled that time vividly; the fight with the serpent as they strove to hatch Thulor's successor.

"What are you hinting at, Wizard?"

"It sticks in my mind that she calls you Father-King and I am Dragon-Wizard. Your daughter is referred to as the Dragon-Mother."

"Thulor chose her to protect her daughter," Westron reminded him.

"She is neither warrior nor sorceress or to my knowledge a mother." Roman pointed out.

"But she speaks to dragons and has dragon sight" Westron countered.

"And dragon secretiveness and dragon deceit?" Roman suggested.

"With plenty to spare. I think she did indeed teach Petulor well. I sensed that the dragon knows more than she was telling us."

"As did I, Majesty, and I fear for your youngest daughter. Will those draconic qualities be enough this time?"

Westron did not answer - with perfect recall he remembered the visions that had come to him before Petulor's birth. He had seen Maeven riding at the head of an army - then it had been one of many possibilities.

"I hope so, Wizard."

CHAPTER 20 - Rhovert and Atlantis

When Rhovert left King Sevin's palace after two days of discussions, both he and the king were satisfied with the agreements they had made. He returned to the border with the same two men who had escorted him from there. The only difference was, they now treated him like the high ranked noble he was.

Atlantis was waiting for him at the Declanese border post, now the only place where people could cross. The King had wasted no time moving his troops to the border. She had observed the troops arriving, and had been watching the on-duty wizard using a strange device on each person and cart that had approached the border.

When Rhovert rode into view, she mounted her own horse and rode to join him. They approached the wizard together. He didn't even need to touch them for the rod device to emit a brilliant white glow.

"Ah!" the wizard exclaimed, drawing the nearer guard's attention. "It's never done that before."

Rhovert looked down at the man and explained. "It is because my companion and I both wear dragon talismans. They are charged with dragon magic and the rod responds to that. Have you noticed any other effects?"

"Hey! Who you be to ask such things?"

"You are talking to the Prince of Thulor, wizard," one of his escorts stated. "He is the one who provided the design of that device to your master, along with a working device."

"Well then," the wizard was genial now. "I have indeed noticed other effects. One traveller wishing to cross the border to here, caused it to turn a sickly purple. The man tried to keep going when we denied him entry, but he...well, grabbed his own throat and passed out. Dead! We checked for one of those demon creatures the king mentioned. He had one, so we killed it quickly."

"It's well you did. It would have found a new host when the one it had started to cool. You do not want to be controlled by its master."

Rhovert saw that the warning had been understood. "Were there other noticeable effects?"

"Only a pale white glow when three scholars requested passage into Thulor. Do you know why that is my Lord?"

"I can only guess that it has a way of knowing those who have evil intent," Rhovert told him. "It also must know those the dragon favours. Were the scholars Declanese?"

"No, my Lord. They said they came from Aqualica, to the south."

"Now, that is interesting," Rhovert admitted. He saw a small group of travellers approaching, and moved back to let them pass. The wizard moved to check each of the men, women and children. The rod stayed the colour of the dull worked metal. From what Roman had told him, before he left, no glow, meant innocent of any ill intent.

He headed back to the road, only to have the wizard trot back to him.

"My Lord, I am also to provide travellers into Thulor with a glamour to repel the interest of bandits. It will last three days."

"That will be most useful, wizard. Thank you."

Atlantis kept her questions to herself until they were a half hour's ride inside Thulor's border. "How did you and King Sevin get on?"

"Well enough. Your brother provided an orb for wizard Indra to enable communication. It was well accepted. Father was able to vouch for me via that device. Did you expect me to have trouble?"

"Well the king doesn't like...the sort of people you act like at court."

"He gave me a good look over. The wizard took longer to be sure."

"Roman always said Indra was a crotchety old bastard. And he always said Roman was a smart-alec upstart. It seems they kept rubbing each other the wrong way. Indra is known to dislike young wizards who think they know everything and anyone who doesn't learn to get the most out of their magic. And he lumps charm witches in with them. Indra thought Roman a wastrel because he chose to return and be a farmer."

"Your brother must have been on his best behaviour, then. He only complained that Indra had startled him. However, watching Indra, he might have mellowed. He was obviously impressed with both the orb and its use to provide long distance communication, and with the rod device for the wizards at the border to use. So, how did things go with you?"

"Well, Gisella and Wystan really hit it off. Krit is delighted to have been asked to teach him too. Horus was so much more noticeable than Wys so he was not the centre of attention."

"I thought that dog would stay with you."

"I wasn't sure, and in truth, I think the creature was torn between staying and going. I told him to guard Wys."

"The more protection that youngster has, the better," Rhovert agreed. Then he fell silent.

This time, Atlantis waited only ten minutes before asking, "What has you so thoughtful?"

"Father wants more details than I sent in my letter."

Atlantis knew exactly what part of his letter was meant. "The bit about his grandson?"

"Uh huh. I told him I will tell him more when I get back. Wants us to go straight back."

"So, why is that bothering you?"

"I can imagine what he is going to say."

"You don't need to care what he says. Things are the way they are," Atlantis said tartly. "So you and I have not been able to give him what he wants. Ven did. He should be grateful for what he has."

Rhovert grinned wryly. "You'd think so. But he can be darn contrary at times. He has never commented on how I behave at court. Yet on the subject of getting an heir, he keeps alluding to that not being a reason not to."

"I wonder what he has seen?" Atlantis commented. "From something Roman said, I think he saw Wystan. Maybe has seen another child?"

"He won't share such things with me," Rhovert predicted. "Anyway, I still haven't worked out the reason for some of his requests to King Sevin. It is partly understandable – that certain people can have free movement between Declanor and here, envoys for instance. But who else might he be referring to?"

"So you and I, like you said. I'd include Roman and Gisella, since he knows we are from there. It would cover Wystan, but your father didn't know of him when we left. Who else? Those scholars?"

"Could be," Rhovert considered. "They made that rod glow a little. But, how did Father know?"

"Does it matter? At least they can stop agents of the serpent. I hope none have gone there."

"Ciabolo would be a fool to start anything there. He wants Thulor. If he can get entrenched here, then he could look further."

"I overheard the mention of that trader who died. That sounded like what happened to Jerint Hardacre."

"Yes, so in that case the man was dead a long time ago and never knew it," Rhovert decided. "So, I suppose we have to take the direct route back?"

Atlantis shook her head. "Not a good idea. Even with this glamour, I don't want to tempt attack. There are still a lot of bandits around here, and they will all be looking out for us." She was going to say more, but she had just experienced a sudden chill, such as she felt just before a premonition. It wasn't as strong as the one she'd had on the way up. "Let's go towards the west," she said slowly, in a voice that didn't sound like her own. In fact, she was still trying to make sense of what she was seeing. This vision seemed to be like she was flying over the land – like a bird. The vison faded and she shook her head.

"West it is then," Rhovert agreed. He waited for Atlantis to say more, suspecting she'd had another vision, but she stayed mute. "So, we bypass the trade town. That's fine. I can wait to have a word with Arlen."

They turned onto the westward road and found a place to stop, rest the horses and see to their own needs. While they were eating a snack made from the provisions King Sevin had provided for them, a bubble popped into view in front of Atlantis. Rhovert gaped in surprise, it was very like the effect of the orb he'd given Indra. He heard his consort say, "Roman, what is so urgent that you risk scaring our horses, and straining yourself to say it?" and gathered that this form of communication was familiar to her. He kept out of the bubble's field of view, and listened to Roman's disembodied voice.

"Whatever did that fool prince tell his majesty that has him in a dither?" Roman demanded.

Rhovert decided he was going to join the conversation, and walked over next to Atlantis. "A dither? Since he got my letter, or I said I wasn't giving details?" he demanded.

"From a few days ago," Roman admitted. "We got your letter just before you reached us from Declanor."

"Did he tell you to find out more details?"

"No. But he is acting strange and I don't know why."

"If I tell you what's going on, will you promise not to tell him?"

"Why? What have you done?"

"Promise, or no deal," Rhovert insisted.

"Okay, fine! An unconditional, I won't tell your father," Roman agreed.

"I told him he had a grandson in my letter. I refused to give him details when he was speaking through your little orb thing. I told him he had to wait till I got back."

"Do you mean that my sister is pregnant?" Roman's face lit up, with mischief.

Atlantis answered that. "No! And get that smirk off your face. You know I like the idea of being pregnant even less than I did of getting married."

"Ah, but you did let the king talk you into marrying that fancy clothed prince."

Rhovert growled and Roman's grin widened. "So, if she's not pregnant now, and I'm damned sure she wasn't when you left, what's the story? I did hear you say has, not going to have."

"Think about it, brother," Atlantis said sweetly.

"Well..." Roman lapsed into silence and Atlantis grinned at Rhovert. "The king did mention getting flashes from a talisman that he didn't know the bearer of. He thought a bandit might have stolen one."

"I don't know what he sees when he sees things," Rhovert admitted, "But what has that to do with the subject? All the talismans we know about are accounted for. So that's not it. Anyway, why wasn't he getting flashes from the one you have when Tormore had it?"

"You know, I never thought of that. I must ask. Anyway, he gets regular reports from Finora and Leanne, and Maeven, you know about that, but Arlen has hers."

"You are totally dense at times, Roman GoldDreamer. Don't you remember what a certain wizard did to Ven?"

"She said..." Roman began, but he stopped.

Atlantis whispered to Rhovert, "I think the game token just dropped."

"Ah, so, this has been a well-kept secret since before the old dragon died," Roman looked at them accusingly. "So where is he?"

"With Gisella, now," Atlantis told him. "I told her not to tell you unless you knew first. So don't be cross with her. The king isn't letting you do your husbandly duty, and she has always wanted children."

"And you have promised to say nothing," Rhovert stressed. "I will explain when I get back."

"So when will that be? I was told to tell you to hurry it when I next caught you."

Rhovert considered what to answer. Atlantis had only been able to say that she just knew they had to head west. "We won't be taking the direct route, since the bandits will be looking for us. I haven't been through the western towns since all this business with the Serpent started up again. So, we will be going that way."

"Whose idea was that?"

"Mine," Atlantis admitted sharply.

"You having premonitions now?" Roman asked with concern. "Petulor came here. One thing she admitted was that she was powering the amulets again. Prompted by something Maeven said to her and I recall that the talisman the king gave you gives warning of close dangers."

"Yes it does. In fact the first one saved our lives. That was about a week ago. The latest one wasn't so intense, just a vague need to go west."

"Then you shouldn't discount it," Roman advised. "The Queen, when she had it was always right. So, can I tell the king that much?"

Atlantis looked at Rhovert before answering. He nodded, and she was about to say, "Yes," when she was hit by another vision, a stronger repeat of the one she had just referred to.

Rhovert, seeing her expression, answered for her. "Yes, tell him. And Roman, has there been any word of trouble out that way?"

"Nothing that stands out," Roman considered. "Why?"

"I think we need to get back on the road," Atlantis told him. "We need to get somewhere fast."

"One last thing," Roman said quickly. "All of us should be able to draw on the power pooling here. Through the talismans."

"We can vouch for that," Rhovert said, recalling the fight with the large bandit group. He had begun to pack things back into their saddle bags.

"Go!" Roman ordered. "I will tell the king and try to get onto you in the morning." The bubble popped.

"Handy way to communicate," Rhovert remarked, as he mounted his horse. "How does he do it?"

"He knows me, and Gisella well. I don't know that he can to it to anyone else. But it takes a lot of energy."

"Perhaps that's why I had to get that orb to Indra."

"Maybe." Atlantis had her mind on other things, and while she was tying the refilled water sacks to her saddle, she blurted. "I have no logical reason to think this, but I somehow think that the reason we have to go west is related to the talisman. The eighth piece."

She mounted and they both spurred their horses to a trot.

"We have to find that piece. If we are to defeat Ciabolo, we will likely need it. We were lucky last time. I hate to think some bandit has it. Surely though, they couldn't use it?" Rhovert thought aloud.

"I don't know,' Atlantis admitted. "What did you say about the one Roman has?"

"The son of one of father's advisers had it. He was a wizard, but after he was dead we realised he was delving into dark magic. We think, as does your brother, that he thought he could send a demon through a scrying crystal, to the bearer of the others. He tried it on Ven, probably because she ran out on him. Father discovered, from his spymaster, that she had been lucky. The demons found her, but they could not get to her. We still don't know why."

"And your father had no flashes from it?"

"No, but if he kept it locked away, there would be nothing to see."

"You are probably right. So, where did he get it?"

"Huh! You have me there. I don't even know if father knows. He had me going through all the books and scrolls he found in Tormore's house, and he questioned Rolliver too. Nothing suggested where the talisman he had, came from. The only thing I found that might have been significant, was a scroll that had recorded the properties of all the pieces. I do know that the pieces were passed down in the royal line. Father has scholars trying to track down when that piece and the other were lost."

"I'm not royalty," Atlantis pointed out. "Neither is Roman, and your father gave Ven's to Arlen."

"Well, yours was once my mother's, and traditionally worn by the Queen, who marries into the royal line."

"Well, that explains one, even though I got it before he made us marry."

"Maeven and Arlen got close," Rhovert said delicately. "They have Wystan in common. Maybe that counts."

"Who would normally have the one Roman has?" Atlantis asked, her mind still puzzling the question.

"Someone in the family," Rhovert guessed. "But as far back as I learnt the family tree, there has never been more than four children in each generation. Mine came from grandfather, Leanne's came from Uncle Edmond, and the others came from father's cousins."

They had travelled some distance along the main westward road, but Atlantis had slowed, and seemed to be looking for a particular side trail.

"Here," she directed, as what she saw matched the image in her vision. "Fodder's trail." She continued their conversation once they were trotting again along the new trail, heading north-west. "So, two of the things have been missing for generations. Where did they come from?"

"A previous dragon mage, maybe?"

"When? I know I used a piece of Thulor's shell to sort the ones we had."

"Are you going to keep gnawing that puzzle all trip?" Rhovert asked.

"I take it that you don't know or have forgotten anything else of use," Atlantis teased.

"I might recall something else, but if your mind is on an old puzzle, mine needs to be alert for trouble," Rhovert growled. "Why don't you ask Roman to find out what my father knows, next time he contacts you. He might be told more than father tells me."

CHAPTER 21 - Rhovert and Atlantis

Atlantis barely had time to warn Rhovert to get his horse off the track before six galloping horses appeared just ahead of where they had been. One reined in hard, gave them both an intent visual examination, then demanded, "You seen any scruffy types along here?"

"No one on foot or beast," Rhovert said in a surly growl. "What these oafs be?"

"Thieves and murderers. They escaped from the town yonder. They be dangerous."

"There a bounty on them?" Rhovert asked.

"Aye, a silver piece each."

"We be looking too, then." Rhovert nodded, let the rider go on, and walked his horse back to the trail. In a soft version of his normal voice, he said, "A change from bandits." He saw his consort's expression and asked, "What?"

"A silver piece. Someone must want them badly. Do town head men usually pay that much for escapees? I didn't think they dealt with murderers."

"They don't. The Lord to whom the town is beholden usually does."

"Those riders were in identical garb, but did they look like the Lord's men?"

"No. What's got into you?"

"Those men want the escapees badly. But I got a picture of the men they were chasing. Three scrawny, dirty, rag clad dungeon rats. I doubt they have seen daylight for years. If they committed the crimes claimed, it was a long time ago."

Rhovert did some rapid thinking. "Lord Mitkin's keep is out this way, not close though. If the town the riders mention is close, it may not beholden to him. It might be why it has its own soldiers. Do you think this is related to your other puzzle?"

"I don't know. Look for a place to pull off, right off the trail. I want to try something. I might be able to get Roman to contact us."

"Why?"

"I didn't like the way that guard looked us over. Did you?"

"No. So what do you plan?"

"To get Roman to organise for some of the guard to follow us."

"You are beginning to sound like Father, do you know that?"

"Sorry, but I keep getting these 'feelings' at the moment, rather than visual flashes. The reason isn't clear. What I have to do, is."

"Okay, do you want to head to that town? I think it is Ackbridge."

"Yes."

The clearing was small, but it had a spring that fed into a rock basin, and plenty of grass. The horses began grazing as soon as they had dismounted. Atlantis went to one of her saddle bags and searched through it, finally pulling out an odd doll-like figure, made from straw.

Rhovert ground tethered the horses, and looked back at her. She was looking around, and had one hand on her talisman. He reached for his own, which felt neither warm, warning of danger or more than normally cool.

"Any luck?" he asked.

"I think so," Atlantis said absently. "Why don't we each have a trail bar while we wait?"

Rhovert made no comment, just did as she suggested and went to fetched one of the pressed dried meat bars for each of them. It was an odd request because he knew that Atlantis preferred to go hungry rather than eat them, unless they had been softened by cooking. At the same time, he was quite sure that some power was working through her for a particular purpose.

Atlantis took her snack, just as a bubble appeared in front of her.

"What do you want?" Roman's voice was brusque.

"Can you relay a request to the border guard post to send a troop to Ackbridge? They claim to have had an escape of a few thieves and murderers, but I am sure that at least one is neither."

"Consider it done. How fast?"

"By this evening," Atlantis said. The bubble popped.

"Talk to me, wife," Rhovert directed.

Atlantis merely beckoned for him to follow. She led the way through some underbrush, and stared at some bushes. "It's okay. We're friends. I have brought you some food. Only trail rations, but I can get you a blanket."

The man who appeared from under a bush, had long tangled grey hair. His skin was pallid, and looked loose as if he had once been a bigger man. The wrinkles were outlined with dirt. He saw Rhovert and ducked back under the bush.

"It's okay," Atlantis repeated in a quiet calm voice. "I know what the horseman said you were, but I don't believe it."

The voice was little more than a croak. "No one believe me. Not in a dozen years."

"Did you kill anyone?" Rhovert asked bluntly.

The man tried to straighten up. "No Sir! Nor steal. Milord said I had something belonging to the king and he took it from me. Put me in dungeon. He wanted to use me."

Rhovert abruptly pulled his talisman from under his shirt. It had grown so hot it was burning his skin. "Stay here, I will go back to the horses."

Atlantis told the man, "Hide!" She had heard the chattering birds suddenly go quiet. She tossed her ration bar under the bush and drew a knife from her belt sheath. She muttered the words of a spell, as she touched her hot talisman. The soft exclamation from under the bush told her that the invisibility spell had worked. She whispered, "Stay quiet," to the man, and thought strongly, "Don't let this man, or myself, be found."

A faint haziness came over her vision just before two powerful looking men, in the same uniform as the horsemen, pushed through the bushes a mere arm's length from her and the hidden man. One held the taut leash of a large dog, who was straining as if following a scent. It and the men were oblivious to the two people right beside them. They were heading towards Rhovert and the horses. Atlantis carefully reached into a pocket and pulled out a small pouch and allowed it to drop in front of where she knew the man to be. She saw the bag being dragged out of sight. "Keep that on you," she whispered. "I'll come back. We need to talk."

Rhovert had been seen and was fending off questions from the two men.

"Not seen, no. Heard them's worth a silver bit," he said clearly. "M'partner will be back in a mo. We'll be looking for them coneys ourself."

Atlantis dispelled the invisibility about herself, and strode out into the clearing from a different angle to where the men emerged. They gave her the same sort of look the horseman had, then did a double take when they saw she was female."

Rhovert smirked at the reactions of the two men. "What's so important about them coneys? Did ya think they could'a turned into a wench?"

Atlantis ignored the men, and went to fiddle with another pouch tied to her saddle. She slipped a small amount of powder onto her hands, then went back to stand with Rhovert. The dog was allowed to come over and she let it sniff her hands. Its handler quickly dragged it back, but it didn't go back to sniffing the ground, as it had been before.

"Man came this way, we followed his trail," one of the strangers stated.

Rhovert shrugged. "That hound still got his nose on it?"

The dog handler gave a sharp command to the dog, which gave the ground a cursory sniff, and sat down. He glared at the two travellers. "Seems he's lost it."

"Three types on horse came by, just a'fore us," Rhovert said, as if thinking. "P'raps they found him and tossed him on one of their horses."

The two men whispered together then the handler said. "P'raps they did. But if not, you watch out. Man's a wizard, he could take yer mind over."

"Huh!" Rhovert said as if disbelieving. "That'd be a trick."

"Musta dunnit to get out," the other man confirmed.

"Right! I won't hold you further," Rhovert told them, mentally commanding, "Get going, well away from here."

He took a water skin and had a mouthful while the men watched. Then the one with the dog snarled, "Find the scent you stupid beast."

Atlantis kept a straight face as she watched them go out to the track. The powder on her hands, with such a meaty scent to attract the dog, had an under scent that would saturate the scent receptors. They'd not be able to smell anything else for the next few days. She gave Rhovert a glance before silently following the men to be sure they were going away. When she returned half an hour later,

Rhovert had company in the form of half a troop of the Kings Own Guards. Arlen was leading them.

"Lady Atlantis," Arlen greeted her with a bow. His troop kept straight faces, some of them had practiced against her in the past. "Can you please assure your friend that it is safe to emerge?"

"Yes," she said at once, recalling that she had left the invisibility spell on him and told him to stay. She went alone, and spoke softly to remove the invisibility. "The men with the dog have gone. It is safe to come out and tell your story."

The man had seemed to be asleep at first, but he rolled and looked up at her. "Many men come on horses. Don't let them have me."

Atlantis knelt down and said, "Yes. They are people I asked to come, so that you can tell your story. They have the authority to overrule the people who kept you imprisoned. Please? I am your friend and I don't want you to be afraid."

"My leg. It has gone all stiff."

"I may be able to help a little with that," Atlantis pulled out her talisman.

The man stared, wide eyed when he saw it. "No! Go away!" He tried to struggle away. Atlantis grabbed his hand, and thought of the man being healed. She felt the sense of a breeze blowing through her. The man's expression changed to one of awe and relief.

"May I...see that?" The man pointed to the talisman.

"This? Yes." Atlantis took the leather strap from around her neck, and put the talisman in the man's hand. He squinted at it, then ran a finger over the raised runes.

"It's like, but not like..."

"You've seen one of these before?"

"Yes. I had one. That is why they took me."

"Ah!" Atlantis let out a breath of understanding. "Then that must be why I felt I had to come this way. Can you stand now?"

Arlen had given his troop permission to relax. Two of them were squatting around where they were trying to start a small fire, another had a metal pan of water ready to heat. Three were leading horses to the spring to drink. Rhovert and Arlen were apart, talking intently.

"Someone is thoughtful, they'll have a brew going soon," Atlantis said neutrally. "For now though, I will introduce you to a few people. Oh, I'm Atlantis. You met my mate Rhovert before. He is with Captain Arlen, the leader of these guards."

Seeing the uniforms of the guardsmen, the unkempt man began trembling.

"Will you share your name?" Atlantis encouraged.

After staring at Arlen, he ventured, "Gamman. Gamman Mogray."

Atlantis made the introductions, and didn't mind that the man pressed against her. Rhovert let Arlen take the lead. He greeted the man as if he were an important townsman, not as if he was a thief, murderer or wizard. Then he told his men, "Keep watch. We don't want anyone else getting close enough to overhear our conversation."

The guards obediently moved out to circle the clearing. Arlen gestured for Gamman and Atlantis to be seated on a downed tree limb over to one side of the fire ring. He and Rhovert, squatted on their haunches facing them.

Atlantis spoke first. "Gamman here, once had a talisman, different to mine."

Rhovert was immediately interested. He reached for his own and took it from around his neck. It was now very cool, but then it was near two others just then. Gamman went wide-eyed again and more so when Arlen produced his own. Gamman moaned with fear.

"My friend, you have no reason to be afraid," Rhovert assured him.

"But...but...the great lord who took mine said it belonged to the king and that I must have stolen it."

"Did you?" Rhovert asked gently.

"No! My pa gave it to me. He got it from his pa."

"I believe you. What did it help you do? Each of the eight pieces aid the bearer in different ways."

"Eight? Well – I'm a carpenter. It helped me pick good wood – without flaws. Didn't need it to carve. Warned me of trouble."

"Yet they caught you any way," Arlen noted.

"They had a wizard with them, and I had to warn my wife, to get away with our boy," Gamman said. "They had fast horses, and I could only run. We got away on the two old cobs we had, but they caught up. I'd told my wife to hide. I don't know what came of them."

"We can ask the guard to listen out for them," Arlen assured him. "Tell me about the lord who accused you if you can. I know it has been a long time."

"Not long enough. His face is burned into my memory. So is his chattel, the mayor."

"The mayor of which town?" Rhovert asked.

"Where I was kept," Gamman said. "Not sure I ever knew the name."

"We are near Ackbridge," Rhovert suggested.

"There is a bridge there. Magicked to drop bandits in the river."

Rhovert glanced at Arlen who confirmed he'd understood the warning.

"Why do you even believe me?" Gamman said suddenly. "You must be king's folk if you have them things like mine."

"We are," Rhovert admitted. "That is why we know that if a talisman had accepted you as a bearer, you must be special indeed. Our talismans have stayed cool around you – the sign of a friend. Tell us about the great lord."

Slowly, in a voice that was still hoarse sounding, Gamman told his story. Atlantis moved once from beside him to fetch the water sack for him to have a drink. She had noticed that he was sounding better since she had left the little sack of dragon shells with him. Another sign that he was special – the shells were reacting to him and healing him.

Gamman had not forgotten the events leading to his arrest and imprisonment. He had thought often on them over the years, trying to make sense of them. When he got to the description of the great lord, Rhovert swore.

"So that's where that bastard got it. The description fits."

"But...he said it belonged to the king. He was taking it to him."

"It got as far as the town around the palace," Rhovert's face was grim. "I know the King didn't hear of it until more recently. Or even suspect it was nearby. Supposedly, his talisman gives him flashes from the others. Anyway, you don't need to worry about Lord Tormore. He got what he deserved, and his magic killed him some five years ago."

That cause a faint lightening of Gamman's expression.

"He was a wizard?"

"Apparently," Rhovert admitted. "I grew up with him, and never suspected it. He had a dark reason for wanting the talisman. He thought he could use it, but he hasn't a trace of royal blood and it only works for those who do, or those marrying into the royal line."

"But, M'lord, I'm only a poor carpenter."

"If you were able to use the talisman to power small magics – it found you a worthy bearer. Were you a mage as well?"

"No. Not really. Mostly I had a feel for growing things. Or it told me where there were weaknesses – like with the bridge in the town. I think that's how they got onto me."

"Bridge?" Arlen prompted. "You mentioned a bridge before."

"Yes. My boy was about to run on it, and I suddenly felt it was about to collapse. My wife grabbed the boy and I managed to stop it falling. Folk must a seen me do it and told the mayor. Many folk don't like wizards."

"Tell me more about the bridge," Arlen invited.

Gamman did so, and went on to tell what had happened to him after he was caught and put in the dungeon.

"We will be wary of the bridge," Arlen noted when Gamman had stopped talking. He did not let on that he was a wizard. "I wonder if the same man is the mayor there. It seems to me that if he abetted the traitor Tormore, then he is not a loyal subject of King Westron."

"I agree," Rhovert said thoughtfully. "I think I should go ahead and see how I am greeted. I will have Atlantis stay with our new friend, as I doubt he would be wanting to go back there. That town is one that I haven't been to before, and I don't think it is in Lord Mitkin's aegis." He paused, and added to Arlen, "It will be interesting to see how he greets you when you arrive."

Gamman turned and whispered to Atlantis, "You shouldn't go there. The mayor's men are mean fighters. I've watched them, and they don't treat women right. But should you be alone with me? I can't fight."

Rhovert heard him, and broke off what he was saying to Arlen. "My friend, what trouble my wife can't avoid, she finishes. I have no doubts that she can protect herself, and you."

Gamman shook his head, as if not agreeing. He felt Atlantis give his shoulder a gentle squeeze, and glanced at her. She asked, "Tell me about your wife?"

"I don't even know if she's alive still. Nor my boy. He should be almost a man by now. But she'd have gone south to her relatives, if she could." Then Gamman grabbed Atlantis's hand and said, "My Shayla had one of those talismans too. Would they have killed her for it? My boy was only four then, he'd have had no chance."

"What was your wife's name before she married you?"

"Shayla Starseeker."

"She was from Declanor?"

"Yes, but she'd been living in Thulor since she was a child."

"My brother and I are from Declanor. I've actually just come back from there. So, I should be able to make enquiries. My brother is Roman Golddreamer and I think he now has the talisman you once had. He is the King of Thulor's Court Wizard. Tell me, you said Shayla had a talisman. Was she a healer?"

"How could you know?"

"About four years ago, we realised there should have been eight talismans. The king only ever knew of six until Tormore died and we found his. We later learnt that the eighth piece was for healing and anti-magic."

"Anti magic?" Gamman frowned in confusion.

"Undoes magic."

"Never undid the little bits I did."

"That's because you were another bearer. The old dragon, Thulor, powered them. Now her successor, Petulor, has started to do the same. For a time, while she was growing, they had no power at all."

"Such events like you speak of aren't for the likes of me," Gamman murmured. "I was only ever a carpenter. That lord who took it, tried very hard to find out why I had it. He never asked me if I knew of others. If he had've, I'd've told him. I couldn't not tell him."

At that, tears began leaking from his eyes.

Atlantis said softly, "I think, even though he'd had taken it from you, the magic in it was protecting you. The king gave me this one, after Thulor died, and it is only recently that I have found power coming back into it."

"Yes, it was only recently that I found I could do some little magics again. That Lord, he did something to me. Made it so I could hardly walk, and I had to obey the mayor. Didn't want to make magic things for him – wood things. That feeling went away back a few years. Maybe when the dragon died? I tried to run away then, but I was too weak. They put chains on me then."

"It might have been when Tormore died that the magic tethers went away," Atlantis considered. "How did you escape?"

"I called the plants," Gamman said. "Got the roots to grow so they cracked the walls. Others got out too. I didn't care if they were real criminals. We'd all been there a long time."

"Do you know their names?"

"Inky. He was a teacher. Clay, he was a builder. Okko, he used to have a real good memory for things that happened, but he went addled. We had to look after him, make him eat. Might have been others, but I don't know."

"Did the mayor have uses for them too?"

Gamman nodded. "But I don't know what. T'was another wizard who made sure he couldn't tell."

"I think I have heard enough," Rhovert said, startling Gamman. "Ackbridge definitely needs to be investigated. I wouldn't be surprised if it is the base of all these brigand groups."

"My lord Prince, I tell'd ye of the bridge, but we was told it was magicked to protect the town from brigands. That's why it could be vanished like, when people are on it."

"After what I have heard you tell, I am more than convinced that it is to protect the mayor and his cronies from the likes of us," Arlen stated. "Thanks to you, we are warned."

Rhovert asked, "Do you want to stay here, or come closer to the town?"

Gamman trembled and Atlantis said, "We'll stay here."

"We will put wards up around the clearing," Arlen said. "I will also leave two men with you."

"Will that give you enough men if there is trouble?"

"The rest of my troop are already on the way. The apprentice wizard will be able to cloak their movements, as I will for us. I don't want them warned."

"Tis, if your brother gets in touch, find out what he knows. Don't tell him what we are doing, just that we have a lead on the eighth talisman. I will provide details later." Rhovert was already unloading all non-essential packs from his horse, including extra supplies. When Arlen finished laying his protective wards, he was mounted and ready to go. As usual, his leave taking was little more than a decisive nod.

When the sound of horses was gone, Gamman mused aloud, "How can it be that I am a relative of the king?"

"It is probably very distant," Atlantis guessed. "The king reckons Roman and I must be too. I am not sure I believe that either. Anyway, it isn't important. Are you still hungry? The pot is boiling, and I can do something better than tea. Soup perhaps?"

"I'm not used to eating much."

"Soup then. I'll get it started. Why don't you rest until it is ready?"

As she had thought, even with the healing effect of the dragon shells, or perhaps because of it, the man was exhausted. He was soon asleep. The two guards patrolled the perimeter, while Atlantis alternated between stirring the pot and pacing around the fire. Her mind was going over everything Gamman had said. She hoped his wife and son were alive, but what Rhovert had said about his father having flashes from one that suggested bandits had it, gave her a bad feeling. She thought too, of the others that had escaped. The riders had said three, had one been caught? The poor addled one? Without conscious thought, she reached for her talisman. If they were there because they were also victims of Tormore, the king would want to talk to them too. She sensed nothing, but had a feeling that something would be looking for them. Had she sensed Petulor's mind?

CHAPTER 22 - Maeven

It had been ridiculously easy to get removed from the women's quarters. Once Maeven had learnt more of the language, and convinced the women there that she did not want to be queen, and the signs of ill treatment had more of the women becoming nauseous, they had begun to accept her and ask what life was like in Thulor. It also helped that they detested Jilli, who had only stayed with them a short time. They had hated her for over four years and were happy to do things she would dislike.

Maeven had noticed an oddity on Jilli's neck. It seemed like a gem, embedded in or stuck to the skin there. She asked the women about it. The more recent additions to the king's harem said it had always been there. The few who had been there before the previous King's death, said it had come on her when the new king had brought her back with him. Those few, luckier than many of their predecessors, also revealed, "The king has one too."

"But what are they?" Maeven insisted. She only received shrugs. She had to leave off asking, but next time El Rasho took her, she decided to study it. His ...whatever it was...was not as noticeable.

As a point of trivia, to get the women gossiping on another subject, Maeven suggested that the things Jilli and El Rashi had might be the reason why the king and the hated concubine could not engender. It made them impotent.

Her suggestion was immediately backed up by the oldest of the wives. "He's only ever fathered daughters," one said. "The mothers are sent away with their babes."

"But he gives them gifts of gems too," a younger one piped up. "I'd have a girl, just for that."

Something in the expressions of the older few suggested they knew differently. Maeven decided not to ask when one of the older ones said, "There have been no babies since the Thulan bitch came."

That was enough confirmation of the effect of the things, so Maeven said, changing the topic again, "Jilli was only ever a chamber maid in Thulor."

Not long after that, Jilli had flounced in, causing all the women to stop talking. She glanced around, suspiciously, but the women went back to talking, of other things. Maeven knew why she was there and merely got up and went over to her.

"Oh, good. Something different to do."

Jilli scowled at Maeven's pretend eagerness. She flounced out again, and Maeven had to trot to keep up.

"Were you all talking about me?"

"You? No. Why?"

"Never mind."

"They are a bunch of bored women. I was telling them about Thulor."

"That you are nothing but a disgrace of a princess?"

"Of course not. Who'd believe it? You know they have a pecking order in there. I'm just the latest new face."

That seemed to satisfy Jilli for a while. Then she said, accusingly, "But they were all listening to you!"

"Yeah. Like I said, they're bored. They all want their turn at getting the King's attention. That is their only use."

"Rashi doesn't need them. The only reason they are still there is because it builds his reputation."

"Well, his interest in me is giving them hope that he might start looking at them again."

"They will figure out eventually how wrong they are. Anyway, how come you're so eager? He likes hurting you."

"You like it that way. I've discovered I do too."

Jilli stalked on in silence, delivering her to the slaves for the usual pre-tryst cleansing, and telling the servants to deliver her when they were done.

Maeven didn't need to be told that her former maid was in a foul mood because of the thoughts she'd had planted in her mind. Nor was she surprised when Jilli wasn't present for the torture session. She'd decided that the woman only enjoyed it when she thought the king's victim hated it. And in fact, although she detested having to be with the king, she had discovered that swallowing some dragon shell before the event, did blunt the worst of the treatment.

However, the following day she discovered the outcome of her latest ploy with Jilli. Two of the kings guards, entered the women's quarters and strode directly towards her. All the other women moved back as far as they could – distancing themselves from the one who looked about to be punished. Maeven stood facing the men. They didn't ask her to come with them, simply grabbed her and began to drag her. She decided to say nothing, and see where they were taking her – it was looking to be a section she had not seen before.

King El Rasho was lounging on a throne like chair, in what Maeven decided was a small audience chamber. Here he had her brought to a position four arms lengths from him, and he just studied her for a long time. Then he gestured to someone – and the creepy wizard appeared. His eyes were brown, so Ciabolo was not controlling him at that time.

"It has come to my attention," El Rasho said without preamble, "that you are working to disgrace me in my own palace."

"And how can I possibly do that?" Maeven retorted. "I don't speak your bastard language, and you and your creepy wizard are probably the only ones besides your common whore that speak Thulan."

"Apparently, you were talking well enough to my other women to be planning some sort of rebellion."

Maeven laughed. "Like I said, they don't understand me. If they were listening to me it was because they were so bored that hearing any new voice is more interesting than their tired old babble between themselves. Besides, you have no idea what nastiness a room full of jealous women can create. They have a pecking order in there, and in their eyes, I am the lowest. Trouble is they also see me as your new favourite, and hate me for it. Their only duty, which they cannot perform, is to please you. So now, they also think you are about to ditch that chamber maid, Jilli, and when you tire of me they will have another chance at you."

"I also hear that you intend to escape and are learning your way around by listening to them," El Rasho persisted.

"Do you think all your fancy guards are stupid, and let me wander around? I have only been in three places, no, four, since I've been here. I have seen more of this place in the last half hour than I ever had." Maeven let the king digest that. She saw the scowl on his face.

"You got yourself far enough around the last time you were here!"

Maeven just shrugged.

"Wizard, put truth spell on her," El Rasho ordered. If he hoped to force her to tell what he thought she'd deny, well, he would see.

"Are you planning to escape?" El Rasho demanded after the wizard nodded.

Maeven felt the magic on her as an itch on her scalp. She didn't bother to lie, but she could twist the truth or not tell all of it – and he would have to believe her.

"Escape? The first chance I get, I'll be gone!" she admitted readily, although a thought occurred to her that she wanted to consider, later. It was the idea of why Petulor had meddled when Arlen had visited her. "As for giving you a bastard, if I had my way, you'd rot. I'm just enjoying making your whore take second place. Obviously, she is barren. You should have kept trying with all your wives if you really want a son. And they way you treat me, I'm not likely to conceive."

"You know, I can have you whipped," El Rasho reminded her in his silky voice.

"Yeah, and I can see you coupling with me afterwards, getting my blood all over you...It might be worth it. It would make sure I couldn't conceive for a very long time."

"Silence!"

Maeven shrugged, she had just learnt something. He might like watching her being whipped, but he wouldn't touch her that way – it fit with her having to be bathed and oiled before she had to endure him.

"What makes you think you are so desirable?" El Rasho taunted.

"I must be, you keep coming back for more," Maeven said with a shrug. "I'm told, though, that some men don't care what a woman looks like. I mean, when you're not around, Jilli has fun with whoever is free."

El Rasho lunged from his throne, and had his hands around her throat. Maeven just stared back at him. She knew he needed her more than she needed him.

The creepy wizard moved just as swiftly to prevent the king killing her. He whispered something in his ear, and it wasn't a pleasant reminder it seemed for El Rasho released her and scowled. When the wizard turned to look at her, she saw the man's eyes had changed to orange. Ciabolo was in charge now.

With a tone and expression that could only be described as sulky, El Rasho announced, "You won't be going back with the wives."

"Great! Back to the dungeon. That's just as good."

"No! I'm going to have a special room for you. Guarded by my guards, and by magic. If you have to go out, you will be guarded, but you will eat well, get exercise, everything my old nurse tells me a woman needs if she is to get pregnant."

Very deliberately, Maeven acted less smart mouthed, so when she said, "I'd like that. It will make your whore furious," – truth spell or no, El Rasho didn't believe her. His smirk seemed forced. It was as if he wanted to suggest to her that he had ideas to make the prospect of decent quarters a torment. He would probably figure out ways, Maeven decided.

"You'd better be sure your guards don't decide to try me out when you aren't around," Maeven told him. "They might be more potent than you. With me in my own space, no one will see what they do."

The evil glitter in the eyes of the wizard was also intriguing. Was that something that he definitely didn't want? Why? He'd brought her to Vatarik, insisted the king got her pregnant, so whatever his reason was, it was important to the slimy serpent. She'd think on that too. The question was, if she was already pregnant to Arlen, was that going to play into his hands? Surely, he wasn't thinking to force his way into the body of a child? That idea sickened her, and her expression must have betrayed it. The wizard merely nodded, and told the King, "Make sssure ssshe isss well locked up and unable to make alliesss."

Maeven's new quarters were a small windowless chamber with a side room that was for bathing and had a privy as well. The rooms were lit during the day by light reflected on a series of mirrors from outside. By night it needed candles, but an intentional 'accident' with one had resulted in the candles being replaced by brighter wizard lights – like those Atlantis had once shown her. Initially it was airless and musty, and the mage tether they had put on her wasn't long enough for her to reach the privy or the wash water. Although she didn't think it fair to the servants, the intentional torment that kept her from the bathroom, neither humiliated her nor made her regret the new quarters. Three years living in a cave without such amenities, had inured her to that. The smell she left was foul, but twice a day, servants cleaned the area and lit sweet candles. Still, it made her next ploy believable.

By careful use of the bath powder, that she had just been able to reach, she made her face, arms and hands pale. She acted like she was on the verge of being sick, although denied any ill effect.

Outside, two guards were always on duty. They were only allowed to let Jilli in, and she had fallen for the ruse, even to believing she had a raging fever. She had heard of the mess that the servants had to clean up, and not being aware of the mage tether, thought Maeven also had a stomach bug.

Maeven had merely said, "It's your dear Rashi's idea of keeping me well enough. He has no idea at all! My body is so busy dealing with sickness – it won't nurture his seed."

Assuming Jilli had told El Rasho she was ill, might have explained why he left her alone for a few days. When he had demanded her presence again, Maeven had disgusted him further by being sick over him. He had sent her away before he could perform his intended torments.

Back in her quarters, Maeven asked for the fire to be lit, even though she wasn't cold. She hoped that El Rasho would think her really sick.

It seemed he was indeed worried, for a short while later an old woman bustled in, followed by her two guards. She turned on them.

"Out! Unless you wish to catch whatever has caused this woman to be ill. As you can see, she is in no condition to do anything, let alone run away."

The guards hurried out and the woman turned to Maeven.

"You, girl, over on the bed. Let me look at you."

Maeven obeyed, and the woman put a hand on her forehead. The touch was gentle.

"We'll have that fire out, girl! You need to cool down."

In a suddenly lower voice she asked, "Why ever are you fouling the floor?"

Not knowing the local words for 'mage-tether', Maeven stood and walked as far as she could. The woman nodded knowingly.

In her loud voice, the woman ordered, "Get that dress off. I'm going to check you all over. You have to be fit and well to give the king a son."

Maeven dared to say, "I don't want to do that."

"Nonsense, you silly girl. The king's interest is an honour to you and your family. You could have been married off to some old doddard to act as his nurse or bed toy."

The words were harsh, but the woman's expression was sympathetic. She said quietly, "It's better that you let him have his way. He will lose interest soon enough."

"No, his master wants him to hurt me too."

That made the woman take a step back. "Like that, is it?" She had Maeven stand up and turn around. "I see you have been a little fool," she said loudly, but her look was not one of censure. She said softly, "I can't interfere."

Maeven asked softly, and gestured, "Can you get them to remove the mage-tether?"

A terse nod preceded, "I will tell him that you need plain food, nutritious, nothing fancy. A well-lit, and well aired room, and some task to keep your mind busy. It is only common sense if he really wants a child."

"What if he's impotent?"

"Hope that what he believes is true, that you are not barren and he can do his dynastic duty."

Maeven kept her real hope to herself. That the king's brother, had beaten him to the goal again. She should have had her bleeding days by now, but she still had a few doubts. The treatment she had endured since arriving might have affected them.

As if reading her mind, the woman loudly quizzed her about her woman's cycle. Maeven mentally blessed Reyna for teaching her about that, and ways to prevent conception. So she was able to be convincing, saying that she had just ended her bleeding days before she had been abducted to Vatarik. If the woman was to report to El Rasho, as Maeven believed, she would tell him that her fertile time was within a few days. With luck, she would insist on the improvement in quarters and conditions to increase the chance of conception.

And so it turned out. She was moved to a room with a window, barred, but it could be opened. The mage tether was removed, although both window and door were magically guarded. She was given three small meals each day, basic fare, but still better than her diet of hoppers and roots. Finally, she was given coloured silks and canvas to use to make tapestry cushions.

When Jilli saw the new quarters for the first time, she growled. "Don't get too comfortable, bitch. Rashi still prefers me."

"You can have him. I would have preferred you had already given him a son, then he wouldn't need me."

"How did you get them to give you a new room to foul?"

"I didn't. You'd told me often enough what your Rashi thinks of me. No, some old hag of a woman insisted on all this if he wanted me to conceive. Damn well wish she hadn't."

"Didn't know you could sew," Jilli tried again.

"Can't. Hate it in fact. It was more fun making all those other wives jealous of each other. I'm going to be bored stupid."

A faint smirk returned to Jilli's face. Now she believed that Maeven hadn't wanted to be in a room by herself.

"How long have you had that thing at your neck?" Maeven asked.

Jilli felt her neck as if she had forgotten about the neckpiece. "The former king gave it to me," she bragged, dropping her hand and seeming to forget about it in the same instant. Maeven studied it while Jilli seemed to have her mind elsewhere. Whatever it was, it might look like a rare bauble, but it made her uneasy.

"Well, is he expecting me today?"

"No. He's away for a day or two. He told me to make sure you are doing all the old nurse told you to."

"You'd better tell him that I am," Maeven threatened.

"Naturally," Jilli lied with a smirk. "Anyway, if you are so missing Rashi's attention, I know of guards that are almost as good."

"Might be fun. One of them might be more potent than your Rashi and get me pregnant. He won't know."

Jilli was sure to tell El Rasho that Maeven had made that suggestion again. It would make no difference, El Rasho would keep being ruthless to her anyway.

Two days of virtual solitude were a relief. Her only contact with others was when servants came with her food or to fix the fire and clean her rooms. Generally it was two from the same group of four doing the tasks. Usually a young one and an older one. Maeven didn't try to make conversation with them, and they were not meant to look directly at her. When she had tried, just once, the two servants had gone rigid as if expecting trouble. That reaction was probably not surprising if the only time they were addressed directly was for punishment. She had seen the same reaction when a young slave was punished for talking to one of El Rasho's other wives.

Seeming to ignore them had another benefit. All the servants knew she was from Thulor, and did not expect her to understand spoken Vatarin, or only a little bit at least. Whenever she spoke to JIlli or El Rasho and servants were around, she spoke in Thulan.

So, sometimes, when they came in, she'd pretend to be doing some women's makework, sewing or embroidery. She would be in the main room of the suite, and when they were cleaning her bathing room, they dared to chat in low voices. Often it would start with the older servant instructing the younger in some aspect of her duties, but soon tended to turn to gossip of happenings in the citadel. They had no idea that the room subtly reflected their voices to where she sat. And when their master was away they were more relaxed. The doings of El Rasho, his wizard and Jilli were frequent topics, and often they mentioned her too. The king was not well liked, he treated servants harshly, but there was nothing they could do but endure it. It seemed that knowing the king was still not able to get his newest 'wife' pregnant was a source of malicious scorn. That he treated her as harshly as themselves, was to them only fair. The wizard was one they all tried to avoid, they knew of servants that had vanished without word or sign. Jilli was detested for her arrogant manner, and her foul temper when the king went away and did not take her.

The chat gave Maeven warning. When she tired of, or was refused by the few Kings guards that had not gone away, and her rampant lust was unsatisfied, Jilli was apt to come in and be unpleasant. The first time, she had started to punch for no reason except El Rasho was 'favouring' her. The servants had heard that none of the guards wanted anything to do with her.

The low voiced words, "...so often away..." caught her attention. Away, meant out of the citadel, like now, not just leaving her alone. She was beginning to think he was tiring of trying to hurt and humiliate her, but what the servants were repeating – snippets overheard of conversations of the citadel guards, confirmed that he and the wizard had gone off to hassle the Thulans. Their conclusions, based on the mistaken belief that the Thulans were the cause of all the bad things in Vatarik, were totally erroneous. With her own wider world view, Maeven added the snippets differently and inconspicuously drew on the magic guarding her to perform a memory spell. Any such information, might be valuable if she could ever get word out to her Thulan kin.

Her only warning that El Rasho was back was when the servants herded her into her bathing room for what she now called her 'pre-torture' cleansing. She hoped he wasn't going to perform his latest punishments in her rooms. At least when she was taken to his chamber, she had a change of scenery. In this instance, going to him would show her the way from her new room, but him coming to her would leave an unpleasant taint in her new space.

Two of his guards came and forced her to walk. Each had a grip on one of her arms. She recognised the chamber before being forced inside, but this time there was a portable screen hiding half the area. In addition, the old woman who had helped her before, stood by a low table that had a wooden mug on a tray. When she entered, the woman took the mug and came over to her.

"You are to drink this."

"What is it?" Maeven asked, only to feel something hard whack the back of her legs. They stung, but she did not turn to glare at the guard.

The woman just gave her a hard stare. "It is a posset to help you conceive. Your fertile days are now."

No doubt, she thought, El Rasho had ordered it, and she had no choice about taking it. However, if the woman made it, it was probably safe to drink. She did, and was amusingly surprised that it tasted pleasant. After a moment, she began to feel her body relaxing. She glanced at the woman as she handed the mug back, and gave her a brief smile.

When the woman had taken mug and tray from the room, El Rasho gave his guards a nod, and they dragged her towards the curtain, which El Rasho shoved back to reveal a wooden construction that completely puzzled her. All she was sure of was that it had multiple places a person could be shackled to, as the guards were already doing to her. In moments, her back was against a thick plank of wood, surprisingly smooth, and her arms and legs were spread wide.

Had he tired of banging her onto the ground when he tried to impregnate her? She saw El Rasho reach for a lever and the wood turned her around. Another lever brought the board parallel to the floor and then spun her around at that angle. When he slowed it, she was dangling from the wood by her arms and legs.

She heard laughter, even as the blood roared in her ears and pain shot through her joints.

Finally, she was standing again on her feet, but trying to dull pain, and not be sick. It would serve the bastard right if she was. She heard El Rasho order the guards out, and dreaded what would come next.

He grabbed her chin and lifted it up. "This device, is called a mating cradle. It is used to train whores for pleasing rich clients. It is also used to discipline wives who refuse to do their duty to their husband. I haven't even begun to show you the basic positions."

Maeven forced nausea away and tried to talk. Her face was slapped, and El Rasho reached for what looked like a leather belt, but wide like a sash. He didn't explain what it was for, just wrapped it around her and the wood, from her navel to under her breasts. When he tied it in place, she became aware that it had metal reinforcing the shape.

"I am allowing myself three whole days to experience every position."

"I'm honoured that you cared to do all this for me," Maeven said, making her eyes seem big and innocent. Jilly will be so jealous."

"My favourite does not need such discipline."

"No, I guess not. She's always in heat, except when she has a go with your guards. Is she going to beat me first? I enjoy that."

"No," El Rasho said with a trace of a snarl. "I have other plans for you."

"I can't wait," Maeven forced herself to say.

For the next three days, true to his word, Maeven endured being forced into countless uncomfortable or degrading positions, while the king used her. Each time, when he was spent, he would change her position. He would leave her alone, until he was ready again, when he would release her and have her cleansed again. After the third time, Maeven began to smell an odd scent on him, and wondered if it was a medicant to make him able to perform with her.

Even so, at the end of three days, Maeven could hardly walk when the guards dragged her, still naked as she had been since the torture started. Jilli forced her way in, shoving her rival aside.

Maeven found the energy to say, "Wow, that was amazing."

Jilli's counter was a gutter level curse, but her attention was on El Rasho, and she began to harangue him. Maeven was not surprised when he slapped her and his tone when he chastised her verbally suggested he had no interest in her just then. It caused a bubble of amusement to surface in Maeven's mind. Maybe the bastard was well and truly worn out – but had he had enough of her yet?

Once Maeven was left alone after the end of that third day, she thought it was safe enough to let her thoughts drift. It was only her conviction that Arlen, formerly El Haba, Prince of Thulor, had again made her pregnant that had enabled her to endure the past days. The dragon shell powder she had taken with water on her return to her room helped with the pain, but did nothing against all the deliberate humiliations. She forced her mind away from them. Thinking of them did her no good at all. Instead, she told herself that child within was actually Arlen's, and she truly didn't want to risk it, be it a boy or a girl. In fact, even less than El Rasho would want to risk what he would think was his heir.

Perhaps, after it became obvious she was pregnant, El Rasho would treat her more gently, or better yet, ignore her. But, as things stood, she'd have to endure two more weeks before they expected her to miss her cycle. If she hadn't had it before then, her last doubts about being pregnant would be gone. One question still nagged her. Why did the serpent want a child of hers? There was no guarantee that it would be magic gifted. El Rasho was no wizard, even though his brother was. Did they have the same mother? If she could get the servants to talk to her, she might find out. Or maybe that wasn't a good idea, she didn't want to get them in trouble.

She decided what she would try for next, settling on getting Jilli to suggest she be forced to take exercise – more than what could be done in a small room. So far, her manipulations had worked. Jilli did not even suspect what she was doing. She was always in too much of a hurry to gossip to her Rashi, maliciously suggesting ways to further discomfort her hated rival. And El Rasho was too intent on punishing her, too arrogant to think that she was anything but demoralised. He hadn't even remarked on how fast she was recovering from his attentions. The residual colour from the bruises seemed enough to make him gloat. He also saw her as small, undernourished, and therefore weak. He had no idea how three years of rough living had toughened her. The idea that she had her own agenda, and he was obeying it, would make him laugh. He wouldn't think she could escape from him either.

Maeven's other hope was that the creepy wizard would keep away from her too. He was nasty enough when Ciabolo wasn't in control of him. When the serpent was, he would be remembering how she had tricked him before.

CHAPTER 23 - Rhovert and Arlen

Rhovert was only familiar with Ackbridge from the trade road approach, coming down from the north. In any event, he had not been there for over five years. However, several of the guardsmen with Arlen came from the area and they knew of various ways to enter the town.

"What do you think, Captain? I come in via the southern trade road?"

"Yes. A travelling merc, stranger to these parts, wouldn't be expected to know the little ways. I'll send Fernin and Cathak follow you some distance back. The rest of us will split up and take the other two ways. Kolti, which bridge do you think would be magicked?"

"Sir, if I'd had one magicked, I'd have both bridges done. But from what the old guy said, I would say that was the back bridge. The river goes into a lake back that way."

"That was my thought," Arlen admitted. He turned his attention to Rhovert. "What reason will you be giving out as your reason for being there?"

"I'm an out of work merc and I don't want to hire out to another Great Lord."

"You want him to try to recruit you?" Arlen asked with raised brows. "If he is working with bandits, you will need to be careful."
'

"I'm already sure the mayor is a traitor," Rhovert growled. "Can you put on me a spell to block truth spells?"

Arlen murmured something, then Rhovert felt a flash of cold, then all seemed normal. "Decide your story, run through it in your mind a few times on the way. Then, if they slip you a truth serum, that will be what you remember and tell."

Rhovert nodded. "How long will it take to get to the trade road from here?"

"A quarter candle mark," Kolti estimated. "Fernin can show you the way."

"Fine. I'll go in, and give me half a candle mark before you come in. I shouldn't alarm anyone much on my own, but if the mayor is spooked by a troop of guards, I'll try to duck away with him."

Rhovert turned onto the trade road, acknowledging Fernin's hand signal for good hunting. He trotted until he saw the trees starting to thin out, then slowed to an amble. When the view opened up to reveal a moderate sized town, he took a good look around. Smoke came from various chimneys, people moved about, but often glanced around. Children played, but stayed close to the brick and wood houses. He could hear the sound of metal being hit, probably coming from the blacksmith's forge. He saw a large number of horses in an enclosure. The sound of birds and an occasional whinny of a horse seemed normal, but he had the impression that the locals were trying to act as usual but expecting trouble. Were they worried about the escapees?

He spotted the most elaborate house, and identified other buildings, before heading to a stabling yard where a small herd of horses stood together. No one came to help him with his horse. Often one of the local lads did so, hoping for a coin or two. Here, the youngsters just looked his way, then away again or sidled off. So he tethered the gelding to a rail, but on the outside, then whispered a quiet command in its ear before settling his weapons in place and strolling to the house he had decided would belong to the Mayor. It was built entirely of brick, not half brick and the rest wood.

He was allowed to come no closer than ten arms lengths to the house when two bully boys emerged and blocked his path.

"Where you think you're going?" one demanded.

"To talk to your Mayor," Rhovert said, standing his ground.

"He ain't hiring," the second bully boy claimed. "This be a well behaved town."

"Huh!" Rhovert snorted. "I hear ye ain't got enough guards to stop prisoners escaping."

Low snarls came from both men, and Rhovert smirked. "Exactly. Now, I want to see the Mayor, lads. I reckon I can guard a jail alright."

"He's not in," the first one tried again, but his words were an obvious lie as the Mayor, in his opulent clothes, emerged from the manor. He was eyeing the rough looking merc as if sizing him up.

"Some jerk wanting –"

Rhovert spoke louder, cutting the other man off. "Looking for work, I is. Don't want to work for them great lords. Annoy one, and they all know about it."

"You were kicked out?" the mayor asked suspiciously.

"Ah, it was just a misunderstanding," Rhovert seemed to bluster.

"What kind of misunderstanding?" the mayor snapped.

"Only a little one..."

The mayor gestured, and a rangy figure in a long cowled cape, bearing a staff, emerged from the house. Rhovert eyed him, guessing he'd be a wizard, and acting wary. His amulet warmed beneath his neck cowl.

The figure stopped beside the mayor, muttered something inaudible and stamped the ground with the heel of his staff. Rhovert felt his head itch.

"What's your name!"

"Berto," Rhovert said, he could feel the compulsion, but it hardly affected him.

"Where'd you come from? Why did you leave?"

Both wizard and mayor would believe he was telling the truth, and Rhovert had no trouble telling his rehearsed tale of woe. They did believe him, and even snickered when he admitted, "How was I to know the flirt was the lord's daughter?"

The two men conversed briefly in low voices and then the mayor decided, "I will talk to my guard master. Why don't you go have a drink at the Leaky Bucket. On me."

The man tossed a bronze token and Rhovert lifted his hands to catch it. "My thanks, my lord mayor." He grinned widely, and asked, "Is there somewhere I can feed and water my horse?"

The mayor gestured to a hut on the far side of the smaller enclosure. "See the stable master."

Rhovert turned to walk back to his horse, and as he went, he felt his head stop itching.

After arranging for his horse to have a feed, he followed the stable master's directions to the tavern. He had seen dozens of horses in the yard adjacent to the stables, and so was not surprised to hear lots of loud voices from the tavern. He was heading there, when he passed a huge building with tall wide doors. He glanced in, seeing piles of bales and bundles, and hessian bags full of who knew what. He didn't betray any obvious interest, and kept his eyes on his destination.

The sign outside showed a bucket leaking water, although he noticed it was painted over an older picture that may have had a bridge as part of the design. Time later to puzzle over that. He strode in the open door, finding the place packed with men dressed in a range of styles and degrees of shabbiness, and inside the noise was deafening. Not put off, Rhovert pushed his way through to the bar and caught the eye of the barkeeper.

"An ale." He tossed the token at the barman.

A huge mug was plonked in front of him, Rhovert took it and appeared to take a huge swig, before looking around. "Great stuff," he toasted the man, who then moved off.

He would have said the barman was surly, but when he studied the drinking rowdies, he decided he knew why. They were all the same type of people as the bandits he had fought recently. He looked more intently, not all were bearded, and scruffy. He saw a clean shaven young man, he recognised from his father's court. He began to notice the men nearby beginning to jostle each other roughly, and decided to edge away from the impending fight. As he moved through the crowd, who barely noticed him, he again felt his head itch. When he reached the wall near the kitchen, he leant there to listen and watch. From watching the various groups manoeuvre at court, he decided that here, there were three separate groups within the room. Bandits, he was certain, and jealous of each other. Maybe, that was the reason for the magic.

"Psst!"

Rhovert looked to the door and saw the tavern keeper gesturing to him. He moved to just inside the kitchen.

"You not be one of them," the man said in the local dialect. "You shouldn't stay."

"I'm not, no. What's going on?"

"What you see. The rabble stays here, while their leaders and the mayor agree on supplies and rewards. Was four lots due to come, but one lot's not turned up."

He might have said more, but someone called for more ale, and he went at a run. Rhovert followed him, but only back to the door.

He studied the nearest patrons some more, looking to see if any had the little controlling demons. Some did, he decided. Then he wondered why none of the men had decided to wander outside. Were they getting free drink? Or was the magic to keep them within, and keep them from fighting?

He decided he had seen enough there and finished his drink. When he tried to go out the door, he felt a solid block where air should be. He summoned the Tavern keeper.

"That wizard got us trapped here?" Rhovert demanded in a low voice?

The man gave a terse nod, then grabbed him. "Come with me."

Rhovert let himself be pushed through whatever it was that blocked him. There was a flash of heat, then pleasant coolness.

"If you be just looking around like, you'd best keep going. You know what them inside be?"

Rhovert nodded.

"We folk, of the town, can't leave here to tell. Normally, wouldn't let you too, but they be busy today. Maybes you can."

"I heard three prisoners escaped."

The innkeeper gave a twisted smile. "Mayor thought them all too addled to try anything. His dungeon had old magic protecting it. Don't think the new wizard wanted to meddle with it. T'was the weirdest thing though. The wall just fell down. Took the whole side of the mayor's house..."

It was Rhovert's turn to smile faintly. "Can you pass the word to all the good folks to keep out of sight?"

Widened eyes were the only reaction he got, as the man studied him, nodded, then whistled. A young boy came at a run, the tavern keeper gave him low voiced instructions, shrugged at Rhovert, and sent the lad off.

"How many guards does the mayor have?" Rhovert asked.

"Too many, but half are out hunting, some are trying to erect a new wall. I think that's why the mob are cornered."

"Right, I'll just be looking around. You be careful," Rhovert warned.

"I should be telling you that," the other retorted softly.

Rhovert kept to the edge of the road while going back to where his horse was tethered, He saw that the doors to the supply warehouse were now closed, and he grinned. If the people inside were townsfolk, they probably wanted to keep the goods if the bandits were removed.

Arlen's arrival with five of his men – all in the uniform of the King's Guards – had the Mayor hurrying out again. This time with four bully boys, but no wizard.

Rhovert had his own ideas as to why the Mayor came right out to meet the King's Guards. Same reason he himself had been greeted outside. If the man was receiving stolen valuables, he would want no outsider seeing things inside his manor.

Arlen looked around before dismounting, saw Rhovert lounging by the stabling yard and imperiously beckoned to him. Rhovert slouched over.

"Mind the horses!" Arlen commanded at his most imposing.

Rhovert nodded, and seemed to be mumbling something. It didn't seem like the Guard leader was listening as his attention seemed to be on the Mayor who was bowing obsequiously because Arlen's rank was obvious from his uniform. He was however, and heard Rhovert's warning about the tavern full of bandits, the guards out hunting, those fixing the wall and the wizard.

"I need a word with you, good Sir," Arlen told the Mayor. "And your advisers, if you would be so good as to summon them." He began to walk into the mayor's ornate manor, causing the mayor and his men to trot after him. Only two of his troop followed – the others went around to the back of the manor and later returned.

Rhovert saw two more men arrive at a run and go inside the manor, and idly wondered how they had been summoned and how many others were inside the manor. He kept a lookout, aware that many guards were absent, and they may not be stopped by the other troops watching the edges of the town.

A quarter candle mark later, Arlen emerged, and gestured for two more of his group to go inside. To the other he said, "Keep watch out here and stay alert."

To Rhovert he said, "I have put a mage bonds on all the men, the wizard included. There are some items on a table that look like records. If we want to examine them, and anything else, I think we should remove them from in there before examining any spells that might be on them. The men outside, who were working on the wall, are being held by the roots from some ancient tree. Do you want to question them now? They will likely want to talk to get free."

"If they will stay that way a while, I think we should deal with the brigands."

Leaving the horses lightly tethered, Arlen followed Rhovert.

"If you go in, only the tavern keeper can get you out," Rhovert warned, adding to the terse information he had given before.

Arlen studied the building, his eyes seeming to go out of focus. He came back to himself. "That isn't the work of the wizard back there with the mayor. This is a high level, multi-layer spell. It is the work of the Serpent, but probably able to be triggered by that other wizard."

"Can you add a sleeping spell to the containment spell?" Rhovert suggested.

Arlen considered, then took off his talisman and handed it to Rhovert. "That might alert the caster, so to be safe, I will use only my own energies. Take that and wait back near the horses."

Rhovert did as directed, suspecting that Arlen was not completely sure he would not attract attention. He watched as his companion faced the tavern, then made his arms fly wide, like he was casting a net. He felt a slight jolt that told him the magic had taken hold. Arlen returned and took his amulet back.

"If the Serpent or his agent checks on them, he will feel the spell," Arlen warned. "Let us find out what the mayor knows, and quickly."

They both went inside the manor and found the guards watching the men Arlen had put mage bonds on. The prisoners now also had physical bonds and the wizard was hooded.

In the instant Arlen recanted the immobilisation spell, a high pitched screech and a loud, thumping "whuff" was heard. In the Mayor's formal room, green fire erupted in the fireplace and something large and ugly flew rapidly around. Arlen began incanting spells. Rhovert raised his sword as the creature neared and sliced through it. It was a demon, larger than any other they had seen, except Ciabolo himself. The body fell to the floor, and Arlen sent mage fire to burn it before it might heal itself and recover. Then He snapped, "Nevin! Go and see what happened outside."

While Rhovert watched for any more unexpected creatures, Arlen tossed something into the fire place that doused the green flame. Then he checked the mayor and the wizard. Both were unconscious, and neither slapping nor shaking had any effect.

Nevin returned quickly. "Captain, the tavern is burning and the flame is green."

Rhovert ran out, heading that way. He was relieved to see the inn keeper outside, just watching the fire.

"What happened," Rhovert asked.

"Damned if I know," the man said. "One instant the men inside all turned to statues, and a little bit later, something dark was flying around the room. I ran, and I'd watch my own tavern burn to be rid of those bastards."

"It is as well that you got out, but that green fire is nothing I want happening. It isn't natural. How do you folk put fires out?"

"There be buckets out the back, near the river. Folk will be coming up soon."

In fact the first men and women were dragging buckets up. These tossed the water on the walls of the tavern, for an instant the flames went out, but then they returned.

Rhovert saw that the wood wasn't turning black or being consumed, and suddenly cursed. He recalled what the green flame meant – the building was one large demon portal. He halted the next bucket bearer, and jerked her talisman from around his neck. He dunked it in the water, and when that bucket full hit the wall, that section of wall did not turn green again. He couldn't stay there and do that to each bucket, and thought of the small pouch of crushed dragon shell he carried in his pocket. He gave it to the tavern keeper and said, "Sprinkle a tiny amount of this into each bucket. Bring the bag back when you are done."

The effect was the same as if he had used his talisman, except that more of the structure lost the green flames.

"What kind of magic is this," the tavern keeper asked.

"Dragon magic," Rhovert told him.

It only took two more buckets to banish all the green flames outside. The water bearers began to murmur.

"Bring some buckets inside," Rhovert directed, as he went to the kitchen entrance and through to the area of the bar. Green fire still glowed in the three fireplaces, and he saw a dark figure dragging someone towards the nearest fire. He felt one of the bucket bearers behind him, and turned to take the bucket. He trotted with it to the fire place and directed the water at the dark shadow. The creature shrieked, and vanished. The man he was dragging dropped to the floor, part in and part out of the fireplace.

"Throw water in each of the fireplaces," Rhovert called, as he crouched next to the fallen man. He felt to see if the man was breathing, and he was, but he didn't react to being shaken. From that angle, he could see several other prone figures. He went to the next one, and when he shook the man, he began to moan, "No, no, no."

Rhovert hauled him to his feet, but the man's eyes went to the uniformed guardsman who had followed Rhovert.

"I give up! I surrender! I beg the King's mercy."

Rhovert righted a chair, that had fallen nearby and shoved the man into it. "Stay there! Move before I say so and the only mercy you will get is at sword point. Look up!"

Startled, the man did, seeming to expect the flying creature to be waiting for him. Seeing nothing, he looked back at Rhovert with uncertainty. But his merc rescuer was already looking under one of the still upright tables.

"Out!"

"My Lord, Mercy!" that one also tried, but he was obeying the command.

"Only if I am generous," Rhovert growled. "Well, you have the look of Artur Hornfoot. Why are you here?"

"I...I came to see my brother. He told me to meet him here."

"You are one lucky bastard. Go sit with that guy there. Don't think of leaving."

As Rhovert went back to the first man he had checked, both he and Nevin heard something scuttling under the tables.

"Come and show yourself," Nevin commanded. "In the name of the king."

Three figures, not one, obeyed the command. Each held his hands up in a gesture of surrender.

"Name!" Nevin barked at the first man.

"Edrik, Guardsman."

"Where are you from?"

"Yewstream. Just south a bit."

The other two, Girdy and Fellet, had come from the same place.

"Why were you with the bandits that were here?" Nevin challenged. The three men all looked at the floor, knowing the fate of brigands.

"Well?" Nevin snapped.

"Theys promised us a share of their loot if we joined them," Edrik said, still looking down. "Thought we'd stay a bit then go back home. Our families be nearly starving, we can't grow anything, and the coin we was promised would let us buy food. What we saw those others eating each day would have fed our families for a week."

"How long were you with them?" Nevin asked in a more moderate tone.

"Only since they came through our farm and took most of our last geese. They said we had to be taught stuff here before they'd let us start earning."

Nevin glanced at Rhovert, who had the King's authority to judge and punish.

"You be lucky, by the dragon," Rhovert said, drawling as his Berto persona allowed. "How be it you didn't turn like statues?"

The three men shrugged in unison, then Girdy suggested, "We didn't drink the ale they gave us. The god says it muddies the mind."

"We pretended to," Fellet said. "Because they said it was good stuff, brought in just for us. I think he meant the whole lot who were here."

"Where'd you put the drink," Rhovert asked.

"In the corner, where the wood is stacked," Fellet admitted.

"Get it," Nevin ordered, and the scared man scuttled to obey, hoping obedience would help save them from hanging.

When he returned, Rhovert took the mug, even though it was being held to Nevin. He sniffed the brew, and tasted a drop from a finger he dunked within. He pulled a face.

"Yon tavern keeper has better that this," Rhovert snorted. "This be like horse piss. Fit only for drunkards."

Rhovert wondered if the drink had been drugged. He gave Nevin a subtle sign to bring the men with them.

"Right, come with us! If you stay, and not run off, you might have a chance to save your skins."

Rhovert murmured to Nevin to have the prisoners tied to the rails of the horse yard, and he went back into the manor. Arlen had been busy – a pile of things were stacked just inside the door, and he heard steps hurrying from upstairs. Two guardsmen were coming down carrying pillow covers full of odd shaped items.

Arlen gestured to a side room, it seemed to be the records room. Rhovert looked at what could be seen, and decided what they wanted to take out. On the table was a large parchment book and it seemed someone had been writing in it. Over a dozen more were in a wooden cupboard, which had the doors open – any protective magics dormant. Rhovert gestured to them, and Arlen had his men take them outside. Other things caught his interest, artefacts, boxes of gems and coins, some with filled purses inside.

"I have the authority to confiscate unlawfully acquired wealth," Rhovert noted. "Do you have any doubts that this was gained by dishonest work?"

"None," Arlen stated. "I have witnesses to the mayor's offer of a bribe to stay away from here. Those caskets are spelled."

Rhovert lifted on of the ornate boxes. His fingers didn't itch, like they usually did when he touched a magic object. He was about to comment when the lookout rushed in.

"Captain, three men have just ridden from the stables, and taken the north road."

"Sound the alert," Arlen directed. "I want those men returned here before they can take a warning anywhere."

"I should have thought," Rhovert muttered. "The tavern keeper said the group leaders were talking rewards and supplies. The mayor probably told them to leave before you went in. And I wonder what happened to the fourth group that was to have been here today."

"Let's get what we want from here and start to question the prisoners we have," Arlen proposed.

A sense of urgency made Rhovert agree. He grabbed the parchment book, and others from the cupboard, passing them to other guards. Arlen directed his men, "Take that stuff near the door out to the horses and keep guard. There may be more people around here that we haven't accounted for."

Both Rhovert and Arlen took up as much of the gems and coin as they could to pass to the next guard in line.

"I have never had a premonition before, but my back is itching like fire. Can we move these men out of here?" Rhovert asked.

"Yes."

As they leant down to grab hold of the helpless men, the sense of immediate danger intensified. Arlen yelled to his troop to get out and drop to the ground, he and Rhovert kept dragging the mayor and his wizard, but an explosion, originating from the room they were just leaving caught them and tossed them across the street. The mayor and the wizard did not come with them.

"Well!" Rhovert said once he had his breath back. "That was unexpected."

"Someone got a warning out, or we tripped something," Arlen said. "Jusden, go check the men behind the manor – the trapped ones."

Rhovert commented, "That box you said was spelled, wasn't when I touched it. Could your spell to counter the mage bonds have countered all the ambient magic?"

Arlen considered that, but only shrugged slightly. "Let's see if the mayor is still alive."

They both went to where they had been blown away from their prisoners. The two men were not there, so they tried to enter the building. They had to stop at the doorway. Whatever had caused the explosion, had caused the upper floor to drop down, and anything that had still been up there was now no more than fragments. Arlen checked for more magic traps and then decided. "We'll need to go through this mess to find the bodies of the other people who were here and try to identify them."

"I'm surprised the walls contained the explosion," Rhovert mused aloud.

"As am I," Arlen agreed. "Unless it was the old magic at work – like that which trapped the mayor's guards."

"Likely we would have been badly hurt had the walls blown out, so maybe it was dragon magic," Rhovert considered. His guess seemed to be confirmed, when Jusden returned to report all the mayor's men were dead and the plant roots had retracted from the bodies.

"Have the bodies brought around here. I want the men identified," Arlen directed.

Jusden trotted off just as three horses bearing King's Guards from Arlen's second group trotted into town with the riders leading horses with the brigand group leaders tied to their saddles.

They stopped next to Arlen, and reported, "The north bridge went down, just when that green fireball occurred. These three were hurrying so fast they didn't see it wasn't there."

Rhovert let Arlen hear the report, he had his hand on his talisman. It was still warm. His skin began to itch. He began to look around, turning slowly. Some of the townsfolk were beginning to venture out until Rhovert called to them to stay inside. All vanished again in moments. From the stable master's hut behind them, came a scream of terror. He raced there, sword ready to use. Two of Arlen's guards followed closely.

One puffed, "More of that damn green fire, like in the house before it blew up."

The glow was visible through the open window. Apart from the screaming, there was the sound of things breaking and something like a strong wind.

Inside, something flew rapidly around the room, seeming to drag with it anything that was not fixed to the walls of floor. Items hit the walls and bounced then joined the swirl again. Rhovert took out the pouch of dragon shells and threw a handful of the fine sand like particles into the whirlwind. Flying items dropped, a dark shape seemed to be sucked into the fire. The screaming had stopped, and all else went quiet. The room was an unholy mess of broken furniture, personal belongings and food stuffs. The stable master was unmoving under a pile of debris.

The fire in the grate was still the lurid green, and Rhovert stepped gingerly on the mess to get close enough to throw more dragon shell into it. The glow died immediately, but to be sure the demon would not return, he took hold of his talisman and ordered, "Fire, die!" and the fire, back to orange, died immediately.

"The man is dead," one of the guards reported.

"We were too late," Rhovert growled, as he went to the other windows and opened the shutters. He used the natural light coming in to scan the mess on the floor. The two guards were ashen faced.

"This is what a demon rage looks like," Rhovert said quietly. He continued to scan the floor, until one of the guards said, "Sir, look there."

The man looked ready to be sick, at the sight of a hand clutching a piece of fine fabric. Rhovert picked up the grisly object and examined it. He kept his thoughts to himself as he decided the fabric could have come from the mayor's formal robes. His talisman had cooled, and he knew the danger had gone, and the dark shape had come in with the mayor, and both had gone through the green demon portal.

He wondered if the stable master had tried to kill the demon, or to rescue the mayor, and died for the effort? Had the wizard been a demon under an illusion? Had the demon taken the mayor onto a more distant fire? Questions kept pouring into his mind. How wide an effect had Arlen's magic had? It had gone at least as far as the bridge....

"Atlantis!" Rhovert exclaimed. He turned and ran outside, straight to his horse, and delayed only long enough to check he had all his weapons and to yell an explanation at Arlen.

CHAPTER 24 - Atlantis, Rhovert and Arlen

Atlantis had given Gamman some of the soup she had brewed and was about to put a second pot on the fire when she heard and felt the explosion. One of the guards pointed to the green glow. It sent shivers down her spine. She had seen Ciabolo, the Serpent, appear through a wall of green flame. At the thought, her talisman grew so hot that she had to pull it from within her shirt. It was almost glowing white, so hot it was. She spun around, grabbed the pot of water and vegetables and tossed it on the fire. The flames wavered, but were not doused. Sword in one hand, she searched her pocket for the pouch of crushed dragon shells, then she recalled she had given it to Gamman to mind.

"I need that pouch I gave you. Now! Quickly."

The man searched. "I...I must have dropped it," he said shakily.

"Go look for it," Atlantis directed, sensing now that the magical protections had gone. She didn't need to say anything to the guards, their eyes were already darting everywhere.

Two figures appeared, right over the fire, momentarily disoriented. They dropped, but were not burned by the fire. Atlantis ignored them for the moment, her gaze on the circling dark shape, a demon. The creature squealed when her sword slash just nicked it. A foul smell pervaded the air. Gamman curled into a ball, covering his head with his hands. The guards slashed at the demon in turn. One managed to swat it to the ground, and put his sword into it until the creatures body had finished fuming into nothing.

Atlantis spun around, just in time to parry a slash from the stockier of the two unexpected arrivals. The dagger missed her by the merest fraction of an inch. The man seemed shocked by her rapid reflexes, and cursed as he barely managed to avoid her return attack.

"A sword bitch," Mayor Amblin leered. He grinned maliciously. "I know what I can do with you!"

Atlantis had no time to watch what the other figure was doing, but she saw flashes of light in the corner of her eye. The two guards were not able to get close to the other man – a wizard, she guessed.

He wasn't paying her any attention. He probably thought the mayor could deal with her, but he was watching her eyes, not her hands, and between one moment and the next, her free hand grabbed a slender dagger, held in an odd grip. She manoeuvred her opponent so she faced the direction of the wizard. The mayor thought her sub-audible muttering was a prayer for help. He was wrong. He saw the dagger and ducked when her hand moved to throw it, and didn't see that it flew straight into the back of the wizard. Instead, he thought Atlantis was distracted for that instant, and tried again to overpower her. He moved her around, caught sight of a guard forcing his sword into the wizard's neck and swore, trying even harder to frighten her.

He didn't see that same guard put out a foot to trip him, but he felt the tip of his opponent's sword at his neck.

"Immobilise him. I think the king will have a lot of questions for him. He will be lucky if he only sees the inside of his majesty's dungeons. More likely, his neck will be stretched until it finally breaks."

"Mercy, mercy," Mayor Amblin began to blubber.

"Not my call," Atlantis told him. He served the enemy of the kingdom. "Check his neck," she told the guard who had finished tying the man's hands and feet.

"He's clear, Lady."

"Well, that tells us something," Atlantis smiled grimly. "Who are you?"

"M...m...Mayor Amblin."

"Of Ackbridge?"

"Yes...yes. Please, you have to believe me, I didn't want to do what the wizard said. I had no choice."

Atlantis caught sight of Gamman, slowly standing up, straightening. He walked over, looked down at the Mayor, and spat in his face.

Instantly, anger replaced the pleadings for mercy. "You!" He looked at Atlantis. "You harbour a thief and murderer."

"And what are you?" Atlantis challenged in turn.

The man snapped his mouth shut.

"I see," Atlantis said evenly. To the guards, she said, "The wizard is dead? Good. Watch this one. If he as much as tries to roll over, hamstring him."

Rhovert arrived at a scene that at first looked innocent. Then he saw the body and the prisoner. He rode closer and dismounted. He met his consort's deliberately neutral gaze.

"Well, it seems you have caught the two who escaped the King's Guards," he spoke with equal neutrality. "Mayor Amblin, we meet again."

"How did you escape?" the prisoner demanded.

"You are not in charge anymore," Atlantis told him, moving her sword deliberately close to his privates. She went on, telling Rhovert, "He does not have an incubus, but he travelled here through a demon portal. It is likely that his true master does not know of his plight?"

"What are you talking about? The wizard is dead. He forced me to go with him."

"And his tongue is as twisted as a snake," Atlantis continued. "What happened yonder?"

"Later. I want him strung over a horse and returned to the village. The rest of the Captain's troop will be arriving soon. They can take this one to the palace with the other survivors."

Rhovert glanced at the prisoner, who for an instant wore an avid expression, which returned to mere anger. He resolved to warn Arlen. "Pack up here, all of you. You are to come to the village."

The two guards each had a body slung over the rump of their mounts. For Mayor Amblin, it was a most unpleasant experience. The dead wizard was beyond caring. Gamman rode behind Atlantis, he spoke for the first time since the Mayor and wizard had appeared. He whispered, "You won't let him go will you? He's evil. I could tell you so many things."

Soft as his voice was, Rhovert heard and said quietly, "He will be lucky if he leaves here alive. I intend to have answers from him."

Atlantis asked him, "What other survivors?"

He explained about the three bands of brigands that had been in the town, and how most of the brigand rabble had vanished through the green flames in the tavern. "We found six that had been unaffected, and caught the three leaders of the brigand groups."

"I wonder where those that vanished went," Atlantis said musing.

Rhovert shrugged. "I will get Roman to spread the word."

Arlen had everything under control when Rhovert returned. His initial troop had been augmented to full strength. He saw the prisoner and the body and nodded his approval.

"Well done, Berto. Naylor, you and Ghent, take the prisoner to join the others."

The townsfolk who had been in a half circle in front of Arlen, recognized the mayor and greeted him with cat calls. The man tried to adopt his usual strut, until he realised he was being led to the stables. He roared with outrage when he was shoved into a stall, whose usual occupant had only recently vacated it.

To the townsfolk, Arlen continued his instructions. "I will ensure that everything you have to tell me is recorded. The king will wish to know all of it."

Rhovert, still unrecognised by any of the subordinate King's Guards, kept near Atlantis and Gamman, waiting for him to be free. One of the guards murmured, "The six survivors have been talking non-stop. It's all being recorded. Some of the women here are good at writing, one is some kind of priestess."

Gamman's head jerked up.

Later, after the long day of questioning, searching, recording statements, the townsfolk gathered in the meeting hall, worried about the town now the dubious protection of the mayor and his wizard was gone.

Arlen promised them that part of his troop would remain for a time, and that the supplies that had come in for he brigand groups could be shared amongst all the townsfolk. Much of that had been grown by the locals themselves.

The women went off and prepared a mini feast for everyone, including Rhovert, Atlantis and Gamman along with the King's Guards. The tavern keeper returned to the meeting hall with a small barrel of wine.

"Been saving this," he admitted. "It be too good for the regular rabble or that snake of a mayor."

When he reached Gamman, his eyes widened in surprise. He filled a glass and passed it to the haggard man, then gave his shoulder a sympathetic squeeze.

While waiting for the women to bring food, Atlantis brought

Rhovert up to date on all she had learnt. She had been with the women writing down what the townsfolk had to say, but also making notes of what Gamman remembered.

"Amblin was in it deep and willingly. He kept the best of the loot the brigands brought in, even though he was meant to pass that on to his master. When women captives were brought in, he used them too. He has been here almost twenty years, acting as eyes and ears for our enemy. From what I have heard, he has some deep antipathy towards your father. No one liked him, but none dared to speak against him. It is as the inn keeper said, he provided some protection for the town, and the rabble was mostly kept under control – except when he wanted to make an example of someone. He took a lot in tithes from the town – food mostly. They never starved, but never had enough surplus to earn extra coin for luxuries."

"Has he admitted everything he did?" Rhovert asked. He'd not had a chance to ask Arlen about that.

"He had no choice – Arlen put a truth spell on him. He may have thought he was protected, but not with Petulor providing the power for the spell. He won't escape the noose. And we had a quick look at the parchment books you saved. He was keeping two sets – one for the king's tithe, and another with the true figures of what he got from the brigand groups he organised. He was also getting paid by his master, who did not hear of the little extras he kept for himself. What he said has been backed up in part by the six who survived in the tavern."

"One was a court noble's younger son," Rhovert told her bleakly.

"Yes, a young hot head – but he became the most useful. Thanks to him, and what his brother had boasted about, we know exactly how the bands were deployed, what they were told to do, all of it. We can use that knowledge to look for signs of similar set ups in other areas."

"That is a lot to pass onto Roman for father to hear," Rhovert sighed.

"You can take the transcripts," Arlen suggested, coming up to them. "You were going back to the palace weren't you?"

Rhovert glowered. "Not that damn fast! And not until I have talked to you about my sister."

"Ah, yes, indeed," Arlen murmured, turning away. Suddenly, the day's victory seemed hollow.

CHAPTER 25 - Roman and King Westron

King Westron looked out from the window of his private suite, watching an unusual fluctuating green glow emanating from beyond the high protective stone wall. The wall was also the limit of the magical protection spells on his palace. He finally summoned one of the few servants remaining in the palace, and instructed him to fetch his wizard.

Roman GoldDreamer arrived at a trot, having just come back from a check of his magical wardings about the palace.

"What do you make of that?" Westron greeted him by pointing out the window.

Roman looked and studied the phenomenon. He hadn't noticed the odd light, but then he had been close to the inside of the walls. Against the overcast sky, the light was noticeable from up high.

"I don't like it," Roman admitted, talking slowly as his mind began thinking. "We know there are chancy creatures out there, and the little demons. That looks like the glow from fires that have been repurposed as demon portals."

"Then what can be done about them?" Westron demanded.

"Well, put the fires out," Roman began. "Maybe sprinkle dragon shell dust at the centre of each. Success will depend on the strength of the demon's magic."

"Do you really think that what is out there will let us put out their fires?" the king asked ironically.

"We might be able to get someone out there to sprinkle shell dust," Roman considered. "I'll go out and see what is happening."

"Not you, wizard. Send one of the guards out, but not in livery."

"As you wish, Majesty. I can put a seeming on him so anyone who sees him, thinks he belongs there."

"A wise precaution. Meanwhile, once he's out looking, can you make these clouds rain?"

"Something is holding the rain," Roman said after a while. "But maybe I can peck at it and stop it."

"You do that, wizard. And tell the guard to report to me when he gets back inside."

The man returned after an hour had passed.

"I had a swarm of them little flying demons zooming at me like moths to a torch," the guard was telling Roman as they entered the King's suite. "Good thing you included that repelling spell or I'd've not come back."

The guard bowed when the king turned his way. "Sire."

"Come in Raydon, tell me what you saw out there." Westron gestured to chairs, as he seated himself. "I heard you mention lots of little demons..."

"Yes, Sir! More than normal, but I can't tell if they came through those green fires or just was attracted from elsewhere."

"Something was coming through those fires?" Westron queried, sensing the unsaid.

"I think so, Sire. The compliment of people out there now has doubled since this morning. The newcomers are just lying around the fires like they'd just stepped out and collapsed. Scruffy looking blighters. Some have the look of Vatarins, but all might have been brigands. Still had weapons on them."

"Interesting. Were there demons on the newcomers?"

"Most, yes. Only just infected, I'd say. Some were well entrenched," Raydon gave his opinion.

"And in your opinion many were Thulans?" Westron asked for confirmation.

"Yes, Sire."

Westron sighed. "We need to find a way to neutralise the creatures."

"I am looking for an answer, Sire," Roman assured his king.

"And the shell dust did work? I was noticing the green glow reducing."

"Oh, yes, Sire. The rain reduced the size of the fires, and they changed back to normal fires after I tossed a palmful of the shell dust into them."

"No one tried to stop you?"

"Oh, I had the soldier types that had been here already, wander over. I pretended to be checking on the arrivals. They didn't even comment about the change in flame colour in my wake."

Roman chuckled. "That fits with what I know of the Serpent. He wants obedience, not intelligence."

"Well, those new mouths are going to need to be fed. Which

means more trouble for the townsfolk and the nearer farms," Westron commented. "Was there anything else of relevance, Raydon?"

"That was all, Sire."

At Westron's gesture of dismissal, Raydon pushed himself up out of the chair, bowed and left the room.

"Are we to expect more enemies to arrive that way, wizard?"

"Not unless they make fires in new places, Majesty," Roman considered. "The fires have been burning since the weather got cold. Now that dragon magic is blocking the demon magic, I doubt anything else will come through."

"Have you heard anything more from my son, wizard?"

"No, Sire. Not since my sister mentioned a lead to the 8th talisman."

"They were going to Ackbridge, you said. It's meant to be under Lord Mindon's wardenship but it's a long way from anywhere. I wonder how long it has been a base for bandits."

"Rhovert and Arlen will find out, Sire. Has your talisman shown you anything about that?"

"No," Westron growled. "If that 8th talisman is there, I would think it would react to the nearness of the other pieces. We will see what is found there. Now, leave me in peace. Come back when my son has deigned to send a report."

Rhovert went back to the King's library of scrolls continuing his search for information useful to the current situation. He paused when he felt the tug of the magic link that he had always had with his sister. He put the scroll he was scan reading down, and spoke the words of his communication spell.

He saw his sister's face appear on the round bubble, and knew his would be seen in the paired bubble near her.

"What can you tell me, sis? His Majesty is in a right state of frustration with your fancy Prince."

"There's a lot, Roman. We have been getting statements from townsfolk, and from some who are prisoners. They'll all be sent to you."

"Aren't you coming here now?"

"Eventually," Atlantis said, and Roman could tell she had shrugged.

"Just the highlights then," Roman urged. "We've had some weird stuff happening here today. I did wonder if it was connected to what you were doing."

"Weird? How?" Atlantis asked.

"People who look like brigands turning up – coming through green fires."

"Oh! I'll tell Rhovert. But likely they did come from here. He saw what were three bands of brigands here, in the tavern. They were spelled to stay within. Arlen added a stasis spell to those on the tavern, then something happened and the whole building was covered in green flame. Inside, something was dragging men into the fireplaces."

"So that town is a brigand base?"

"Not any more. We have the mayor as a prisoner. His wizard was a demon in human guise, but he's dead. The mayor's name is Amblin. You might ask his Majesty if the name means anything to him. The guy has been supplying the bandit groups for five years, although he has been in charge here for a two score of years. Arlen put a truth spell on him, and he has admitted everything. He didn't have a little demon incubus, so he was doing all of it willingly. Some of the locals claim he hates your father for some reason. Oh, the dead wizard was calling himself Goldfire Honeywell."

Roman couldn't control a laugh. "I met him once, just before my wizard master sent him off. He was a nasty one then. I wonder when he was taken over by the demon?"

"It doesn't really matter," Atlantis told him. "Now that he's dead."

"Did you find out anything about the 8th talisman?"

"Yes and no. I am not used to the visions I am getting and maybe I misunderstood, but then again, we found out that three prisoners had escaped from Mayor Amblin's deep cellar. One of them had minor magic and did something to make the nearby tree roots grow and grow and break the dungeon walls. He recognised our talismans, because he used to have one himself, handed down from his pa and grandpa. The mayor and a great Lord took it from him and imprisoned him."

"The 8th piece?" Roman asked with avid interest.

"No, I think it was the one you have now. Rhovert recognized the great lord from Gamman's description."

"Gamman?"

"Yes. Gamman Mogray. He was a carpenter, and could put magic into things he made. Somehow, the great lord found out he had a talisman, and wanted it. He accused Gamman of stealing it. But he didn't know that Gamman's wife also had a talisman. I think she had the 8th piece. She was a healer, but after so many years, he doesn't know where she is, or if she and their son are still alive. Her name was Shayla Starseeker, and I think she might have been related to one of the dragon priestesses."

Roman bit back a comment. Since the King had started getting flashes from the various talismans, he had been getting them from one that suggested it was being worn by someone in a bandit group. If Gamman's wife was alive...she was probably little better than a whore now.

"When will Rhovert be ready to talk to me?"

"I don't know. They have been so busy."

"Alright! I'll settle his Majesty as best I can. He's been like a fidgeting flea since the mention of a grandson."

Roman went to update the King, and expected the growling response of, "I want him here! I'm not paying him a stipend to lounge around and ignore my orders."

"I'll take notes when he gets in touch," Roman suggested, to placate his king. "Although written statements will be coming."

"You do that," Westron agreed. "Damned whelp!"

"Well, his detour has proved a win for us, Sire," Roman pointed out. "I hope it removes the brigand problem from the south."

"I wouldn't want to guarantee it," Westron warned. "It only rids the area of the Vatarin infiltrators. Thulan brigand packs may still be there. However, with the Declanese closing and guarding the border, there will be less trade or traffic down that way, and we will be sent word of odd happenings. Maybe fewer poor folk from that area will go missing – and likely becoming soldiers to fight us."

"Do you wish me to get a report of missing people from all parts of Thulor?"

Westron considered that. "I already know many are such in the north. More than half the men in the raiding groups Leanne and Finora have encountered up there are Thulans – bespelled or with demon controllers. But yes, the extent of the problem needs to be known. And when you next speak to my older daughters, tell them what has been happening here and down south. Have them keep alert for a resupply location for the bandits they are flushing out."

"Yes, Sire," Roman confirmed. "Do you want me to have a meal brought up here, and a potion to help your joint aches?"

"The potions don't work, and before you say so – I will not spend every waking hour down in the dungeons. Yes, bring food, and bring yours here too."

Roman was glad to rise and stretch his legs. He wondered what was occupying the king's mind. It had to be so fascinating that the king could forget the nausea that had kept him from eating for several days. He let his mind recall all the things Atlantis had mentioned from Ackbridge. Even considering each thing as he trotted down to the kitchens, gave him no ideas. The king was back to keeping thoughts to himself, although three years of being close to the king had allowed him to make guesses on many occasions. It had been easy to see that the news of his youngest daughter had hit him hard, but not the nuances of why. Well, the servants would be relieved that the king wanted food.

Westron, who had been quiet all during his meal, put his eating utensils down on his plate, and pushed them away.

"Any news of Gwillard Ley?" Westron asked, as Roman finished his own meal.

"He is coming from West Kerdale, bringing much of his library – or so I was told. He should be here tomorrow or the day after. Half a troop of soldiers from the guard post are coming with him, and the guard's wizard has put an illusion on the cart. When they get to Drange, they will let me know and I will tell them the way in. Whatever did you ask him to do?"

"Never mind. Are any others of my scholars still within a day's ride?"

"There are two downstairs, going through all the scrolls in your library – looking for ways to help your aches and to rid those who are afflicted of the little demons. They are frequently in touch with colleagues in other towns, discussing ideas."

"Have one of them see what can be found about Gamman Mogray," Westron directed.

"The man Rhovert found?"

"Yes – since he had the talisman Tormore got his hands on, that one you now have."

"Handed down from father to son," Roman prompted.

"I want to know when and how it got into his family."

"I will put Zeb and Jackary onto it. Though personally, I want to know how Tormore came to learn the man had it. There was nothing about it in his private journal that we found."

"Indeed," The King agreed, remembering their earlier investigation. "And I am sure that one was never in the possession of bandits."

"That eighth piece – the healing one – what did you see in the flashes?" Roman had an idea he wanted to explore. The king hadn't said much about it.

"Just a lot of dirty men, and lots of blood."

"Do you think the person who had it was using it to heal?"

"What makes you ask?"

"I was just thinking that Atlantis mentioned that the wife of Gamman Mogray also had a talisman. He doesn't know if his wife still lives. She might be living with bandits, and being forced to heal them. I cannot see any that are part of a bandit rabble, being able to use it. Unless one with dragon blood, as Petulor stressed, is with bandits."

"Make that something else to tell all troops – search all captives and look out for a talisman."

"Yes, Sire."

Later, once his magic had opened the talk bubbles between the palace and Ackbridge, Roman sat at a table taking notes. He was mildly amused when Rhovert began to speak without any of the usual courtesies, or waiting to let his father ask questions. His voice did sound tired as he reported his actions, observations, events and conversations.

Roman had to write fast and it was a boon that the dragon magic below the castle could be used to augment his energies and speed his writing. Rhovert gave his father no chance to ask questions until the end. There was so much to consider, but finally, Westron ran out of questions and commanded, "I want you to come directly back here. My Guard Captain can handle anything else that comes up."

Roman heard a vague murmur from the bubble before Rhovert spoke again.

"That is our intention unless something else untoward happens."

Roman decided that was a good place to end things, and popped the bubble, then sank back into the chair, flexing his hands that had cramped from the extended session of note taking.

CHAPTER 26 - Leanne and Finora

The sword found the man's heart and as he fell, something began flying in mindless circles. Leanne recognised it as being one of the ugly little demons.

Finora was already incanting the attraction spell and this was conflicting with the demon's intense compulsion to find a new host. As she increased power to the spell, the demon drew closer and closer to the silver orb and was sucked into the receptacle. She sealed the two halves of the receptacle together and placed a locking spell on it and put the silver orb into a bag with many others.

Leanne was already battling with another brigand, a clumsy fellow who barely knew how to defend himself. Finora used her magical senses to search for more of the little demons. She spotted another liberated demon flying around the village square and began another attraction spell.

Leanne finished off her opponent as Finora snapped the second silver sphere shut.

"Another poor sod that ought to have been back home somewhere ploughing!" Leanne muttered in disgust, not even out of breath.

The sound of the fighting around her had changed in a way that only an expert fighter would be aware. Leanne glanced around; her troopers had the remaining brigands, those that hadn't fled, occupied.

"Can you sense any more demons in this group?" Leanne asked her twin.

"No. There were only two this time." Finora confirmed.

Leanne let out a piercing whistle. The rest of her company of fighters knew it was the signal to indicate that their opponents were no longer in the thrall of the demons.

Of the enemy group, once fifty strong, only ten remained fighting and they all chose to drop their weapons and surrender when their opponents offered to spare their lives.

Leanne let her second take charge of the prisoners. They would be questioned later to find out if any of them had information of value. For the meantime, they were offered the chance to earn royal pardons by fighting for Thulor.

Mostly, the men they questioned were appalled at suddenly finding themselves fighting against skilled opponents. Their minds might well have been asleep since they were taken from their hometowns, which in any group were widely scattered.

Some of them were more than enthralled farmers and traders. Occasionally, one of the prisoners turned out to be a political opponent of the despotic King El Rasho, conscripted into his army to be killed fighting for Vatarik. These ones, when their memories returned, were more than willing to tell anything they knew and to switch allegiance to Thulor. The farmers, knowing they dare not return to Vatarik, accepted the offer of earning a place in Thulor.

Whenever Leanne heard new evidence of El Rasho's excesses, she berated herself for not killing him when she had the chance.

Now that the sounds of fighting had stopped, some of the braver villagers were venturing out of hiding. Leanne strode over to the boldest group, which included the village headman.

"You'll need to burn or bury the bodies," Leanne told the group. "Anything of value on them can go to the town."

"They fouled the well," one of the group reported savagely.

Finora didn't need to be told what to do. She walked over to the well, set in the centre of the square and took several pinches of herbs from a pouch at her waist. She crushed the dried leaves together and sprinkled them into the well, accompanied by a low voiced incantation.

The stench of rotting garbage, which had been wafting up from the well, was slowly becoming fresher. She returned to the group around her sister.

Finora waited for her sister to finish talking to the men before she gave them her advice.

"You'll need to get water from the river for now, and boil it before drinking it. By morning, the well water will be clear again."

Leanne gave a piercing two-note whistle and immediately her troop moved up into ranks of two ready to return to their hidden camp. As they strode off, the grateful townsfolk gave them a ragged cheer. Apart from the well, damage to and loss from the town had been minimal as help had been fast in coming. It meant that the townsfolk were able to do the clean-up – mainly tending their few dead, and burning the bodies of the more numerous dead bandits. Anything they found on those dead was finders keepers.

That had been Finora's doing. Knowing that a band of brigands was active in the area, she had spent hours scrying for signs of their camp. She had failed, concluding that something was protecting it as well as she was doing for Leanne's base camp. It was chance that had given her sight of the rabble on the move, and more luck that she had been able to identify their likely destination. The troop had set off within moments of the sighting.

Now, Finora was feeling every bit as tired as the troopers who had been fighting. Forcing demons, even small ones, to go into the globe shaped demon receptacles took energy, as did keeping a degree of protection on her sister and herself. She was glad when they reached the glade where those in the troop with sufficient rank had their horses tethered.

Once back at the camp – Leanne had her second in command, assign the new recruits to tents and sub-troops. Those that were once farmers, would need to be trained to fight, since any skill that had been forced on them was now gone. Those that had been Vatarin soldiers, would still need to learn the troop signals. All would be told what was expected of them and the penalties for not obeying the rules.

Finora headed directly for the tent she shared with her sister, but stopped when she heard a soft cooing coming from the top of the command tent. She looked up and saw one of the magic protected messenger birds perched there. From a pouch she carried, she drew out a handful of grain and held her palm out to the bird. It flew down at once, avidly hungry. It didn't fuss when Finora used her free hand to remove the tiny scroll from its leg. Leanne saw what she was doing and came to see what the message was. Finora passed the roll of flimsy parchment to her twin and examined the bird.

"This little fellow has a few singed feathers," she remarked. "I guess it was lucky it wasn't worse. Whatever attacked it with magic almost removed all the protection. What does the message say?"

Leanne was still reading the tiny, but precise and neat script. "It's from Arlen. He says Maeven has been captured by Ciabolo in his serpent manifestation. He wasn't able to prevent it, and neither was Petulor. Father refused to let him go after Maeven."

"Arlen has been down in the south," Finora considered thoughtfully. "If that is where this happened, it means Ciabolo is getting stronger."

"I wonder if Arlen was sent there because that was where Maeven and Petulor disappeared to, or to keep him well away from potential bounty hunters and his brother's desire to kill him," Leanne mused. "Father was right to refuse to let him go after Maeven. He's too valuable as a source of information about Vatarik. I wonder if father will send us north again? I'd like another go at El Rasho, and this time I won't let him stay alive."

"I'll contact Roman and find out if he knows anything more. I don't think even Maeven deserves to be his prisoner now he he's king and a tyrannical despot. He won't have forgiven any of us for outsmarting him."

"No," Leanne agreed scowling. "And I wish him all of Maeven's wretchedness. Three years! She and Petulor managed to stay so well hidden that no word came of her. Why was she suddenly so stupid as to let herself be found? Petulor can't even be old enough to mate yet and surely she knows she has to ensure her successor."

"Maeven, no doubt, had a compelling reason," Finora shrugged.

"A really cock-eyed one," Leanne growled in frustration. "Now she can be made to tell all she knows about Thulor." With a sudden surge of movement, Leanne turned, saying, "Oh, go and do what you need to do. I'll be seeing what I can learn from our newest recruits. I'll need half a dozen more tokens for them. You can do that later, get onto Roman first."

"You won't need me?" Finora asked.

"No, we got all the little demons, and young Tyrell is well able to do truth spells."

Finora knew her twin was as concerned for their younger sister as she was herself, but Leanne expressed it as anger – thinking of the situation in terms of the Kingdom's safety. She kept it inside. She and Maeven had never been close, but the girl had proved herself loyal – had stepped up from just being a spoiled brat.

Inside the tent she shared with her twin, a large one as was appropriate for the troop's commander and the troop's sorceress, she prepared a shielded circle around herself before sitting on a padded cushion and beginning the ritual to contact her father's court wizard. First she lit a small brazier, and let the tent fill with fragrant smoke. She added a touch of peppermint and pine and began speaking the words of a summoning spell and prepared to wait. Roman would answer if he were not busy."

Five minutes later, Roman's face seemed to hover in the smoke. His voice sounded like he was there in the tent.

"Finora! Is something the matter?"

"Yes. Arlen sent a message that Maeven was captured. What is father going to do about it?"

"Ah! Well…"Roman's face turned to profile, as if he was talking to someone. He probably was and Finora guessed it was her father, King Westron, and he was telling his wizard what to say.

"The King has matters in hand," Roman said when he turned back. "He wants you and Leanne to continue what you are doing. He has other agents who will go into Vatarik. He asks to know where you are camped now."

"Ferndale," Finora said at once. "We will be here a few more days then moving onto Silver Creek."

"Right! I have made a new device that will make communicating easier. I will send one up to you. Rhovert went down to Declanor with my sister. He's took one there for my old master, Indra."

"So, do you know anything more about Maeven?"

Roman frowned faintly. "Nothing definite."

Finora sighed. If there was more to be told, he couldn't tell her if her father was nearby. She tried another tack. "Arlen saw Petulor."

"Yes. She couldn't fight the Serpent, so she came here to take her anger out on the Vatarins surrounding the palace. Once she'd calmed down, she showed us that magic is pooling in Thulor's crypt. She says she is sending power through to the talismans as her mother used to do. She says all of us should be able to draw on the magical pool through the talismans."

"Even Leanne?" Finora asked.

"Yes. I would say it would be like having a potion to do magic. It should also extend your stamina."

"Interesting," Finora mused. She had never been aware of power coming through her talisman, but then, the old dragon, Thulor, had been ancient. Her mind decided that information was very useful.

"Will you tell us if you hear anything else?"

"As usual," Roman agreed, and his face vanished.

Finora doused the brazier and muttered, "As usual! He'll only tell us what father wants us to know." She stood up, removed her protections and opened the tent flap to let the smoke dissipate, and went to find her twin.

"Well, now I know I wasn't imagining things this past week or so," Leanne admitted. "I am glad Roman thought to mention it."

"More likely father told him to. To distract us."

Leanne snorted. "True, but that means Maeven has been gone at least that long. Can we even be sure she is still alive?"

"Let's hope she is and doing all she can think of to annoy El Rasho," Finora wished fervently. "I wonder if father will get someone to try to get one of Roman's new devices into Vatarik."

Leanne considered. "Probably not. I doubt Maeven will be kept in luxury. Where would she hide it?"

"She used to do small spells," Finora reminded her twin. "Though she doesn't have a talisman. Ah well."

The troop broke camp two days later, after raiding the brigand's camp. They'd had no trouble finding it for the brigands who had fled the fight had been back there and gone. Anything of value, or that was edible, was taken. Only broken equipment, excess tents, broken weapons and rubbish remained. Leanne ordered her troops to glean anything they could use, even if it needed repairing first. So the tents, that had been slashed by the deserters, were taken down and folded. Metal things were collected, either to be traded at the next town as metal, or if it was weaponry, to be mended and used. The rubbish was either buried or burnt.

The newest recruits did not take part in that raid, but none had seemed interested. They probably had nothing personal there in any case. While the troop was away, Finora watched the recruits being tested for weapons skill, and when she had made more of the magic tokens, she gave one to each. She felt nothing but gratitude from each of them. Being alive, and able to start a new life, was more than they had expected. Each felt they had narrowly escaped being hung. More so, when the few troopers who remained in camp whispered to them who she was and who the commander was. They knew well the usual fate of brigands in Thulor.

It was not until they were on the road, with the mounted officers leading the foot soldiers, that Finora had the time to study the newcomers more carefully. She had set a light illusion on the company, and was alert for magical trouble, but there seemed little likelihood of any.

"Something disturbs me about that black haired one," Finora commented to her twin as they rode at the rear of the company. She nodded in the direction of one of the recruits.

Leanne spurred her horse to pass the group so she could speak to her second at the fore of the group.

"The dark one, what did he claim to be?" she asked without preamble.

"A trader from the north of Vatarik," Sub-captain Clee reported at once. "He was on El Foulness's death list for passing treasonous messages."

"He rides better than those farmer types," Leanne commented thoughtfully.

"Fought better too," Clee recalled.

"A trader would have more opportunity to practice," Leanne supposed.

Another voice entered the conversation. "Captain, that one you speak of is smarter than he lets on and he is carefully watching everything."

Leanne recognised the voice, but didn't turn to look at the speaker. "Do you think he's a spy, Nels?" she spoke quietly.

"I would be wary," Nelsi suggested.

In the past two years, Leanne had come to appreciate the little master thief. He was ostentiously her chief scout, but under that title, chief spy and assassin. If anyone would recognise another spy, he would.

"See what you can find out, Nels," Leanne instructed. "Don't make him suspicious. Remember, we need to get agents into Vatarik too."

Leanne, moved her horse out of the way of those following and dropped back to ride beside her twin. Nelsi had already positioned his horse just in front of the dark haired recruit. He had assumed a surly expression as if angry at the world.

Leanne suppressed a grin of her own, she certainly didn't need to give him detailed instructions.

Nelsi sidled into the tent of Princess Leanne and Princess Finora. He was like a shadow in the dark, but no sooner had he closed the flap of the tent behind him than a faint light began to glow between the two cot beds. The little master thief crept close to the light so that he could whisper his report.

"I have convinced the man that I resent my position. I told him that I had the choice to serve in the King's army or in his dungeon. So far he has just listened and not returned any confidences. I am certain that he is a spy. I thought that we could force his hand, perhaps by letting slip some information, something so important that he would want to rush back to his master."

"I think we can arrange something," Leanne mused. "What is your plan for sneaking away if he doesn't ask you to?"

Nelsi grinned, "You can wake up and catch me with my hand on your coin purse!"

"But you know the company rule, Nels. Anyone caught thieving from their shield mates receives five lashes," Finora reminded him.

"And before that, you'd have me chained out in the cold!" Nelsi grinned again. "The threat of a flogging and the King's dungeons would be a perfect reason to escape."

"Does nothing scare you, thief?" Leanne growled softly.

"Some things do. Wizards for instance. Them and their truth spells."

"I can put a simple shield spell on you," Finora offered. "It will protect you from coercion spells."

"Mistress Finora, please .... I have no wish to betray Thulor."

Finora chanted quietly, a faint glow settled over the thief and then it vanished.

"I have something else for you," Finora said. She produced from a bag beside her bed, a small glowing stone. "Take this too, Nels. It is spelled to glow in the dark but it will also help us follow your track."

Nelsi nodded.

Leanne spoke then. "You can pretend to have read a piece of parchment in here that suggests that we will be going to Trevale in a half score of days and that our Father the king will also be there."

Nelsi nodded. "I can work on that idea. Perhaps I can pretend that I know a way to find the secret way in and out of the besieged palace."

Leanne felt amongst her pack of clothes and drew out a small coin pouch and passed it to the thief.

"Remember, we need to confirm where they have taken our sister – and a safe route there and back. Anything else that you learn will be useful."

"Where is the spy?" Nelsi asked.

"Still in his tent," Finora assured him.

Moments later, Leanne bellowed for the sentries. They came at a run to her tent and saw her holding onto a struggling man. It did not seem to matter to Leanne that she was in her long sleeping gown.

"Have this man chained to a tree outside. I caught him stealing from me. Tomorrow he is to be punished in front of the whole company."

"Yes, Captain."

The sentries took control of the prisoner and withdrew towards the centre of the camp. The core of her troop guessed what Nelsi was up to, and made no comment. Those she had recruited away from El Rasho, took events as they seemed.

Finora, still magically watching the spy, saw him sneak from his tent and creep behind it. He was careful to keep a row of tents between himself and the sentries as he came and hid behind a bush within earshot of her tent. She gave her twin a hand signal, one that meant listeners.

"Horrible wretch!" Leanne said in her normal voice. "Now we will be lumbered with a prisoner. I wish we could just run him through with a sword and be done with it."

"Well we can't!" Finora sighed. "We'll just have to take him with us to Trevale. Father can decide his fate himself. After all, he made the deal with the wretch – so the wretch can face him with his failure."

"Well, he won't be so cocky in the morning," Leanne said finally.

The sisters lapsed into silence for a while.

"I think he's taken the bait," Finora said very softly. "He's creeping towards the fire. Nelsi is almost loose."

The little thief had waited until the camp had gone quiet again before beginning to work himself loose. The sentries, mostly recruited in the field, were well trained in the art of tying up prisoners and would normally expect no trouble from the weedy looking thief. They had already gone back to their positions on the edge of the camp. If they had any inkling of the skills of some Master thieves to free themselves from such bindings – they would not have taken their eyes off him.

Therefore, when the spy crept over to the thief, Nelsi threw off the last of the ropes.

"What do you want," the thief demanded in a low whisper. "Besides to lose your tongue if you yell for the sentries."

"I was coming to free you," the spy admitted.

"Obliged, but I don't need yer, I'm off."

"Wait! I want to get back to my family. Want to come along? I need a guide to get me to the border."

Nelsi coiled the ropes and shoved them under his jacket. "Which border?"

"North, back to Vatarik. I can't go direct though."

"Reckon I will then, anywhere but south or east!" Nelsi agreed. "And far from here. I don't want to be a guest of King Bloody Westron."

The two men slipped like shadows through the camp and even the sentries didn't see them.

Finora gave her twin a touch signal saying all was well.

"I'll send a message to my guild and to Roman –warn everyone to watch out for that stone," Finora promised.

"Reckon Maeven is worth all this trouble?" Leanne said. "You'd think she'd have the sense to keep within Petulor's sphere of protection. Surely she knew El Foulness would be hunting for her."

"She has a soft spot for children," Finora reminded her twin.

"She has a death wish if you ask me," Leanne growled.

"I would have done the same," Finora argued.

"Dammit, so would I, but you and I can at least defend ourselves. I wouldn't bother with this spying business if I didn't feel anyone should have to endure El Foulness's hospitality."

Chapter 27 - Del, El Rasho and Vorman

Vorman heard the sentry's alarm and stood up, pushing aside Del's ministrations. He listened to the whistle cadence.

"I'm well enough for now, boy. Get me a cleaner vest."

Del obeyed, then put his medicine and healing bag away. Vorman's stitched ragged slash, from his fight with one of the other brigand leaders, would hold. Well, it would if he didn't try to take on another fight that day, just to prove his superiority. The blood soaked rags and bandages he rolled into a ball and took with him to the laundry of the commandeered farm house. The girl was there. The daughter of the couple who owned the farm. He tried not to look at her. From her look, he knew that she loathed him, as much as she loathed all the men who had already used her to slake their lust. He wanted to help her, but Vorman had her tethered to the house. She could only go to the kitchen, the laundry, and the privy. She had to sleep in the kitchen, and since Vorman had come, never alone. Her mother was no better off, and was only allowed the extra freedom of being able to scrub all the usurped rooms. The farmer was no better than a drudge for Vorman's band – worse even than Del was now.

The worst of it was, he could feel her mixture of terror and pain, shame and the burning need for rebellion. He wanted to help her, but Vorman had not forgotten how he had helped that other girl, years back. What he had threatened to do to Del if the girl got away, had Del himself terrified. He knew how hopeless she felt. Hadn't he wanted to escape all these years? He'd thought when the half mad hedge wizard had died, the mage tether would have broken, but it hadn't. Whatever was still holding him, was holding the girl and her parents too.

Del found a bucket and filled it at the well outside, then returned to the laundry. Perhaps the girl would come to see he wasn't like the others. He would not try to touch her. He started to wash his rags, borrowing the hard soap the girl used.

"Why don't you just let him die?"

The girl's hissing voice was only just loud enough to hear.

"Can't not," Del said without looking at her. "That ugly thing he wears – he can make me do what he wants."

"Does he make you lie down for him?"

The shudder that went through him was obvious to the girl. "He ain't since he figured me a healer."

"Why do you stay?"

"Can't leave either."

They both heard loud voices and went back to ignoring each other.

Del wanted to keep a low profile. Vorman might protect him from the rest of his rabble, but the visiting other brigands included others that wouldn't care if he was male, only that he was young. At least he had free range of the house and nearby sheds and outhouses. It gave him plenty of places to hide.

The farm had been prosperous and productive when Vorman had set eyes on it and decided he wanted it. In the three weeks since they had been there, the place was already showing signs of neglect, and brainless vandalism. There had been three sons too, but one had tried to ride to the nearest Lord's manor for help. He'd not come back, and Del had seen one of the rabble wearing the boy's clothes. The other two were tied up in the cellar, neither resigned to obeying Vorman's orders, despite a thorough beating that had nearly killed them. Somehow, they were immune to the vile magic produced by Vorman's dried rat's head.

Once he had pacified the farm. Vorman had sent out messengers to the other bands that had been drawn to the area by the rumour of riches to be had. He had got enough of an idea of what the set up would be and intended to seem to be the top dog. He wanted to appear smarter, colder, and more efficient than the foreigners who already knew the important foreign visitor who was soon to arrive and set them to work. After all, he had the advantage of being a Thulan and not a stranger to the land. He had already found and bound to him, some of the locals who knew the area very well. His unusual fetish for clean clothes, even though not as fancy as those of the foreigners because they had been taken from the farmer, was to seem prosperous.

Del slipped outside once he'd hung his rags to dry on a rack in the laundry. In spite of the faint thawing earlier, the girl spat at him as he left. He didn't try to change her opinion. Only if he could free her, would she believe him better than the others.

Outside, the current hopeful for the role of chief of the bands was brawling with his latest opponent. Vorman had been the previous contender, and if his boasts to Del were truth, he had allowed himself to lose and seem out of contention. Most would think his wound would keep him sidelined for days, but Vorman had Del, and he now claimed to have figured the other man's weaknesses.

Putting bits of overheard talk together, Del guessed the important visitor was on his way and Vorman planned to be victorious just as the visitor arrived. He was glad, as Vorman's secret weapon, that he was not expected to heal the other losing contenders. Not wanting to be around any of the visitors, he went across to a small grove of trees, which was at the limit of his mage tether and watched the fight. The current contender, one of the foreigners, was already bleeding badly but seemed to have energy to spare. It had to be an act though, surely he was tiring, as he had already defeated three others besides this one and Vorman. That must be part of Vorman's plan, he decided, as his master told the farmer to bring a bucket of fresh water to the area near the brawl. When it arrived, and placed on a tree stump, Vorman did something to it. His hands went nowhere near it, but one went to where he wore his rat's head amulet. Del's own talisman began to heat up.

Movement along the road, a few leagues away from the farm, caught Del's attention. Twelve guards around two riders. It had to be the important visitor and his entourage. The guards moved to show the nearest of the centre horses – a huge creature, all black, that moved like a thoroughbred. The other was just as big, but brown and more highly strung as judged by its mincing gait.

Watching the horses was more interesting than listening to the inciting talk between Vorman and the foreigner who had beaten him. They were well past Vorman's claim that he had never conceded defeat and intended to finish what he had started, and the other's retort of having more than enough guts to finish him off. The man took a dipper of water from the pail so temptingly placed and swallowed it in four gulps. He poured another dipperful over his head and launched himself at Vorman without warning.

If only the man did have enough in him to kill Vorman, Del wished. Maybe then, he'd be free.

The riders approached up the narrow unpaved laneway. They halted at the edge of the arena and watched. The avid look on the face of the black clad noble on the black horse gave him a pain in his gut. His companion, a non-descript man with a vacant expression looked around and when his eyes were directed at Del, they took on an orange gleam – just for a moment. Del wanted to think it was a trick of the sun, but the sun was behind them, and his amulet was burning hot. These people were dangerous.

Vorman seemed to be unaware of the newcomers as he sent his opponent sprawling and leapt onto him and made to look like he was about to kill the man. He even jerked around when the black clad man spoke. The voice, too far away to hear the words, sounded unctuous and oily. He shivered when the voice was suddenly loud enough to hear. "Let us spare the man, he has been a worthy opponent and you are the victor. I need all the strong, clever leaders I can find and there is plenty for all."

After a deliberate pause, Vorman looked at the rider, nodded, and rolled off his opponent. He stood, but did not offer his hand to help the man up. Instead, he greeted the newcomers and let the man's cronies help him up and insist he accept things for now.

Del heard Vorman calling for him and felt a hard jerk on the mage tether. Resigned, he obeyed, knowing that if he dallied, he would be beaten. As he approached, he heard Vorman ordering the farmer to tend to the visitors' horses. The man's expression brightened for a moment. Del was just glad he hadn't needed to do that task. The two new horses looked like they wanted to rear, scream and bolt.

"Boy, run and tell the leaders of all our guests that the important visitor has come."

For that, Vorman allowed him a longer tether, since the six other groups had camped well away from each other while still on lands belonging to the farm. Running, even though the command was being forced on him, felt good. Even having to hear all the insults shouted at him, things none of them had dared say in Vorman's hearing, didn't deflate his mood. He waited only a moment to see that the people were going to obey, before running off to the next camp. After leaving the last, the drag on the tether eased, and Del could slow. Testing his limits, he decided to go back via the stream where the two horses, seemingly calm, were drinking.

"How did you calm them devil's beasts," Del asked, quiet enough not to startle the horses, but the man jumped. He relaxed quickly when he saw it was Del.

"They be good if you treat them right," the man said. "You remember that, sonny."

"Yeah, I will," he agreed, moving close and daring to run his hands over the black horse's smooth, though sweaty flanks. A vague sense of pain caused him to continue feeling over the horse until he stopped at the stallion's rear left tendon. The farmer stopped rubbing hands over the other beast to watch as Del put one hand to his neck, holding his talisman, and the other over the injury. He sent healing energy through his hand.

"You're not like those others, sonny. Why do you stay with them?"

"Can't leave. And now they know I'm a healer, they treat me better."

"You should let them rot." The farmer spat on the ground. "They be little better than rabid beasts."

"I know," Del admitted, sighing. He saw signs of beatings on the man's face, and offered, "I can heal your face."

"Why would you do that, sonny?"

"They shouldn't treat you that way."

The man considered. "This is nothing. Can you do anything for my girl, or my wife?"

Del felt his face redden, knowing what was being done to them. He should have thought about that sooner, except he'd never been allowed to be near them long, until today when Vorman was distracted.

"Maybe I can...but it may not be enough. Do you get to talk to them?"

"Now and then," he admitted. "I can't go in the house, but I can sit outside windows."

Del grinned, the man wasn't defeated. "Tell either one of the women to look for a packet of herbs in...in the drawer where the powdered soap is. And if anyone asks about them, they should say I told them to add them to make the food more flavourful. Them rabble are used to that, and will recognise the taste."

"What will that do?" the man asked.

"Maybe little, maybe much. I might have to experiment to get the herbs right. I'll mix them and try to slip them to the laundry next time I've been fixing the rabble."

"You got something to rid my girl of a babbee?"

Del had to think, for that had never been something he needed to know, and his mother had died when he was too young to need to know. "I don't know. I learnt stuff from my ma, years ago, and bits along the way. Never that though."

"Ah well," the man said. "Maybe nature will do it for her. You'd best get back, and so should I."

The visitors were in the farmhouse parlour when Del returned. Vorman called for him as soon as he entered the house.

"You boy, I have invited our guests to stay for a meal. I want you to oversee it being made. You know what tasty herbs to add to the old woman's bland food. My guests are used to the best."

Vorman dropped his voice to and undertone, "And I want to put my guests in a suggestive mood..."

Del understood and said, "I will see that the wine is the best of what you brought here."

"See that you do, boy, or you will feel my displeasure."

It was like the fates had heard him and wanted him to help the farm people. He didn't show his glee, but kept his usual surly expression, and went towards his pallet in the farmer's bedroom.

He only had time to grab some of the herbs he needed and a bottle of the best wine, Vorman was making his urgency known through the tether. He went into the kitchen, ignored the woman's scowl as she took a few moments rest. She scowled harder as he went to where she kept her best serving ware. She probably thought she'd hidden it so well the rabble didn't know of it. It was still there because Vorman wasn't going anywhere yet. He found a delicate glass wine server, recognisable because Vorman had stolen things like it from a Lord's retinue. Into that, he poured the wine then found three highly polished wooden mugs, and a polished wood tray to put them on. He glanced at the woman as he added herbs to each of the mugs. Her eyes had grown intent – perhaps he had her interest, and would listen to her husband later.

On the tray, one mug was set slightly apart from the other two. Vorman's had herbs in too, but not the one that he hoped would make his guests susceptible to his ideas. Del wasn't dressed to be a serving lad, but he did recall the exaggerated carry on amongst the rabble when they had unpacked their loot from the wedding train for a Lord's daughter.

Vorman didn't thank him, but chastised him for looking so filthy, and told him to wash up before the evening meal. He had shivers, seeing the avid look on the face of the black haired visitor. He knew that look, and his fear was confirmed when he passed the farmer on his way to the pump. He slowed as the man said, "You'd best be scarce later, sonny. I heard that dark one asking about you. I judge him a nasty one – worse than our master."

"Unlikely," Del muttered. "But I know what you mean." Would Vorman let the visitor play with him to further his ambition? He hoped not. He hurried away, gave himself a quick wash, and headed to where he had a small sack of better clothes. Once changed, he sorted through his supply of dried herbs and considered what he had seen growing in a small garden near the kitchen. For his mixture, for the evening meal, he'd use fresh where he could. Fresh was always better, and would hide the slightly astringent taste of the lust inhibiting herbs. He intended to double the dose of that. Then he went to the kitchen.

"They gone all la-di-dah now," the woman accused, when Del mentioned the herbs to put in the food. "I know what I'd like to put into it. But they's never complained up to now. Who's the noble?"

"I don't know," Del said. "But my master wants to impress him."

The woman made a rude noise. "What you got in that mixture? I saw you in my herb garden."

Del saw no reason not to tell her the main ones. She snatched his pouch of herbs and sniffed the contents, and her eyes took on an accusing glare. In a low voice, Del added the name of two other herbs, and when her expression didn't change, he whispered, "Turns lust to dust and blunts anger."

"I must remember that mixture," she muttered. "I don't have all that here."

Del told her what the other two herbs looked like and usually grew. He'd not seen any around the farmhouse, but if he got away a bit further, he would look for some more. He was able to rest while the woman prepared food for the noble guest and his retainer, and the leaders from the other brigand groups. The twelve guards from the visitor's retinue ate with the rabble. Their food was less fancy, but had the same 'tasty' herbs added. Del didn't mind helping to cook that while he was ostensibly watching the old woman.

He had to help take the food into the parlour where someone had assemble a large table, and then stand near Vorman and the man in black in case they wanted more wine. When the man in black started to grope him, and he jerked, Vorman pulled tight on the magical tether, so he had to take it, even though shivers kept running up and down his back. The torment lessened as the men drank more of the wine, but he knew Vorman was only pretending to get more inebriated.

Once the meal was finished and the wooden platters cleared away, Vorman sent him to his bed. While it was a relief to get away from the man in black, for a while, he doubted it was permanent. That one was staying the night, in the best room...the farmer's bedroom where his bed was...and he could not even leave that room to go to the privy. The mage tether was like a leash on a vicious dog.

It was well after sundown when Del heard the meeting break up. The other leaders wasted no time leaving to return to their camps. Vorman came into the bedroom. "Get up boy, we're sleeping elsewhere tonight."

Del had been feigning sleep when his master came in and kicked him in the ribs. Any thought of relief at not having to stay in that room fled when he saw Vorman's expression. His guts went into a knot, as he was dragged to the next best room, and Vorman kicked out the current occupant. The chief should not be feeling any lust at all, not with the amount of the inhibiting drug in the food and drink. Well, Vorman wasn't drunk, although he smelt of wine. He was well pleased with something though. Perhaps that was strong enough to overcome the herbs. Del hoped the man would fall asleep soon. Or had he not taken any of the last round of wine with the sleep herb in it?

As soon as Vorman fell into a satiated sleep, Del slipped out of the room and went to douse himself under the pump outside. He had hurried through the kitchen, not wanting to see any of the men having a turn at the women, but on his return, he saw the older woman was alone on her pallet on the floor. Of the girl there was no sign. He was too tied up in his own humiliation to worry about her. Vorman had added new degrading torments, things he had said the little whore – the younger girl – had done to him. All he wanted to do was find somewhere to hide until the visitors had gone.

The pull on the mage tether was impossible to resist, even when he held his talisman and wished as hard as he could. He had to leave his hiding place in an empty cupboard and venture outside.

The visitors had not gone, they were standing by their horses, and the dark haired one was talking to all the leaders. Del saw Vorman glance at him, and then turn his attention back to the noble. As he edged around the attentive group, as far away as he could, he heard snippets of the conversation. They were getting orders about what this foreigner wanted them to do. The odd thing was, all of them, even Vorman, and the man he'd beaten the previous day, were still and listening, not pushing and shoving each other. Then he saw the orange eyes of the other one, the one you tended to forget. He quickly looked away and concentrated on memorising the face of the noble. Black hair, curled and neatly combed down to his shoulders, not matted like Vorman's. A thin black moustache and a pointed beard, eyes that were brighter than normal...

The eyes strayed in his direction during a pause in the chatter of the mixed bandit leaders. Del turned to look at a tree in which two birds were squabbling. His amulet had grown hot, as if the man's very gaze was dangerous. Still looking away, he put his hand in his pocket and took his eyes from the birds to scuff a toe in the dirt until he found some stones suitable for his purpose. . If he was going to disobey Vorman's command to stay close, he'd need an excuse.

Using every bit of stealth he had learnt in five years of trying to avoid the attentions of the bandits – he moved to a point beyond the tree with the still squabbling birds.

Loading his sling with the two stones, Del waited until an inner prompting told him to throw. Two birds fell, one to the ground, the other to be caught in a fork of the tree. It was a moment's work to recover and twist the neck of the first bird; and only minutes to climb the tree and copy the gesture with the second.

"That was skilfully done," the greasily smooth voice of the noble spoke from behind him.

Del jumped, the hair on his body was trying to stand on end and a rush of cold raced from his head to his feet.

"Thank you, Great Lord," Del said, trying not to show his fear of the man. His amulet was so hot it might as well be glowing.

"You're Vorman's boy," the man continued casually.

Del simply nodded. It was no use mentioning that Vorman wasn't his father. In every other possible shade of meaning, the statement was probably true. He was a mixture of slave, fetcher, messenger, body servant and sometimes surrogate female.

Then, since his 'magic' had returned, the chief had made it plain to his rabble that the only person allowed to touch Del, was himself. He had become, once again, the chief's most prized possession.

"You remind me of someone," the Great Lord said, staring at him with those deep black eyes.

Del remained silent, and endured the man's stare.

Abruptly, the Great Lord turned and strode away. Del let out the breath he was holding and drew in a lungful of fresh air.

The Great Lord was calling for his retinue and preparing to ride off. Vorman watched them leave, and from the way he then strutted towards his 'boy', he was very pleased about something. Del's stomach turned queasy. He hoped Vorman didn't want to celebrate again, like last night. Relief flooded through him when Vorman ordered him to roust the rest of the rabble, the 'lazy sods', and have them come to the house. With a glance at the two birds he had killed, he nodded.

"Oh, go give them to the old woman. Tell her to cook them for my lunch."

Vorman glared at him until he got moving.

"Oh, yeah," he said, tearing his eyes away from Vorman's neck, and the oddity that hadn't been there the previous night. Did he dare ask what it was? Something in his mind said, "No", and he decided that playing stupid was a very good idea. He ran into the house and was greeted with a hiss from the old woman. He gave the birds to her and Vorman's order, and she spat at him.

"What did they do with my girl?"

"What?" Del asked.

"Those bastards! What did they do with her?"

"I don't know," Del told her. "Really."

"Your that slimy bastard's boy, why don't you know?"

Del wanted to tell her what had been done to him, but when he tried, his tongue was stilled. She began to curse him, and all he could do was turn and run. He kept running until he reached the river. A lot of the men slept there – only Vorman and Urdich, his second in command, slept in the house. He arrived as some were stumbling into the cover of trees, only just awake. He went to some just stirring and shook them awake. "The chief wants you all up at the house, now, not later. Where are the rest of you?"

"Barn," one man managed to give an answer.

"Hurry and get up," Del told him, before trotting back towards the house.

The barn was where they were keeping all their horses, and he had not yet been allowed in there, but having to go and look for the men Vorman wanted, was apparently enough to allow him within. His eyes had to adjust to the dark, but the groans of men waking with a headache led him to the rest of Vorman's rabble. They all just stumbled to their feet and reeled out the door. Del, no longer being forced to do an errand, followed them out, but something else tugged on him. He followed the feeling and went around to the muck pile. There, tossed like a bucket of manure, was the girl. She wasn't dead, not yet, but her moans were so soft as to be like a faint zephyr of wind. Del dragged her onto cleaner ground and looked her over. There was so much blood, that he knew there was no hope for her. Still, he tried, he took out his talisman and sent the healing energy through her, wishing her better. All it did was make her voice a little louder.

"Mama?"

"No, it's just me, Del."

"Mama, I don't feel well. Will you hold me?"

Del only dithered for a moment, before lifting the girl so he could hug her.

"Mama, I'm sorry. I didn't want to do it."

"No one will blame you," Del said. "They should have left you alone."

"I'm going to die. I know it. But I'm sorry I couldn't get the boys free."

"You tried. You have been a very brave girl," Del told her, and he felt her body relax from the rigidity of the pain, and her breath stilled. After a moment, he checked her breathing and then for a heartbeat. Gently, he put her down, and pushed aside long buried memories of his mother's death.

He made a silent vow to himself, that somehow, everyone who had a part in the girl's death would pay dearly. Vorman, first and foremost. If he hadn't put so many spells on him, he would have been able to help the girl. He would have welcomed a beating if he had managed to let her get away. It would have been a victory.

He hadn't been long with the girl, for when he got back to the farmhouse, the rabble were milling around, still more asleep than awake. Vorman had not yet got their attention, and only did so when he let out a bellow.

"Listen well you lot. We have work to do." He drew out a rolled parchment and opened it up on the ground. He crouched beside it. "This be a map of our territory. From the border to Herron's Fort, and the Thul River to the razorback range."

Del, curious in spite of his anger and sorrow, wriggled in between two of the men Oggy and Nanti. He saw the symbols and writing on the page – he understood some, but really couldn't read much. He was about to back away, when something in his mind told him that the sinuous black line was the road they had travelled before coming to the farm. A spot on the map began to glow, and the thing in his head said, "That's where you are." Del was jostled out of the way by the others who probably had less idea of what they were looking at than he did.

"What we gotta do, is work, like usual. We gotta feed ourselves after all, and those soft foreign types have to as well. No more supplies coming for them. That's just the basic stuff. We've got extra jobs, since we be knowing this area."

Del snorted softly and muttered, "Not that damn well we don't."

"Sometimes that noble foreigner be needing to bring people into Thulor. People that don't like the current rulers. Or he might need to get people out. When we do them jobs, we will get paid in luxury stuff – the types of food the likes of us never get, and wines – even better than what you all got drunk on last night, all sorts of stuff."

The men were suddenly more awake, and began to ask questions.

Vorman held up his hands. "First, we gotta learn our territory. All the safe places we can duck into at need. And if we come across easy targets, we take them. We gotta make stashes of weapons and dried foods in places."

Del decided he had heard enough. He wondered if any of the rabble would point out how Vorman always claimed he'd never serve a master other than himself. As he wriggled back out of the group, he heard Vorman boast of being the foreign noble's number one agent. Perhaps that was equally good – the best of both ways. And all the other groups had their own territories, well away and elsewhere – all along the Thulan-Vatarik border. No fighting for territory, and if Vorman was to be believed, his territory was the cream of the lot.

The men went off gabbling excitedly. Del didn't find the future so great. His situation wouldn't change. He fingered the sling in his pocket, imagine Vorman as his target...and sighed. Unless he could be absolutely sure his shot would kill the bastard, he didn't dare try. And if he did kill the bastard, Urdich, or one of the others would proclaim himself chief, and Del would be back to being a bone to fight over - unless the spell that kept him tethered broke when Vorman died. Then he would run away, and never let them catch him.

Abruptly, he saw himself as an outsider might – someone who stayed with this thieving murdering rabble because he wanted to. The King's men, if they came upon the rabble, would assume he was one of them, even if he had never killed anyone. He'd be thrown in the King's dungeons, and hung and no one would care. Maybe he should have died when his mother did, not go along with the only person who had seemed to care about him.

The odd voice in his mind said, "You were only a little boy. You could not know."

Until it was too late, Del thought. He still wasn't even full grown. He couldn't take on any of the rabble in a fight. And now, it seemed, Vorman was wholeheartedly embracing treason. Helping some vile foreigner to take over Thulor. Traitor's didn't even get a trial, they was just hung, right away.

As if to echo his thought, he heard Vorman saying to himself, "And I will be the new high lord of Herron's Fort."

Suddenly, everything he'd endured from the time of his mother's death came back to him. Right up to having the girl die in his arms. That death was too much. He knew the rabble killed often, but so far they had kept him away from the worst sights. He was as bad as them, he hadn't helped the girl.

A rough hand grabbed him as he was about to run off. "What's got into you, boy?" Vorman demanded. Just his voice set Del off, kicking and punching. He was too angry, too overcome with ill memories that he wasn't hearing anything. He just wanted to get away, to the hells with the consequences. It would be better for everyone if he was dead.

Another rough hand slapped him hard, then lifted his feet off the ground. Del was only vaguely aware he was being carried inside, and then only for a moment aware of his danger. He felt himself hit the sharp edge of some stairs, and was unconscious before he hit the ground at the bottom.

How long it was before he roused, he did not know. Something was touching him. It took him a while to realise it was someone's foot. His head pounded like a huge drum, and he only had enough strength to grasp his talisman. Slowly, the pain went away as the cool breeze blew through him. He tried to sit up, only to find he was still giddy. He could see nothing.

It took a while to understand that someone was talking to him. "Who are you?"

"Del. Who are you?"

"We belong here. How did they get you?"

"Ah...." Del didn't want to say he was one of the rabble. He realised he'd been thrown into the same cellar as the two brothers of the dead girl.

"Are you tied up?" he was asked.

"No," Del realised.

"Can you get us free?" another voice asked.

"Don't know. Where would you go? You can't be thinking you can get away."

"You don't need to know what we plan – unless you come with us."

"I can't. They got a magic tether on me – like they do for the old woman and the old man."

"What about our sister?"

"She...she had one."

"Had one?"

"She...she's...dead."

Two hissing sounds were just audible. "I'll kill the bastards," one voice declared.

"You... you can't. There's... too many."

"Our parents, are they still alive?"

"They were. Unless they find out about the girl and try something."

Del didn't mention the men who had been at both the woman and the girl. He didn't want these two to die as well. He needed to think. His hand was still gripping his talisman, and he felt the breeze blow the fogginess in his brain away. "Do you get fed down here?"

"Once in a while. We can't tell what the time is down here."

"Can you move around?"

"Some. We are tied up like animals, but we can move to the bottom of the steps and to the edge of the cellar. They couldn't make us docile like they did the folks and our sister."

"If you was loose, you couldn't escape through up there," Del warned.

"Can't anyway. Brit's leg is broken we think."

"But there's another way out," one of the voices said, followed by, "Shut up, stupid. He could be a trap."

Del managed a sick laugh. "They won't hear about it from me," he promised. "But if that is so, maybe I can at least help you. Keep talking. You with the broken leg."

"What for?"

"So I can find you. I can help with the leg, and if I can help you get away, well, it will be one in their eye."

Del inched his way towards the voice, not trying to stand, just lifting his bottom off the rough wood planks enough to scrape across them. Finally he came to a stop, his leg touching one that was stretched out. He edged around so he was sitting next to it, and could feel along it. He found the break at the same time as the voice said, "Ouch. It still hurts."

"Stay still," Del directed, and he put his free hand to the talisman. Thinking hard, he asked the powers that helped him to heal, "Please, help this boy heal. He needs to get free and bring help to his parents.

And justice for the girl and their other brother.”

Even before he finished his plea, he felt the cool breeze. A slight jerk of the leg suggested the boy felt it too. Del distracted him by asking, “How come you didn’t get one of those magic tethers?”

The other answered. “Some whys it didn’t work. That tall bastard tried.”

Del didn’t admit he’d seen that, but the why would be useful to know. Maybe it could help him think of a way to get rid of the one on him. “How’s that feel?” Del asked when the cool breeze seemed to taper off.

“It don’t hurt none,” the voice admitted. “Now we just need to get free.”

Del reached to get to his boot. He now had a sharp knife in a sheath there. Nanti had given it to him on the road up. He’d never shown it to any of the others, and he was sure Vorman didn’t know of it. Now he had it in his hand, he felt for the hand of his patient. “Here. Use this.”

Another hand took the knife, and from the vague sounds of movement, was already working to cut the rope. Del, thought to himself, “Don’t let anyone come down here until they get away.”

“Why did you help us,” One voice asked. “You’re one of them.”

“I’ve had no choice. You do, and I couldn’t help your sister, or parents. If you get out, don’t try to free them. You can’t. Last two he magicked, died when they tried to escape.” That brought on another awful vision. The one that hadn’t died right away, only lasted a week before dying in some sort of convulsion. “Reckon he probably spelled the tethers to kill any who try to help.”

“We can’t just do nothing.”

“Best thing be if you get right away and bring King’s guards.”

“What about you?”

“They need me. I be their healer when they near kill themselves. And if you go out some secret way, I won’t know. How long was I out?’”

“For a bit. Don’t know.”

“It was morning,” Del remembered.

“Then we might get someone with our food soon. No one’s come yet.”

“I’ll play unconscious,” Del said. “Won’t have seen either of you in this dark, or even know you was there. Do they use a light to come down?”

"Only a dim one. We can look tied up if they come too soon."

"You be careful, and keep the knife. You have to bring help. The rabble are going to help some foreign noble take over the kingdom."

CHAPTER 28 - Maeven

If asked, Jilli would probably sneer and say that El Rasho's new favourite was a scrawny bitch and her use was limited. In fact, she was insanely jealous of her former position of being the king's only lover. She knew he was determined to get that sorry excuse for a princess pregnant, for some obscure reason. He said it was revenge, but he was doing to that bitch what she wanted him to do to her. It was all very well that he needed to get an heir, but while he hadn't, he had a reason not to let himself merge with the creepy entity that had once possessed his father. And Jilli shuddered at the thought of being pregnant herself.

Equally true, although she didn't realise it, was the compulsion on her to lust after powerful or handsome men. When that lust got so powerful, she sometimes lowered her standards, just to ease it. Only now, no male that she tried to seduce, wanted any of her. That caused her to be in a powerfully foul mood, and she blamed Maeven, her rival. The servants bore the worst brunt of her temper, but did nothing to ease her discomfort. She had visited her rival, without guards present, and thought to beat her to a pulp. Had got in a few decent scratches, but then... she wasn't sure. Something stopped her. It must have been some spell the creepy wizard had on her, for he turned up and had her dragged out like she was a mere servant. He'd put her in the dungeon for a whole day and let the other scum in there have a turn at her. After the twelfth, at least the agony of unfulfilled lust had eased, but when she came out – she knew the servants were silently laughing at her and the wizard was watching her.

She knew she had been warned, but she could not help herself visiting her rival, just to torment her. The bitch was probably the only person in the citadel that didn't know what had been done to her.

When she began coming everyday, and El Rasho wasn't summoning her, Maeven guessed he was probably away somewhere, though she preferred the malicious idea that El Rasho had worn himself out.

There was often a smell about him that reminded her of some medicant. Having Jilli as a visitor was better than seeing no one, and their verbal sparring was currently Maeven's main entertainment.

"Is he fed up with you or something?" Maeven prodded, three days after El Rasho's marathon attempt to impregnate her.

"No! He's away."

"Huh! He must have satisfied his inflated ego with me."

"He calls you a scrawny sheep."

"Well, he's no better than a bull in a fairy circle. If what you think is the truth, surely he would have taken you to forget about me."

"He would have, but that creepy wizard sent him off to attend his other duties."

"Doing more rabble rousing in Thulor, is he? And the wizard went off after him?" Maeven's suggestion was based only on servant gossip.

"How would you know that?"

"A good guess. Your Rashi got his royal backside kicked last time he tried it."

"No thanks to you!"

"He deserved it. He tried to get me then, but I was too smart."

"You ran like a coward!"

Maeven laughed.

Jilli retorted, "Not so clever now, are you?"

"Oh, I don't know. Anyway, when is he due back?"

"When he gets back. Why? You in a rush to be beaten to a pulp again? You already look black and blue all over."

"All to the good," Maeven said cheerfully. "While my body has to keep healing itself, it doesn't have the reserves to keep a parasite alive. Your Rashi probably spoilt his chance, and it will be a month before it is the right time to try again. Before that, it will be a waste of time, or so that old woman seemed to imply."

"What do you know about being pregnant," Jilli sneered. "Is it something your ineffective father bothered to explain to his motherless daughters? Or did he expect your unnatural sisters to do it?"

"I listen to servants," Maeven said, then inwardly berated herself. She hoped that Jilli didn't take in the full implications of that.

"Servants? They are the most superstitious idiots around. Some think you get pregnant from sitting on a privy seat after a man sat there."

"So, you know better?" Maeven insinuated. "Then why aren't you pregnant yet?"

Jilli had no answer, so she changed the subject – back to insulting Maeven. And when that didn't reduce her rival to tears, she flounced out.

As the time since El Rasho had gone off stretched to two weeks, visits from the old woman became more frequent. There would be the same questions about how she felt, the same hands on examination of her breasts, more questions that made little sense but she assumed were to indicate if she was pregnant. Like did she have a craving for any particular food? What a silly question – of course she did. She much rather have food prepared as they did in Thulor, to the spicier ones the Vatarins preferred.

She did lie when she said her breasts felt normal. It was not her intention to admit they were sore. Not yet anyway. The old woman could wait, and so could El Rasho.

Thanks to her friend Reva, and recalling the same feeling the first time, she knew that was a sign of being pregnant.

During yet another haranguing session, when Jilli was again feeling the frustrations of rampant unfulfilled lust, Maeven decided to distract her.

"Why don't you send him a message saying you think I am pregnant? Then, when he gets back, he won't want me and you can have him to yourself?"

"Are you pregnant?"

Maeven shrugged. "I damn well hope not. I don't want a brat, and particularly some bastard of his."

"So what good would it be to say you are?"

"I can pretend for a bit. I've heard that babies often spontaneously abort in the first month. And as far as his attention, how it had been isn't the best way to ensure successful fatherhood."

"Then he's have to try all over again."

"Only during one week in a month."

Jilli must have been desperate enough to consider it. "You'd do that? And I'll have him for the rest of the time?"

"He'll be all yours," Maeven invited, not saying it wasn't up to her, or that she wished El Rasho onto her all day, every day.

"But when you do get pregnant, that ghastly thing will still have to wait to take him over..."

Maeven wasn't sure Jilli realised she was speaking aloud, so she added softly, like a wisp of thought, "Since babies can die for no reason, he'd have to stay out until the baby arrives."

Jilli growled. "I don't have a way to contact him."

"Too bad," Maeven tried to sound disappointed. If he was still away, he must be off doing no good in Thulor. Well even if she were still in Thulor, where she belonged, what could she do? At least here, amongst Jilli's spiteful taunts, El Rasho bragging, and the guards gossip as filtered through the servants, she was gleaning information, that hopefully would come in useful. And in turn, she could plant erroneous ideas in the head of El Rasho and the obnoxious Serpent.

Deciding she'd had enough of Jilli for a time, Maeven said, idly, "You know, I know how to get that wonderful, blissful feeling – just as two women together."

The hoped for reaction was instantaneous. "What? No way! Get away from me."

The last thing needed was for Maeven to take one step closer to her. Jilli turned and fled.

When her prison door had slammed shut, and she'd controlled her laughter, Maeven went back to sit in her chair, murmuring, "I wonder how long that effect will last?"

Her mind turned to think of what she might have to endure once it was obvious she was pregnant – which hopefully wouldn't be until her belly began to enlarge. One thing she had decided, she was not going to tell El Rasho anything. She would pretend to be totally ignorant of any sign of pregnancy. He'd find out soon enough, when the old nurse figured it out, and then he'd be unbearably smug.

The question in her mind was whether he would stop his attentions when he did find out. Had he tired of having to mate with her? From Jilli's comments, what he liked was the idea he was hurting her. Well, he was doing that, but she had ways to distance that, and recover fairly quickly afterwards. She had been trying to give the idea she was enjoying his attention, as well as trying to make Jilli jealous. That hadn't seemed to do anything to get him to give up. *What to do...*

A faint smile followed a sudden idea. If he did try to keep hurting her, and forcing himself on her, well...pregnant women were often queasy...

The first time she had been pregnant, she recalled being nauseous for a time. Then she had put it down to the memory of what she had endured. This time, if he came to annoy her, could she contrive to be sick over him? If it was likely to happen again and again, would he want to avoid her?

It would give her the chance to continue insinuating that rough treatment was likely to abort the child. The old woman, would at least continue to insist she had decent food, rest and living conditions.

That got her thinking again. The room she had now was decent enough, but she was tired of being there most of the time, with only detested needlework, and short sessions of needling Jilli and eavesdropping on servants to break the monotony.

Once they knew shew was pregnant, that creepy wizard and his demon occupant would likely want to speed up his plans. Now, if they were busy elsewhere, and she could walk around outside of the room, or spend time in the garden, she might be able to pick up even more snippets of information.

Maeven considered. Maybe, suffering from nausea, and being 'forced' to exercise, could seem like enough punishment for a while. That is what she would work on next.

CHAPTER 29 – Rhovert and Atlantis.

"What now?" Atlantis asked, turning her back on a capricious breeze that was raising dust. Rhovert sighed, and stared at the pile of rubble that had fallen down, blocking the entrance he usually used to go in and out of his father's palace. This new collapse had only occurred during the short period they had been away. "We could just march up to the main entrance," he suggested wryly.

Atlantis gave a quiet snort, which might have been blowing dust from her nose. At least half of the unholy, semi-visible creatures besieging the place had their attention focussed there.

"There are other ways in," Rhovert told his consort. "But I don't want to draw attention to them by checking them out. Let's go and wash the road dust from our throats. We might as well spend the coins we earned. The locals around here probably need them more than we do."

Even though the king had ordered them to return directly from Ackbridge, Rhovert had not intended to ride day and night to do so. In fact, when they had come upon a trader's wagon under attack from bandits, they had joined the fight and hired on as extra guards. The slower pace had suited him and given him a chance to listen to the trader's gossip. After five days, the dust was an excellent disguise. He and Atlantis looked like a pair of mercs.

For her part, Atlantis did want a drink, but she said nothing as they passed two taverns that were doing a flourishing business. Many of the patrons hanging around the door probably belonged to the besieging army. Instead, Rhovert went to a quieter part of town and took the horses to stable at the rear, then entered from there.

"Why do those others serve the rabble?" Atlantis finally asked.

"Did you really look at them?" Rhovert asked.

"What?"

"A lot are bespelled farmers. Thulans."

"And those brigands from Ackbridge," Atlantis countered.

"Yes, alright, but my point is – if they have coin to spend, that will help the locals here. Father isn't having his soldiers kill them, because a large proportion are just sword food. They would not be here if they had any choice."

They stopped speaking as they entered the tavern, for both were instantly aware of the heads turning to look at them.

A few nudged companions, and returned to their own conversations. These had recognised Rhovert's merc persona.

To reassure the rest, the man behind the bar bellowed, "Hoi! Berto! Been a while since you graced this place. What do you want?"

"Something long and cold for me and my partner."

They moved between the patrons at tables, to reach the bar. They perched on tall stools as their drinks were decanted into stiff leather mugs.

"What's new, Brennan?" Rhovert asked as his drink was pushed towards him, and Brennan looked with raised brows to learn what his partner wanted. He made no issue of the fact she was female.

"Cider," she said quietly, and she turned to watch the other patrons without making it obvious. She took her drink gratefully, relishing it, even as part of her mind was anticipating a proper hot bath to clean off the week's worth of dust.

"Hello, darlin'," a far from sober voice asked right into Atlantis's ear. "Why don't you and I go and find a room together?"

Atlantis put her drink on the bar, picked off the rude hand squeezing her leg, and said, "Why don't you let me help you back to your chair?"

Slipping off the stool, she stood taller than the man, and when she took his arm, it was to half support him back to the chair he had vacated. "You just sit there and dream about it, okay?"

"Whatever you say, darlin'."

Another of the men nearby started to rise, as Berto drawled, seemingly to Brennan, "Met her on the way, I did. She's deadly with a sword – legendary. We have a truce..."

It was hint enough to make the second man drop quickly back onto his seat, and to dissuade any others trying to get favours from the woman.

Those that knew Berto began whispering, "That Berto, he's an expert with all sorts of weapons. You can't see all he's got, until they get you."

Brennan was grinning when Atlantis sat back on her stool. He went back to his interrupted conversation.

"Well, like I said, Berto, you've been away a while. You won't find much work around here. King's not trying to kill that army. Many of them are farmers, just in from the country, and some come from here in the town. All his nobles and their guards have fled back to their manors. There's lots of chancy creatures about, but they don't stray far and don't want what we offer. There's human scum and foreigners too. Those types we don't encourage in here. Other places aren't so picky. The scum like crawling over the rubble looking for stuff the king's folk left behind."

Brennan was full of the sort of information Rhovert needed to know, and had proved to be a totally trustworthy man. He knew who Berto really was, and had never let the knowledge slip or even to brag that he'd had the Prince of Thulor as a customer.

In a pause, while Brennan served some of his other customers, Rhovert took several more long swallows of his ale. When it was safe to talk quietly again, he asked, "How's the goat woman?"

"Dead this year past. Had to find a new cheese seller and their stuff is not half as good. They reckon it is to do with that new weed that's taken over everywhere."

"She had no dependents," Rhovert persisted with his questions.

"No, or at least I never heard of anyone coming to take the place on. The scum looted it, and the house is a wreck. I doubt even the most desperate would stay there now. It is too close to all them odd creatures."

Rhovert nodded. There should be no one there. He let Brennan move away and chat to other patrons, finished his ale, and when Atlantis had finished her cider, gave her their private signal to leave. No one was interested enough to watch them go.

The sun had gone down while they were in the tavern. This part of the town that surrounded the palace didn't have gas lamps along the streets so the glowing things they saw were some of the chancy creatures Brennan had mentioned.

Rhovert touched his talisman and concentrated on the idea that the creatures needed to move away. That the creatures they watched were dangerous. Atlantis touched hers and spoke the words of a spell her brother had devised that would make her and Rhovert less noticeable. They had left the horses at the tavern stable. Berto had a long standing arrangement with Brennan.

They made sure there were none of the creatures around before Rhovert pulled Atlantis off the main street, with its row of run down or derelict houses, and onto a path that ran next to a collapsed shack. Only the last traces of daylight and the starlight illuminated the damage. Not far away, and backing on to the small garden, was the palace wall.

"Do we have to go in there?" Atlantis whispered.

"No, through the stable. This is the way Maeven always used to go in and out. I don't think she ever realised that Father knew of it too."

The third of the stalls had escaped the worst of the vandalism, although nothing remained of the old woman's buckets, stool or other equipment. If any animals had been there, they'd probably been killed and eaten.

"She kept a few cows that gave milk," Rhovert explained. All that remained was the lingering smell of old manure and rotting hay. He then whispered the words for a 'reveal all' spell, one Finora had taught him. Looking around, and seeing no glowing shapes, reassured him.

"There are traces of old spells," Atlantis whispered. "Was the old woman a witch?"

"I wouldn't know. If she was, it was a minor gift – but then, her cheeses always lasted longer than anyone else's." Rhovert had gone to where a heavy manger was pushed against the side of the stall. He shoved it aside, trying to minimise the sound of it scraping on the stone floor, and crouched down to brush filth from part of the ground. An age blackened iron ring sat in a depression of a wooden trap door. He didn't try to lift it right away, for it would have proved impossible until he moved a particular brick into a gap in the stone floor.

"If you use enough force, you can get the wooden door up, but you'd only see a hole filled with dried cow dung pats. Moving the brick, moves a false floor, and that gets you to where there's a ladder going down. In you get, I'll follow."

Atlantis wriggled so her saddlebags didn't catch on the sides of the open trap door. When she reached the dirt floor below, she moved aside to let Rhovert drop his bags down. He paused, when his head was low enough, to relock the trap door. Meanwhile, in the deep dark, Atlantis fiddled in her saddle bag, her fingers seeking one of the wizard balls she always carried. The faint rustling sounds, brought Rhovert to her.

"What are you doing?"

"Looking for one of Roman's wizard lights."

"Leave it for now. I know my way through here, even in the dark. Use one hand to feel along the wall, and slide your feet along the floor. The roof has partially collapsed in a few places, so it is better not to have a light down here that might be seen through the chinks. The part of the palace above us is rubble, but things still move about up there when it is dark."

"Why not fix it?"

"Any repair work would draw attention, and for now, all the really bad nasties are concentrating on the other end, where they know people still are. It makes this way in and out a lot safer."

True to his word, Rhovert led the way along the narrow tunnel that took several twists and turns along the way. He stopped when his hand contacted a wooden door and frame. The last few yards had been sloping upward, so there was no ladder to climb at this end.

Rhovert fumbled with the catch and the door opened, letting in a dim amount of light.

Atlantis looked around. They seemed to be in a store room, and the light was reflecting in from another room. Rhovert went out first, into what was the servant's kitchen.

Two of the King's Own Guards met them with swords drawn.

"And who do we have here, slinking in like thieves?" one asked conversationally.

"If you can't figure that out, Toltee, I will tell your wife you wear pink underwear."

"And I don't let her forget how she washed them with her new red scarf." Toltee grinned broadly, and when he sheathed his sword, the other did as well. Rhovert nodded at the younger man, a son of one of the other, older guards.

"His majesty is wearing out the carpet in his apartment," Toltee told Rhovert. "Don't be surprised if that wizard of his has orders to drag you there. He told us that someone friendly had passed through his wards. He didn't say you had been brawling in the dirt…" Then he recognised who was with the Prince. "My apologies, Lady Atlantis, I wasn't implying…"

Atlantis chuckled. "I know what we look like. I suppose we won't have time for a long, luxurious, hot bath."

A wry grin accompanied a head shake.

Rhovert took his consort's hand. "Let's get this over with. Toltee, can you see to it that our bags are taken up?"

He saw the man nod, and drew Atlantis out into one of the servant's passages. They did stop briefly in the servant's wash room, to get the worst of the dirt off their faces and hands, then trotted to the stair case that led up to the second level, and where the king spent most of his time. At the top of the stairs, a short, solid figure hurried towards them. He gripped Rhovert's shoulder with one hand and pulled Atlantis into a bear hug with his other arm.

"Glad to see you back, safe and well," Roman Golddreamer told his sister. "You too," he added to Rhovert. "It has been damn hard to keep my mouth shut these past few days. Your father is like a fidgety flea, waiting to hear what you have to say."

"I don't suppose he will let us clean up properly first?" Rhovert asked, as a means to test his father's mood.

Roman, like Toltee, just shook his head. "Maybe…if you had arrived three days ago."

Rhovert gave a half stifled laugh, to cover the fact of being envious of how Roman had greeted his sister. He had long given up any expectation of an equivalent greeting from his father. However, when they entered his father's private apartment, it was enough to see some of the worry lines leave his father's face.

Atlantis eased into the room, and watched as the king confronted his son. The two men were unalike in looks, but in some other things, very alike.

Westron was a tall man, solidly built, and two inches taller than his son. His once dark hair was now steel grey, and long enough to need a head band to hold it off his face. Despite his age, he had lost none of his air of authority.

Rhovert had dark hair like his father, but his graceful build had come from his mother. His stubbornness, was equal to his father's. Just then, he was staying quiet, not even greeting his father, and once the king had finished giving him a thorough look over, he turned to approach where she had moved to lean against a clear piece of wall.

Wordlessly, he held his out his hand, palm up. A gesture of deference to a lady, to take his hand. Keeping her own expression as neutral as her consort's, she placed her hand in his and allowed herself to be escorted to a chair. His gaze was intent, but if asked, she would guess he wasn't even seeing how dusty she was, or even that she was in her preferred style of clothes – tunic and breeches. And damn it, she knew what he was thinking and wondered how long it would be before Rhovert stopped keeping him guessing.

"Are you well, My Lady?" he asked her.

"I am in excellent health, Sire," Atlantis answered politely, aware of the King's excitement and wondered how Rhovert was going to tell him about the child they had found.

"And my Grandson?"

"He is well," Atlantis began but stopped when she saw Rhovert frown slightly.

"Father," Rhovert interrupted, "The child is not ours. He is about four years old and I have no doubt he is your Grandson. Petulor vouched for him."

The King stared at his son.

"If he is my Grandson, which of my daughters was his mother?" His voice was dangerously soft.

"Father, I think you know!"

"Maeven is his mother!" Atlantis told him, in no way cowed by being in the King's presence. "He can't have been more than a week or two old when I first met her. She had him fostered by a couple in that hill village where she had been living."

Between them, Atlantis and Rhovert told the King all they had learnt about Wystan. As they talked, King Westron turned away from them, perhaps so he did not betray his feelings. He said nothing until Rhovert finished his tale.

"Now I know what was so important to her that she nearly didn't give me her oath."

Atlantis shuddered and Rhovert held himself rigid. Both knew how close it had come to Maeven being hung as a thief, murderer and traitor. With only moments to spare she had given her oath of fealty.

"Am I to take it that you have still not sired a son?" Rhovert was asked.

"No, nor a daughter!" Rhovert clamped his teeth together to stop himself uttering a vile oath.

The King sighed. "Then it seems that my daughter has given me a gift beyond price. Wystan, named after my Great grand sire. A wise man and a wizard. His father – is Arlen?"

"The boy didn't know," Rhovert said, his tone more moderate. "But I had little doubt. He has the Vatarin cast to his features, and had begun to display a stong ability for magic. And yes, Arlen admits paternity. He said that he and Maeven had come to an agreement, but she was taken off before she could confirm it."

"You say he has no knowledge of his status or rank?"

"Yes, Father."

Atlantis added, "And I impressed it upon Gisella that he would be safer in ignorance."

"Wizard, would your wife be able to keep such a secret?"

Atlantis answered for her brother. "Sire, I have no doubt of it. She misses her husband, regrets that she has no chance yet for a child of her own. In the short time we were there, Wystan had taken to her and she to him. She would do nothing, say nothing, to endanger him."

"Can your brother in law train him, Wizard?"

This time Roman answered. "Krit has only a little magic but what he has he uses most efficiently. Wystan can learn from him that you don't need to hitch a cart horse to move a butterfly."

King Westron turned back to face his guests. There was a faint smile on his face and if his eyes were a trifle moist, no one commented.

"That little village is not a suitable place for the boy. The King of Declanor has promised to aid us. Rhovert, please contact King

Sevin and ask this favour of him. To place the child high in his court but keep his rank unknown. To teach the child statecraft and other kingly subjects and protect him in every way he can. It will be suitable if Lady Gisella accompanied him."

Roman knew it would be his part to facilitate the conversation between Rhovert and Westron's Declanese counterpart, once this discussions with his son was over. He'd need to give his wife a warning of what was planned too. However, he wasn't ready to go to fetch his message ball – wanting to hear what Westron would get Rhovert doing next.

"Sire," Atlantis asked. "Do I have your permission to seek for Ven?"

"No! I wish you to stay with my son. I have not given up my hopes for a true born heir. And I do not wish my son to starve if he must travel on his own away from towns."

"I can look after myself!" Rhovert muttered.

The King ignored his comment.

"Lady Atlantis, while Petulor is sure where my daughter was taken – we are not prepared to send an army into Vatarik. I must hope my youngest daughter has lost none of her cunning, and continues to be a thorn in the plans of the Serpent. Her unorthodox beliefs can benefit us there."

Atlantis bowed her head, considering her next words. "Even if she is being ill-treated?"

"In these times, everyone must do what they can. It is war, even if it has not been declared. Maeven gave me her oath. I do not doubt it. And I believe you will agree, she has never aspired to be a delicate court lady. In any case, I have sent three agents into Vatarik, each carries one of Petulor's scales. If they are able to deliver, even just one of them, we will have a way to be in touch with her. I do not believe that bringing her out at this point will be the best option. In fact, since they took her there, they will not consider that she could be a spy."

It was no use arguing with him, Atlantis knew – he usually got his way. But he was right. Maeven was tough in all ways that mattered.

Rhovert added, "Arlen believes that Ciabolo will want to merge with his brother, in the way that he did with their father, even if El Rasho has no magic. So far, it seems that El Rasho has resisted, using the need to sire an heir to ensure succession. If he heard that Arlen got Maeven pregnant, and she insisted she had aborted the child, he might think he too could make her pregnant."

"So you think that will keep them distracted," Atlantis asked.

Rhovert blurted a laugh. "You know what she's like, she can twist your words right around, and is stubborn enough to find ways to prevent them getting what they want."

Atlantis did know, but she was uneasy about Maeven being so close to Ciabolo.

It was as if Westron felt her unease. He began to speak slowly, as if thinking, "There might be other reasons to wish for a child with dragon blood, perhaps one who could use dragon magic...."

Roman gave the king a speculative glance, waiting for him to say more. When he didn't, he suggested, "A child would be of little use for some time..."

"And we already have someone with the blood of Vatarik," Westron finished.

Rhovert looked from his father, to the wizard and back. "And what advantage does that give us?" he demanded.

Westron merely shook his head, the vision that had come upon him, had faded.

"Time might tell us that," Roman offered.

With an effort, Rhovert cooled his frustration. "What do you need me to do, father? I'd like to keep moving around, seeing what needs to be done."

"I will let you know. For now, you can send a message to Arlen. I want words with him."

"In person?" Rhovert asked. He had said all he was going to say of his own private talk with the former Vatarin.

"Yes, in person!" the King confirmed. "I think things will quieten down in the south now the border is closed to traders. I can use him elsewhere."

"Very well," Rhovert agreed, glancing at Roman, and getting the silent message that he would do the summoning. "Anything else?"

"Stop shedding dust on my carpet," Westron commanded, by way of a dismissal.

Atlantis merely rose, with a grin at Rhovert's expression. His father knew how to rile him, and right then, he seemed about to explode. He didn't though, just turned, gestured to her, and strode out. Roman followed them both.

"I'd like to –" Rhovert began.

"Hitting a king is a bad idea," Roman inserted quickly. "However, I think I know where you and your sisters get their attitude from."

"If I ever get to be as intransigent as him –"

"I will let you know," Atlantis said sweetly.

Rhovert deflated.

Atlantis went on, "Were you going to mention more of the conversation you had with Arlen?"

"No, only as much as I did. The rest was private, just him and me. I know father trusts him, but I was keeping an open mind. I wanted to be sure he hadn't tricked her again, somehow, and then sold her out to Ciabolo."

"But he said his brother and Ciabolo would kill him on sight," Atlantis argued.

"Unless that was a ruse."

"No! From what you told me, Ciabolo nearly did kill him, and he was the one to put Wystan onto Petulor to get him away."

"I know that. Now I have the full story. I wanted to be sure that Maeven did trust him. After all, she saw a very different side of him."

"And are you satisfied?" Roman asked him.

"I am, and by the sound of it, Petulor is sure. She would like them to have more children of mixed blood."

"Too bad they didn't get the chance to arrange that," Roman sighed.

Rhovert shrugged. "I'm for a bath. What about you, Atlantis?"

"Good idea," Roman said quickly, while giving his sister a sly glance. "You will need to look like a prince when you talk to King Sevin, and you heard your father's comment about a true born heir."

His grin widened when Rhovert growled, "I'll talk to you later," and his sister thumped him on his shoulder.

Feeling much better after they had removed the travel grime, donned clean clothes, and eaten, Rhovert and Atlantis went to find Roman.

He was not in the rooms he had been using and Rhovert had to ask a servant to direct him. He was surprised to realise that the wizard was now occupying the suite usually assigned to the King's chief advisor. It made sense, for really, Roman had been that almost since he had first helped the King.

Though, recalling how the room had looked when Col Tormore had resided there, it was now Spartan indeed, but also, more comfortable.

"How long have you been in here?" Atlantis asked. "You never said anything about changing rooms."

"Not that long. The offer was made just after the last of the Lords left, but I wanted to be sure there was no lingering spells on the room – considering who the previous occupant's son was. Anyway, the idea had been around longer than that, but some of the nobles were making it clear that they thought wizards should stay in closets – out of sight. Even the King's court wizard."

"Maybe, especially the court wizard," Rhovert suggested. "Particularly if they had a guilty conscience, and feared you could read minds. Who were the worst?"

"Old Tarthal and his arrogant son, as well as Lord Kilkennie. They don't realise that it is not my place to gossip about their liaisons. The servants do enough of that, and unless the servants remaining here have relatives in their retinue, who is to know? They both sent their wives and staff back to their manors, as soon as the last conclave was officially over."

"Are you sure that's all it is?" Atlantis asked, having had a flash of something, too fleeting to catch.

"It's most likely. Why?"

Atlantis shook her head. "Where do they live?"

Roman mentioned two manors and Rhovert added, "Out to the east. Kilkennie's land borders the great lake. Tarthal's is north of his."

"On the border?" Atlantis persisted. "With Vatarik?"

"No...not quite. There is a huge stretch of dense forest between him and the border. It's reputed to be impregnable. What are you trying to puzzle out?"

"Nothing in particular. I have never gone that far. Never seen a really huge lake either. Does it stretch up to Vatarik?"

"I'm not sure. I know it borders that forest for much of its length."

"Do people travel on it?"

" I guess people must try it now and then," Rhovert said. "I heard that anyone that does and goes out of sight of the edge, never comes back."

"I would still like to see it."

Recalling the odd compulsion that had led them to Ackbridge, he said, "If father hasn't any more definite task for us, we'll go that way and do a circuit of the northern manors on the way back. I know father has troops all along the border, but I haven't heard about any trouble out that way. So Roman, is it likely to be too late to contact your old master?"

Roman rolled his eyes roofward. "I swear the man never sleeps, you know. And he will be sure to tell you if it is too late to talk to King Sevin."

"He's really got you pegged," Rhovert jested.

"Oh, he's not that bad. My little glass ball really impressed him."

"Plus, you are Thulor's court wizard, equal to him in rank," Atlantis teased. "That should count for something."

"Not with that old curmudgeon. He must be at least two hundred years old."

"I doubt it," Atlantis argued. "He is an awful snob. Anyway, brother mine, are you going to give Gisella warning of how the wind will be blowing?"

"I did that while you two were getting civilised. By now, she is probably about to whelp a litter of kittens from nerves. It is a big step up from farmer's daughter to the King's palace."

"She was living here!" Atlantis protested.

"So I reminded her," Roman assured her. "I also told her that she might only be a herb witch, but the work she did that night Petulor was born, in saving so many lives, has made her something of a folk hero. I didn't tell her all they were calling her, but none of that was that she had been hiding like a coward, as she claims. She went downright silent, then told me I was having her on. What she had done was no big deal. It was just doing what she had been taught to do. So, I told her that being the wife of Thulor's court wizard puts her far above most of the women in the King's court."

"Did that help?"

"She liked the idea, and laughed when I said not to tell anyone that I didn't earn my position, just got dragged into it."

"Well, you are doing a good pretence," Atlantis teased. "But just so you don't keep bragging, are you going to contact King Sevin or not?"

"Me? Brag? Not a chance," Roman countered as he drew out his glass ball and concentrated on it. When it began to glow, he spoke the words of a spell.

Minutes passed before the crotchety voice of Wizard Indra was heard in the room.

"Oh! It's you! What do you want now?"

"Master Indra, I am contacting you on behalf of Prince Rhovert. He has matters to discuss with His Highness King Sevin."

"Oh, very well. But I warn you, he might be too busy."

"If need be, Wizard Indra, I will be happy to wait. The matter is extremely important, but not urgent." Rhovert saw the old wizard react to his words. The sound that came then was like a growl, and the wizards face vanished from the glass ball. However, when he looked into the ball, he had the impression that it was being carried. Listening too, gave the same impression, other voices came through briefly, as well as the tones of Indra's voice. A high pitched shriek startled them all, as the image in the ball jumped.

Clearly then, they heard, "Prince or no, young man, if you try that again, you will spend a week unable to sit down. Be gone! You should be in bed. Go back to your nurse."

In a low voice, Roman murmured, "King Sevin remarried about ten years ago. That scamp must be the youngest Prince. The others are fully grown men. You might suggest that Wystan could be a companion. Farthing is about eight, but from what you said, Wystan is old for his age."

"Worth a thought," Rhovert agreed, as they waited.

"Prince Rhovert," King Sevin's voice came clearly. It followed some moments of low voiced conversation between him and Indra. "I understand you have an important matter to bring to me."

Without going into the actual details of Wystan's parentage, and saying only that he was the next heir after himself to the crown of Thulor, Rhovert outlined his father's request, adding the suggestion that Roman had made. He then waited as Sevin thought it through.

"It might be a good thing at that," Sevin said finally. "Farthing is getting reckless. The only boys near his age are older, and they egg him on. Maybe the responsibility for mentoring a younger boy will help settle him. You say this boy is a sensible lad?"

"He was fostered until now in a hill village on our side of your border. With a lot of straight laced, parochial –"

"Spare me. I know the ones you mean. They are a breakaway group of some new god-creator religion. Ones who felt our ways were too liberal. Yes, I'll take the lad on. He can have lessons with Farthing and see how he goes."

"He will need to have his magic trained," Roman reminded Rhovert in a voice that wasn't quiet enough to be unheard.

"Can't be a worse student than you, young upstart," Indra retorted immediately.

"No, Master, on the contrary. He is likely to keep you on your toes. He has been with my brother in law for less than three weeks, and he has already mastered a lot of small magics."

Sevin asked, "You have advised his guardians of this?"

"Yes, Master," Roman confirmed.

"I will dispatch a carriage to collect him, along with his foster mother. It will arrive in three days."

"Thank you, sir," Rhovert said respectfully. "One other thing. There is a dog that has adopted Wystan. If that will not be an issue."

King Sevin waved his hand, brushing that concern aside. "Is it well behaved?"

"Yes, Sir. It is also big enough to be extra protection for the boy."

"All is well then. Assure your father that I will do him his favour, and give him my regards."

The light went from the globe when the conversation ended. All three in the room relaxed.

"I'll tell Gisella when to expect company. She will need all that time to pack. I just know she will have bags and bags of herbs she will insist on taking."

Atlantis stood up, and wandered over to where she saw a wine sack slung over the pint of a chair. She opened the stopper and sniffed.

"It's barley water," he said, not looking her way. "With some of Gis's herbs in it. Want some?"

"I think I will. Do you have any wine for visitors?"

Roman chuckled. "It's in the chest by the window. The servants take it from your father's private hoard. It's even better that the stuff he gives his Lord's when they visit."

"Or gives his children, I bet." Rhovert laughed as he went to help himself.

Roman finally ended his quiet talk with his wife, all the way down in Declanor. He appreciated how his guests had moved across the room, and sat quietly talking between themselves. He missed his wife, as much as she missed him.

He turned around, and found Atlantis offering him a drink of the barley water.

Rhovert had followed, and he sat down in one of Roman's chairs. "So, how are things here? I saw the extra soldiers outside – recognised the type."

"They came through green fires," Roman said, and he saw Rhovert nod.

"So, here is where they were sent."

"And probably all infected by little incubi by now. Those creatures are a real plague around here."

"And are you any closer to finding a solution?" Atlantis asked.

Roman shook his head. "Gis suggested chopped onion or garlic," he told them. "But they only work until the stuff dries out. While it's fresh, it stops the things attaching, but once they have, it does nothing, except lull them to a limited degree. It is still better to keep away from them. I can't think what else to try."

"What about that purple weed?" Atlantis suggested. "It's pungent enough."

"Did you see much of it down south?" Roman didn't answer the question.

"We were keeping well away from cultivated areas for the most part," Rhovert admitted. "All I really noticed was one or two of the plants on the edge of a clearing."

"Now, that's interesting. Everyone I talk to is convinced that the reason it is growing rampant around here is because of the sickly pall that's everywhere. Perhaps the tree canopy filters it?"

"Or the stuff stays low," Atlantis countered. "The ground is higher in the south."

"True. Whatever the reason, the pall is the Serpent's doing. It reeks of dark magic. The black clouds blow over frequently – bringing new pests, new blights. As soon as we find a counter for one lot, new ones show up."

"But the weed is a problem?" Atlantis prompted.

Roman growled. "The farmers and their families, work from dawn to dusk to keep the stuff out of the fields. The crops they get are marginal at best, sometimes they are so wrong looking we need to burn the crop. When we get a period when the air is clearer, that damn weed grows really fast. It is a fight to keep the good plants clear of it. As for using it to send off the demons, it's more like to attract them."

"What about father's edict to stockpile last year's harvest in the manor granaries?"

Now Roman grinned. "The Lords are praising the King's foresight. The serfs are spending half their time in the fields and the other half earning extra rations by serving in the Lord's garrison. The woman and children are helping to tend the fields and animals. As far as I can tell, no one is actually starving, but no one is ever really well fed. I would be wary of anyone that seems well fed."

"And here?" Atlantis asked.

"Here? With so few people still living in the palace, our supplies will last a while. We have been helping to feed the town's people."

"Why does the king stay here?"

"Where would he go?" Rhovert countered his wife's question. "If he went to any of the Lord's they would feel obliged to hold grand gala's in his honour. No one has enough spare time or food for that."

"It's not just that," Roman broke in soberly. "He is the last defence for the magic that is pooling in Thulor's crypt."

"He could let me do more," Rhovert said passionately.

"You are doing a lot," Roman hurried to assure him. "You are keeping him aware of events in his kingdom that he doesn't hear about from his troops or his lords. And, very few people know where you are travelling. The serpent craves the magic in the crypt. If anything happens to your father, protecting that will fall to you. At the moment, the enemy's chancy creatures and conscripts are concentrating their attention here. It means the lords and everyone else don't have to face them."

"That is all very well, but I feel like I am being pushed away, to safety, like an unbreeched child. The serpent and his creatures are as good as walking all over us."

"It is hard to fight an enemy that won't show itself," Roman reminded him. "We have yet to know what form Ciabolo has taken, since King Malokin of Vatarik was killed."

"Arlen said about some hedge wizard," Rhovert inserted.

"For now, maybe. He will want someone stronger before he begins his real move. In the meantime, the more we can do to thwart his preparations, the better. In case you have never considered it, the king is not calmly letting him do as he pleases. You, your father, your siblings, by your very existence, are a threat to the serpent. Or why else have so many attempts been made to kill you over the years? That is why the king is so insistent about having the royal line continue."

"Dragon blood?" Atlantis suddenly said. "Do you think there is more to that term than being in favour with the dragons?"

"Like what?" Rhovert asked.

"Oh, like, maybe dragons can shape themselves as humans?"

"Right and maybe mere humans can fly," Rhovert retorted.

"I was just trying to figure out where the term came from. Great grandfather wrote down some old legends passed down from generation to generation. Some suggest that a long time ago, people prayed for protections against demons and the dragons came and presented themselves to the king."

"Then why are there so few dragons around now?" Rhovert moderated his tone to one of someone asking an obvious question.

"People hunted them," Roman suggested. "Once the demons they scared off had been gone for a time, and people forgot what they had done and only knew they took too many domestic animals."

"And they turned themselves into people," Atlantis finished quickly.

"Goats more likely," Roman snorted. "Dragons are as ornery as goats. And did you know, goats will actually eat that purple weed?"

"Huh!"

"It's true," Roman insisted. "One lord is building up his goat herd, to help keep the stuff under control. Mind you, he knows he needs to keep them tethered out of reach of the good crops. Perhaps you should suggest that to the lords you encounter."

"For that suggestion wizard, you can tell father of King Sevin's response. I'm for a late supper and bed."

Roman smirked as Rhovert led Atlantis from the room.

CHAPTER 30 - Leanne and Finora

The brigands raiding in the bounds of the manor of Lord Falston of Silver Glen, were a canny bunch. They seemed to know the movements of both the Lord's soldiers and Leanne's troopers, avoided the areas where they were patrolling, and struck hard and fast at some other location. All of the small villages that looked to Lord Falston had suffered losses.

Leanne and Finora had been at a strategy meeting at the manor, and were returning to their camp. With their minds working on the new ideas, they didn't immediately see Nelsi hovering near their tent. When they did, they quickly summoned the new recruit who was doing duty as ostler, and had him take their horses. With quick strides, they went towards their tent.

"You're back again," Leanne greeted neutrally. Nelsi grinned.

"And you've improved the food around here," the little thief commented.

"Lord Falston is happy to keep us supplied while we sort out his persistent brigand problem," Finora told him.

"They too clever for you? I expected you to be at Miner's creek by now."

Leanne growled softly. "Apart from having the chance to belittle me, what has you so chirpy?"

"You have a visitor." Nelsi shrugged in the direction of the cook fire. "Found him on my way back. He expected you to be elsewhere. You changed the spell on the token's then?"

Finora laughed. "Yes, you sneaky man. I decided I didn't want your friend sneaking back and finding us asleep."

"No chance of that," Nelsi said, sobering.

"Glad you think so," Leanne told him. "The visitor – he's one of Father's messengers?"

Nelsi grinned again, he knew she knew, the man was a guild bonded thief.

"Send him to our tent and keep any listeners away," Leanne directed. "I'll hear what you have to say after I hear him out."

A few minutes later, the newcomer coughed politely at a point just outside the tent flap. He heard the invitation to enter. He bowed to each of the women, knowing they were both royalty. He was waved to a seat.

"What do you have for us?" Leanne asked in a low voice. Even though the man was a thief, he was likable. He grinned now.

"I bring you a gift from the court wizard. He tells me that you..." he gestured to Finora, "...need to activate it by saying..." he quoted a three sentence spell before continuing. "That will cause the one at the palace to activate and form a connection."

The thief seemed to produce a soft leather pouch out of nowhere, and passed it to Finora. She rolled the perfectly round glass ball out onto her palm. "He also said it is no longer safe to send pigeon messengers."

"I was coming to that conclusion," Finora admitted. "Do you know what has been attacking them?"

The man shook his head. "The unattached little demons might be getting hungry."

Finora shuddered. "Have you more to tell us?"

"A great deal, your ladyship," the man admitted. "And a few things the wizard mentioned as we parted that might interest you." A tightly rolled scroll appeared like the pouch had. This he gave to Leanne. "Firstly, his majesty has sent three from my guild to take objects into Vatarik, into the new king's citadel, on the orders of the dragon."

Leanne's eyes widened, as she considered the implications of that statement. "That is dangerous," she commented.

"That is why three are going. Three chances, I heard."

"Let's hope all three get in and out safely," Finora spoke softly, like a plea to whatever gods were near.

"Amen to that, Prankster bless," the thief agreed. "And to another end, I am told that the King's envoy to Declanor has been doing some effective bandit eradication down south. Amongst the rabble, he identified several young nobles that once graced his majesty's court."

Leanne growled, "The serpent has corrupted too many of our people."

"Captain Arlen has found and broken up the supply base being used by many of the groups down there. Ones, it seems, that contain many Vatarins, and not those that are Thulan rabble. His majesty suggests you should look for indications of a similar system up here. There is a summary of what he found on the scroll."

"Anything else?" Leanne prompted when the man fell silent.

The man shook his head.

"I don't suppose you will tell us where you are to head next?" Leanne asked.

The man grinned. "Oh, I am going back to my wife for my little one's birthday."

The usual lack of an answer still got a chuckle. Thieves were secretive about their own business.

Finora told him, "Go and help yourself to food and drink. We will be getting more supplies from Lord Falston in the morning."

The thief slipped out of the tent as Nelsi slipped in.

"How much did you hear?" Leanne demanded.

"Most of it," Nesli admitted.

"Have you picked up anything about a central place that supplies brigands?" Leanne asked.

"No... but I will listen out. I did hear that bands from the south were moving up."

"Since Arlen broke up that group in Ackbridge?" Leanne suggested.

"Maybe," Nelsi considered. "I was just thinking that we were never aware of caravans of goods heading south frequently, and I haven't heard how the supplies were getting to Ackbridge. Have you heard?" He saw Leanne shake her head. "Well, if it is overland, for groups coming up – I would think a supply point would be nearer the border."

"Makes sense," Finora agreed. She was watching Nelsi's expression. She thought he seemed to be trying to remember something.

Leanne merely said, "That would be a good reason for us to get nearer the border." She caught her twin nodding agreement. "We know all the Vatarin soldiers are not coming in on the main trade road through Thul Run."

"They'll be using a smugglers trail," Nelsi suggested absently. "Or..."

Leanne waited for Nelsi to go on, finally prompting, "Or?"

"Well, I heard that a bunch of brigands vanished from the tavern in Ackbridge. I didn't hear how, but I also heard a whole bunch of extra brigand types arrived at the palace about the same time.”

Leanne swore, “Dragon dung! I wish father would tell us everything that is going on. Fi, next time you speak to Roman, see if he knows anything more.”

“Assuming father isn’t around when I try it,” Finora told her. “Nels, do you know what father sent into Vatarik?”

The little thief’s eyes gleamed. “Scales. Three of them, from the dragon.”

Finora felt a surge of relief. “Then Maeven has to be alive still. Only someone with the blood of Thulor, could make use of them, or the magic in them.”

“I think it is to try to have a way for the dragon to know she’s okay. The wizard said she can’t go into Vatarik. At worst, if your sister gets them, it might provide some protection and healing.”

“And let her do little magic things again,” Finora chuckled.

“How did you hear all that?” Leanne asked.

“From my master,” Nelsi admitted readily. “He didn’t know much, just what I told you. He came through at night, on his way to Vatarik.”

“Well, at least father is sending the best he has,” Leanne remarked as she began to carefully unroll the scroll. Nelsi’s master, the leader of the Thieves’ guild, was also the king’s spy master. He was also the thief who had trained Maeven, and didn’t always agree with the king withholding knowledge from the two Princesses - if the information might increase their effectiveness or keep them safer. With that understanding, Nelsi shared all the information he received, and in turn learned of the details of all official communications to the troop leaders. That way, he knew what things to listen out for.

Finora waiting for her sister to finish reading, asked, “Nels, did you happen to hear how our sister managed to let herself be caught?”

“Don’t you know?” The little thief was surprised. “I thought it was common knowledge...or at least nothing that had to be kept secret. She went to help a child who was being stalked by one of the big black cats.”

Leanne’s head twisted to face Nelsi. “What the heck did she think she was doing? Wait! She was in the south. Those creatures are usually only up this way.”

“Fact though. And there have been other reports of the creatures moving south."

"Was Arlen around?" Leanne made it sound like she was accusing him of something.

"He had gone back to that hill village to talk to her. Or so I heard."

"That stupid, stupid, brainless wench!" Leanne exploded. "I told you, Fi. A stupid cockeyed reason! Those parochial old farts up there don't deserve her consideration."

"It was for a child, Lee," Finora pointed out.

Leanne ignored that and went back to reading the report about events in Ackbridge. Finally she handed the scroll to Finora, who passed it to Nelsi to read.

"What are the main points?" Finora asked, although she intended to read it fully herself later.

"At father's request, King Sevin has fortified his border with us. We are to report the incidence and numbers of those little incubi or succubi demons we find. Likely the brigands down south will move north for richer pickings, so we are to check any dead or captured brigands to see if one is wearing a talisman like ours. Rhovert and Atlantis found the guy who had Roman's one before Tormore stole it. His wife, who ran when this Gamman Mogray was captured, had another. They don't know if the woman is still alive, but father has been getting flashes from one that seems to be from amongst bandits."

That had Finora's attention. "How long was the man imprisoned?"

"Over twelve years, so that traitor Tormore must have had it for a long time before he tried to use it."

"Well, we can look. I doubt we overlooked it at any time. Our talismans would have reacted."

Leanne snorted, reminding her twin, "Until recently, since Thulor died, they have been as unreactive as plain rock." She saw Nelsi hand the scroll back to Finora and said, "Well, sergeant, you certainly heard a lot of things when you were, presumably, in Vatarik."

Finora asked, "When did your master go through?"

"Only a week ago," Nelsi told her as he saw Leanne begin to scowl.

"I expected you back a couple of weeks ago. I know how long it took us to go in, all the way to the citadel, and come back."

"My master ordered me to report," Nelsi shrugged. "The matter was urgent, and I did have maps of Vatarik and the route that spy took me, and some useful passwords. That route was not one my master knew of, but he said there were likely lots he still didn't know."

"I would be interested in any maps that show routes across the border," Leanne said pointedly.

"No need my lady. The king gets told of every new one that's found, and he has a troop watching each one.

"Men that would be more useful going after the bedamned brigands. Can't father see they are not coming in over the hill borders?"

Finora contradicted her, "Father may well have seem something to suggest they are." She turned back to Nelsi. "Tell me about this route. Did you go all the way to the citadel?"

"Actually, no. I was three quarters of the way there when I had a bit of luck. Met up with some brothers with a grudge."

"Brothers?" Leanne queried, her brows rising. "Like of the local chapter of your guild?"

A grin was confirmation. "It seems El Rasho treats my brothers even worse than people think your father does. Lots of them have been conscripted, or beaten to death by his bully boys. You need to be careful about them. They are like vipers, sweet one minute, attacking the next."

"Noted!" Leanne said tersely. "Get to the point."

"I got to Treffin Zyg. I think you know it. The town is surrounded by chava bushes."

"Yes, that stuff is delicious. If we'd not been in a rush last time we went through I would have bought some."

Finora nudged her twin, to get her focussed back on the point. "So you know the way there from, where did you cross the border?"

"Near Florin Peak. The trail to there is marked on the maps, and my brothers have promised to plant your trail markers the rest of the way to the citadel."

"You said the spy wouldn't be a problem. Is he dead?" Nelsi looked at Leanne and said, "As dead as that haunch of cow that's smoking over the fire."

"Should I ask how it happened?"

Nelsi produced a crystal earring on a gold chain. "It might be because he lost this and didn't get believed by the self-important King's men."

"And that is?" Leanne prompted.

"Rank insignia of El Rasho's spies. Thought it might come in useful."

"It might at that. So, you reported to your master when you got back, gave him the trail map. I assume you have other copies?"

Two scrolls suddenly appeared in his hand. "If you have to go in, I can guide you."

"Father won't let us, but it relieves me that his messengers have that much."

"All good," Nelsi agreed. "Now, did you miss me? You must have – you are letting some brigands pull their noses at you."

"Don't start!" Leanne warned. "Yes, we could well use your sneaky ways. This group is well organised, and their camp is well hidden."

"You might let me go scout around Scrubby Hollow," Nelsi suggested. "My master and I heard cows mooing when we went that way. We had thought to camp in some caves near there, but we didn't think the cows got there by themselves, or would be allowed to stray."

Finora just shook her head. "Yes, Nels, we did miss you."

"Get out," Leanne ordered. She watched him leave.

"Sometimes I think what we are doing is too little too late. As soon as Ciabolo thinks he is strong enough, he and El Rasho are going to come over the border with a huge army. This bandit business is just to soften us up, spread out father's soldiers, and give them time to conscript our innocent farmers and traders. Father should be training more soldiers..."

"Except, we need all our farmers at work trying to grow enough food in spite of the nasty magic blights the Serpent keeps sending out way," Finora pointed out.

Her sister growled, frustrated. "I wish the cowards would show their faces..."

Leanne stalked out of the tent, going off to tend to other things. Finora sighed. The two of them were making a difference, but they could only do so much.

She went to sit in a folding seat, to read and note the points Leanne had not found as important. One was the description of how a stranger, a hedge wizard, had been over shadowed by Ciabolo and then changed into the form of a giant serpent – which swallowed Maeven. It was an aspect of their enemy's power she had not been aware of, and she would need to think about it. Another part of the report negated her idea of a way to remove the incubi demons. Her father had tried taking a demon controlled prisoner down into Thulor's crypt and the magic pooling there. Demon and host had died.

Finora told herself there had to be a way to help the poor controlled peasants, she just had to find it. At the end, she idly turned over the parchment and saw a post script, and wondered if Leanne had seen it. Roman, who had written the report, mentioned how a large number of Vatarin soldiers – former brigands, but no doubt they were soldiers, had appeared around the palace, arriving through green fires. She knew what they were... demon portals. So if they could move men from the south to the centre of Thulor, what else could they move that way? Supplies? Animals? Was that how Ackbridge had been supplied? It made sense – there had been no sign of regular convoys of stuff going into that town. If they went north, they would need to look out for that, as well as physical routes over the mountain border.

CHAPTER 31 - Maeven

When the old woman asked her to pee into a clay basin, Maeven just shook her head and did as she asked.

"What did you want me to do that for?"

"To tell if you are pregnant."

"I don't feel pregnant," she said to be perverse.

"Every woman is different," she was told, as the woman carefully carried the basin out.

"How soon will it tell you?" Maeven called after her.

"Soon enough."

When the woman was gone, Maeven muttered, "Don't tell me then! I didn't need to pee into anything to know I was pregnant last time."

Which, she admitted, was true enough. She had been much further along before she found a healer to tell her what was wrong with her. That woman had at least given her a charm to ward off the nausea. During their talk, the woman had heard how the child was conceived, and delicately offered a means to be rid of it. She had considered it, but only for a moment. How could she kill it? It would make her no better than the bandits she had recently outsmarted. Just thinking of saying yes had made her throat close up. Then the reasons to keep it had come into her mind.

Deciding to keep it, had brought on the knowledge that she could not go home. She would be a disgrace, not for being a victim, but for being where no well bred girl should have been. If anyone knew she was also a thief, back then, they would say it was karma. Either way, she would be a disgrace.

Her only regret was knowing she could not raise her son herself. She had watched Wystan growing, from her cave up the hill and when she had crept downhill to the furthest limit of Petulor's protection. When she had finally met her son, she had known that her instinct was right.

At least she had stopped Ciabolo taking him. She wondered if Arlen realised who Wystan was, and if the boy was still safe in the hill village. Or if Petulor had got him away. She had to believe he was safe. If El Rasho, or Ciabolo in his hedge wizard suit had done anything to him...they would have used the fact to torment her... even if they didn't know she was his mother.

Two days later, the old woman returned.

"Well?" Maeven demanded, wondering what kind of spell had been done.

"The frog laid eggs."

Maeven stared at her. *What was she on about?* "Is that some hocus-pocus you did?"

"No, it is a useful way to check for pregnancy," the woman told her quite seriously. "By putting some of your pee into the back of a female frog. If she lays eggs, the pee came from a pregnant woman."

"What a load of goat manure," Maeven told her. "What do frogs –"

"Be quiet you silly girl. I did not expect to see a result so soon. It tells me that you've been pregnant longer than two weeks."

Maeven shut her mouth.

"I don't know what you are playing at girl, but Rashi won't be pleased if he finds out."

It was a risk, but, "He doesn't have to find out. He just wants a son. Did your frog tell you if the child is a son or not? He's only ever had daughters before. So if I have a girl, he might send us away."

"Do you really believe that, girl? Considering how he covets you?"

"No. But he will likely kill a girl child. I had that impression from the older wives. They don't believe the mothers go home with jewels and presents either."

By the frown that appeared on the woman's face, Maeven was sure that she knew that as fact.

"Are you going to tell him this news?"

"No," Maeven told her. *Did she mean boast about being pregnant, or admit the child wasn't his?* The latter would be suicidal, and the former, well, he didn't deserve the courtesy. "No, so you can wait a few days and tell him you think I am pregnant, but you need to wait longer to repeat that pee trick to be sure. And your Rashi, being a man, will be totally clueless about such matters. He is going to be unbearably smug as it is. And regardless of whether I tell him or you do, it isn't going to make him be nicer to me."

The woman sighed. Maeven glanced at her.

"It is a dangerous ploy, child. There is an old way the rulers of Vatarik can prove the bloodline of the heir. If they invoke that and find out the child has no Vatarin blood…"

"They won't find out," Maeven said flatly. "And to prove the child's bloodline, they will first have to test the worth of the current king. And I don't think your Rashi is game to do that. No, even if I give him a son, nothing will change. I doubt there is anything you can say to change that. However, at the moment, once he finds out and becomes unbearably smug, he will be too full of himself to realise that he is actually in my power."

The old woman gave her one long last look and left her alone.

She probably decided not to tell El Rasho right away, or he and that hedge wizard were off somewhere again. It was a whole week later when El Rasho and his wizard off-sider came to interrupt her solitude. Having heard the lock opening, she had quickly gone to her chair and settled herself with her feet on a stool.

"I suppose you've heard about the dratted parasite growing inside me," she challenged before El Rasho was ready to gloat. "No wonder I am so exhausted, I feel I need to sleep all day."

"You should greet me as your majesty," El Rasho told her, trying to dominate her.

"You should be calling me, my lady," Maeven retorted. "After all, none of your other wives or whores are pregnant. I outrank them all."

The hedge wizard, eyes glowing the orange that betrayed Ciabolo was controlling the man, watched the exchange.

"You are no lady," El Rasho said, intending to belittle her. "Just Thulan trash."

"Seems that's what you like these days," Maeven retorted. That comment was ignored.

"I have been talking to my old nurse. She tells me that being tired is common, but you must get exercise, fresh air, eat well, and keep clean. I will have my real favourite see that you do."

"Jilli? Yeah, sure. Do her good to go back to being my maid. I can make her dizzy watching me going round in circles in here to get exercise. But with her around, the air isn't very fresh. She reeks with the odour of lust."

A very quick direct glance at El Rasho showed her an odd expression. She wondered if mention of Jilli's unbridled cravings annoyed him. But a moment later, his face was again smiling smugly.

"No. I am feeling magnanimous. I will let you go into the Garden of the Wives – with guards."

"Well, I'm hoping you are running true to form and it's a girl. But yes, the garden will be a nice change. I can doze in the sun."

"Indeed, but to earn that privilege, you will have to walk around first. Wizard, can you create a spell to make this wench walk around for an hour each day? Say between the second and third candle mark in the afternoon."

"Sssertainly."

"So, will I be allowed to walk anywhere I want? I would like to see more of this place. I don't even know where the front door is."

El Rasho studied Maeven's mock innocent expression. "Wizard, you will also see to it that that this wench will only be able to walk in the garden, and other places where my wives are allowed."

He smiled widely when Maeven scowled, thinking he had out witted her.

"Better than this stuffy room," Maeven muttered under her breath.

The face of the nameless hedge wizard, still with glowing orange eyes, wore a feral grin.

"I intend to be sure that you take care of my son," El Rasho warned her.

"What makes you so sure it is a boy this time? It won't be my fault if the parasite is female."

"I don't hold with that old wives tale that the man's seed determines the sex. It is a tale put around by weak females who cannot produce a male child."

Maeven shrugged. "Well, if it survives nine months, we'll see. Will you be snuffing me out if it is a girl?"

"That would be more mercy than you deserve."

El Rasho turned and strode from the room. The wizard eyed her for a long moment before mouthing the words of a spell. The words were in Ciabolo's hissing tones, and Maeven felt a flush of heat as the spell settled on her. With a malicious grin, the hedge wizard, now brown eyed, followed El Rasho out.

"Well," Maeven murmured aloud. "I wish I knew what he said, and if its only about me getting exercise. That is what I wanted them to do, but I was thinking I could figure a counter spell. I will have to think on that..."

She repeated the words she had heard until she had them memorised, word perfect.

"So, he'll have to put a spell around anywhere he doesn't want a Thulan nosey-beak to go. That will tell me where I will want to be looking. So I will just have to see what the spell does, and then figure out how to change it a bit."

She didn't have long to wait. Soon after eating her small and plain midday meal, and right on when the hour chime resounded through the citadel, her feet began to move on their own accord and she was suddenly standing and marching on the spot. Her guards must have had instructions, for a moment later they opened her room, a sullen Jilli with them.

"Come on bitch. I'm supposed to see you have your walk."

"I'm ready. I hope you are fit enough to keep up!" Maeven headed to the door, and Jilli had to trot after her.

It was soon apparent that word of her pregnancy had got around. The servants they passed, would normally have turned their gaze down as soon as they saw people of high rank. Now, they saw her and they were staring at her as if she was the Queen of Vatarik. Or, it might have been they wanted to enjoy the sight of Jilli having to trot to keep up with her, and the scowl on her face. She was far from fit. It seemed she had done little exercise that wasn't horizontal, since she had arrived in Vatarik.

Maeven didn't slacken her pace, although she did wonder if she could.

"Are you going to slow down, Bitch?"

"Can't," Maeven called over her shoulder.

"Why are you going this way?"

"Why not?"

"Rashi's suite is this way."

"So? Then what is that chamber you and he usually..."

"Shut up! That was the old King's suite."

"Well, fancy that. I would've thought dear Rashi would have moved in there full time."

"He decided not to."

"I might see if he will let me have that suite now I am senior queen."

"You are nothing, bitch! Anyway, I doubt you'd last more than a night in there on your own."

"If he's not in there, I can't see a problem."

"That's just it, you can't see them."

"Them?"

"You'll be in trouble if you keep heading this way."

Maeven wanted to know more about the mysterious 'them', but decided Jilli wasn't going to say more. I might try to talk to the other wives, in the garden. Maybe they know something.

"Why would I be in trouble? That creepy wizard put this spell on me," Maeven said truthfully, and then added the lie, "I can't control my feet, or where I am going. Anyway, the gutless creep was told to make sure I couldn't go anywhere they didn't want me to be."

"Him? He's useless."

Maeven knew better, but since being back in Vatarik, she had pretended to be unaware that Ciabolo manifested through the creature when he chose. As if the hissing wasn't a dead giveaway. Or does Jilli really not know what is wearing the creature like a tunic?

It had been a pleasant discovery that she had not met a barrier while walking around. She had deliberately set out towards where she remembered El Haba's suite to be, assuming correctly that El Rasho's old suite was in the same area. She wasn't planning on actually trying to go in...not yet anyway.

A seemingly strangled sound made her slow slightly and turn around. One guard was trying to kick and punch air, as if something had stopped them.

"You can wait there," Maeven told them. "Jilli will make sure I keep away from the king's personal space."

"You'd better," Jilli muttered.

"Totally last place I want to be," Maeven assured her. "And I hope I don't have to hang around here. I am looking forward to resting in the garden. What else is in this slum corner of the place?"

"Nothing much. Empty rooms. The wizard's trophy room."

"Trophy's?"

"Lots of ghastly creatures, pinned to the wall. Oh, and there is a way down to the dungeons. The ones where they torture spies."

The shiver that went through Maeven was noticed by Jilli. "Want to go look there?"

"Oh, not today. Besides, I don't think the spell will let me go there."

Maeven decided it was time to get back to her guards, but she chose to go a different way back. She came to a door, and as she passed, her skin itched. She slowed.

"You said you didn't want to go there."

"Doubly no! That used to be his brother's room."

The guards were visibly relieved when she reappeared, and the two men moved so she could feel their breath on her neck. They directed her subtly by crowding her on the side where they didn't want her to turn. In that way, they were shepherded to the Garden of the Wives. Once they had gone in, the guards seemed less stiff. They did not come in, but passed on the responsibility for them to the Eunuch guards that emerged from their shelter. These huge men, naked to the waist, and showing off their bulging muscles, were the only ones allowed in the garden when any of the wives were there. They oversaw any servants that had to go in.

Maeven, still feeling the compulsion to walk, began a circuit of the garden. "You don't have to hang around," she suggested to Jilli. "I'll just be circling the garden until this damn spell stops."

"I may as well," Jilli said grumpily. "Rashi went off somewhere with that wizard."

Well, that was probably why my little experiment wasn't interrupted by their nastinesses, Maeven thought.

Putting a grin on her face to mask her sobering thoughts, she began a circuit of the garden, refreshing her memory from the last time she was there. She was also considering trying a little magic, and hoping she still had enough residual power to succeed.

"If you had to walk around this mausoleum, where would you prefer to go?" Maeven asked Jilli.

"Here, and I wouldn't be ruining my feet with walking."

"Alright, where do you think I should go?"

"In the east wing. That's where all the women live and they have indoor galleries."

Maeven hid a grin and silently mouthed the words of a spell. "In the space of thirty heartbeats, you will forget where we went today and recall only going where the wives are allowed."

For a moment, she considered being more detailed, but it was probably better if Jilli came up with the where.

Maeven tried a test. "I'm surprised we didn't see anyone else in the galleries."

"You wouldn't. Between the second and third chime, the wives have an afternoon sleep. Most of the servants do too."

"Why don't you?"

"Same reason as you. We came from Thulor. Besides, I'm not a servant. And I'm Rashi's favourite, not one of the wives."

That sounded to Maeven like Jilli thought she was above the wives. Well, she could think what she wanted. She was doing the duty of a wife, and maybe, the spell thought she was one. Perhaps that was why she was able to go where her guards couldn't...because even though it should have been off-limits, she was with one of the other 'wives', even if it was one who was allowed in more places. Did Ciabolo have a false idea about Jilli?

"Where should I try to walk tomorrow," Maeven asked. "The galleries again?"

"Why should I care?"

When Maeven finished her first circuit, Jilli left her to go and collapse on one of the reclining lounges. That suited her, and when she was a little distance way, although still in sight, she slowed her pace. She still couldn't stop, but if she kept moving, the spell did nothing to force her faster. With a hand down beside her, as if she had put it in the pocket of a pair of her altered men's breeches, and picturing the action in her mind, she cupped an invisible pouch. Then she murmured a spell that would enable her to bring that item out into sight. The pouch materialised from that 'there but not there' place her spell had put it.

Keeping her hands out of sight of the eunuch guards that were watching her, and from Jilli too, Maeven took a pinch of grainy pulverised dragon shell from the pouch, put it into her mouth and then re-hid the pouch. Back where Jilli was, she took up a glass of water that had been placed by a servant since she'd been there last, and washed the stuff down her throat, as she moved on.

Immediately, she felt a sensation like a cooling breeze inside her, and maybe coincidently, she stopped walking.

Jilli began to rant at her for taking her drink. Maeven ignored her and pretended to walk off, murmuring a repeat of the spell she put on Jilli, to be sure it worked, and to specify that she be vague about where they had walked, and to say that they had been stopped by something and went somewhere else, ending up in the garden. Jilli grunted, and murmured something akin to what she had been told in the spell. Then, Maeven finished with, "When I count to three, you will remember what I said and forget that I took your drink."

Maeven went off to stroll across the garden, and glanced back to see JIlli reach for the half-filled water goblet and refill the glass for herself. She grinned when Jilli drank from it, when normally she would not. Well, it served her right. She should have told the servant to leave two glasses.

As if the spell had finally worn off, Maeven turned back and went to collapse on a second of the lounges, with an audible sigh of relief. Jilli snickered, and made rude remarks, but they were ignored. Maeven was only acting as others would expect. In fact, after swallowing the shell grit, she had felt herself re-energised. While she was allowed to rest there for a while, she rehearsed the words she would use to form a spell on the guards. She doubted that Jilli would want to stay there much longer, but that wasn't a problem. Maeven had decided she was going to act exhausted, for Jilli would report that to El Rasho as soon as she could, and he would smirk and feel he had made her day miserable.

Jilli only gave her five minutes to rest before jumping up and stating, "You've done your exercise. Time you were back in your cage. Come on!"

As if it was an effort Maeven rose, watched by the eunuch guards. They turned to go back to their well-hidden quarters once the women were out the gate and in the aegis of the King's Guards.

"Take her back where she belongs," Jilli ordered before flouncing off.

Maeven went deliberately slow, until she was out of sight, then stopped and looked at the sole of one of her feet. "I'm going to have blisters," she said to no one in particular. It made the two guards chuckle. With their mind distracted, they didn't hear her murmur her spell to make them forget they had not had their eyes on her all the time during the earlier part of the hour. "You will say that you followed me to that barrier, I could not pass it, and then I found my way to the garden and went in there."

The two be-spelled men, repeated what she had said. Then heard, "You do not want to say I went beyond, it will mean harsh punishment."

Both men, like rigid statues, shuddered, and Maeven ended the spell, and was back to walking slowly when they returned to awareness.

Once back in her room, she let them see her collapse onto her bed, as if exhausted. They too could report that she had no energy left, and had fallen asleep.

In fact, she was far from wanting to sleep. Let El Rasho gloat if he wanted too. Her initial survey had given her plenty of ideas on how to manipulate her circumstances. Things she was taught by her former thief master, Nayfor, were already filling her head. She was already getting wizard and king to thinking one way, when the truth of how she felt was altogether different...and now she knew places she wanted to check out. They would have to be tried when she knew the king and wizard were away.

If she were found in forbidden areas, she would need some excellent reasons, like, "I can't control where I go. I have to force myself to go elsewhere." Or, "I thought I was only allowed to go where wives go. It must be because Jilli comes here."

Amusement bubbled inside her.

CHAPTER 32 – Leanne and Finora

A minor altercation drew Leanne's eyes to the edge of the camp where her troop were settling back into their tents. She wanted a wash, but as was her habit, she let her sister do so first, while she ensured all was well in the camp.

Heading to where she heard shouting, she caught sight of two figures running away, towards the creek. Several of her troop took off after them. They had come from the direction of the supply tent. By the time she walked there, she heard cursing as two captives were alternately shoved and dragged back to the camp.

Checking first to see if the supply tent's lock had been damaged or broken, she strolled over to where the two captives were sprawled on the ground and ringed by armed men. She made no secret of studying the pair. Both were young, tallish, but gaunt and pale, despite the grime that suggested they hadn't washed in a month. One moved to hold his leg, as if it pained him. The other glared back at everyone, angry it seemed, at being caught.

Setto, one of the older troopers, said, "Captain, I saw these going through my tent."

The eyes of both of the men, really more like boys, widened when they realised she was the captain that they'd been told would have them beaten.

The one with the uninjured leg, rolled, crouched and threw himself at her feet. "Mercy, Captain. We beg your help."

Rough hands dragged him back. "None of that, Sonny! Do ye know who's feet you are soiling?"

"Enough, Setto. Help them into the clearing." When she saw one of the two helping the other, she added, "Gently."

She turned and strode that way, but decided to detour via the tent she and Finora shared.

Putting her head through the flap, she spoke to her twin. "Fi? Sorry, but I need you outside."

Finora, already preparing for her bath, redressed in a long over robe and came out. By then, the two captives had been sat down on a large log, and the men surrounding them had grown to most of the camp.

"Have you searched them?" Leanne asked.

Nelsi, moved closer to Leanne and showed her a knife. One of the boys suddenly felt around his ankle, and his face went red and then paled.

"It has the crest of Lord Vivarin," Finora murmured.

Turning, Leanne said, "His manor is in the south. So how did this get up here? These two don't look like brigands." Finora shrugged slightly.

Leanne asked the question of the captives. "This knife belongs to one of the King's Lords. How did you come by it?"

Now both where chalk white in the face. "We didn't steal it," the slightly taller, possibly older one, insisted immediately. "We was given it. So we could escape."

"From where?" Leanne pressed.

"From our folk's root cellar," was the unexpectedly candid reply. "Can I get some water? My brother's been sick and feverish these past few days."

Leanne nodded. One of the camp orderlies trotted off. "Perhaps you should start at the beginning. Why were you in the cellar?"

It only took the mention of a group of brigands riding into the yard of their farm for everyone in earshot to suddenly become still and intent.

"Our older brother tried to ride off for help, but an arrow got him before he got out the gate. We was grabbed too, and the leader called to his wizard. They put some spell on the old folks, and they stopped struggling and became all quiet and docile. They acted real stupid and dull witted."

"And what about you. Did they try it on you?" Finora asked, and she saw the boys eyes go wide again. He did know who she and Leanne were.

"Think so, but we could still struggle, and we got free. Tried to run for it, but more of the bastards came out of everywhere. Brit and me, we tried still, but one hit Brit and he was out cold. I couldn't leave him. Then we was tied up and taken inside, and shoved down into the cellar. Brit fell and broke his leg."

"And one gave you this knife?" Nelsi placed a subtle emphasis on the word 'gave'. Leanne recalled that as a master thief, Nelsi did not treat unaffiliated thieves with sympathy.

"That was later. Don't know how later. We was kept in the dark for so long."

"Can you describe the one that gave it to you?" Leanne asked, her tone gentler than it had been. She now had the knife in her hand.

"No, Mam. It's as dark as a pit in the cellar. But...his voice sounded young, about our age. He got shoved down the stairs too, and musta knocked himself out. We thought he was dead, it took so long for him to wake up."

"He was one of them. The brigands," Brit finally spoke up. "Said they had some tether thing on him, like our folks got. But...he did something and my leg stopped hurting so much and it was less broken. We couldn't have got away before that, though I told Alec to go without me. But he wouldn't."

"How did you get out?" Leanne asked as if casually interested.

"Cellar has another opening," Alec said. "Comes in from near the fields. Once we got the ropes cut, we went that way, but we waited until dark. We've been looking for help since, but we keep needing to hide from chancy looking people, like those at the farm."

"You were lucky then," Leanne commented.

"We's good at hunting," Brit said proudly.

"But with all those strangers, no game stayed around. We had to act like hoppers and burrow out of sight."

"Can you tell us where your farm is?" Finora asked.

"You will come to help us?" Brit blurted. "They was eyeing out Mam and sis in a nasty way..."

Alec nudged his brother, and said, "The farm's out from Rowan Flat, near the Red creek."

"How long have you been running?" Leanne asked. "That is over a week's hard ride from here."

"We's couldn't go fast," Brit hung his head. "My leg's not so strong yet, and we had to find food, and keep hiding. You've got to help our folks. You're King's Guards, aren't you? That's your job isn't it?"

Alec, now staring at the ground, said, "They might be dead by now. The one who helped us said our sister was."

"We are part of the army. We're on border patrol," Leanne told him. "And yes, we are hunting brigands. We will help your folks, but not right away. We have business around here to finish first."

"But you have to..." Brit said, eyes watering.

Finora spoke gently. "We will have to hope they want them as servants. If, as you say, they were made docile, it will be some protection. They won't try to get away, or fight them. Are you hungry?"

That question distracted both young men. Their stomach's growled in unison.

"We will get you something for now, and later you can share our fire and meal," Finora promised. "Now, please wait here. I might be able to do something about that leg."

The camp orderly returned with journey bread, cheese and apples. Both young men grabbed from the tray as soon as the orderly moved away. Leanne gestured to her twin and they moved away. Nelsi received a nod from Leanne. He would ensure they were still guarded, but also try to see what else he could get from them.

When they were out of earshot, Leanne asked her twin, "Did you pick up anything?"

"They are what they say they are, and look like."

"So, is that another lot, or are they the ones Nelsi saw, but have moved on?"

Finora considered. "Likely another group. We know many groups came up here, and from what we have been seeing lately, they each have claimed a stretch of territory. I had the impression from the older boy that they were tied up for two or three weeks. And they haven't been travelling very fast to get here."

"So one lot of the influx of brigands decided to use that farm as a base. Lazy bastards. I will send a rider to Langdon's group. They are nearest, and can get there and have a look."

"I'll see if they will talk freely to me. They recognised us."

Nelsi watched the boys eat. "Seems like you ain't eaten food for a week."

"Mmm, only some old berries," Brit said with mouth half full. "Them brigand bastards hardly gave us any food."

"I'm surprised they didn't just kill you when they couldn't tether you."

Brit just shrugged and kept stuffing his mouth.

When Alec had finished his mouthful, Nelsi asked, "Tell me about your folks. Are they smart?"

"I suppose so. Pa always seems to know what needs to be done," Alec considered. "The farm does well enough."

"That might be why those vermin decided to move in. Were they both born around here?"

"Lots of folk know them both when we take stuff to market," Brit mumbled, still chewing.

"Actually, I think Pa came from the south somewhere." Alec had a thoughtful expression. "I remember some woman come...his sister, I think. She knew lots about animals. Told Pa things to try to make then fatter for the market, and how to raise the orphan sheep. Some folk thought they were right crazy for trying it because no one had ever done them."

"Do you recall her name?"

"Too long ago. Seems all I recall is it was long," Alec said.

Since Finora was heading back with a healer's kit and bandages, Nelsi stopped his questions. Already he had an idea. The farmer might have been from down near Declanor, the sister might have been one of the reclusive Dragon Priestesses – he didn't know enough about them.

"Olaf, our healer will be here shortly," Finora said with a cheerful lilt. "But if you have been able to walk at all, that bone must have begun to heal. Olaf will be able to tell if the mend is straight."

Brit swallowed and said, "It still hurts. When I can, I've used a stick to help me keep off it, but we've had to run a bit."

"Let's hope you haven't added to the damage."

Olaf, still dusty from their recent engagement, came from the tent of one of the men who had been injured in an earlier fight. At least there had been no deaths or serious injuries that day. The encampment had been small, and taken totally by surprise. All had surrendered and were now going to be working for Lord Edgent as field labourers.

Brit, having helped finish off the last of the food, obediently lay down so Olaf could examine his injured leg. Even though he was gentle, when he reached the sight of the break, Brit yelped. Olaf kept his hand there, and seemed to go off into a trance.

"The bone has fused back into place, but the muscle around the break has taken damage. I am told you had some healing done already?"

Brit repeated the story he had told Finora.

"Well, lie still. I am going to do more of that."

Finora put one hand on the shoulder of the kneeling medic, and the other clutched her hidden talisman.

Brit had closed his eyes, but after a moment, they flew open. Alec, peering with concern at the proceedings, asked, "What's wrong?"

"I feel it again."

"What?" Finora asked.

"Like a cool breeze is inside me."

"It's just the healing," Finora assured him.

"But before, when I was little and needed healing, it always felt warm."

"I see," Finora remarked. "It might be because I'm a sorceress, adding my power to Olaf's."

Brit's eyes widened and Alec moved uneasily. "You do magic? Then the kid must have been too."

"Kid?" Finora queried.

Alec explained, "Brit and I kept making up nasty names for the brigands. We called them goats, and the boy was a kid – a young goat."

"Anyway," Brit interrupted, "before we went out, like I said, he did some healing on my leg so I could at least walk."

He watched as the healer and sorceress gave each other an unfathomable look. "What did I say?"

"Are you sure it was a young man who helped you? Not a woman? You said it was pitch dark," Finora asked.

"It was," Alec insisted. "When they did decide to give us food, they had a really dim torch, but we had a glimpse of him then."

"Did that rabble have women with them?"

"Didn't see any," Alec said, and Brit nodded agreement. "We was surprised to see woman fighters with you."

"Young man! If you don't keep still, your leg might heal, but be twisted," Olaf growled.

Brit subsided, but Alec demanded, "Why aren't you going to ride straight out and get those brigands?"

"Steady, lad," Finora urged. "Captain Leanne has sent a message rider to another lot of King's Troops, that are closer to your farm. They will scout the area and report back."

"But out Ma and Pa…" Brit pleaded.

"We will do ourselves no favours rushing off without preparation," Finora told him. "Plus, we have just got back from clearing out another nest of traitors. Some of our people have minor injuries, and all of us deserve a decent supper."

A new voice had Alec twisting, and Brit wanting to. "And we are not finished here," Leanne told them. "We found a camp where they were training peasant farmers, some even younger than you pair, to fight against Thulor. However, those that give the orders must have got warning and taken off. I want them. And, if Langdon can't handle things at your farm, I will hear about it."

"But what if they kill the one that helped us?" Alec asked. "He can't have been really one of them."

"They get given the option to surrender," Leanne said, not adding that the poor magicked ones had no mind of their own to choose with.

"What if they make him fight? Even if he don't want to?"

No one answered that question. It was an all too real possibility.

"Let us worry about that," Leanne said finally.

CHAPTER 33 – Leanne and Finora

The small scouting party of King's Troopers withdrew to their forward camp. Captain Langdon dismounted and helped Alec down from behind him. "See what I mean? The place looks deserted."

Leanne asked Alec, and Brit who had ridden behind her, "Did you notice anything out of the ordinary?"

Both boys considered and shook their heads. "Looks like it ought to at this time of year," Brit said.

"Well, if that rabble has been there a while, making your Ma and Pa slaves, who would be tending the fields? That kind of rabble don't want to do honest work," Langdon said bluntly.

"But it does look like it should."

"Have you been having trouble with that purple weed up this far?" Finora asked.

Two voices said, "Oh!"

Leanne nodded. "Fi, did you see any signs of illusions or other magic?"

"Just that barrier. A hedge wizard could do that field illusion with very little power."

"Can you take that barrier down?" Leanne asked her twin.

"Do you think they are still there?" Langdon demanded before Finora could answer.

"I am sure," Finora asserted. "That barrier is not the work of a hedge wizard. It keeps people in and stops others coming in. It the rabble were not still there, why waste the magic? And the two boys came out – it can't have been there then."

"Your scouts might have been spotted, Lang," Leanne suggested. "They might have been on edge since the lads escaped."

"You are probably right," Langdon agreed. "It makes sense that they left the scouts alone, knowing that the barrier would deflect almost everyone around it."

"Sense, yes..." Leanne mused. She turned to the boys. "Where did you say that cellar came out?"

"In the back paddock, at the back of the shed," Alec said.

"When was it last used?"

"Last harvest. That field was ploughed and left fallow."

Leanne nodded, keeping her thoughts to herself.

"I wonder what would happen if an innocent traveller came looking for eggs of something?"

No one answered, and the lads forgot the idea when Leanne said "Go off and get fed."

Once the boys were out of earshot, Leanne outlined her plan.

"Lang, can you find a suitably dull looking peasant to go and try to buy some eggs or something? Not right away, we will let them have the idea we have gone first."

"I've the very person," Lang assured her.

"Good. I also want you to keep an infrequent check on the place. From the road. Just one scout, like you think the family have just gone away for a few days and you expect them back any time."

"I can get one of the juniors to do that," Langdon agreed. "Do you think the whole lot are holed up in there, waiting for us to lose interest?"

"Holed up? Probably. It is debatable as to whether they think we will lose interest. I want them to think we didn't see anything suspicious and are not thinking of going right in to be sure no one needs help. I don't think they will want to leave their comfortable camping place and go back to toughing it. I also can't see them lying low for too long. The real master behind these bastards wants maximum activity, preying on locals to keep us busy, and seeing how many of our farmers they can enthral for the enemy's army. This lot will be wanting to amass wealth for themselves too, not to mention that they will need food. If they use up any supplies here, they will have to go out for more – unless they are being supplied like they were in the south, and being supplied here."

"It would be good if we had them too afraid to come out," Langdon sighed. "Was there more?"

"That back paddock, has been tramped around since it was ploughed. It wouldn't surprise me if they discovered the tunnel and are using it themselves. Any activity there won't be seen from the road. I want to sneak two or three people in to look around. At that time, I'll get you to be more visible out on the road. They will have to keep their attention on you."

"They'll be sure to have scouts outside the barrier," Langdon warned, but Leanne just nodded.

Finora added, "If they are going in and out, still doing raids, they will probably have at least some of their horses kept outside the barrier."

"I will make sure my scouts are aware of that," Leanne said. "Lang, if you find out anything more, send a report. Otherwise, report in seven days. Once I bring the rest of my troop up, we will go in."

Langdon remounted and rode off, and after he was gone, Nelsi sidled up to his Captain.

"There were watchers on us," he reported. "I think one followed us."

Leanne smiled grimly. "Well then, we will strike camp, and head back to our main camp – all nice and leisurely, as if this was a dead end."

The main camp was being struck, when the dusty messenger arrived. He was on foot, but not so out of breath as to have travelled all the way on his feet. Nelsi made a quick sign as the man looked around, and as the man headed for the command tent, he caught up.

"I'll show you the way," Nelsi offered, to the dull witted, seeming peasant. The man could act that way, very well, but he was actually another guild bonded thief.

"What did you see?" Nelsi asked in a low voice.

"They have guards around the tunnel end, right enough. Some have come out on horses, from near the shed. They've some sort of signal when they want back in."

"Did you see the barrier come down?"

"Yes, but only in a small section between the shed and the tree on the right. It's like your lady thought. That back paddock, the real place, is full of the weed, until the barrier goes back."

"What about the signal?"

"They seemed to pull on something. Heard a bell ring, way off. Reckon its just a bit of rope strung from there to near the house."

"You game to go in?" Nelsi asked.

"Too right!"

Leanne felt exposed without her twin watching her back, but Finora had a more important task. She had at least placed a glamour on the six who were to penetrate the house through the tunnel. Thanks to Nelsi, the messenger Ronan, and one of their newest recruits, they knew what to expect in the house.

The leader and his servant slept in the main bedroom. The wizard in the one that had been the eldest boy's. Only one other slept in the house, likely the second in charge. The rest of the rabble, Nelsi had counted twelve ruffians and two dozen bespelled farm boys, were spread out by the river, under trees, in sheds or the stables. Her troop had an excellent mental map of the farm and where the supplies were kept.

Their first task had been easy. The four men meant to be guarding the tunnel entrance had been asleep, and were now trussed and gagged and hidden in a grove of trees, a distance from the farm boundary.

Finora had neutralised the small section of the barrier used to get horses in and out. It also revealed the tunnel entrance, allowing Leanne and her small group to enter the tunnel. They were invisible, but had to move quietly, and at that hour, two hours before dawn, they encountered no one in the narrow passage way.

They came to the huge trap door that led up to the kitchen, and Leanne waited there until the nudge of a thought from her twin told her the full barrier was down. At that moment, three dozen mounted troopers began a noisy charge towards the house and Leanne's group swarmed into the kitchen and quickly spread out through the house.

A swarthy man charged out of one of the bedrooms. He ran straight into an invisible trooper. The confusion was momentary, a second ruffian guessed accurately and stabbed at the unseen assailant, who became visible as he died.

Outside, shouts, screams and the clash of metal weapons, indicated that the mounted troops were engaging the newly roused men.

Leanne went after the man who had killed her trooper, and quickly realised that something had neutralised the glamour. She had seen him send off a runner, a young slender boy, who appeared to be unarmed. He called out to another, and something unseen seemed to explode, the pressure wave blowing her into a wall, and darkness threatened to overcome her. She reached for her talisman and drew on its power to regain some strength. She had just enough energy to roll as the brigand slashed with his sword.

Somehow, instead of piercing her side where the two parts of the leather armour joined, it slid between hr and the armour at the front. She felt blood oozing out and feigned dead. As she lay still, calling on more of the power of the talisman to help her heal, and some to repel her attacker, she heard the man cursing her for an unnatural bitch, then calling for someone as he ran out the door. Leanne thought urgently of the need to be back up and fighting – the cool breeze increased on strength, her energy returned.

Finora's concern came sharply. "I'm okay," she thought back. "What's happening?"

"A lot of the rabble are racing for the stables. Langdon is sending men to surround it. The rest are fighting the green farm boys who must have been magicked because they are acting like berserkers."

Leanne recovered her weapon and raced out, heading for the stables. She saw Nelsi, waiting out of sight, and called, "Tell the troops to stun, not kill, those poor lads if they can."

"The sorceress is planning something," Nelsi called back.

"And so is their wizard that stable door is glowing," Leanne called a general warning. She neared the stable and called, "I want that door open, use a wooden battering ram."

Six troopers dismounted, kicked at a horizontal fence rail that was once the trunk of a slender tree – six inches in diameter.

External to her current purpose, Leanne was aware that the noise of fighting was quietening as the farm boys were stunned unconscious. Berserker or not, they were no match for the highly trained fighters.

The stable door went down, Leanne led her troops inside, saw a man on a horse and went for him. He whirled his horse, blocking her attack with skilled sword work.

He yelled, "Boy! Get the wizard away."

A second horse trotted to where a cowled man was swaying on his feet. The rider looked like the messenger that had gone off from the house, and he reached the man whose hands were glowing as he chanted some spell. One of the troopers picked up some half dried dung from the floor and hurled it. The wizard was distracted for a moment, and a blast of power came at him from the door way, causing the boy to cover his eyes and the air around the wizard to glow. Finora, clad in tunic and britches, with the glow reflecting off the earrings of her profession, came into sight, but before she could send a second blast or construct a barrier, the wizard sent a blast of his own. He began laughing as all the invading fighters went down.

Leanne tried to get right back up, fighting some sort of invisible tangling. She was aware of the boy on the horse trying to get him up on his horse, and the leader yelling, "GO, go, go!"

Only then did she see the flare of green light that was a demon portal. All the horses that had brigands on their backs, raced into the green fire, telling her that they had lost their fear of the strange manifestation.

Finora, having partly replaced her magical energy, recovered first. She knew her twin was alive, so she checked the other five men first. Alive, stunned and already stirring. Then she went to her twin.

Leanne was trying to catch her breath and Finora helped her sit up. She saw the green fire, already fading to weird embers. "Any chance of getting through that?"

"Not if you are sensible," Finora told her. "We don't know enough about demon portals to be sure we would come out in the same place. And you had better believe they will have guards where they emerge, in case we did. Are you hurt?"

"Just a scratch," Leanne said. In the intensity of the fight, she had forgotten the earlier wound. It wasn't hurting her. More men were entering the stable and Leanne called out, "Seal that fireplace, and make sure all other fires are out and drenched. I don't want them to sneak back here to get us. Where is Nels?"

"Here, Captain," he called, soberly. He was coming back from taking one of the dead troopers into the house.

"What's the damage?" Leanne asked.

"Four of us dead. Six of the farm lads. We have the rest disarmed and under guard. The owners, husband and wife, were hiding in a cupboard."

"How are they?"

"Confused. I don't think they recall much of what happened since the rabble came."

"Where's Langdon?"

"Out doing a thorough foray – making sure we have them all."

"When you see him, tell him I want a report."

Finora added. "And he is in charge until I see to the Captain's wounds, and she has rested."

"What? I'm okay," Leanne argued.

"Look at your tunic and tell me that again," her twin countered. "I reckon that bastard got you. I can't tell how bad, or where until you get that armour off. And your eyes aren't quite focussing, are they? What happened in the house?" She was helping her twin limp towards the house.

"That damn wizard blasted me into a wall," Leanne recalled.

"No finesse that man. Brute force only," Finora growled. "I don't think that outer barrier is still up, although I haven't checked. Before he went, that wizard was getting magic returning from somewhere. He was glowing."

"Do you think they will have left any traps behind?"

"Not magic ones. I reckon he must have been pulling magic from all the protections. Others? Probably not. The rabble moved around freely, and after you attacked, there was no time. We caught them sleeping. Lang knows to look for physical traps, and I will look around later – just in case."

"I'll be fine for a time," Leanne said. "Get me to the house and I will sit near the door, to see what is happening."

"You need to move as little as possible," Finora stressed, and she caught Nelsi's eye and ne nodded. "I want to check over those farm boys. Check they don't still have spells on them."

Colour and sense were returning to the faces of the farmer and his wife. They came out and were huddled on the same long seat as Leanne.

"Couldn't leave, we couldn't," the farmer said. "I could only go as far as stable, and the nearer sheds. Couldn't go inside. Wife couldn't go further than the pump. Bastards, one or nother, had her every night, And our girl..." he began to cry.

Tears were falling down the wife's face too. She was looking around, as if to see her.

"We can't find her. Did they take her with them?"

"No," Leanne said immediately. She saw Nels's face as he shook his head, then shrugged in the direction of Langdon.

Leanne gestured the other troop leader over, and asked the question.

"I'm really sorry, Sir, Mam, We found the lass's body, out beyond the stable. We have wrapped her properly and placed her in the room that had been hers. We can help you with the burying."

The woman began to cry softly, and the man's eyes were watering. "Our boys? What about them? They were put in the cellar."

Leanne smiled. "They got out and found us. Now things are clear here we will send for them."

"And our older boy? Did you find him? He rode to get help. They shot him. Did you find him?" the farmer asked.

"We will look," Langdon promised.

"I'll go with ye," the man insisted. "I saw where he fell down. Though I don't know that I want to stay here now. What if them ruffians come back?"

"Where would we go, Mattis? This is your land, been in the family since you grandsire won it."

"But Bessie, think of all we've been through."

"I won't think of it! Other women have had to marry brutes, and endure it every night. Them's gone now, and at least I have a kind, loving husband. And women go through worse'n that bearing their man's littles. Least, I'm beyond that now."

Langdon coughed politely. "I was going to ask if my troop be allowed to base ourselves here. We won't be any trouble. We get our own supplies, plus the rabble left a lot of stuff in the sheds. And, in quiet times, if we be so lucky, some of my lads were farmers and they could help ye."

"What of our cow, and the chickens?" Bessie asked.

"The cow is with the horses. At least one of the rabble appreciated its value. The chickens...no idea. Either eaten or fled."

"Bessie be right. This be my place, and I'd be right glad to have you here," Mattis agreed.

"Great!" Langon told him. "You and I can discuss a stipend, later."

"I heard your lads talking," Bessie said then. She wiped her eyes with the very dirty sleeve of her over gown. "This lot that was here, was only one of many. Will other lots arrive?"

Leanne leant back, feeling her left side stiffening up under

Finora's herb infused bandages. "Yes, there are still a lot of little and not so little bands around, although we and other troops have been hunting them and have captured quite a few. However, I would be remiss if I said you would be fully safe. In general, things are likely to get worse in the near future. We think Vatarik will be bringing an army into Thulor, somewhere along this northern border. It would pay for you, and others like you, to store what non-perishable foods you have, and have them well hid."

CHAPTER 34 - Del

Vorman spared no mercy for the King's trooper he'd killed. He ran for room he'd been sleeping in and kicked Del awake. "Grab my stuff, boy. We're leaving."

Hearing shouts, screams and the clashing of metal swords, Del guessed why. He was already shoving the few things Vorman had out of his pack, back into it, even though he had not consciously told himself to do it.

He, like all the band, slept in his day clothes. It wasn't the first time they'd had to run at a moment's warning. He himself owned little of value, except his medicines and healing kit. These were together in a small bag with the coins Vorman had given him before they came north. The command now on him allowed him to get those too, since he told himself Vorman valued them. The chief was already yelling for his wizard, a new addition to the group, and probably the reason why Del felt had had no control over himself. Vorman's horrid amulet, only had the power to keep him close.

Del hefted Vorman's heavy pack onto one shoulder, and grabbed his own. It slowed him down, so he couldn't race for the kitchen as his body wanted to do. Reaching there, he saw a head starting to rise from the cellar and he dodged to the laundry, currently deserted, and paused to see what was between him and the stables. He hurried as best he could, obeying the nuance of the command, to keep to cover. He also somehow knew he had to go and saddle as many of the horses as he could. Naturally, the first ones were to be Vorman's, the wizards and his own. Obviously, Vorman had no stomach to fight an overwhelming number of King's Troops. He might boast he could beat any dozen of them...

Del heard Vorman yell an order to the new fighters. "Kill! Kill the intruders."

His words rang with the amplification of magic.

Fighters? Those poor kids knew less of fighting than he did.

Then Del heard a single clear note from Usif's horn. Withdraw! He's leaving those poor farm lads to be slaughtered, he thought with despair. Only so much a fight spell can do for them.

The two dozen recent conscripts had barely learnt how to hold a sword, let alone use it.

In twos and threes, Vorman's original rabble, and the louts he'd attracted since being there, raced into the stable. They began saddling their favourite beasts. Vorman came in last, dragging the wizard.

"Get the portal open!" Vorman yelled into his ear. "To the fall back camp."

He seemed to shake the wizard, who turned and directed muttering and gestures towards the rear of the stable. A blaze of green fire, suddenly erupted. The newer horses, recently acquired, began to snort and whinny, causing their current riders to rein them harshly. They settled only a little when directed to follow the horses that were now familiar with the cool fire.

The wizard went back to what he had been doing. Vorman, now astride his dark brown stallion, held him upright. "Hurry, man!" he was urging.

The wizard kept muttering, making gestures with his hands, pointing in all directions as if calling or gathering something.

Outside the stable, the sounds of fighting were decreasing, and a glow was increasing in the area of the closed wooden door.

Just as a loud regular battering began, Vorman repeated his urging. The wizard was jerking, and beginning to glow!

Del waited near the fire, the strange space warping portal he had hoped never to venture through again. Things happened quickly then. The door to the stable flew open, half a dozen well-armed and armoured fighters raced in. The leader was a woman, and Vorman cursed. Vorman whirled his horse, sword already drawn, and took the woman on.

"Boy! Get the wizard away."

Del rode his horse to where the wizard was teetering, and prayed the man could get himself up between himself and Vormans pack. He did. Del felt his skin burn as the wizard hurled a bolt of magical power the fighters. They went down. Vorman roared, "GO!"

If he had his own will, Del might have tried to surrender, and even that brief pause caused pain along his nerves. It was a sensation he had long associated with Vorman's amulet.

Just before he spurred his horse into the fire, he saw a brilliant flash of white. Then he was through the fire, racing along a narrow canyon with Vorman's beast right behind. The wizard was now like a dead weight on is back.

The canyon widened, Del slowed his horse, and Vorman reined his in alongside. He reached over to shake the wizard. Getting no response, he cursed and roared, "Six of you lot go and guard the fire pit. The rest of you, set a watch on the road entrance."

The men raced to obey, and Vorman reached for the loose tunic of the wizard and dragged him off Del, and barely holding him so he didn't fall too hard from the horse.

"Get him to one of the caves, boy. When he wakes up, he's to put his wards around this camp."

Then Vorman seemed to contradict himself. "See to the horses first, Boy. Leave them saddled for now, just in case. I don't know what those two damn bitches can do."

Del who had dismounted, stared at Vorman. Had he heard right? Did Vorman run from a couple of women?

"Unnatural bitches," he cursed under his breath as he stared around. "How did they find the way in? Those wretches must have found them. I should have killed them!" He swivelled and eyed Del. "This is your fault, boy! Somehow, you helped those wretches escape. Well? What are you waiting for? The beating you deserve?"

With a shake of his head, Del too the reins of the two horses. There was a small corral not far away with some late season grass. He'd have to fetch water from the trickle stream to fill the trough. Freeing the horses, he retreated through the gate and lifted the log back onto the y-shaped supports.

On the way to check which cave to put the wizard in, Del noticed Vorman pacing up and down a stretch of road, an angry frown on his face, and still muttering.

Vorman's compulsion had lost much of its force now, and Del's mind gave him some malicious pleasure.

Reckon he's trying to think what to say to that creepy noble patron. Won't be that he ran away from a bitch fighter, just because the other bitch got the better of him. Not that he left two dozen mindless farm boys to cover his retreat. Probably he'll complain of how useless they were. Glad I ain't him right now.

Del sobered quickly. He probably wouldn't want to be himself later, if Vorman needed a punching bag to relieve anger.

"Might as well start a cook fire," he considered. "Bring out some of the stored, dried meat and tubers and add some of my herbs... and get some of the stored ale out, and add something there too. Can't hurt..."

Del curled up into as small a huddle as he could. Which wasn't as small as once possible. He didn't want to be seen hiding behind the scrubby bushes, but he couldn't see if he had to keep his head down. He would be fine there, so long as Vorman kept pacing just on the other side. Vorman had not let him get further than five feet from him since they had come to the canyon. It made using the privy pit awkward. He had to go when the chief did.

His herbs had helped that first night, it had curbed Vorman's temper. Since then, his anger had simmered, and he always seemed to be muttering to himself. Del had heard enough to know he was rehearsing his excuses for the...he wasn't calling it a defeat, but a cautionary retreat. Likely, his noble patron would still be angry, but maybe less so when he saw the gifts Vorman had for him. He had fluked two very lucrative ambushes. He hadn't wanted to summon his foreign patron until then.

Del felt his talisman becoming hot, and risked a peek. As he expected, the bonfire in the fire pit had changed from orange to green. He likened it as an open door from the pit of hell.

Only Vorman and Usif, were in sight. The others had made themselves scarce, and Del wished he could. He hid his head until he heard the snorting of two horses, as they reared briefly, after coming through the flame.

To give the chief credit, he stood his ground and betrayed no fear as the tall black haired foreigner swung from his horse and strode towards him. Del could see a faint glow about him, and felt the tingle of magic. He tightened his grip on his talisman and thought – let me see what he truly looks like.

The showy display of athletic health, was an illusion. The man was overweight, and flabby, but even so, he still gave of the sense of power. Not magical, but as if he had the right to absolute rule. Or believed he did.

Talking into Vorman's face, the new arrival challenged, "Why did you call me here, to this barbaric backwater? What is so important?"

Del risked another look. The wizard with the orange eyes, was watching and listening intently, still on his horse.

"As you can see, Lord, we had to move," Vorman said as if it was no matter. "Please, rest. These logs are of a comfortable height. Boy! Refreshments."

Del felt the pull and obeyed. He found he could move further away now, but only to where he had been told to put a bottle of the wine they had recently acquired and the freshest sweet candies taken in the same raid. He hoped he would not have to serve it, but he doubted he could avoid it. He gathered the serving plate and the three glasses and brought everything to the section of flattened log that served as a table. All the while avoiding looking towards the visitors.

He returned to hear soft, venomous words, almost hissing. "So, the leader was a woman, an unnatural female, and protected by a sorceress... Tell me more."

Del put wine beside both visitors. The noble sampled it at once, but the wizard was intent on the report. Vorman stated facts, although phrased to put him in a better light. He let his anger and dislike of the women show, not quite demanding his patron do something about them.

The noble put down his wine with a force that would have broken the cup had it been glass. "I know those bitches. They are your King's unnatural issue." His anger at some memory seemed to resonate with Vorman's.

The other, the wizard, said, "So, they are around here. We will pay you well if you can capture them. Continue with your report."

Vorman continued to tell of the rout, and the logic of preserving experienced fighters, at the expense of green farm boys was not questioned.

When the discussion paused, Del heard, "You! Boy! How do you think they did it?"

He looked up, saw the orange eyes on him. He stammered out the first thing that came into his head. "We was asleep, near morning. They musta found a way in through the cellar."

"Did you know about that way?"

Something clamped his tongue until he had a safe answer. He hoped he looked stupid.

"Only thought roots be in cellar."

"You even been in there?"

"Only once," admitted in a small voice. He guessed they were wondering if he'd let the boys loose.

Vorman smirked, and explained. "The little twat got drunk, and needed a lesson."

The noble laughed, but the wizard's eyes still bored into him. "You are not a fighter. Why not? Are you a coward?"

Vorman inserted the answer quickly. "The boy's something of a healer. Too valuable. And he's a runt. The farm boys were more use than him in a fight."

The dark haired noble laughed. "He'd better not help those bitches if you get them. I have my own ideas of what they deserve."

"And they will get what is coming to them," the wizard said with deadly promise. "However, maybe it would be better to wait...just a little longer. Let them think they are doing some good up here, protecting Thulor from the likes of those farm boys. Doing that, we will know where they will be, and we can work our plan in another location. Don't try to take them on, just keep aware of their movements. When the time is auspicious, we will have them. They will be overconfident, unsuspecting."

Vorman gave a feral grin. "Doing that, will severely curtail how much we can contribute to your campaign, but my men will do as you ask."

The noble waved that concern aside. "We will send you supplies, every other week...to here?"

Vorman nodded.

"And that way, you can do hit and run raids to keep those bitches hopping. Spread fear and panic."

"I will provide some magical artefacts and a wizard to teach yours how to use them," the orange eyed visitor promised. "Those bitches must stay alive until I am ready for them."

Del, who had again edged out of sight, and out of the minds of the visitor's, felt his head prickling him. This stranger had to be a wizard, and just as obviously had a potent antipathy to the two Thulan women. And the thought of Vorman having access to even more potent magic, made his guts turn to water. He was relieved when the two visitors reactivated the green fire, and rode back into it.

"They didn't promise us more fighters," Usiv muttered when he dared approach Vorman.

"We don't need them. We're better off on our own – less useless mouths to feed. Those farm boys were more of a problem than a help."

Usiv grunted an agreement.

"We've supplies on hand," Vorman considered aloud. "Too bad we had to leave stuff behind. We had best lie low for a bit – see if the bitches come sniffing around."

"Don't see how they'd know where to be," Usiv pointed out. "They hadn't the guts to follow through the portal."

"No, that's true. But we know how close we are to that farm, so we will be careful."

CHAPTER 35 - Maeven

It was bad luck that she had just slipped her guards when she walked into the creepy hedge wizard. She noted at once that he had a new staff, elaborately carved with runes and other arcane symbols.

"What do I see here?" he snarled, grabbing her.

"I'm lost!" she snapped back at him. "I'm under a compulsion to walk around for a candle mark each day!" Her feet continued to try to walk, even though she was being held. "Or don't you remember?"

"This part of the palace is not for you to be in."

Maeven already knew that, which was why she had headed there, again, at a time when she believed the King would still be absent. And she would keep coming when she could until he realised that having his spell on her, let her pass his wards – the ones that should stop her passing into the area.

The wizard knew she was under a spell; but he wasn't going to let that excuse her. A glowing line of power flew from the end of his staff and circled her. Maeven soon discovered that it acted like a leash.

"Impressive," she commented, "for a mere hedge wizard!"

"My master rewards me well for the use of my body."

"I see," Maeven replied, feigning calm. "I don't suppose you could guide me back to where I should be? The candle mark should be up soon and I have no idea where I am. Besides I am really getting very tired - this wretched parasite inside me..."

The creepy hedge wizard scowled at the reminder, he would not have an excuse to harm her whilst she was carrying the King's child.

Without further conversation he stalked off, forcing Maeven to walk fast to keep on her feet. He took her in the direction of the King's audience chamber.

When El Rasho saw her being dragged in, he arbitrarily dismissed all the remaining commoners. Those leaving took away the vision of a slender, woman, dressed in the robes of a Royal Wife. And since the gown was filmy and really hid nothing of her shape, they would see the start of the round bulge of her belly.

"She was about to enter your private quarters," the wizard reported.

"Really?" King El Rasho said silkily. "I knew you would come to want me in time."

Maeven merely stared at him as her feet kept trying to walk.

"Take that stupid spell off her," El Rasho snarled at the wizard.

With relief, Maeven felt her feet stop, but that was all she had to be glad about.

El Rasho was removing his fancy Robes of State, eyeing her all the time.

Maeven had the sinking feeling that her immunity to his physical subjugation of her body was about to end and to fight what was coming would merely arouse him further.

"My old nurse tells me that it is quite safe to bed a pregnant woman. I have never tried it. In fact, she says that pregnant women are not necessarily delicate and fragile objects. I think it is time you had another lesson - in obedience."

Maeven continued to stare at El Rasho as if she was unconcerned. She had plenty of practice at hiding her feelings.

Her mental inner rebellion simply told her to say," Perhaps I am one of the fragile ones. I hope I am; I won't mind losing your bastard."

Her words made a hit. He had wanted her for a long time, to have in his power. But now he was forced to be grateful to her, even while hating her. By now, Maeven had him figured out, thanks again to Reyna's advice.

She filled her eyes with tears but nothing more. If she fought him, pleaded with him, or even remained impassive, he would hurt her more. This tactic made him gloat because he owned her and he was humbling her, but it did not rouse his desire to hurt her more than by entering her unwilling. That much she could bear. She consoled herself again with the knowledge that she was not the only woman who had to endure the attentions of a 'husband' she detested.

The King was claiming her as his wife. In spite of the fact that under the old Vatarik laws, she was his brother's wife. But then, since he had claimed the crown, El Rasho had made and broken any law he chose.

This time the 'tear' tactic had a different effect. El Rasho paused as he reached for her and studied her for a long time.

"You are not scared of me!" he deduced.

Maeven shrugged. He was not completely correct, but close enough.

"I've got you figured out," Maeven said flatly. "You like to hurt me. In that, you are no worse than any other man who has had me. But the more you hurt me - the greater the risk of making me lose your bastard."

"You've implied that already," El Rasho said thoughtfully. "I'm not going to give you any chance to harm my heirs."

Maeven caught the plural and betrayed her surprise. "What do mean?"

El Rasho nodded with a smile. "My old nurse believes you are carrying twins."

Maeven swore a curse that was straight out of the gutter, then added, "I hope they are both girls!"

"Girls are of no use to me. They shall not be permitted to live."

"Good, I won't get saddled with them."

"What are you planning?" El Rasho thought aloud. "In everything you say, you claim to hate me - yet you have made no attempt to escape. I want to know why. Wedek, put a truth spell on this wench."

Maeven cursed inwardly, she had forgotten the wizard for a bit.

Within moments, as Wedek incanted the spell, Maeven felt the itch of magic increasing beyond that of the tether spell.

"What were you doing, trying to enter my apartments?"

"I wanted to look and see if I could find anything to use against you."

"Are you working for your father?"

A laugh escaped her. "Your pet wizard dragged me here. I was living at the furthest reach of my father's kingdom. And I haven't seen him for three years."

That was the truth; let them digest it.

"What do you want to do to me?"

"I hadn't decided. I simply pictured my child on the throne of Vatarik, with me as regent."

El Rasho continued to question her ruthlessly, but he learnt nothing more specific about her intentions because she hadn't formulated any. Finally, he stopped and considered the answers he had got.

"You and I are a lot alike. You are out to get whatever you can for yourself, aren't you."

"The only thing we have in common," Maeven snapped back, "is we have both spent time in my father's dungeon!"

"We also have our unborn children in common."

Fortunately, that comment was not phrased as a question and she did not have to answer.

The king indicated for the spell to be lifted.

"You are an argumentative brat!" El Rasho accused. "What could I offer you to have you work in harness with me?"

"Nothing, you bastard."

El Rasho smiled a knowing smile. He believed he knew how to handle her now, but trusting her was another matter.

"Wedek, where is our mutual friend?" El Rasho asked obliquely. He did not wish to grant the Serpent the honorific of 'Master'.

"What do you wissh?" came a different voice from the throat of Wedek.

"I wish to give my wife a gift worthy of a - Queen."

Maeven did not understand the oddness of the phrasing of the request. It was almost as if he was speaking in a secret language.

The voice of the Serpent had made the hair on her body want to stand on end. She struggled against the mage-leash without success.

Wedek passed something that glittered to El Rasho. At first glance, it looked like a huge diamond with a strange orange glow coming from within. It was a perfect match for the neckpiece that Jilli wore and Maeven wanted nothing of it. She struggled fiercely, keeping her attention on El Rasho. That was her mistake; Wedek came up behind her and used his staff to render her unconscious.

Maeven roused in time to hear the Serpent say, "Sshe will be obedient now - my little demon friend will make ssure of that."

"Excellent," El Rasho purred. "Guards!"

Two figures in rich silken uniforms entered the audience chamber.

"Take my wife back to her quarters."

When the guards had departed, supporting the barely aware woman, El Rasho spoke to Wedek.

"Find those who were guarding her. They are yours to do with as you please."

Wedek-Ciabolo smiled an evil grin of anticipation.

Maeven woke with a pounding headache and had to send a servant for something to dull it. The pain was so bad that she had to lie down. She couldn't even think. When the pain potion finally eased it, she still felt dizzy and nauseous. Standing up left her on the verge of falling or fainting.

Suddenly she remembered the diamond like object and felt at her throat. There it seemed to be stuck to her. She pulled at it but doing so hurt dreadfully and it felt as if something was burning her.

"Oh, dragon shells!" Maeven muttered. Now she knew what the diamond like object had contained - one of Ciabolo's little watch demons.

It wasn't hard to figure that they didn't trust her, or Jilli either it seemed. Maeven wondered for a moment if there were any female demons and if there were, were they dominated by the males. Then she realised that El Rasho also had one of those diamond things. That raised the interesting notion that Ciabolo did not trust him. How and why he had received one was something to consider for a later time.

Her most urgent consideration was to determine how much control she still had and what she could and could not do.

Firstly, she called in more servants to have a bath made ready. Soaking the object had no effect on it. Then she went through her improvised exercise routine, the one she hoped would keep her supple in spite of her increasingly bulging belly.

When the hour for her walk arrived, she led her new guards on a tour of the palace, deliberately going again into the forbidden section. A glance at them showed their consternation. She guessed they had been told not to let her walk there. The demon, though, did not seem to be affecting her. Well, she had been thinking her usual litany of, 'Jilli is a wife, she goes here, so I can too'. She didn't stay long before scampering back into the custody of her guards, then continued walking in a very thoughtful frame of mind. Did the nasty little creature only react when it knew she was doing what they didn't want her to do? Or rather, understood her mind thinking that?

The nausea had not abated by the following morning and persisted all that day and all the one following. Finally she summoned the old woman.

"Yes, I know pregnant women suffer from nausea, but I didn't have it before so why should I suddenly get it now?"

Maeven wanted to scream at the old woman, and tell her that she had never suffered from that problem. However, if she did, everyone would know that she had been pregnant this long before.

"Ok - I'll try the tissup-tea!" she said instead, only so the old woman would stop lecturing her and leave her alone.

After she had waddled off to fetch her remedy, but before it would be ready, one of the black robed servants entered her room unannounced. He was so quiet, that she would not have heard him except for her keen hearing.

She spun around, and had to grip the chair to stay upright. There was something different about the servant. It took her but moments to realise that his movements were stealthy, like a thief, not bowed by fear.

As if to confirm her guess, the servant stood straight, looked directly at her. None of the servants dared to be that familiar. They would at most give her a quick glance then look down again. He made the hand signal that identified bonded thief to bonded thief. Maeven let her eyes grow wide and her mouth form an 'o' but did not return his signal. She was no longer a bonded thief.

The man however was confident that she understood what he was. He put his hand into the pocket of his servants robe and brought out a black object that looked like a gigantic beetle carapace. He placed it in her hands and for an instant Maeven was filled with a surge of familiar power - dragon magic - and her nausea and dizziness vanished.

The relief was not to last; the thing at her neck roused, burning her neck and making it hard to breathe. She dropped what she knew had to be one of Petulor's scales.

"Put it in the red covered basket," Maeven whispered to the thief spy.

The man obeyed at once and with that little bit of distance between demon and dragon magic, Maeven managed to breathe again.

"I have come to free you if you wish," the man spoke very softly.

An overwhelming sense of homesickness made her need to sit

down. To be away from El Rasho's deliberate tortures, his forcing himself on her, the wizard and his master – how often had she wished for that?

She couldn't count them all. What would happen if she agreed to go? What if the attempt failed? The so far nameless thief would die – that was certain. What would they do to her?

Not too much, at least not right away. Not until after the child was born, if it was male. Then they might kill her. Or he might get to considering physical ways to stop her – like breaking her legs and letting them heal wrong. Trying not to think of such ideas, she thought of how El Rasho had asked if she was spying for her father. He should have asked if she had been spying for herself.

Finally, Maeven shook her head. "Doing that would put you in danger. The Serpent has put one of his watch demons on me. I don't know what might alarm it and bring him after me. I am being treated well enough for now...and I can be a spy they don't suspect."

She didn't really want her family know she was pregnant again, though the word was sure to get to them now, and he would assume it was El Rasho's child. Everyone was meant to think that, and she was sure there was more to it than Petulor's cryptic, "the fate of two kingdoms shouldn't rest on one child."

"I have a chance to learn the weaknesses of the enemy. I will stay, for whilst they concentrate on me, they will leave others alone. Tell your master that the serpent is not yet as strong as he was, but he is building his forces. He hasn't merged with the new King..."

Swiftly, Maeven related a myriad of facts and observations. She kept to the most important details, it gave the thief more than enough to remember.

"Dragon-speed," she said finally, and watched as the thief became the picture of a palace slave, even his body language was different.

Maeven felt revitalized. Her father had found her. Petulor had sent one of her scales and even if she could not touch it, she was not completely alone anymore.

The little watch demon had quietened down again, once the dragon's scale was a little distance away. However, the power in the scale was still easing the nausea and dizziness. She would need to keep it near her, but not too close. She used her follow spell on it, and when it moved with her, smiled and added the invisibility spell to it.

She would have to tolerate the obnoxious demon creature, until she could find a way to have it removed, but so far it had done little to her.

CHAPTER 36 - Maeven

Maybe El Rasho wasn't aware of it, but when he told Wedek to remove the 'walking' spell, it hadn't been just for that moment. He must have assumed that was what had been done, for the guards still arrived at the end of the second hour after noon, and it suited Maeven to act as if the spell was still active.

First, she would walk around the citadel, gradually learning the greater layout. When the king and his wizard were away, she would duck into the places she wasn't meant to be in. Her new, regular guards no longer worried, for she had put a subtle compulsion on them – to not make a fuss and tell no one where she had gone.

On one day, she had gone to the door of the suite El Rasho used when alone. The spell on that was mechanical, and she easily mastered it. There did not seem to be anything of interest to her. She had no use for the more opulent furnishings that had replaced those his brother had, and nowhere to hide the little trinkets she could have taken. She could have made them invisibly follow her around, but that took magic, and she was hording what there was of the magic in Petulor's scale. Besides, should the magic run out, everything would appear and drop to the floor. That's what had happened while she was in the cave with Petulor, before the dragon was old enough to learn how to power her spells.

Getting into the rooms that Wedek-Ciabolo had claimed, was harder. She had, on one occasion, managed to get into one of the rooms, but almost immediately, an inner prompting had made her scurry back to her guards. Next time, that room had not opened, before she had needed to hurry away – the time Wedek had caught her. What she had seen in that one glance was enough to see that it was even more opulent that El Rasho's. It seemed that Wedek had not been lying when he said he was well rewarded by his 'master'. There had been many gem encrusted items of precious metal, silver and gold figures, and that had only been from a narrow slit view. The stuff must have come from Ciabolo's hoard under the lake.

At other times, during that hour, when she had finished learning about a new section of the citadel, she went to the Garden of the

Wives to enjoy the fresh air and sunshine. Always, she did a lap or two around the garden as if still being forced to walk. Generally, that hour was when the other wives had a siesta. However, the new guards had no idea of the usual routine, so Maeven gradually stretched out the time until after the end of the third hour. Now it was a regular thing, and the other wives had discovered her there, and came as a group to talk to her. They fluttered around her, knowing that she was now the pre-eminent one amongst them. She was bearing the King's child. They had heard the gossip, that she was bearing a son, maybe two.

Maeven could now have simple conversations with them, and when she didn't know the words for something, young Isala was happy to translate. It gave her more status amongst the women.

All in all, the interaction was a pleasant change to just having her own company in the solitude of her own rooms. The question was, how long would she be able to keep it up before El Rasho found out and stopped it. That, Maeven decided, would be when Jilli figured it out. Her former maid hadn't bothered her for a while, so she inserted a question about that to the other wives and that had them all gossiping like a gaggle of spiteful geese.

Most of what they knew they had heard from the servants since Jilli usually stayed away from the wives. What seemed to be a consistent thread was that El Rasho had tired of her constant demands and she had been sent to entertain his senior officers. Some versions had it that she had been promised a gem for every man she had. That part Maeven doubted, but she didn't say so. It was likely more true that he and the wizard were away so much now, that she had voluntarily gone to the officers as if she was a camp follower.

There had been a new story that Jilli had slipped and broken her ankle while trying to do something and now she was confined to her room.

That made Maeven shiver, wondering if the accident had actually been El Rasho punishing her. If it was, he obviously didn't care that she was in turn taking her temper out on the servants and making constant demands on them.

Whatever the reason, Maeven didn't miss her. She was finding the women much better company after finding out she was nothing like Jilli.

Some of the older wives, the ones who had been there when El Rasho's daughters had been born, warned her that even if she sired a son, she would not have any say in raising him. There would be a nurse, then teachers. Even the baby girls were kept away from their mothers until they had recovered enough to be sent away. The implication there had been, 'and never seen again.' One even remarked that the gems one wife had received, were identical to those the previous mother had been given.

As time went on though, Maeven sensed a gradual return of the nausea and dizziness that had begun when the little demon had first been put on her. She still had Petulor's scale invisibly following her, but it seemed it was losing its power to help. What was worse, she found herself snapping at her servants, at the other wives too, when she had no reason at all to do it.

Even when the old woman came to fuss over her, she would be short tempered, and it worried her enough to ask why she would be acting that way. All the woman could say was, "It is because you are pregnant. You need to rest more."

It might well be true, Maeven considered. Her belly was increasing in size, so much that she no longer doubted the prediction of twins. Her doubting side thought it might be some spell to make everyone hate her. It was certainly a reason for El Rasho, on his increasingly few appearances, to slap her around, and hit her, even if he chose not to couple with her.

He had, however, developed a fascination with her huge belly and she had used that distraction as a chance to put a spell of her own on him. It was one Atlantis had told her, back when she was first a prisoner in the citadel. A spell to inhibit lust. It seemed to be working. Unless it was the way he was nearly always drunk, or affected by some medicant. She wondered if her jibe about joining Ciabolo was haunting him.

From always going out when she could, she began to spend more time in her rooms. She had given up the pretence of the spell still working, and even had to force herself to eat, drink and care for herself. The old woman kept at her, providing brews to help the nausea, and having the cooks prepare daintier foods and tempting snacks.

A fresh batch had arrived just before Jilli limped in with help of a cane. She took one look at the food and would have swept the dishes off the table if the old woman had not grabbed her wrist.

"How come she gets such nice stuff," Jilli demanded. "I had to have servant's stodgy food. She's only a brood ewe and I'm Rashi's favourite."

The old woman was stronger than she looked, Maeven realised. She was feeling horrible, but still managed to find amusement in the confrontation. She was about to say, "Are you? You are not the one bearing his son," when the woman said as much and added, "She must eat to stay healthy and strong. She is eating for three now."

Maeven did add, "And they might both be sons." She saw the red flush on JIlli's face as the old woman called for the guards to have her removed.

When the room was quiet again, the old woman sighed and asked, "Must you antagonise that one?"

It brought her to her senses for a moment, but thinking on it, Maeven decided, "It makes no difference if I do or not. She will still run to her Rashi and make up stories about me."

"You have not learnt, even now, you foolish child!"

"Learnt what? That he will never stop hating me?" she retorted. "Nothing I can do will make him, or the creature that is occupying his wizard, like me."

"No! I mean that there is much worse that they can do to you that than have so far. Have you considered that?"

She hadn't. "Well, get them to keep her away from me."

CHAPTER 37 - Maeven

The second thief arrived several days later, and approached her during her period in the Garden of the Wives. He carried a tray of refreshments, but still managed to make the thieves sign look like a natural part of serving her a drink.

"A second gift lies with the first," the thief, an older man this time, whispered from under his hood.

Maeven seemed to ignore him.

"Be warned, that which feeds on you, will not affect you on your own. But it will make you obey its master."

Maeven felt suddenly cold. She had still hoped otherwise.

When her face was looking away from any possible chance of a guard seeing her lips move, she asked, "Can they be removed?"

"So far, we have no knowledge," the man admitted. "It has proved necessary to kill the hosts, while they are bespelled by magic. The creature then dies with the host and cannot infect other innocents. Death is a kindness."

"I do not have that option," Maeven said without emotion. "But I am warned..."

Maeven turned and held out her glass but asked not for water.

"Can you leave me a weapon?"

"Yes. Or I can bring you out."

"No. With this thing on me...I do not know what they will make me do, and I don't want to risk being forced to betray my kin."

The man accepted that without a movement or change in expression. He poured a second lot of water into her glass.

"Have you seen my master?" the man asked unexpectedly. "He carried a third gift."

"No, when should he have come? I only have one gift, plus the one you mention."

"Do not concern yourself," the man told her.

"You should leave!" Maeven saw the eunuch guards reacting to someone at the entrance.

"One more thing, Princess. There is a new sign. It is like the greeting sign, but reversed. Use it, and any bonded thief will aid you."

Maeven spotted Wedek approaching and spoke normally.

"...And have the water changed in my quarters - the last lot tasted as if beasts had washed in it."

The disguised thief did not bow to her but turned away to obey the command. He did bow to the one who was the King's wizard.

Wedek ignored the servant and fastened his cold eyes on Maeven.

"The King has returned. You are to come to him at once."

Maeven had no reason to disregard the order, but even her slight and deliberate hesitation to obey, caused the demon to rouse and add it's coercion. Her recent week of peace, whilst both wizard and King were away, was over.

She was led to the King's Chambers and as soon as she had entered, two of El Rasho's enforcers grabbed her.

"I hear you are acting like the Queen of Vatarik," El Rasho accused in his silkiest voice. She had been dragged to within a man's height of the King. "Do you think you are better that my other wives?"

Maeven was sure that Jilli must have been talking to him. Her mind was ready for an argument and she didn't censor her words.

"I don't consider myself your wife! And I don't care to be compared to those that do. They have nothing better to do than find imaginary distinctions between themselves." Maeven told him.

"Do go on," El Rasho invited. There was quiet menace in his voice.

Maeven had no choice, the little demon was rousing further, and her nausea increasing.

"They consider me an upstart outlander. Unfortunately, for them, I'm carrying your brats. By all their definitions, I out rank them all. When I have to spend time with them, they all fawn around me, hoping my influence will bring them to your attention. Sometimes I find it amusing to play their little games. Your whore is just jealous of losing their attention and yours."

El Rasho walked forward and slapped the face of the 'upstart outlander'. "I will tell them that you are nothing more than a stable sweeper in rank."

Maeven's cheeks stung, but she continued to face the King of Vatarik. "I already know what you think of me."

It was meant to sound defiant, but a sudden cramp in her stomach made her want to double over. It was another sign that one of Petulor's scales was no longer enough to lull the little demon and make her feel well. Would being near two of them help at all?

The guards kept her upright and she managed to say, "Tell them what you will; it will be a relief to have them ignore me."

She spoke through a wave of pain worse than she had experienced before. She wondered if the babies were wanting to come already, and it was still too early. She took several breaths before she could continue.

"Though they are too stupid to believe it. After all, their only purpose is to get heirs for you. If they believed you thought so little of me, they would have no incentive to please you."

A more intense wave of cramping overcame Maeven, and it was obvious she was in pain, though she was biting her lip to avoid crying out. Someone began to shake her.

"What is wrong with you?" El Rasho demanded.

If Maeven had not been feeling so terrible, his concern would have amused her. "I think the babies are coming, but it is too early."

He was angry; his eyes were flashing and flicking around his chamber looking for the cause.

"Summon the healer!" he told one of his attendants.

"Have you poisoned yourself?" he shook Maeven again, causing her to gag.

"No," she said with no force to her words.

"Wedek, go and search the women's quarters for traces of poison. Search this one's room too."

"There was a servant giving her a drink when I arrived to bring her, Sire."

"Find out who that was," El Rasho ordered. "You," he turned on the guards holding her, "put her into a chair before she fouls the floor."

Wedek went off, intending to make a very thorough search.

Maeven was not dismissed, and was forced to endure the worsening cramps and potions that did nothing to ease it.

She tried to focus on the idea that someone was trying to poison her. It was more than possible. Funny thing was, El Rasho was the only one she could be sure was not.

His anger was real. He liked seeing her suffer, but he was the only one allowed to cause it.

A seemingly endless time later, Wedek dragged in a pale shivering woman, dressed, as Maeven was in almost transparent white silk.

"I found this Majesty," Wedek handed El Rasho a small vial. "It was in the pocket of this one's robe."

Maeven looked up, and identified the youngest of El Rasho's wives. Isalla was barely fifteen and the only one who was nice to her.

"No! Not Isalla, she wouldn't poison me," Maeven protested between cramps.

"Quiet, woman," El Rasho ordered, sending the command through the demon at her neck. She tried again to protest, but no sound came out, and the cramps got even worse.

The girl looked about to faint as El Rasho questioned her. Wedek seemed to be enjoying her terror.

The girl spoke in a different Vatarin dialect to the one Maeven was learning but was obviously protesting her innocence.

Maeven believed her. There was no way the girl could have poisoned any one and Maeven never ate and drank in the presence of the other wives. No, she was not being poisoned. The cramps and nausea had only begun when they had put the demon on her, but El Rasho wanted a scapegoat - a reason to do something.

"No!" Maeven protested silently, as the knife was forced into her hand.

"You will obey me! This woman has been judged guilty of poisoning you. You will carry out the sentence of death."

The horrible truth of the old woman's warning was brought home to her as she watched from some far corner of her mind as her hand grasped the knife and her body began to walk towards the girl. Tears streamed from her eyes as she buried the knife in the girl's heart. The body dropped taking the knife with it. There was laughter from the King and his wizard. The truth of her position almost broke her spirit. She had been made to kill an innocent girl. Her only near friend here and she hadn't been able to fight it.

"Return woman," Wedek ordered.

Maeven's body obeyed, even as her mind wanted to rebel. What other horrors could they make her do?

The twisted satisfaction on the Kings face, mirrored by the wizard, sickened her further.

"You are totally mine, bitch of Thulor," El Rasho gloated.

He was satisfied that the woman knew what she had done for tears still streamed down her face. He knew she realised the extent of his control.

"Repeat after me. I pledge to serve the king of Vatarik; I pledge to obey his every command..."

Maeven found herself repeating the words that would make her nothing more than a chattel of El Rasho and the forced oath had the power of magic behind it. It made her forsworn. She had given her oath of obedience to her Father, to the kingdom of Thulor. This oath bound her to Thulor's darkest enemies and would make her act against her own kin.

Darkness closed in on her mind, and the spark that was a princess of Thulor became no more than an irritation in the body of a demon.

CHAPTER 38 - Maeven

The servants noticed the change first, but only spoke of it amongst themselves. They had grown used to the how the King's chief wife had become a tyrant, demanding and unreasonable. After some weeks, the demands lessened as the Royal Wife kept more and more to her bed. Then, almost overnight, she stopped noticing them at all. On the first day, it was simply a relief. Until the food taken in for her had to be removed, hours later, picked over, but hardly any eaten. They never made the connection that the only parts taken where those easily identified as meat. They were taught to obey, not to think.

As this trend continued, one of the servants, newer and less mind-trained, noticed their charge was visibly losing weight – it was enough to make her afraid. If the Royal First wife died, bearing the king's heir, the servants would be punished. She tried to insist that the Chief Servant say something to the former Royal nurse, and received a beating for her trouble.

For three days, the servant couldn't work, and as a result was not given any food. On the third day, though, she was recovered enough to try to find the old woman herself, only to discover she had come down with some respiratory illness and had taken to her bed. The Nurse, as a servant of high rank, slept in a section of the citadel where lesser servants were not allowed. She went back to work to consider the problem, finally deciding that expressing concern to a fellow servant, one of the duller witted ones, about the health of the nurse who was meant to be tending the pregnant royal wife, and at a time when the chief servant would hear, would force him to act.

So, when the next lot of food was returned, and the servants that day put it where they could finish it later, she said, "Again? I guess we will have to wait until the nurse is better." The man she spoke to stood straight by the wall, waiting for an order and showing no sign that he was listening to her. "At least she makes the woman eat. But since she's ill, it probably isn't a good idea she go in. I hope someone is looking out for her. If she dies, who will be seeing that the king's sons are born healthy?"

The Chief Servant came and gripped the neck of the woman's robe. "You will go and tend her! On half rations for your impudence. Take this!"

He pulled out an odd coin from his pocket and shoved it in the face of the one he held. When she took it, he released her with a shove and she knew to scoot out of his way immediately.

The old nurse lay on her bed, too weak to do much else. Her breathing was harsh and wheezy. Yet when the other servant came in, her mind was alert enough to act on the unexpected help. In moments, she had the visitor preparing a tonic, using the small cooking fire in her room. Her status as a former royal nurse, was higher even that the Chief Servant. The finished brew eased her breathing and put colour back in her face. Only then did the lower servant tell of her concerns.

"A day or two won't hurt," the old nurse said. "By then, I will be fine, thanks to your help."

Once back on her feet, the old nurse went to the quarters of the first wife and examined her. She saw the pale, slack features, the loose skin where the flesh had shrivelled. The she noticed the bright glow emanating from the neck piece. What she saw frightened her and sent her scurrying to her old charge who now was King.

"Rashka!" The old woman strode past the guards, right up to where El Rasho was duelling with the Captain of his armies.

El Rasho snarled at the old woman but continued to fight.

"Rashka!" the woman said more sharply.

"What is it, old woman?" El Rasho snarled again, waving the sword in her direction.

"The mother of you children is dying."

"WHAT! Have all my wives brought before me; I will have the truth of who is still trying to poison her."

"There never was any poison. You know that!" the old nurse argued fearlessly. "And I know you have kept her away from the others and all her food is tested for poison."

"Then what is wrong, old woman?"

"It's that demon on her. It's male!"

"They are all male. It hasn't affected that other bitch from Thulor."

"No, that one is still obeying the commands of your father, to lust after anything male and powerful; she has never been pregnant either."

"What has that got to do with anything?"

The nurse gave her former charge a look that suggested he was a very dull student."

"The demon is male. Your wife is a pregnant female. The two are incompatible. The demon is trying to make her body its own. If the demon stays on, your wife will die. Your sons will die with her. It will have to come off, now!"

El Rasho, suddenly pale faced, turned to the Guard Captain. "Get Wedek here. Are you sure of this, old woman?"

"Yes, the symptoms started when you had that demon put on her. They have got steadily worse."

Wedek performed the summoning that drew the demon away from the woman. When it was once again fully occupying the crystal faceted orb, he severed the magic attachment and slapped a seldom-used healing spell on the site the demon had touched.

The woman lay, still unconscious, on the bed in her chamber.

"Why doesn't she wake?" El Rasho demanded.

"She will need time to recover," he was told bluntly. "Let her rest here in her chamber. We will fill it with soothing aromas."

"See to it old woman." El Rasho stalked out. The blank faced wizard followed.

The old nurse dug into a pouch at her waist, pulled out several pinches of herbs, and began to burn them in a small brazier near the bed.

Then she carefully covered the woman who was bearing the heirs of the king and settled down to wait and watch.

After several hours, it was obvious that the woman's body was breathing more regularly but she still did not wake.

Maeven had sent her mind away from that of the demon, into the one place it had no conception of; that in the mind of a male demon, did not exist.

She was still aware of the forces battling in the rest of her body, but she was drifting in the warmth of her own womb, sharing the watery dreams of her babies and shielding them with her presence.

The boy was sleeping with his thumb in his mouth. The girl, with a spark of magic in her, seemed to be aware of the other presence.

Maeven let her mind send them soothing reassurances and urged them to hold on; they were precious and she loved them.

She did not know how long she had been drifting in that state before she became aware of the calmness in the body around the womb. When she did, she let her mind venture out slowly, cautiously; creeping like a thief through her own body. Finding no trace of the demon, she ventured further.

Finally, she opened her eyes, and for a while, her body felt like an unfamiliar garment that had been dumped in a heap. Eventually her mind re-gained control of it and her first action was to feel at her throat for tactile confirmation that the demon had gone.

The movement drew the old nurse's attention, and she spoke softly. "Yes, the foul creature is gone. Can you manage to take some broth?"

"Water?" she asked in an almost inaudible voice, and without opening her eyes. She felt a reed placed to her lips, and tried to suck. She couldn't, so the woman dripped water into her mouth until she could.

"Only a little for now," she heard as the reed was removed. "Try some broth. You need to put more meat on your bones."

Maeven tried, knowing the woman was right, but even a little made her feel like it wanted to come back up. She lay still, hearing the woman moving around, rustling through her few possessions. The woman made a satisfied sound, and her steps came close again.

"Here, girl, put this in close to you."

The gentle hands tucked something hard, but covered in cloth, over her huge belly. Immediately, Maeven felt the sensation of a cool breeze flowing through her. Her eyes flew open and she saw the smile on the woman's face as she nodded to herself.

"How did you know?" Maeven asked.

"Now is not the time, girl. Rest, let yourself get better."

For a long time, as she lay too weak to move, realising she was alone, she was content to let the cool breeze that was the dragon's healing magic flow through her.

"Petulor?" she thought, picturing the dragon.

"Dragon-mother?" was the immediate, although faint reply. It came with the sensation of love and relief.

"I need an ally here. Can you help?"

"Yes! Be patient, one will come. Must you stay? They don't treat you well there."

"I can't escape, Petulor. There is a magic barrier around the palace. They think I can't sense it. I can be of some use here – even if it is only distracting them so others can fight more effectively. Besides, they have put a magical binding on me, to obey the King of Vatarik, even though I swore to obey my Father."

"You should leave there," Petulor insisted.

"I don't want to have to fight against my father! And, right now, I am too pregnant to do much and they have stopped tormenting me. Please get someone here. The king of Vatarik will not let my daughter live – I have to get her away."

"Keep one of the scales close to each child," Petulor instructed.

"How did you know I was having twins?"

"I saw!" Petulor sounded smug. "The dragon-friend that you call Reyna, had twins. Dragon magic makes you human women more fertile."

Maeven kept a straight face. "Is Wystan safe?"

"I took the son of Father King to him."

"Rhovert?"

Maeven received a wordless affirmation.

"The child is safe with friends in Declanor. I can venture there, but not into Vatarik."

"You don't want to!" Maeven thought back. "Someone is coming."

Petulor had the last word, "Practice your magic."

Maeven forgot any aggravation she had felt towards the old woman when she realised that her intervention had saved her life. In her role as nurse and midwife, she was fearless – even in the presence of the King. She was even influencing her former charge to leave his pregnant wife alone. When she claimed that her patient was still very weak, Maeven played along, though being near Petulor's scales had returned her strength to nearly normal.

The woman was the one who suggested that Maeven begin to sew clothes for the second child and obtained materials and threads for the task. On another occasion, she brought with her the traditional robes, worn by the Princes of Vatarik.

"I can't do work that fine," Maeven told her, as she admired the rich white fabrics with tiny pearls sewn into sun shapes and sun rays."

"It won't matter, only the elder son will wear these. The lesser will not."

"What if one or both are girls?" Maeven asked her, and watched her closely as she waited for an answer.

The woman didn't answer directly.

"The previous King was the youngest of six boys and seven girls. He had two boys; three girls were stillborn."

"Why did the youngest son inherit?" Maeven found herself asking.

"Three sons were killed fighting the northern barbarians, four of the girls were killed when their town was overrun by the same barbarians and the youngest three girls fled with their mother when their father died. Malokin became his father's successor because he was the first to engender a son and heir. It is an old, old law."

"So, if El Haba had sired an heir first, he'd be king now?" Maeven asked.

"He was named traitor."

"What if he had a bastard before that?"

Maeven sensed the old woman's interest.

"I am sure he would have told his father."

"Would it have made any difference to the way he was treated?"

"Perhaps some," the woman conceded cautiously. "If he knew he had a son, he would never have sworn to serve another king."

"If he had not been treated so horribly by his father, brother and the Serpent, he probably wouldn't have anyway," Maeven said, then she sighed. "Never mind, it's such a totally useless fantasy. If he'd been treated better he would not have changed from the bastard that raped me five years ago."

The old woman was visibly startled. "Habi did that?"

"Yeah, and his brother was really mad. He wanted me first."

"Then you are Habi's wife!"

If rape and marriage are the same thing in Vatarik, Maeven thought. "It seems to me that El Rasho does not care about such details now he is King."

The old woman's face went into hard lines and her lips thinned. She might have been angry about what she had just learnt, but she said nothing against the King.

Instead, she gathered up the gowns and prepared to leave. Before she left, she said, "Habi is better off away from here."

Maeven cautiously deduced that El Haba had been her favourite. It led her to wonder if the old woman could be made an ally. Even if she was the only other person to know the truth – that by the old laws of Vatarik, El Haba was the true king – then her vow to obey the king of Vatarik should apply to El Haba, not his brother.

Relief flooded through her. There was a chance that she could get around any commands that El Rasho gave her. Time would tell.

CHAPTER 39 – Rhovert and Atlantis

From the moment they entered the lands overseen by the old Lord Tarthal, Atlantis felt prickling along her spine.

"Do you remember those feelings I was getting on the way to Ackbridge," she asked.

Rhovert reined his mount to a halt, and Atlantis did the same beside him. "What are you sensing?"

"I don't know. My back is prickling, that's all."

After looking around to try to see if they were being watched, he said, "Why don't stop to rest the horses? There is a small stream not far ahead."

"We can eat too," Atlantis suggested. "You aren't expected at Tarthal's manor at any particular time, are you?"

"No, but if he has watchers out on the road, they might be who you are sensing. They don't know that I am the prince, so they shouldn't be too paranoid about receiving me. I am merely passing messages from the king and offering to take back any needs he has."

"Maybe going as 'The Prince' might be better. Then they would not expect you to notice anything they try to hide."

"No..." Rhovert disagreed. "Let's get to the stream and talk there."

They sat on an opened travel rug, close to the stream where the water flowed over a rocky bottom. In a low voice, Rhovert was saying, "I think your brother distrusted both Tarthal and Kilkenny, so I am not about to distrust your sense of 'something'. We'll need to be alert. We should aim to arrive in the town near dusk. It will be a logical reason to stay at the inn overnight."

Atlantis nodded. They had done the same thing on many occasions. At the inn, he would speak to the men, and the next day, when he went to the manor, she would find a way to speak to the women. Often this would be while washing clothes, and usually, the women were more inclined to talk.

"When you go and see Tarthal, make sure you have the protection spell activated," Atlantis said abruptly.

"I will," Rhovert promised. He saw her realisation, that what she had blurted was a forewarning prophesy.

The sun was almost down when they saw the first of the houses. A child playing outside suddenly raced inside. Rhovert dismounted, and while Atlantis still rode, he walked his horse. When they were almost at the house, a man came out. One hand was behind him and Rhovert guessed he had a knife there.

"This is an odd time to venture here," the man, a stout peasant wearing brown homespun tunic and trews, challenged.

"Yes, it be that," Rhovert agreed. "Hoped to have been here soon after noon. My horse picked up a stone and went lame."

Atlantis dismounted and moved into sight. The man glanced her way, then turned back for a better look.

"Mam, this be a chancy time to be out."

"Is there an inn? And somewhere the horse can rest?" Atlantis asked, after nodding at his warning.

"Aye, there be that. Keep on the road to the centre of town. Ye have business here?"

Rhovert, playing his merc role, kept his answer to, "I do. I have reports to take up to the manor."

The man took a couple of shuffling steps backwards. "Reports?"

Rhovert was being careful, but something prompted Atlantis to add, "Yes, from his majesty, King Westron."

The man's eyes widened. "And ye take reports back?"

Rhovert nodded tersely.

"Do ye intend to see the Lord tonight?"

"Think I need a cleaning up first," Rhovert suggested.

The man nodded, as if agreeing. "Then ye'd best be on your way. If ye be expected to report back to the king, maybe you won't have trouble."

The man spun and hurried back into his house. Atlantis glanced at Rhovert as they tugged the reins to make the horses walk. They were both between the horses, and able to speak softly. "Why do I get the feeling," Atlantis began slowly, "That people who come here, don't leave?"

"What did he say to give you that idea? It makes no sense." Then the thought occurred to Rhovert, "Unless they want people, any people, for some purpose. Like sword fodder for an invading army." All he said aloud was, "I wonder if people are vanishing from up here."

"Likely," Atlantis considered. "There is a lot of it happening along the border. Your sisters keep finding bespelled Thulans, and haven't been able to find where they are coming from. The poor peasants have little memory when the controlling spells are removed."

The first thing Rhovert noticed when he entered the inn was the scarcity of patrons. When his eye passed over each in turn as he looked for the innkeeper, he saw that all of those present were disabled in some way. Not to the point of being physically helpless, but certainly were not able to fight. He stopped his scrutiny when he saw two men talking. One glanced his way and nodded.

The man in the leather apron began to walk nearer. The other slipped out through the kitchen. Rhovert walked to meet the first man. "Are you the innkeeper?"

"Aye. I be Talkus. What can I do for you?"

"If you have a room for me and my companion, and a stall for a lame beast, I'd be in your debt."

"Not if you pay me five coppers, laddie."

"How much more for two meals tonight and breakfasts in the morning?" Rhovert asked with a faint smile.

"Two copper bits, and drinks are a bronze bit each."

Rhovert felt in a pocket inside his tunic and sorted out the required coins, then added a copper bit extra. He handed them over.

"Stables around the back. There's hay and a pump for water. Ye need to tend your own beasts."

"That's no problem," Rhovert assured him. "I'll see about the room when I have seen to them."

Atlantis was waiting with the two horses, gently patting each on the nose, and not expecting trouble. Yet within two minutes of Rhovert entering the tavern, she was aware of two men approaching. They wore the livery of Lord Tarthal, and might have been crossing the road to go to the inn. When they stopped to examine the horses, she stopped moving and stayed quiet. If they were just looking, and moved away, well and good. When they began to untie the reins from the tethering post, Atlantis emerged from between the animals.

"Good Sirs, if you wish to be arrested and hung as horse thieves, I will be sure to let Lord Tarthal know."

The two men startled, and final saw her. "We weren't..." one began.

The older one said, "We were going to take them to the stable. It is not safe to have horses out this late."

"Your concern is noted," Atlantis told them. "However, surely you would let the riders have time to arrange for their own stabling so you would have no need to pay the fee. And surely you saw my companion entering the inn as you walked over."

That speaker had begun to smirk, thinking her a guileless traveller. Then it faded. "Hey! You're a female!"

"Well, I'm glad I haven't turned male – and before you begin to worry, I do not need your protection, my partner is returning now."

Rhovert heard the last part of the conversation and guessed the two supposed guards were chancy types. When they saw him, with his weapons harness on and the weapons in full view, they quickly nodded and walked off.

He made no comment about them then, just announced, "Got a stall out back and a meal. Have to tend the beasts ourselves."

Only when they were alone in the stable did Atlantis relate the whole encounter.

"The lord's men? Acting like horse thieves? Or instructed to appropriate likely beasts?" Rhovert considered thoughtfully. "I am sure our friend along the road sent someone to warn Talkus, maybe the guards were warned too? Can't see them waiting out in the cold each evening to wait for travellers." His glance at the dozen empty stalls, and the single horse already dozing in another, was enough to let him guess travellers to the town were few.

He continued thinking as he groomed his horse. "Did you notice how the man we met walked stiffly?"

Atlantis murmured an affirmative.

"Well, everyone I saw inside, except maybe Talkus, would also be ineligible for the Lord's guards."

"There could be reasons," Atlantis proposed. "For us only seeing the infirm, I mean. We are strangers."

"And they only have our word for why we are here. I am sure the man we met was interested, and I'd bet that Talkus knows what we told him, for all he never mentioned it."

"Do you think he might think, we might be involved in taking people? Might that be why there is no horse boy?"

"I don't know. I think we should put some of your brother's gadgets to work. On the stalls and on the horses. I would sleep out here, but I want to talk to the men and I don't think you should be out here alone." He shook his head as she began to protest. "I know you can take care of yourself, but I don't want anyone to know that."

"Fine! I get enough sleeping rough that having a decent bed and a meal I don't need to catch, is appreciated. Do you think they will try again?"

"Hard to say," Rhovert said, then gave a low chuckle. "It really depends on how smart they are. However, we should bring all the packs inside."

After a brief wash with cold water and a towel, and a promise of a hot soak later, they left the room they had been shown to, and made their way down to the small dining area that led off from the bar where the men were drinking. Their saddlebags were still up on the sleeping level, and the room supposedly locked, but if it proved otherwise, anyone touching their things would have some nasty surprises.

Talkus came over with a meal – chunky pies, vegetables and a chunk of yellow cheese.

"Ale?" he asked.

"One for me, and a barley water," Rhovert requested.

The innkeeper nodded. "Heard you had a bit of trouble before."

"No trouble," Atlantis assured him.

In a lower voice, Talkus said, "The lord's men check out all strangers. Theys don't want brigands coming in and talking what little we've got."

"Has there been trouble like that here?" Rhovert asked.

"Brigands? Oh no. The old lord still has some wits. We've had no brigands attack here, nor have any of the smaller villages."

"There's been a lot elsewhere," Rhovert said. "The other lords have drafted the able bodied men to help protect their people. It seems that must be so here too."

Rhovert had kept his tone even, and wondered if he had guessed right.

"Oh, aye...drafted. And those still here have to work twice as hard to feed them, and ourselves. Here, you eat that while it's hot. You'll want a bath later?"

"Yes," Atlantis said firmly.

Once alone, they ate without discussing their thoughts. They were aware that some of the other patrons might be in earshot. Talkus, might have been checking them out, or trying to warn them, but he still wasn't sure of them. Rhovert was keeping his ears pricked for the conversation between the other patrons, but this tavern wasn't like others they had stayed at. The talk had been desultory when he had first arrived, and now it had devolved into furtive whispers.

"Finish up," Rhovert urged, giving no reason.

"You getting visions now?" Atlantis asked, finishing a mouthful.

"No. I just had a glimpse of those two guards heading up the stairs."

"I'll wrap the rest of the pie in my kerchief and finish it later."

They were just reaching the upper floor when a screech, like a rabbit screaming, pierced the air. They raced to the third door along the passage, their room, with their boots making a racket on the wooden floor. Inside, they saw their bags had been dragged towards the window, which was now open, and on the floor, a spreading blue stain.

Atlantis checked the street and saw no one running off. Rhovert said, "The locks are intact. Whoever did this will have the evidence on their hands. Good thing I sent off all the reports from the last guard post."

Atlantis chuckled. "Blue hands will be hard to hide. I think I had better go see the innkeepers wife and see if she has what I need to remove the rest of the dye before it stays permanent."

"And I'll go down and have a few drinks. You can have the first bath."

Atlantis knocked on the kitchen door. The two women there

stopped talking and turned. The younger one flushed. She looked to be just out of childhood.

"You'd be wanting your bath then," the older one suggested.

"Soon. I actually came to ask if you can spare a cup of brown vinegar, some lemon grass and pond wort."

The list was repeated as the inn keeper's wife considered it. "Aye, I have all that. Why do you want it?"

"Have you had any need to send anyone to our room?"

"No, I was to wait until asked, and bring water and towels then."

"Good, because we met some would be horse thieves when we first arrived, and they just snuck in to check our packs. The scream you would have heard a while ago, was a warning triggered when they tried to open our packs. The would be thief will have blue stained hands from touching the mage lock. Unfortunately, some of the blue stuff got on your floor. Those ingredients, when mixed in warm water, will neutralise the colour."

"Won't soap and water do it?"

"No, that will simply make it stay. That's why I was going to clean up the mess for you."

"That's right kind of ye. My knees aren't what they used to be."

"I'll help take up the water," the younger one offered.

"I'll get brushes as well as what you asked for." The older woman bustled off.

She returned quite quickly and put what she had brought on the table, then went to lift one of the water buckets sitting near the fire.

"I can carry the bucket," Atlantis offered.

"But you're a guest," the girl protested.

"But not one that insists on being pampered. I am well able to tote a water bucket."

"Oh, well, if you say so. And I don't even know who you are. I'm Tansy. Talkus is my man."

"And I'm Kellthea. Tansy is my aunt."

"Atlantis Golddreamer."

Kellthea's eyes went wide. "Are you a wizard?"

"Men are wizards, women are sorceresses," Tansy corrected.

"Why do you ask?" Atlantis felt her back prickling again.

"Oh, well, you said you had mage locks on your stuff."

"My brother is the wizard. I'm much better with a sword."

Atlantis was trying to recall if her great grand sire, the wizard Gold Dreamer, had ever travelled up this far. It seemed that Kellthea had recognised the name. Something made her hold back on asking if she was right.

Kellthea proved to be stronger than her slender frame suggested. Like Atlantis, she easily carried two of the buckets up the stairs. Tansy brought up the cup and scrubbing brushes.

As soon as she saw the stain she exclaimed, "Oh, what a waste! Such a lovely colour – if only it would dye cloth."

Kellthea rolled her eyes. "She loves blue! What is the dye made from?"

"My brother isn't telling, but when I tell him the mess it made, and how I had to clean it up...and how nice you were about it, I might see if he can send you some. I doubt the idea of using it to dye cloth has ever occurred to him."

"That's a man for you," Tansy chuckled.

Roman GoldDreamer's counter for the blue dye didn't work immediately, and the stain did need scrubbing. Atlantis mentally rehearsed what she intended to say to him. She guessed though, that he would brush that aside and only comment on the fact that his traps had worked and their packs had not been searched or taken.

"What's it like where you come from?" Kellthea asked as she helped to scrub the wooden floor.

Diverted, Atlantis told her, "I come from Declanor."

"But you travel with the King's messenger!"

"Yes..." Atlantis wondered if Rhovert had announced his role to the innkeeper. "How'd you know that? Berto wasn't going to make a big deal of it."

"I heard Dekker tell Talkus. Dekker's pa lives at the edge of town."

Atlantis chuckled. "I had the feeling we were expected here. I assume the Lord's guards heard that way too."

"Oh, no! There wasn't any of them around."

"You heard."

"Yes, but I was just going in to talk to Aunt Tansy. Dekker would have made sure not to be overheard. They must have just seen you arrive."

"Maybe, I guess." Checking strangers in case they were brigands sizing up the town, she thought. The two of them were too well armed and dressed to be brigands. "I think that's the best we can do. I hope the rest will fade. And now I am more than ready for a bath."

On the way down with the now empty buckets and the borrowed brushes – the dirty water had been poured down a pipe to go to a cistern under the inn to be filtered – Kellthea had more questions.

"Have you ever been to King's Town?"

Since that was the town around King Westron's palace, Atlantis answered, "Quite a few times. Though these days it isn't the best place to be. Lots of chancy creatures and Vatarin fighters are besieging the palace."

Atlantis wondered why the girl's cheeks flushed. She asked in turn, "What's it like living here. The place seems quiet enough."

"Oh, I don't live in town, but with people my mother knew. It's just that there aren't many women there and those that are...are old!"

"And there are no young men there?" Atlantis guessed.

"No. Just a few scholars. Oh, I'm not saying they aren't interesting..."

"Just old?"

"Yes."

"There are young men here?"

"Used to be. Some years ago. That's why I begged to be allowed to visit my aunt."

They had reached the lower floor, and Atlantis began to feel a prickly chill and a distinct warmth coming from her talisman. She sensed she was being watched. She startled Kellthea with an abrupt change of subject.

"Perhaps you can tell me where I can get my clothes washed. Berto's too. Not that he particularly cares what state his are in."

Kellthea missed a step then quickly caught up. "Most of the folk do their own. There's a paved area by the river. But there might be some who would do yours for a few coppers."

"Can you take me there tomorrow?"

"Sure." Then Kellthea turned and took the bucket and brushes from Atlantis. "I'll take these back to Aunt Tansy and we'll bring up the water for you."

"I said I'd help carry it."

The girl was edgy now, like she was forcing herself to sound naïve and not look around. Atlantis did, and caught sight of a man heading towards the door out of the tavern. "What's the matter?" she asked in a low voice.

"Aunt said we're not meant to talk to strangers."

It sounded like advice her guardians had told her as a child. Instinct made her say, "Or there would be trouble?"

Kellthea nodded.

"That man that was leaving?"

Another nod. "But I don't know what he was doing here."

"He?"

"That was Volvus, the Lord's son. Oh, he was dressed like a sheep farmer, but it was him! He makes my skin crawl."

Well, Atlantis thought, that makes two of us. Did she dare go into the bar area to find Rhovert and warn him? No, she'd best play the lady for now. Rhovert, as Berto, had been looking out for himself since before she'd met him. And if the man had meant trouble, his talisman would have warned him too.

Atlantis emerged from the relaxing bath, feeling clean and refreshed, and dressed in the lighter clothes she usually slept in. Then she let out the water through the pipe in the bottom. Tansy, when she brought up fresh towels, had explained how the water was filtered to be reused. She was considering the process, while she waited for Rhovert to return.

When he did, she greeted him with, "Learn anything?"

"Lot's of hints, very little straight out information. But there is definitely a shortage of able-bodied young men."

Atlantis told him what she had picked up from Tansy and Kellthea.

"The Lord's son, you say?" Rhovert pounced on that when she reached that point. "What did he look like?"

"Kellthea said a sheep farmer, but all I can tell you is he had a dark brown wool jacket over his other clothes. I also know my talisman was getting very warm."

"I think I know who you mean. I did feel the heat of the talisman when he brushed past me. He had probably been close enough to listen. Well, when I go visit Tarthal tomorrow, I will wait to see if he admits being here. And if I am quizzed about being here, I have my reasoning well worked out."

While she had done her fair share of clothes, washing, Atlantis preferred to pay someone else to do them when she could. This time, she compromised, and asked for help to get Berto's done.

At first, the women seemed uncommunicative, although they had been chatting like magpies until they had noticed her. One did agree to her request, and merely set to work. It was Kellthea who broke the ice. She had some soiled table cloths from the inn, and announced, "Aunt Tansy asked me to wash these, and said you'd help me learn how to do it properly."

The women all knew Tansy, and now they became very interested in this previously unknown niece.

Kellthea gave out much the same information about herself that she'd told Atlantis, and the women started nodding and revealing what they knew.

"That be the group that live near the lake? We rarely sees any of them here."

Another said, "They've not been drafted then?"

Kellthea said, "They're all old!" The women chuckled.

A few of the women were not much older than Kellthea. One said, "There's none here worth trying for. Our men got taken and we've not see them since. My little brother tried to follow them, but he got all beat up and left lying by the northern road."

Atlantis didn't mind being ignored. She was listening and comparing what she heard to what she knew was happening elsewhere. Here things were different.

For one, other lords were drafting men to be trained to fight and protect the towns, but it was on a roster so only part of their time was taken from their usual work. Disappearances elsewhere were random and opportunistic – not wholesale. Lord Tarthal would find little profit in farmers and artisans who could not work their trade.

Then Kellthea said, "Atlantis comes from Declanor and her brother is a wizard, like the wizard Gold Dreamer."

A raspy chuckle preceded, "Tis little's tales girl! Like dragons and orcs and other nasty creatures. Told to keep littles from misbehaving.”

Kellthea flushed, wanting to be considered adult.

Atlantis considered her words. “Before I came here, I didn’t believe that a dragon protected this realm. I thought Thulor, for who this kingdom was named, was a myth.”

The old woman chuckled again. “Hasn’t been that much protecting going on these past years, girl!”

“No, Thulor was old – many, many of our human generations old – and her power was waning. She hoarded what she had left to ensure the birth of her mage successor.”

“Nonsense, girl.”

“No. The creature that is the real cause of all our troubles tried to prevent that, but Thulor had chosen a new champion, and Petulor has grown safely to maturity.” No need to add that no one knew where she was just then, and her champion was a prisoner in Vatarik.

“Huh! You’re having us on,” several other women accused.

“I am not. I am travelling with the king’s messenger, and he will confirm what I said. I just hope that Petulor comes into her full power before the army of Vatarik starts pouring over the border.”

Silence fell. Then the woman who had scorned mention of Thulor, abruptly changed her tone. “We get no word from elsewhere these days, and no traders either. What has been happening?”

“You need to keep working,” Atlantis said as she felt her back prickling again. The old woman gave her a startled look, then began to explain to her how they washed their clothes. She moved closer to Atlantis and said quietly, “Keep your voice low. I am not so old that I can’t hear we will soon have company.”

She did so, knowing that the other women who were now concentrating on their own washing, would hear what she said at a later time. She kept to the main points, the woman listened in silence until the mention of the bespelled farm boys being forced to fight the king’s soldiers, then she hissed.

“So it is to be war then. What is the king doing?”

“I am not privy to all his plans, but I do know he has troops guarding the border, and he has warned all the lords to prepare.”

“Then our lads might be training for that.”

Atlantis feared that wasn’t so, but had no proof. She was spared the need to answer by the arrival of a pair of horse riders. The old woman abruptly changes topics.

"So you're saying that women in Declanor do that? Wear breeches? Like men?"

"Yes, when they are working in the fields."

The two riders reined in their horses and dismounted. The old woman looked up and greeted the men by repeating what she had just said aloud to Atlantis. It was a reason for all to look their way. The men were in Lord Tarthal's livery, but they were not the two from the previous night. While the men were looking at the old woman, Atlantis touched her talisman and breathed the words of a spell. She went back to rubbing soap on her clothes, until one of the men said, "I prefer my women to look like women."

She looked up as the man's eyes slid away from her – the interest deflecting spell having taken hold. The two men studied the group, them led their horses down to the edge of the water, upstream of the swirl of suds.

Most of the women went back to chatting. Talking of dull domestic things, like how many eggs their hens had laid, variations to a recipe, and the antics of their children. Under that chatter, Atlantis continued to talk to the old woman, suggesting ways to prepare for the worst such as trying to put aside food, if they could, although she had already heard of the heavy tithes. It was a while before she realised that Kellthea had slipped away to get more water.

The scream, quickly stifled, had Atlantis on her feet, ignoring the hissed warning from the old woman.

"No one, from the lowest stable boy to the Lord of the manor, has the right to lay hands on a woman unwilling," she said as she identified where the sound had come from and began running along the stream. She ran faster when she saw Kellthea being dragged into a copse of trees.

The man that held her was not having an easy time trying to carry her and keep her from calling out again. His companion, keeping a watch out behind them, saw Atlantis coming and stopped to block her way. He had his arms loosely at his sides and a smirk on his face.

"Well, well. The she-man wants a bit of it too!"

He began to strut towards her, sure of himself.

Atlantis let him grab her shoulders, then let him have a knee in his groin. She twisted free as he writhed. A second kick knocked him down onto the grass and a punch to the face put him out cold. She took a length of twine from a hidden pocket and quickly wove it around his wrists and fingers. He would have a hard time freeing himself.

Then she continued after the other man, who had only gone far enough into the trees to be hidden from the women further down the river.

Kellthea was on the ground, but still fighting. She had been taught well, and Atlantis recognised the moves and knew what she was working to do. When Kellthea kicked out at the man's front, she was in position to follow it up with a kick to his rear. He fell, gripping his painful part, cursing vilely and promising his victim retribution. He did not expect the strong grip that dragged one arm back behind him and held it while another hand forced his other arm to join it. He tried to writhe around, but he felt a knee in his back and something winding around his fingers and wrists.

"Bitch! You'll be up before Lord Tarthal for this. Attacking one of is guards is a serious crime."

"Interesting," Atlantis remarked calmly. "I wonder what the king will say when he hears that one of his lords tolerates the rape of his dependent townsfolk by his guards."

The man stopped cursing abruptly. Something in the confident stance of the two women began to worry him. The younger was now standing and looking down, neither cowed nor frightened.

"Get up!" Atlantis ordered. "Your fellow would be rapist should be rousing about now. You will both be coming with us to the Lord's manor so I can hear for myself that he condones this behaviour."

"You'll wish you kept out of this," the man threatened, trying to get to his feet with his hands behind him.

"As will anyone who condones your behaviour," Atlantis countered. "Do you realise that it is treason to attack a King's Envoy?"

"Who? You? That's a laugh."

"Laugh then! All the way to the king's dungeon. You should hope he puts you there, rather than leaving you tied up outside for the chancy creatures to get you."

His further blustering was ignored, as Atlantis drew a hunting knife out from a discrete sheath. She spoke to Kellthea. "The other one isn't far. If he gives you trouble, I think you know what to do with this."

The eyes of the younger girl gleamed. "I do. My mother taught me from a young age."

"You and I need to talk," Atlantis said. Once again she was feeling the prickling of an incipient premonition. The vision came over her, she saw a younger Kellthea and a dragon. One that was neither Thulor nor Petulor, was brown not black. When it morphed into a human shape, it stopped her in her tracks. But the vision didn't end there. The seeming of the man changed and this one morphed into a demon and she had a brief glimpse of Berto.

Her prisoner might have tried to take advantage of her distraction, except that Kellthea had the knife touching his throat.

"You won't stab me, girlie."

"I don't stab men, only animals," she said evenly. "These days, with most of the useful men gone, women and girls still have to eat and feed families."

He made the mistake of trying to call her bluff, only to feel a trickle of blood start to dribble down his neck.

In another moment, Atlantis was back with it, and began shoving her prisoner back towards the women.

"What is it?" Kellthea asked, keeping up.

Atlantis didn't answer the question, saying instead, "We take him and his mate to the women and have them watch them. I have to get to the manor."

Kellthea didn't persist with her question, just ran ahead to where the other man was awake and cursing.

Seeing the knife in the girl's hand, he obeyed her command to get up, but was unsteady on his feet. When he saw his mate was also tied up, anger turned him mute.

At first, the other women backed away.

"These men will be taken before your Lord. In this realm, what they intended is a hanging offence," Atlantis stated.

The two men tensed for a moment, then smirked – as if the words were a joke that only they "I need to leave them here, while I go to the manor. They won't cause trouble."

She pushed her prisoner down onto the stones, away from the working women. Kellthea directed her prisoner over to join the other, but when he refused to sit down, simply swung a leg around behind his knees, so he collapsed onto the ground. The other women stared at her with fresh respect, and didn't notice Atlantis gripping her talisman and muttering quietly. The words were of no spell she had learnt but she hoped that Petulor's magic would act on her wishes. Roman had often told her most magic worked on intent, not merely words. The men became like man shaped rocks, their mouths open in silenced innuendo.

For the benefit of the women, although she was looking at the men, she added, "Just some minor women's magic. They will stay like that until the counter spell."

With the women eying the men, Atlantis strode off in the direction of the manor house. When she was out of sight, she broke into a run. She wasn't surprised to find Kellthea keeping up with her.

"Who was your mother?" Atlantis asked as she ran. Knowing the answer seemed to be as urgent as getting to where Rhovert was about to meet trouble.

"Dorothea Woolweaver."

"She was a dragon priestess."

"She never actually said so, but...she must have been. How did you know?"

"She trained you, the same way my mother trained me."

"Did she teach you about dragons?"

"I was more interested in fighting."

"I wasn't...until now." Kellthea stopped talking, needing all her breath to keep running.

They both slowed as the manor came into sight.

"There are guards on the wall," Atlantis noted. "Is that usual?"

"My aunt says they are there to protect Lord Tarathal. Though, should the town be attacked, we are meant to go in there for protection. That is where are tithes are being stored, and if need be we live on them."

It sounded like the instructions the Lord's had been given, but Atlantis had heard comments about the harshness of the tithes, although the speakers had been quickly told to keep quiet. Such a need to censor what they said, friend to friend, told her something was very wrong. Even she could see the tithes were keeping the women at a level just above starvation. None of the women that had been doing their washing had much flesh on their bones.

"Where do we go in?" Atlantis asked, trying to hide her inner agitation. "Do you know?"

"Important guests go in the front – where the four guards are. See them? Just along the road?"

"Well, I wasn't invited – only Berto."

"When I bring in eggs from Aunt Tansy's chooks, I go in via the kitchen. Come on, I'll show you."

"Hurry!"

"What's the rush?"

Atlantis wasn't prepared to explain her visons, particularly the one where Kellthea talking to a dragon had morphed into Rhovert fighting a demon. "Later. It might be nothing."

"We need to go around to the side of the keep."

"Are there guards?"

"Probably, but they know I bring eggs."

"You aren't carrying any now."

"No. Wait. I'll pick up a few stones and carry them in my apron."

While she did, Atlantis found the small metal sphere she carried in a pocket. She unlatched the two halves, but didn't pull them apart. Her brother Roman, had placed a powerful charm on it...just in case they encountered a demon larger than the messenger demons and the incubi. Rhovert had one too, but if he was fighting...

CHAPTER 40 - Rhovert

Rhovert, dressed as befit an envoy of King Westron, approached the door of the manor on foot, eyeing the four men on guard. As he came closer, he saw that two were merely watching him. The other two, with thumbs in their sword belts, were more belligerent. He decided he could not have looked threatening, or they would have their hands on their swords.

"Who approaches the manor of Lord Taranthal?"

"I am Berto, envoy of King Westron. Please advise your Lord of my arrival. He is expecting me."

"He was! Yesterday. He is not impressed."

"He will be even less impressed when I explain that you delayed me even further," Rhovert countered.

Although not dressed as his merc persona, Rhovert was not unarmed. His sister, Leanne, had insisted on him having weapons that could be well hidden, but drawn quickly. His hand, was ready to draw one if needed to make his point. The subtle movement, betrayed the body language of a fighter. The guard that had spoken, stopped his arrogant strut forward, and gestured for one of the watchers to take the message within.

"You will have a letter of introduction?" the guard challenged.

Rhovert drew out a scroll, tightly rolled, from a pocket in his tunic. It unrolled by itself, and when the man touched it, he quickly withdrew his hand.

"It's magicked!"

"Naturally," Rhovert commented, as if expecting the man should have known. "However, your lord, as the intended recipient, will be unaffected. That is the reason why the king has something personal from each of his lords."

"Come inside then. I sent Jessop to announce you."

The same guard, who still hadn't identified himself, let the way into the manor and along a maze of passages, to a room at the centre of the keep. Rhovert was sure there would be a quicker route, but made no comment.

Lord Taranthal was seated in a chair that looked too big for him. His clothes too, seemed a size too big, and looked to have been put on hurriedly. Rhovert had not seen the man in person since the night Petulor had been hatched. He now seemed to be a shrunken effigy of that man.

When the lord nodded, Rhovert came forward to an easy speaking distance and bowed. It was that of a king's envoy to a noble of the realm, not quite a bow of equals. He introduced himself, and his reason for being there.

"I am very pleased to welcome news from my king," Taranthal's tired sounding voice answered. "Please be seated and read to me the news my king wishes me to know."

As he was seating himself on the chair angled towards the Lord, Rhovert saw a younger man, flanked by two guards, entering from a curtained off archway. Tarathal saw his attention move, and glanced in the same direction.

"My son, Volvus. He is my right hand man these days. Since I am unable to get around."

Volvus nodded an acknowledgement and said, "You have news from the king? Let's see your introduction, and hear what you have to say."

Tarathal would have waved away the formal introduction, but Volvus had him open the letter and took it once his father had read it. Only then did he gesture for Rhovert to speak.

Rhovert opened another scroll, and seemed to be reading from it, although by then, he knew it word for word. He paused after each point, and glanced at both nobles to see they were listening intently. Taranthal, although leaning forward, appeared to be staring somewhere beyond him. His eyes were milky white. Volvus though, was staring directly at him, like an eagle eyeing prey. For a moment, Rhovert thought he caught a flash of orange in the eyes, but decided it must have been a reflection from the fire – a sudden flare.

When he finished, Taranthal spoke. "His majesty is very generous. But so far, we have had no trouble. I do not see the need to have extra troops brought into my manor."

Volvus took over speaking as the old Lord's breathing became raspy. At the same time, he produced a stoppered vial and handed it to his father once he had eased the stopper out. Tarathal held the vial in both hands and breathed in the aromatic fumes. His breathing began to ease.

"My father's guards are well trained, and we are currently training all the local men of fighting age and fitness. Should the invasion that his majesty has foreseen come to reality, they will be ready to reinforce the manor guards. We will be ready to fight for the kingdom."

"I will inform his majesty of your offer," Rhovert spoke gravely. "Have you any requests or intelligence that you wish me to bring to his majesty under a privacy seal?"

While Tarathal's breathing had eased, his voice was becoming hoarser and hoarser by the moment, and was now almost inaudible. Volvus leaned closer to him. When he straightened, Volvus said, "There is a matter. My father has already written and sealed a missive to be sent. I will fetch it from his chamber. Please do not make my father try to talk. When he has these spells, the remedy makes it hard for him to talk."

Rhovert nodded, but he could see the old Lord was trying to speak. When Volvus and his two guards had gone, Taranthal gestured for Rhovert to come closer. The guard who had originally escorted Rhovert had apparently returned to his post. He glanced right around to be sure, then crouched next to the old man.

Taranthal's gnarled fingers grabbed his wrist, and Rhovert instinctively reached for his talisman, willing healing energy to the man.

"What magic is that?" Taranthal demanded.

"A healing spell the king's wizard gave me."

"Save it for yourself, Berto. I do not have many days left. Tell the king – beware. Those to the north do not wish him well. They have bewitched my son. He is not the man I raised from a child."

Before Rhovert could question that statement, the old man fell forward. A sharp expulsion of air from his lungs, followed as the old hand relaxed its grip.

Rhovert had caught him so he didn't fall to the stone floor, and he felt for the pulse of blood normally felt at the neck.

"Dragon shards!" Rhovert swore under his breath. He eased the old lord back into his chair and before he could straighten up, was grabbed from behind. His talisman flaring abruptly into heat, as

Volvus shoved past him and went to his father. He searched for signs of life, then turned with a surge of anger.

"You killed him!" came the loud, unjust accusation.

"No! He just fell forward, and I stopped him from falling onto the floor."

Volvus was drawing his sword, and Rhovert abruptly broke free of the man who'd grabbed him, and moved aside.

"He was alive when I went out!" Volvus yelled.

"He was an old, sick man," Rhovert countered, keeping aware of the guard and Volvus. The accusation was ludicrous, he was being set up.

"As lord of this manor, I have the right to judge and pass sentence. I hereby deem you guilty of murder and sentence you to death."

Rhovert was reacting, even as Volvus rushed at him. The guard tried to grab him, but found himself swung around as a shield, then released as Rhovert released two wrist knives into his hands. He was already mouthing the words of the protection spell, and just in time. The guard behind him cursed as his sword slid away from its intended slash. He tried again, only to have his sword break when it hit the hidden armour under Rhovert's tunic. Armour that was strengthened as part of the protective spell.

"He's wearing chain mail!" that guard yelled a warning to Volvus. The new lord, threw something with his left hand that hit Rhovert hard on the cheek. A cloud of aromatic vapour forced its way into Rhovert's nostrils, burning them. He risked a quick swipe with his sleeve, to remove the rest of the oily liquid. Already, he was feeling his mind dulling. The stuff smelt like the potion for breathing, but something in it was poison. His own breathing was getting harder, but he knew he had to fight. Volvus was calling for someone, and again, Rhovert was grabbed from behind. He turned the knife to stab behind and heard an oath as the man released him. Then he ducked, just as Volvus tried another slash. His movement gave him a glimpse of another guard behind him, and his second knife, thrown instinctively, found its intended target. The man fell, with the knife in his throat, and Rhovert reached and grabbed his sword.

Only his unexpected agility saved him from a severe whack on his protective armour. He felt the blow, it unbalanced him, but only for a moment, and then he was defending himself from Volvus's insane attack. He concentrated on defence, for the protective spell might make his armour stronger, and himself faster, but Volvus could still get a deadly slash where he had no armour. He was needing all his attention for staying alive.

Atlantis reached the passage leading to the audience chamber, only to have her way blocked.

"His Lordship is having a private audience. You may not enter."

"I am Atlantis Gold Dreamer, and an envoy of King Westron in my own right. I have just received an urgent message that your lord needs to hear immediately."

"Show us your warrant!"

She took it out. It was identical in form to the one Rhovert had produced. The two guards in front of her conferred, and allowed her past. They followed her to the curtain, and it was only when they moved it aside, did the fact of the fight draw their attention. Somehow, the curtain had muffled all sound from within the chamber.

Atlantis moved in, feeling a fleeting itch of magic before it was negated by her talisman. She was grabbed by one guard as the other pushed past, telling her to, "Stay there!"

She saw that Rhovert was holding his own, so she reached into her pocket for the metal orb, She flicked it open one handed, and activated the attraction spell, using the words her brother had taught her. The arm being held, was gripped above the elbow, so that hand went up to her talisman. Her mutterings might have been mistaken for fear, or disbelief, but it was the guards' turn to exclaim in the next moment.

The place where Volvus had been fighting, was now occupied by an immensely ugly creature with a reddish, wrinkled face, two wings tightly furled to his back, and a tail that coiled up against them.

Atlantis saw Rhovert's eyes widen when the handsome but angry face changed to reveal the reddish skin with the underlying purple markings of the true demon form. The two guards with Atlantis would have gone in, but she ordered them to, "Stay back!" and the command held them.

She moved forward, the hand with the open orb, outstretched. She chanted softly to increase the power of the attraction spell meant to pull the creature into the orb. Her whole body was rigid. She wasn't a sorceress, and whilst the spell should work for her … things could also go dreadfully wrong.

A glance from the demon, directly at her, told her it was feeling the pull. She wondered if it yet realised it was showing it's true form. It did realise that Rhovert's increasingly ferocious attack was forcing it towards her.

Suddenly, furled wings expanded and made a powerful down sweep that raised the creature off the floor. Rhovert had to change the angle of his attack and defence, spinning like a child's toy spinner to protect himself. The demon circled him, attacking more fiercely and with greater desperation. It was beginning to shrink in size, as the attraction spell pulled on its essence.

When Rhovert tripped over the outflung arm of one of the dead guards, the demon abruptly changed directions, swooping straight at Atlantis, wings angling to envelop and smother her, while its hand still held the sword.

The wings allowed little air through to her, but Atlantis stood her ground, kept her arm out stretched. Somehow, the demon had managed to stop the attraction spell, and where it was touching bare skin, she was feeling like she was too close to a fire. She couldn't call out, but what gave her courage was the glint in Rhovert's eye as he stalked closer to her.

"Come any closer and I will finish this with the woman's head separating from her shoulders."

There was not a trace of fear or worry in Rhovert's eyes. He had a plan, what it was she didn't know.

"Now! Atlantis," he yelled.

There was nothing she could do, but the demon did not know that. It changed its grip, trying to see what she was going to do. The distraction was long enough for Rhovert to leap forward, and thrust. The demon screeched, and released Atlantis, Its hands went to try and stop the gush of ichor from the slash in its side. The inner flesh sizzled as the air touched it.

Atlantis released her own dagger with her left hand and thrust it into the creature's heart. Then, with a whoosh, the rest of the creature's essence was dragged to the orb, the creature becoming smaller, then insubstantial. The orb snapped shut, and resealed itself.

In an effort to stave off hysterics, Atlantis said weakly, "Did you have to waste time giving it a gut wound?"

"Didn't think you'd want me to skewer you too," Rhovert replied in kind. "Nice thrust with the dagger!"

"Couldn't rely on you getting yours back from your victims in time!"

"Didn't want their incubi to find other hosts," Rhovert countered.

Atlantis took a more careful look at the other dead guards. One had a knife in the front of the neck, the other lower down, in his chest, but a spreading stain of purplish ichor surrounded it.

More guards were staring in, plus the two Atlantis had commanded. Rhovert straightened, and called out, "Come in!"

Four men came in, stumbling when they saw the dead guards and their lord slumped in his oversized chair.

"Lord Taranthal is dead," Rhovert announced. "Poisoned by a substance mixed with his breathing elixir." He went to the chair and found the dropped vial, and stoppered it. He showed the vial to the guards before dropping it in his pocket. "You don't want to breathe in the fumes. They burn the lining of your nose, and wherever they touch."

"But...but...we saw a demon. Where did it go?"

Atlantis brought out the now sealed orb. "It is gone, likely dead and gone. The question should be – how did it come to replace Baron Volvus, and is Volvus still alive."

No one had an answer.

"I was told," Rhovert began, "That Volvus had become an arrogant sort. When did that begin?"

"He always was," one of the new guards admitted. "Even when we were littles."

"Has he been away at any time?" Rhovert persisted.

"Aye, he was. He went to visit his mother's kin. Up north."

"With Kilkenny as overlord?"

"Aye."

"Well, I still have to go there, so I will ask about him," Rhovert told them. "Now, as King's representative, I hereby take charge of this manor in the absence of the blood heir. Is there a great hall in this manor?"

"Aye, just through yonder door."

"Fine. Is there a way to summon all guards, and manor folk there?"

"Aye, Sir."

"Then do that!" Rhovert turned to another guard. "I also want all the townsfolk to be summoned here. Arrange it!"

Atlantis spoke then, "What of those that live out from the town. There is an enclave of scholars. Kellthea grew up there."

"Who?" Rhovert asked, distracted from his thoughts of what needed doing.

As if summoned, Kellthea came into the room, with an elderly man following. She saw the bodies, and slowed, but only her expression tightened.

Atlantis introduced Rhovert to Kellthea, and he immediately directed her to take a command to the enclave for the occupants to come to the manor.

"Berto, Sir, they will probably choose to stay. Most of them are ancient, and they are well protected there. However, if I am not needed, I will borrow a horse and ride there. They should know of what happened here, and they may decide to send a representative."

"Fine, you go and see that she has an appropriate beast to ride." The third guard went off, gesturing to Kellthea.

The man who had arrived with Kellthea, came forward. "Sir, I have heard the Lord is dead. May I examine him? I am the Lord's personal healer. Though there was little I could do for him anymore."

Rhovert drew the man over to the body of Taranthal.

"I believe that the aromatic substance used to help his breathing had an astringent substance added. I may be wrong, but I caught a sniff of it and felt the effect in my nose. Please examine him, but tell no one of your findings except for myself. Later, I will allow him to be moved. For now, I wish him to remain in this chamber."

"I will do as you say, but I don't understand…I compounded the aromatic myself, and only my lord's personal guards were allowed near him."

"We can talk more after I have spoken to all the people in the manor."

Rhovert moved towards the great hall, with Atlantis keeping up with him.

"Taranthel was silenced. He managed to say to me, that those to the north don't wish the king well, and they bewitched his son, who now wasn't the child he had raised."

"I wonder if he realised what had replaced his son?" Atlantis wondered aloud.

"I don't think so, but even though no demon can emulate a human perfectly, Taranthal had no reason to suspect such an event."

Atlantis nodded agreement. "What do we do now?"

"I want you to contact your brother and tell him what has happened here. As much as I want to head further north, we will need to stay here until a care-taker lord is appointed and gets here."

"But that means that Kilkenny will be warned...or is that why you wanted everyone here?"

"Partly, but I suspect it is already too late to stop word getting there. It is more the idea that if Kilkenny's manor is fully under the control of the Vatarins..." he meant Ciabolo and the demons he controlled, "...then this manor is like an empty flask waiting to be filled. Particularly with all the men gone. Did you get a hint of where?"

A flash of a vision came over Atlantis. "North, I think, near the lake."

"We will need to check that out. If they were being trained to fight, they may be almost ready."

"Ready to fight for Thulor or against," Atlantis posed the question, and saw Rhovert frown. She went on, "Can we get one of the nearer groups of the King's Own to come here?"

"They are all needed where they are."

"But is that threat as great or immediate as the one we have here?"

"You have a point. Tell your brother to get the king to authorise it."

"OK. Anything else?"

"Keep people out of this chamber. I think Tarathal's personal guards are loyal, so they can help. Don't let any of Volvus's personal group in. You know the difference in the livery?"

"Yes, Kellthea and I left two of them tied up by the river. They can wait. They will find out soon enough that their protector cannot help them. Later...handle this first."

Rhovert drew the curtain behind him and went to stand just

below the Lord's dais. He watched as off duty guards, the lords other dependents and manor workers began to drift in. From the expressions on the faces, many of which betrayed unease, he gathered that rumours were already spreading. He needed to quell them with the truth, and an assurance of leadership. He began to get odd looks, being that he was a stranger to them all.

In his turn, he was studying each person as they came in. There were probably people who were in Voltus's circle, and they might be the ones to watch.

His elbow was jogged by an older man, who Rhovert recognised as Tarathal's steward. His eyes were red rimmed, betraying his grief, but he was still alert.

When Rhovert turned, the man's eyes widened, but as he opened his mouth to speak, Rhovert said quickly, "I am Berto, King's Envoy, acting on the king's behalf." He had his hand to his talisman, and mentally voicing the spell to test for truth. "I need to be sure of the loyalty of everyone here."

"Of course, Sir. I am at your service, and will obey the new lord as I did Taranthal. Has Baron Volvus been told of his father's death?"

Rhovert sensed no falsehood in the man's speech or manner. "I do not know. That is a matter I will raise later. What I need now is to know is if anyone who lives in the manor is missing when I start talking. I may also need to know about particular people."

The room continued to fill, and when the trickle seemed to stop, the steward listed five names, all members of Voltus's honour guard.

Rhovert bit off the curse he wanted to utter. He imagined the five to be galloping north.

He strode up onto the dais, only because it meant he could get everyone's attention. Instantly, all eyes went to him. He spotted Atlantis looking through the gap between curtain and arch, and gave her a gesture indicating she should scout the keep. Then he drew on the manner of his father and introduced himself.

"I am Berto, Envoy from King Westron. I came here to speak with Lord Taranthal on a matter of great importance. However, I was too late to prevent him from being poisoned. It is now my sad duty to inform you that Lord Taranthal is dead."

Murmurings broke out, and one yelled an accusation, ending

with, "...and where is Baron Volvus? Why is he not here?"

Rhovert had a good idea the caller was one of Volvus's cronies.

"That is something I too wish to know. The man I believed to be Baron Volvus, gave Lord Tarathal his medicant to help breathing, and I believe this was poisoned. When Taranthal collapsed, I was challenged, and my opponent was revealed to be a demon."

Rhovert heard the start of a panic, and went on more loudly, "The demon was killed, and its remaining essence captured. However, the whereabouts of the real Baron Volvus is now of great concern. Now I am told that Lord Taranthal and his son each had their own dedicated honour guard..."

Over two dozen men straightened and moved into a group. They eyed him, they had been suspicious, or afraid he'd blame them for the demon's deception, but when he didn't they resumed their usual arrogance – perhaps now considering themselves promoted to elite.

These ones, Rhovert knew, would need to be handled carefully.

"I will especially need your help to locate Baron Volvus and ensure he is safe."

To all the people as a group, he called loudly, "Are you all prepared to obey the lawful commands of Lord Tarathal's successor?"

Many voices called out in confirmation, some people just nodded.

"All of you here now have a very important role to play, in addition to your normal roles. Until Lord Tarathal's successor is confirmed, this manor is effectively open for invasion. Until the new Lord is confirmed, all orders will come from me. Disobeying my orders will result in harsh punishment."

There were grumblings, but no loud protests. Perhaps they realised the need for a strong leader. And perhaps, those of Volvus's guards still here, were all loyal Thulans. That would need to be checked however.

"Servants, you should all go about your work as normal, but there will be mandatory weapons training for all. I know most of you are not fighters, and have no weapons. However, even pots and pans can be effective weapons." He went on for the benefit of the townsfolk now adding to the crowd in the hall. "I urge all the townsfolk to move into the manor for safety, and go out from here to your daily work. Those that were concerned were advised to set up a system of watchers to warn of the approach of horsemen and armed fighters, and find a way to sound an alarm.

Questions were being called from the newcomers, but Rhovert halted the barrage for long enough to send the on duty guards back to their duty, and those off duty to start preparing for a siege or invasion.

When all but the guards that had been Tarathal's personal guards had left, Rhovert approached them.

"I have heard there is a training place where most of the men from this area have gone to learn to fight. Can we expect them to return here to help us?"

Uneasy glances were shared by some of the guards, Rhovert studied their unconscious mannerisms and waited. Finally, he had an answer.

"We hope what you say is true, Sir. But..."

Rhovert finished what the man didn't say. "You feel it is not so?"

He received nods from all.

Another man admitted, in a low voice, "Especially since who we thought was the baron passing on the Lord's will, wasn't."

"Had you asked your Lord about it?"

"Aye, but he said Volvus was organising it."

"Well, I share your doubts, and we need to find out the truth. We need to be alert for an attack by the King of Vatarik. So far, he is only sending in groups of brigands to vandalise our defences, steal our harvests and valuables and thin out the King's guards."

"We've had none of that here," the first speaker said.

"In other areas, further south from the border, and along the border, the manors have not been spared the brigands attention, and that makes my hackles go up here."

"We are somewhat isolated here."

"All the more likely that enemy will try for here to dig in and begin his campaign. When he crosses the border in earnest, he will come with an overwhelming army. Here, he can assemble it, and run little risk of word getting to the King. And I am sure that a large proportion of that army will be men of Thulor who have been taken unwilling and bespelled to fight against Thulor."

"What can we do, Sir?"

"Well, in addition to what I have already said, I would like all of you here, keep your eyes and ears open, and if anything even slightly seems odd, come and tell me."

"We aren't in command anymore," the original speaker admitted.

Rhovert grinned briefly. "All the better. I will need to check Volvus's guards." He saw understanding on all faces.

Rhovert returned to the small audience chamber to hear what the healer had to say. It confirmed his suspicions. The fake Volvus, had deliberately killed the old lord at that time, and Rhovert was sure he was to be set up to take the blame – had he not first uncovered the demon and killed it. The fake Volvus may have been helping Tarathal's condition worsen over a period of time.

Atlantis followed servants into the room. They had refreshments for Rhovert, she had news from her brother.

Rhovert was ready for a drink, and offered the healer refreshments too. He moved aside to hear what Atlantis had to tell him.

"There is a troop on the way here as we speak. A very capable Captain, with a highly skilled sorceress. They will be here in three days."

Her faint smile betrayed the identity of the troop mentioned. "His majesty is sending for a distant cousin of Tarathal to come here to be caretaker lord, while the whereabouts of the real Volvus is ascertained. He told Roman, to tell us, 'well done' and stresses the need to do the very things you have already considered."

Rhovert smiled grimly, and was inwardly elated. His father rarely praised him. The trouble was, he wanted to leave right away to check out Kilkenny.

Three days later, after the arrival of a tired and dust begrimed troop of twenty four King's guards, and their leaders, his sisters Leanne and Finora, Rhovert and Atlantis were ready to set off. He had only to report what he had done since he had reported to Roman. Leanne had listened, and then said, "Go!" She also sent half her troop with them.

Finora, although tired, announced, "I will go with you."

The decision did not surprise Leanne. Either Finora had mentally communicated with her twin, or the idea had been discussed already.

Rhovert had told her, "I have to admit, I am relieved to have you along. Tis and I have been able to do some spells, but only minor ones."

"I don't know, you did well here, killing that demon. It would have been a major ally of Ciabolo."

Leanne agreed. "Removing that creature is a decided victory for us. Let us hope Ciabolo does not learn of it. However, you need to be prepared for even worse with Kilkenny. He has to be in league with Ciabolo too, and his manor is between here and the border. What road are you taking?"

"I want to check out where the town's menfolk are supposed to be training. If all is well, I will send them back here."

As they rode away from the northern edge of the town, and the last of the grain fields, they saw two riders coming towards them. Rhovert sent two of the troopers to intercept them, but continued on.

"It's Kellthea," Atlantis announced. She then explained to Finora, "She is the daughter of a dragon priestess. She says she has no magic, but I think there is some. She is also half Vatarin."

"Who is her father?" Finora asked.

"She hasn't come out and said."

"What about the other rider?"

"I expect it is a representative of the enclave of scholars where she grew up."

"Maybe father needs to talk to them. Your brother said he is collecting scholars, but has given no specific reason."

"We don't have time to stop and talk to them," Rhovert frowned as he kept riding. "And the stranger rides like an old man."

Finora snorted. "My mentor Ermytrude, wasn't good on a horse, but there was nothing wrong with her mind. You can promise to talk to him after you have dealt with Kilkenny, or he can come with us and keep out of the way."

"Pick up the pace," Rhovert called back to the rest of the party.

They paused where the two travellers had pulled over. One of the riders he had sent ahead told him, "They will ride with us. They believe the training ground is deserted."

Rhovert swore, but in fact, the news was not unexpected.

Only rubbish and a dusty square – barren of vegetation – showed where the missing men from Tarathal's manor had trained. Another area had regular rectangles as patches of dead grass, likely where tents had been erected. The huge cooking pit to one side of the square contained cold ashes and the desiccated bones of roasted creatures.

The troopers Leanne had sent with the group, obeyed Rhovert's instructions to scout the area and hopefully find out the direction the men had taken when leaving. No tracks were found beyond the confines of the camp.

One found an oddity. An erected, rope bound portal, made from tree trunks, over a bed of ashes.

"We have seen the like of this before, Sir. Our quarry of the time escaped through it."

"A demon portal," Rhovert growled. "I have seen it too. The men we seek could be anywhere by now."

"What now, Sir?"

Rhovert looked around, saw that Atlantis was keeping company with the scholar and the girl, and Finora was returning from her own survey of the area. He strode her way.

"What have you found?"

"Residual traces of a perimeter shield, like Lee and I found at a farm near Rowan's Flat. It would have kept the men in, and outsiders seeing nothing. I found two more structures that might have been used as portals – smaller ones – and I made sure they cannot be used again in future. I also sealed the places where fires have been. That's the main fire pit and the one by the first portal."

"So they can't come back here except by foot," Rhovert stated.

"No," Finora assured him. "They won't be able to come here and make it a forward camp or a staging area. Like you said, they will have to come over the border by foot."

"Right! Now to deal with Kilkenny."

"What about the scholar?"

"I don't have time." Rhovert glanced that way and decided, "I'll have Atlantis go and see whatever it was they wanted to show us. You can tell them that's how it is to be. They already know who you are Fi, and a King's daughter outranks a King's Envoy."

"Very well," Finora agreed. As her brother, even though he was in his merc persona, he outranked her. "I suppose, with me and the best half of Lee's troop, you can't get into too much trouble."

"Tis and I did okay at Lord Tarathal's," he reminded her. "But, like I said, I am glad to have you along."

While Rhovert called the troopers into a group, Finora went over to Atlantis.

"Oh, no," Atlantis greeted her. "He is still going on to Kilkenny's manor. Right?"

Finora grinned wryly at her sister in law.

"He's getting more like your father every day."

The scholar lowered his hood to reveal an old, weather tanned and wrinkled face. His hair, though, was still a rich tawny brown.

"My lady, we have not yet been properly introduced. I am Hestnor, scholar from the Deander Enclave. This is my protégé and student, Kellthea."

"Finora, Sorceress of the First Troop of the King's Guards. I am pleased to meet you."

Kellthea betrayed surprise with widened eyes and an 'o' with her mouth. "You are a Princess."

"It's no secret," Finora said with a smile. "However, these days, I am of more use as a sorceress."

Hestnor nodded, both in respect and agreement.

Finora went on, "You can tell what you must to Atlantis, King's Envoy in her own right. Please do not consider it an insult. My father trusts her skill and her memory. She is also the sister of my father's chief wizard, and sometimes advisor. So she is able to get messages to the king, through her brother."

"The Lady Atlantis will be an admirable proxy," Hestnor agreed. He turned to Atlantis. "My young protégé tells me you are the child of a dragon priestess."

"Yes, but she and my father died many years ago."

"And the magic in your line did not come to you?"

Atlantis glanced at Kellthea, realising she had already told Hestnor about her Great grand sire.

"Not the magic, just his wandering feet and curiousity. And in turn, I am very curious as to what you, all the way up here, know of him. Anyway, Finora, tell Berto I am quite happy to leave the next fight to him as he has so many helpers now."

Finora grinned at her teasing thrust aimed at her brother, and turned to join the briefing in progress.

"And we might as well get going," Atlantis announced.

"Just like that?" Kellthea asked. "Without saying goodbye?"

"Berto isn't one for soppy partings. Besides, I will be rejoining him after I have seen what you need to show me."

"I thought, you and he, were…"

"Lovers?" Atlantis finished the thought. "Sometimes." She felt her own face flush.

"I did not expect to meet the King's son, this far from the palace," Hestnor remarked.

Now Atlantis was astounded.

"He is not at all what I heard him to be."

When she found her wits again, she said, "I don't know what you can see that others don't, but perhaps you also understand the reason for the difference. Perhaps the latest rumours being spread about him have not reached here. Last I heard, he had fled south to Declanor."

"Does the king know that you and he…" Kellthea began again, but stopped when Hestnor glanced her way.

Atlantis sensed that Hestnor was about to say more, but spoke first. "The king keeps a lot to himself, but he is hoping for grandchildren, and Prince Rhovert has yet to show interest in any of the lovely court decorations, and Berto knows I have no wish to be pregnant. Come on. Let's get going. Hestnor, you know the way?"

They rode in silence for a time, leaving the flat land and entering an area of low hills.

"Is this the Great Northern forest?" Atlantis asked as the trees on either side of the trail began to get more dense.

"The fringes, yes," Hestnor confirmed. "You need not fear. No one will harm us."

"It continues up to the border, doesn't it?"

"And beyond."

"Berto told me that people go into the forest and never return, and the same about the lake. Those that cross it, don't return."

"There are trails through the forest," Hestnor told her. "However, they are hard to find, since the trees block most of the light."

"What if an army tried to come through, with axes and flaming torches?"

"They will be forced back."

Atlantis sensed his absolute certainty. "But something is going on up this way, with Taranthal's son being replaced by a demon."

Only after she had sad it, did she wonder what prompted it. Hestnor was now staring at her.

"That demon is well contained now," Atlantis assured him.

"This part of Thulor has always been a forgotten backwater, from way back in history and the time of the seven kings," Hestnor commented.

Snippets from her great grand sire's journals came to her mind. "There were eight realms..."

"Yes, and very few can go to the lost realm. Only those whose blood is from the old ones."

"You are intriguing me," Atlantis admitted. "Is that where you are taking me?"

"Yes."

Kellthea gasped. "I'm to go there too?"

"It is time, young one, to know what you are."

Hestnor would say no more. He was proved correct that no one would trouble them on the journey.

"This is where I grew up," Kellthea told Atlantis when they rode through the huge wooden gates in the wall around the enclave. "Since I was little, anyway, when my mother brought me here."

"Who was your father?"

"Mother only ever said, 'He was a decent man, once.' She never gave me his name."

Atlantis looked around. She saw men and women moving around, just as in any town or village, but little prickles of premonition were building up inside her.

"Child, go to the kitchen and see to some refreshments. We will be with Alkinor."

The names Hestnor and now Alkinor, were beginning to niggle her mind, but for a moment, she was distracted.

"Alkinor is the Esteemed Elder of this conclave," Hestnor explained.

Atlantis knew the Thulan language better than most Declanese, but her mind had to hunt for the meaning of 'conclave'. A private meeting? She had taken 'enclave' to mean a town, and it did look like one, but now she wondered what nuances she was missing. She recalled the women she had already noticed. They seemed to have originated in many different lands. Some looked Thulan, others Declanese, some had the dark skin of those from the land beyond Vatarik, and some might even be Vatarins. The men, except for hair colour and skin tone, were of a single type, apparent in the facial bone structure.

Hestnor led her into a large garden, with plants and trees widely spaced. A tall, ancient man, stood erect in the open, watching them approach. Atlantis felt her talisman growing very cold. Closer to the man, the air became warmer, and slightly smoky...like dragons!

A great silvery shape began to gleam beside the man.

"Petulor!" Atlantis exclaimed. The form became fully visible, and moved closer. She wanted to demand answers to so many questions. "Have you heard from Ven?"

The voice in her head said, "The contact is not strong." The silver dragon's tail thrashed around, betraying Petulor's agitation. "She will not try to leave that place yet."

Alkinor spoke aloud. "The time is not right."

He turned back to Atlantis, and now she could see his eyes were clouded, and the oddest impression of an old dragon seemed to enfold him. "Young one, what is your name?"

"Atlantis Gold Dreamer."

"You travel with the son of Thulor's king?"

Either these folk, dragons, communicated mind to mind, or he was a seer.

"Yes. Rhovert and I are mates."

She sensed then, the old man/dragon's elation.

"Atlantis is a true dragon friend," Petulor stated.

"And it is the time foretold when we must once again show ourselves. The pieces are all falling together."

"Is that why Petulor is here?" Atlantis asked, now certain that all dragons liked to seem omnipotent.

Hestnor fetched three large cushions, one for himself, one for Atlantis and one for Kellthea who was returning with a dangling drink filled skin, and a tray of cups and cakes.

Only when everyone was seated, although Alkinor remained standing, did he raise the reason why she, and she assumed Rhovert, had been invited to come.

"I think, young Gold Dreamer, that you have already guessed what I am. If you will not be afraid, I will change so that you see me as my true self."

Kellthea gripped Atlantis's arm. "He won't hurt you."

"If he hasn't spoken to Mortmellor, I'm probably safe."

Hestnor made a sound like a snort. Any curiosity on Atlantis's part, was washed away as a giant head, longer than her height, and a body that blocked all view of the garden, replaced the elderly man. She felt the need to bow.

"Young one, we honour your presence, as your great grand sire honoured us. He gave us the means to protect ourselves, and to hide amongst the humans who once revered us, but later turned on us."

"I knew he could enable mass transformations, but his journals never mentioned...in his journals, there were few mentions of dragons."

"It was best that humans thought us dying out and gone...but that meant the enemy we thought vanquished was emboldened."

"Do you mean Ciabolo? The Serpent?" Atlantis asked.

"His kind. That one is relatively new come, although he is generations old. He has taken on humans as suits of armour. This world is not perfect for his kind. Though the lesser demons do better here."

"Yes, I've seen that," Atlantis admitted.

The great head moved slightly, as if it were a nod. "Then listen to what I will share with you."

She listened. The history of Thulor, before history was recorded, excited her, but, "Was this what you so urgently needed to tell us?"

"You need to understand the beginning," Alkinor chided gently, his cloudy eyes looking her way. "This enclave exists, but our numbers are fewer than in generations past. We cannot fight our enemy alone."

"King Westron is doing everything he can. He has scholars looking ----"

"It will not be enough. He will be missing vital information. Listen well. Even before Exconidor aligned herself with the king of this land, and gave to them the continued protection of her daughter, Thulor, our kind had sent pilgrims to all the human realms.

"As human travellers, they learnt about humans – the good, and the bad. They mated with human females whose inner light shone pure. The young, born to these women, were human shaped and something more than mere human."

"Blood lines," Atlantis breathed, beginning to see a picture, almost too vast to comprehend. It morphed, wordlessly, into a clearer picture. "You spread into all the lands," she said aloud. What she saw in her mind was like a piece of loosely woven cloth, with sections tinged with different colours, at the centre, an area of brilliance. She understood the colours to be the realms, and where she was. "This is the eighth realm!" she realised. "Magic as we know it is coming from here."

"Not all of it. Magic comes from all living things. It flows to us, we concentrate it, and keep a trickle returning."

"Can we draw on that magic?" Atlantis asked.

"I think you already do."

"Thulor's talismans?"

Petulor raised her head. "Of course. The dragon mother reminded me that my mother did that for you."

Alkinor went on. "The talismans are older that Thulor, but yes, they are the foci of our power. Thulor was enhancing the bloodlines – focussing it further in the king's line."

"And in the dragon priestesses," Atlantis breathed in awe.

"Naturally. It spread outward again—"

"You are starting to lose me," Atlantis murmured. "How does this help us now?"

"Young things are so impatient," Hestnor commented. "And I do know that time is short to prepare. I will summarise. A study of the king's ancestors will show that the line of the priestesses, keeps crossing back into the kings line. But the blood lines we started, back in the beginning, also cross back into that. Think of it as a surface of power that your king, and our new dragon mage, can tap into at need. A magic weaving.”

“I’m not magical myself, and I need to explain this to my brother – he’s the wizard in this generation.”

“Do not sell yourself short. You have different skills, but your blood is the same. That is what matters. Just as other young one here, has the blood of the Vatarin kings and of dragons.”

“I have what?” Kellthea blurted. She had been listening to Hestnor, just as intently as Atlantis, and she had known some of it – but not that!

Hestnor leant over and took her hand. “Your mother did not tell you, and that was to protect you, but your father was the former king of Vatarik.”

“NO! Please tell me that’s not true.”

“It is the truth. Why does it bother you so?”

“Because I don’t want to be like that...that ...not-man.”

Atlantis understood her revulsion. She too, reached her hand across. “It is all right. You were conceived before the creature took your sire over.”

Kellthea seemed to gag, swallow hard, and then breathed slowly.

“That was what you feared, wasn’t it?”

A nod.

Atlantis asked, “How did you know of it?”

“Things I remember, from when I was very small. I could see it. See the creature, sitting there as if he was only a normal person. I didn’t know he was a king, and I don’t think I even realised he was my father. Just that there were times when I was with my mother and he was around. I didn’t know why no one else could see what I saw.

“Later, after I had been here for some years, I heard things about the king of Vatarik. And I knew by then my mother had fled from there. Mother never knew what I overheard. Now his heir is causing war and hardship. And that man is my brother!”

“Half-brother,” Atlantis corrected.

“How does that make it different?”

“The difference, young one,” Alkinor spoke up, “Is that your mother, had the blood of dragons and in you, that blood joined the recessive dragon blood in the former king. It makes you, and your friend here, a focus. You can draw on the magic of Vatarik, as Atlantis can draw on that of Declanor."

"I'm no magic user," Kellthea protested.

Atlantis had another vision of what that meant. "Nor am I, but that doesn't matter. Do you want to bring peace to Vatarik? Do you want to remove the tyrants who are oppressing loyal Vatarins?"

At first, Kellthea's expression, already hard, didn't change. "How can I help? I am not a fighter either, merely a scholar."

Hestnor and Alkinor kept silent.

"You need to go to the palace," Atlantis said with growing certainty. "King Westron needs scholars, and there, you bring to the fight the knowledge of Vatarik, and the hoarded dragon magic of that land. I think that is what my brother and I do – bring that from Declanor."

Kellthea looked to her mentor.

Hestnor said, "Yes, It is time for us to leave here."

"Will you travel with us, Atlantis?" Kellthea asked.

She was going to say, "Yes," but a new feeling kept her from doing so. "It depends on what happens at Lord Kilkenny's manor. I am not sure what will be needed there, and afterwards. However, if you are going, you should waste no time."

"A day or so more will not matter. Let me show you around the enclave, and then when the king's son has triumphed, I will show you both a place that is a well-guarded secret."

"As you say," Atlantis conceded. "Where did Petulor go? I have questions for her." Somehow, she had been so intent on what she was learning, she hadn't seen Petulor fade out. She hadn't felt the rush of air that would have occurred if she had taken off, either.

Early in the morning, a week after he had left to go north, Rhovert's horse walked into the enclave, head drooping, and stopped by the stable. Rhovert slid from the saddle, staggering a bit when his feet met the ground.

A man in a striped cloak, came and took the horse's reins, and begin to talk softly to the exhausted animal. He began to lead the horse off.

Rhovert looked around, wondering if he should follow his horse and ask the groom where he should go. Then he saw Atlantis running towards him. Something eased inside him, though the tension headache remained.

He fell into her hug, and held her tight for a moment. "I need a bath and bed," he admitted. "But I need to talk to Roman first."

Atlantis didn't question him. She just tugged on his arm. "This way. We had word you were coming. Wash first, and have a drink. Then wake my brother. Is your report that urgent?"

"Another half hour won't hurt. It is just that father needs to send more troops up here."

"What happened?"

"Later, Tis. You can hear it all when I tell Roman. I left Vander and his sub-troop up there at Kilkenny's manor, to guard the prisoners. I am just not sure we got all the traitors. Finora has gone back to Leanne, and I was told you had come here."

"I have a lot to tell Roman as well, but I couldn't get onto him last night."

Atlantis activated the glass orb, then seemed to look into it as she rotated around. When she stopped, she said, "Hey! Brother! It's morning, wake up." After a moment, when she got no reaction, she gave a shrill whistle. They both heard, "Dragon shards! What the hell do you want? I only just got to sleep."

"Sorry," Atlantis said, with some sympathy. "Rhovert hasn't even seen his bed yet, and we both have important stuff to tell you. Are you ready to write it all down? In case you can't remember it all."

"Yeah, give me a minute."

Rhovert disappeared from the orb's view. When Roman returned to view, he yawned and said, "Keep it short."

"Suits me," Rhovert said as the ball rotated to face him.

A chuckle preceded, "Well, you look like I feel. Talk!"

Rhovert kept it brief. "Kilkenny is a traitor. He gave himself away a dozen times over. Thought himself better than his Prince, or King, though he stopped short of claiming that. He thought he could ignore a King's Envoy, and when I challenged him about that, he realised he had been caught out. The others took out his personal guards, and he still thought he could silence me. When he finally recognised Finora, he tried to summon help. He threw something into the fireplace, and the fire turned green. He was so sure it was his escape route that he ran right into the wall behind it."

Roman smirked as he wrote. "Did you see anything of where it led?"

"I don't think it was going anywhere. Finora had already blocked that fireplace. Anyway, after I had put Kilkenny in his own dungeon, we rounded up the rest of the household and freed the prisoners he'd had down there. One was his pregnant wife, and she confirmed he had been dealing with Vatarik for some years, and he had imprisoned her when she had confronted him about it. Most of the other prisoners were there because they too objected to his dealings. Vander's lot are getting as much information from them as they can and will send it to you."

"Did you find the guards that ran off from Tarathal's manor?" Roman seemed to be fully awake now.

"No, but they had been there. Kilkenny had been warned. That's why you need to get more people up there. The border here, with the lake and the forest, is wide open."

Now Roman could be seen frowning, and rubbing his hand through his bed mussed hair.

"I will tell his majesty, but from what I hear, we have all the King's troops, fully stretched. We could really use Vander's lot back where they were. The brigand raids have increased in frequency, with ambushes on trader caravans, and even the camps of the troops. Something has even stirred up the rabble around the palace. Your father thinks the major push will come soon."

Rhovert cursed softly. "There is only a handful of local fighters still at Taranthal's manor, and no one in the area around that they can call in. They were taken off, supposedly to be trained, but when we found the camp, they were gone."

He mentioned other concerns, and then became aware of an old looking man standing beside Atlantis. Very quickly, she introduced Hestnor, and outlined what the king needed to know.

"Heck yes, Sis, send them here. You and Rhovert had better come with him."

Hestnor murmured, "There is still more you must learn."

Rhovert saw Atlantis nodding, and she told her brother, "We will need a few more days."

"I really should stay up here," Rhovert tried.

"No!" Roman insisted, with unexpected urgency. "No, you need to get back."

"Why?"

Roman changed the subject. "Where are your sisters?"

"Leanne was still at Tarathal's. Finora should be back there now too."

"So half the troop is there and half further north?"

"Yes, why?"

Roman sighed. "Finora told me she and Leanne were heading back to take over Prosper's troop. He took an arrow during a skirmish with brigands. "

"So why does father want me back?"

"It's more than that," Rhovert challenged.

"I think so too, but he is not saying anything. I do know he has been sleeping badly and a few times calling out, like he was having a nightmare."

"All right, but tell him we will head back after we have seen what these scholar types need to show us."

"That will have to do," Roman grimaced. "Look, you get some sleep. His majesty has just got to bed too. I don't dare wake him for at least a couple of hours. You can argue with him then. Though, I suppose he might be able to get some local fighters from between here and there to reinforce that region. I'll get back to you."

The glass orb returned to reflecting the sunlight coming in through a high glass window.

"Dammit! We need to be sure Vatarin's forces can't flood through here."

Hestnor put a calming hand on Rhovert's shoulder. "We can help you."

"Huh? A conclave of scholars?"

Atlantis shook her head, "They aren't just scholars."

"No, only some of us," Hestnor agreed. "But, most of us are dragons."

Rhovert gaped, not believing his ears. He looked at Atlantis, who said, "Shut your mouth. It's true."

"King's son, you have only to ask and we are yours to command," Hestnor said, bowing.

"What can you do?" Rhovert was in between shock and disbelief.

"We are greatly fewer in number than we once were, but we can ensure that none of the enemy - the human kind – cross the border in this area."

"Then, yes, please," Rhovert agreed instantly. "What of the other kind? Ciabolo's demon allies."

"They are our enemies of old. Come King's son, there is one of us you need to meet."

Rhovert really wanted to do as Roman suggested. He was exhausted from days of effort, with little time to sleep. First had been the ride to Kilkenny's manner, then the intense fight against the traitor, the imperative search of Kilkenny's manor, and the long ride back. Instead, he took hold of his talisman and thought, "Give me the energy to listen to what I need to hear."

As he followed the old scholar, he felt the tiredness replaced by energy.

"You knew about him," Rhovert challenged his consort. "But you didn't mention it to Roman."

"Hestnor and Kellthea can explain things when they meet with him, and your father."

"What else did you omit to tell them?"

"Too much for now. I've written it all out and we can take the report with us. I told him the most important parts. But there is still more that they need to tell us, and I can catch you up on the rest when you've had a sleep."

Another shock waited for Rhovert outside. It was one thing to be told that the scholars here were dragons, it was quite another to see the enormous head, attached to an even more enormous body.

Atlantis let Hestnor make the introductions, for her eye had caught a flash of silver in the air and a strong shiver of apprehension raced up and down her spine. As Rhovert bowed to the dragon elder as if he were a king like his father, and spoke in the old language Atlantis had only ever heard when he'd spoken to Petulor almost nine months ago, she watched the silver flash take on a darker shade.

"Petulor," she said to herself, but Rhovert heard, looked where she was looking, then returned his attention to the dragon elder.

Petulor spiralled in to land, and trotted close to Alkinor. She stopped, but wasn't still. Agitated, Atlantis realised.

It seemed that Alkinor was aware of her state, for he raised his head and turned to look at her. Likely thoughts were passing between them. The old dragon looked at his visitors, then his snout twitched in Petulor's direction, as if conceding the conversation to her.

"King's warrior, you have to come."

Atlantis and Rhovert both looked at her. Suddenly, Atlantis blurted, "It's Ven, isn't it? She needs help. I'll come. Let me get my things." She raced off, and Rhovert was about to follow.

"King's son, you must stay!" Petulor said in his mind. "You must hear what father-dragon has to say."

"If my sister is in trouble—"

"You must stay! The King's warrior has been there before, and she will have help."

Rhovert bit off a protest, torn between priorities. He knew Petulor had the right of it. Atlantis had gone in, with his other sisters, right into the king of Vatarik's citadel. They had gone right into Ciabolo's den, brought Maeven out – that time stealing Petulor's egg from under his nose. Trouble was, Atlantis hadn't been his mate then.

He settled on saying, "When I have seen and heard what I need to here, I'm going after her! And no wet eared whelp of a dragon is going to stop me."

Atlantis returned with a hastily packed sack with basic necessities, her sword, and was strapping the last of her hidden knives into place. Petulor nuzzled her, clearly indicating she was to climb onto her neck.

Rhovert heard her make a strange sound, before she straightened her shoulders and climbed up the huge leg and up into a position on Petulor's neck.

"I'll swop places," he called to her, but she didn't seem to hear. She probably wouldn't, since she had wanted to go after Maeven for months. He watched her hug the dragon's neck, and close her eyes as Petulor launched herself skyward. When the dragon was no longer even a speck, he turned to the old dragon.

"What is so important that I have to stay here? My father also wants me back and won't say why."

"There is a place we must show you, King's son. You should rest first. It is a long ride."

He no longer felt like resting, but he realised that his horse deserved a good feed and a rest. He growled impotently, then noticed Kellthea beside him. "We have prepared food for you, and I can tell you some of what you missed hearing."

Rhovert forced himself to let his anger drain away. He should be used to being moved around like a pawn. His father was as impossible as dragons were. He wondered if his father had ever felt that way – helpless to choose between what he wanted to do and he must do for the good of his kingdom.

"Thank you," he said after a moment, nodding for her to lead him to where he needed to go. The where turned out to be a small circular structure. A hut made of willows and cloth.

Inside, he saw a cot covered in rugs, and some of Atlantis's things in a pile beside it. To his left, was a low table set with food and a padded cushion for him to sit on.

Kellthea fetched another for herself, and declined his offer to share his food. While he ate, she shared what Alkinor had told her and Atlantis.

Before she reached the part that had so astounded her, she realised Rhovert was almost asleep. He had stopped eating, with one hand up to his mouth with a part eaten bread roll, and when she stood up, jerked back to awareness. She helped him stand, and walk across to the bed, eased his boots off, and covered him after he all but collapsed onto the cot.

She gathered up the uneaten food and returned it to the kitchen, and collected a clay mug and a skin of water to take back. By then, Rhovert was deep asleep.

Kellthea moved quietly, even though he was unlikely to wake. He had not reacted to her when they met, so maybe he didn't realise she was Vatarin. Atlantis had been more interested in their mutual Dragon Priestess mothers, but the Thulan king and his son had every right to hate the rulers of Vatarik, and their kin.

CHAPTER 41- Rhovert

When he woke again in the late afternoon, Rhovert found that preparations had already been made for his trip to wherever the dragon scholars intended to take him. There was no fuss when he insisted on leaving right away and eating on the ride.

Hestnor rode level with him, followed by half a dozen other men, and he wondered if they were all dragons. He didn't ask, for Hestnor was telling him of the history of dragon kind, from the times before humans came to the various lands. It was becoming clear to him that between dragons and demons, there was a deep, undiluted hatred. He tried asking Hestnor what he was going to see, but was only told, "We must go to the island in the lake."

They couldn't take a boat to go across, but could reach it by a narrow causeway known only to dragons.

When they stopped at a specific place on the lake's edge, Rhovert looked around for the landmarks his escorts had used. They were subtle, but once Hestnor had indicated them, he nodded.

"And the lake is deadly?" he asked.

"Only to those of ill-intent," Hestnor murmured. "However, we do not wish for those that venture here for curiosity, to be endangered. Those who try to cross, ignoring the warnings, end up elsewhere with no memory to draw them back."

That could mean many things, Rhovert decided. He felt sorry for any that might only be foolish, but adventurous kids.

Hestnor seemed to sense his thoughts. "It has always been, that those not of ill-intent, only ignorant, have felt the warnings and retreated. Come!"

The shallow water on the causeway soon soaked through his boots, but Rhovert merely shrugged and kept going. He wanted to see what he had to see and be free to go after Atlantis. Ahead, the island still looked mysterious, with tall pine trees growing close together. The only difference was that there, they seemed to be staring at the narrowest point of what had seemed a much wider island from the point nearest Kilkenny's manor.

When they finally stepped back onto dry land, Hestnor led the way along a faint and narrow track that wound amongst the trees. Rhovert soon wished he could have ridden his horse, but none of the horses would set foot on the causeway, and they wouldn't have fared well amongst the trees. After an hour, they stepped straight from the dimness under the trees, into bright sunlight. As his eyes adjusted, he saw what looked like a solid stone gateway standing atop a stone flagged platform.

"What...is that?" He had a bad feeling he knew, for it made him think of the portals he'd seen at the training ground.

Hestnor confirmed that idea. "It is the first portal. This is how the demon horde came to this world. It is how the first dragons came in pursuit."

"What else can come through?" Rhovert thought to ask, for the area bounded by the gateway seemed to be glowing. Certainly, it was even brighter than the sunlight. "

"Now, small things are coming through. We feel the seal we placed there is weakening."

As if summoned, something like a small black cloud, briefly darkened a section of the glow. It spread out and headed towards them. Before it got very far, a jet of flame came out of nowhere, sweeping across the cloud, incinerating whatever things made it. High pitched screams had him trying to block his ears. Only the far edge of the cloud was not incinerated and the creatures there were fleeing as fast as they could fly. They narrowly escaped a second jet of flame, then abruptly vanished.

Rhovert trotted to where some of the blackened things had fallen. He poked at the mess with the tip of his sword, separating what looked like lumps of seared flesh. His face hardened when he identified the remains as being of demon kind.

"We guard the portal, but we can't catch them all."

"How long have they been coming through?"

"Maybe for the past human generation."

"Is this where Ciabolo came through? You said he was more recent come."

"It is likely. Some event happened after generations of peace. We came here and found the seal had been ... manipulated."

"And you could do nothing?"

"We are not mages," Hestnor stated. "Dragon mages are rare, and by the time the breach happened, Thulor was already ancient. The seal was a combination of dragon and human magic."

"So where do the demon kind come from," Rhovert asked, as another black cloud emerged.

"Another plane of existence."

"You also told me that humans came here. Did they also come through this portal?"

"This and several smaller ones that once linked to it. The smaller ones were weaker, easier to destroy."

"When were they destroyed? Recently?"

"No, when the demon horde came, they flooded through all the portals. The dragon mage, chewed some sacred rock – rock that flew from the stars, and the magic she breathed out with her flame, destroyed the magic that held them together. The magic of this portal though, was too strong."

"What do you think I can do?" Rhovert asked, as he still stared at the portal. "I am no wizard. You should have brought my sister here."

Hestnor shrugged. "You needed to see this, perhaps once again, humans can help us."

"I wish I knew how."

"We know the old magic is fading. It was stressed severely when the event occurred. This time differs from before. Instead of the force coming from beyond the portal, something here is attracting the little pests."

"I think I know who that is," Rhovert growled. "Can't Petulor strengthen the protection?"

"She should not try yet," Hestnor said with alarm. "She is only just old enough to mate and must ensure her successor."

"Could not one of you ...?"

Hestnor chuckled. "Like the young of any kind, she prefers to find a young, virile partner. There are not so many young ones of our kind."

With a shock, Rhovert realised what he meant. Dragonkind, considered my most to be legends and long gone, was in fact dying out.

"So the solution must be one that does not rely just on magic…" he saw with startling clarity.

"Yes," Hestnor confirmed. "Petulor did come here once. She told us that on the other side, where we cannot see, swarms of those little things exist. They are like moths to a flame, or ants to dead meat."

"You said something attracts them," Rhovert mused. "Not just Ciabolo summoning them?"

"That is what I believe. I do not know what, but I think it is this side, not the other, or they would not have such incentive to force their way through to obey the summons."

Rhovert was stuck for ideas. Then a question came to his mind. "Who built that structure?"

"It is the work of humans. The bricks are from clay native to this place. Dragons do not have the means to create bricks."

When Rhovert glanced at Hestnor's human shape, the dragon scholar simply said, "Back at that time in history, we hadn't learnt to change shape."

"This is too much to take in. Does my father know of this place?"

"We have not brought him here. Before this, there was no need."

"The fleeting thought of how much Atlantis would revel in this puzzle, recalled him to where he wanted to be. All the questions buzzing in his mind were secondary to wanting to follow his consort and his sisters.

"My father needs to know this," Do you have records? Written histories? Sketches?"

"Some. Thanks to the humans who have chosen to align with us. But surely it would be easier for some of us who remember it all to go and talk to the king. I have already offered and I can find others who are willing."

"Then, please, do go," Rhovert urged. "I don't know how much power is needed to bring these little swarms through, but dread the idea of more of the larger kind emerging."

"It is not only magical energy that is needed, but a knowledge of the spells that created the seal. If the one you know of as the Serpent, Ciabolo, came through this, then he has some knowledge or had a lucky fluke of mindless desperation."

"That is not what I want to hear," Rhovert admitted.

"Perhaps not, but Alkinor, the elder, believes that the serpent fled from the rest of his kind and came here.”

“Are we also to expect others of his kind to come here?”

“If there has been no other major incursion since that one came through, perhaps the portal on that side is not marked, or the demons on that side are just as glad not to follow.”

“We can’t know,” Rhovert said. “There may be no defined portal there, and Ciabolo did know how to create one.” He shook his head. “Was it Wizard GoldDreamer that helped seal this portal, back in the day?”

“One of his forebears,” Hestron clarified. “Many generations ago. However, the wizard you speak of helped us at a time when the humans had forgotten what they owed us. He taught us how to change shape.”

“Petulor should have made Atlantis see this,” Rhovert finally admitted. “She’d have more ideas to solve this puzzle. And she has her great grand sire’s journals. He may have written something in there that would help. Although, he didn’t say much about dragons...”

“I can see that you are impatient to go off after your mate,” Hestnor spoke with sympathy. “However, you, as the king’s son, needed to see this for yourself.”

“Yes, you are right...and father may have had a glimpse of it via my talisman. Maybe all his scholars will be able to figure out if this knowledge will help us against The Serpent when he brings the armies of Vatarik against us. I have a deep fear that whatever we do will not be enough. He would not hesitate to spend all the humans in that realm to overcome us, and turn loyal Thulans against their own kin. And as you have suggested, this time we cannot rely on dragons to win out for us.”

“And in truth, you should not rely on us.”

“Are you saying you won’t help us?”

“No, King’s son, I am saying his kind has fought us before, and knows how we fight. He does not know how humans fight.”

“He has El Rasho to show him that.”

“The false king of Vatarik does not have dragon blood, and the motivation of the bloodline of Thulor. However, you wish to follow your mate. Come then, we will return to the enclave and we will provide what you will need for your journey, including a guide to show you a protected route across the border.”

Rhovert wasted no time when he was back at the enclave. While his horse was given a good feed, he was collecting everything he had left there, as well as all that Atlantis had not taken with her. Travel food, in hessian sacks, was waiting by the bed – ready for him to leave.

He saw the sense in having a meal too, but he was determined to leave and use the rest of the daylight to start on his way.

The last thing he did was to find Hestnor, who still had Kellthea with him, and apologise for not going with them when they left for the palace. "I should really go, I know the way into the palace, that doesn't go near the chancy creatures. And I don't know how safe it will be travelling with all of the brigand groups up this way. I should be there to introduce you."

"Be at ease, King's son. We have long mastered the art of travelling unnoticed, and you have already mentioned us to the king's wizard?"

"Yes, but not the being a dragon part."

"We will manage just fine," Hestnor assured him. "The little creatures will sense dragon and flee."

"Still," Rhovert thought quickly, then opened one of his packs and felt around. He pulled out one of Roman's gadgets. "Take this with you, he will recognise it and know I gave it to you."

Hestnor nodded for Kellthea to take the object. "Safe journey King's son."

CHAPTER 42 – Leanne and Finora

When Leanne awoke, the air in the tent was already heating up. From that fact, she knew the sun was already high enough to be over the trees. Normally, she was awake at first light, but then, she and her twin had been riding hard for two days and had only arrived the previous night at dusk.

The slight noises she made getting up and dressed, woke her twin.

"You don't need to get up," she suggested.

"We need to make a good impression," Finora countered. "I'm rested enough."

They were dressed in their best clothes – a uniform for Leanne and an expensive robe over trousers for Finora. Her sorceress's earring ready to sparkle in the sun. Her standing a step back on her sister's left was a statement of strength.

As soon as they looked out over the camp, they could see Prosper's Troop was disorganised by his injury and the attack on their camp. However, as soon as they emerged. Prosper's aide raced up to them.

Leanne gave a signal for silence, then said softly, "Sound the rally signal, softly."

It was not her intention to draw more attention to their camp. One group of brigands knew where they were and that was one group too many.

Men came running from all directions, even the perimeter guard. Leanne was not concerned by that, for her sister had not retired the previous day until she had set up a magical perimeter. Not all the men knew her by sight, but within a very short time, Leanne had proved her authority and had the whole camp hopping. All the men were stowing their gear into packs, and dropping tents to break camp. They had fewer horses since the raid, so the supplies and camp gear would be loaded onto horses first. While that was underway, Leanne went into a huddle with the four remaining sub-troop leaders. She had a large map unrolled on the ground, discussing various options of places to relocate the camp. When requested, Finora scryed each place.

"Okay," Leanne said finally. "We'll go here. It's higher in the hills, closer to the border and it will give us a wider field of view."

The men went off to instruct those under them, and Leanne gestured to Finora. Together, they went to where the cooks were packing. They were relieved to see a kettle still on the dwindling fire, and one of the cooks reaching for two plates with left-over cooked sausages and eggs sandwiched between slabs of thick journey bread.

As Leanne ate, she watched the ordered activity. The aide was seeing to her tent, formerly Prosper's, but he had already been taken south to find a healer. Finora noticed the chill first, she shivered and looked around, wondering if it were a premonition of trouble. She concentrated for a moment, sensing the warding around the camp. There was nothing threatening it. Then her hand went to her talisman and she realised the cold was coming from there. Her thought, wordless as it was, had Leanne copying her gesture.

"What now?" she murmured, also beginning to shiver.

One of the troop glanced skywards and yelped, "Flaming hell!"

Leanne followed his gaze, recognised the shape that had to be Petulor, circling above the camp.

"Clear the parade ground!" she bellowed, causing her troop to scatter back to the edge of the clearing.

As soon as there was enough room for the dragon, Petulor spiralled tightly and landed neatly. Her head faced Leanne and Finora. A warm, smoky scented breath wafted around them.

"Petulor!" Leanne greeted the unexpected apparition. She was going to say more, when someone groaned. The sound of someone being sick followed, and then a shaky but familiar voice said, "Petulor, I don't mean to offend you, but if I ever have to travel that way again, it will be twice too often."

Atlantis walked into view, coming around the dragon's giant head, and gratefully taking the waterskin Finora handed to her.

"Thanks," she said after rinsing her mouth out and taking a longer drink.

"Are you okay?" Leanne asked.

"I will be. Even though I feel like I have been dragged through a mountain or two."

Finora stepped on tip toe and looked around. "Is Rhovert with you? Weren't you two planning to head back south?"

"To do what Father wants you to try and do," Leanne added with a faint smirk.

"He might have hoped," Atlantis retorted, "But in case you think otherwise, we haven't spent the last year idling in some fantasy paradise, any more than you have."

"We know that," Finora placated. "So how come you are here?"

"Well, your father may think he's the highest authority in Thulor, and probably is as far as most people are concerned. However, even he will have to fit his schemes to the whims of a certain stubborn young dragon, who just dragged me from the Enclave near Taranthal's manor, for reasons she has only hinted at, but I am sure are connected to Maeven."

"She's in Vatarik!" Leanne blurted. "So why now? Why not as soon as they took her? Is she likely even still alive and sane?"

"I wanted to go then, but your father forbade it," Atlantis told her. "But I have no doubt she is alive."

"And Rhovert let you come on your own?" Finora asked.

"He didn't have much choice, and I bet he will be haring after me as soon as he can. The scholars at the enclave had stuff to tell us and something at least one of us had to see."

Leanne gestured to her aide. He was staring goggle-eyed at Petulor, while keeping well back. He edged closer on seeing Leanne's gesture. She gave him instructions in a quiet voice and he ran off. Then she said, "Rhovert needs to head back south, not try to take part in a sneak raid into Vatarik. He's heir to this kingdom. The only one."

Atlantis stared at Leanne, as if startled. When Leanne began to frown at her reactions, she blurted, "That's not strictly true, but you are right. There is only one of him. I mean, if something happened to me, he could marry someone else..."

"Tis, what do you mean? It's not strictly true...that he's not the only heir?" Finora demanded.

"Yes, what do you mean?" Leanne added her insistence.

"Shards! Has no one told you? Your father has a grandson."

"Congratulations!" Finora said with a grin. "When did that happen?"

"Where is he? Why aren't you with him?" Leanne asked at the same time.

Atlantis held up both hands to silence them. "Petulor? Can anyone overhear us?"

"No, Atlantis," came a smug sounding mind-voice.

"He isn't mine, or Rhovert's. You know Roman said it was a very remote chance he could engender an heir. No, he is about four or five years old..."

"Maeven! But how?" Leanne asked.

Finora was thinking back. "Thul Run! Something happened then. I knew there was something she wasn't talking about."

"Yes," Atlantis confirmed. "It seems she met Prince El Haba after she ran off from there."

"She never did have any taste," Leanne muttered.

"Don't you ever let up on her?" Atlantis snapped back, surprising Leanne into silence. "It was not a pleasant experience, and if you must know, I think the old dragon had a hand in that."

"If she had a child, why didn't she tell father?" Finora asked aloud.

"Sheer perversity," Leanne growled.

"Probably," Atlantis agreed. "Or maybe some dragon inspired instinct to protect him. This stubborn monster here wouldn't admit anything."

"Father-king would not have accepted him then," Petulor spoke to the minds of the three women. "And the boy's father would never have sworn himself to Thulor, had he known."

The revelation that the former Prince El Haba, had fathered Maven's child, was considered by Leanne and Finora. The latter conceded, "Arlen is a powerful wizard, but what was so important about having him on our side?"

"My mother allowed him to wear a talisman for a time," Petulor spoke loftily. As if that should answer all questions.

"Petulor, this isn't getting us anywhere," Atlantis interrupted. "You implied time was short. The three of us are here, like you wanted. Will you please tell us what the urgency is? Not that I am arguing about going, mind you."

"The Dragon mother needs help. I gave Father-king three of my scales. I know at least one was delivered and only two of the messengers returned. I can reach her, but only faintly. And soon, she will need to pass my scale onto someone else who will need my protection more. I won't be able to help her."

"The brat must be developing a conscience," Leanne muttered. "Even if seems she has lost her sense of self-preservation."

"No, Lee!" Finora argued. "We have never given her credit for being unselfish. Remember Thul Run? She may have run from the fighting, but she rescued most of the children by herself, and never claimed credit. And if you recall, she helped by distracting El Foulness and that wizard."

"Children must be the only things she puts herself out for," Leanne proposed.

"They are probably the only people who don't try to make her anything other than herself," Atlantis commented tartly. Then a thought hit her, and all colour fled from her face. "Dragon's breath!" She turned to Petulor. "Maeven's pregnant again, isn't she?"

"What makes you say that," Finora asked sharply.

"Did you hear what happened to her up in that hill village?" Both of her sister's in law nodded.

"Think about it! She stood in the Serpent's way, so he couldn't get her son. It's the only explanation that makes sense. In spite of your comments, Ven isn't stupid. If the scales were her only protection, her only source of magic power, she wouldn't give them away. But if it were to protect her child..."

"Children," Petulor interrupted, raising her snout an inch off the ground. All three women stared at the dragon who blithely went on, "A boy, who will be heir to Vatarik, and a girl who will have no value to the king, and he won't know she has magic."

"So, we have to save Maeven, again, and the babies?" Leanne summarised.

"The boy will be safe enough," Petulor assured them.

"Maeven and the girl, then. It makes my hackles go up to think of the boy being raised and corrupted by El Foulness," Leanne admitted.

"The boy does not have Serpent tainted blood." Once again, Petulor's mind voice sounded smug. "He has the blood of Vatarik, but the Dragon-mother tricked them again. Besides, do you not think we won't have some influence on the young prince through the twin bond with his sister?"

Leanne and Finora exchanged glances and Leanne grinned.

Atlantis smiled too, but said, "I won't ask how you arranged that, Petulor, but we had best get going. I have no doubt that Rhovert is going to be riding hard in this direction, and we don't want anyone trying to stop us."

"No," Leanne agreed grimly. "And this time, if I get close to El Foulness, so help me, I won't hesitate to kill him! Will you be coming too, Petulor?"

"I cannot come. I cannot cross the border. But I know you three have gone in before, and returned, when I was still in my egg."

"We did," Leanne agreed. "We will leave as soon as I organise things here."

Petulor raised herself up onto her four legs and spread her wings. With one powerful down thrust, and possibly magic, she launched herself up above the trees, circled once and flew off, disappearing from sight, rather than into the distance.

"She's big, " Nelsi said, trying not to sound awed.

"Good! You are here. I thought I saw you skulking around last night." Leanne returned to business.

"What do you need, Captain?"

"Do you have anything you need to tell us right away?"

"No Mam. Everything can wait. I have sent all my reports to the king and can catch you up later."

"Good! Fi, can you get the map?"

Finora trotted over to where the aide was buckling the last pack onto her horse. Leanne turned to Atlantis. "Are you positive that Berto will be coming after you?"

"Quite positive."

"He really doesn't have to prove himself," Leanne said. "Alright! I'm not trying to stop him, but if he is to be of any use, he needs a guide who can bring him by the shortest, safest route. Nelsi here has been right into Vatarik, and his 'northern brothers' gave him an excellent map."

Nelsi grinned. "You want to show me where he'll be? Huh? So I can meet him?"

"He's not helpless on his own anymore," Atlantis said for the benefit of her consort's sisters. "But we will likely have a couple of days head start on him."

"I'll find him," Nelsi assured her.

Finora returned with a map and a small sack. Atlantis took the map and unrolled it, pointing to where she had just come from. "The dragon scholars, had a place they wanted to show him. It is my thought that he will go from there to the border, and since he is not familiar with Vatarik, will probably keep near the border until he gets to the main north-south trade road."

"Makes sense," Nelsi agreed.

"Nels, take these with you. You know how to activate them?" Finora passed over the little sack and the thief glanced in.

Nelsi dared to suggest, "I might need a new power stone." He knew the sorceress was not strict about thieves using magic. She believed that her father's spies, should use whatever tools they had.

Finora pulled an egg sized white rock from her pocket and handed it over. "If you use them going to find Berto –"

"Pick them up on the way back," Nelsi cut in.

"Get supplies and get going," Leanne ordered. The thief grinned and trotted off. Then Leanne yelled, "Anders!"

The man hurried over. "Captain?"

"I know I just got here, but I am promoting you to acting captain until I get back. Get to the new campsite, and set up physical boundary warnings. I had intended Fi to use magic too, but we have to go somewhere else. You know how to report to our superior?"

"And to request help, and supplies," Anders babbled, then straightened. "I will do you proud, Mam."

"Do your best to keep the men alive. That is all anyone can ask. Do you have any questions?"

Anders did, once he really took in his abrupt promotion. While Leanne answered him, Finora took Atlantis off to find a horse that had not been taken by the brigands, and was not being used for supplies or equipment.

Finally Anders said, "I still can't believe I was here, near a dragon. I thought they were only a myth."

Leanne understood his awe. "That was Petulor, the new dragon mage – Thulor's successor. Now, I won't make all of the men swear to secrecy about seeing her, but I would prefer they didn't talk about it. It might draw the wrong kind of attention to the troop, and we don't want any more surprise attacks."

Anders straitened even more, salute, and turned sharply – stepping up into his new rank.

Leanne went to organise supplies for their own trip, and made a mental note to ask Atlantis about the reference to dragon scholars – once they were under way.

CHAPTER 43 - Rhovert

The sight that met Rhovert as he crested the last ridge, made him quail. Down below, on a vast plain, stood rank upon rank of men, standing in formation - four per row, twenty-five rows per rank. When he forced the panic from his mind, and observed them further, he realised that none of the figures had moved, and that sent all kinds of atavistic shivers up and down his spine. They were all like the men he had seen in Ackbridge, waiting there until the serpent summoned them to fight.

It was a sight to send a weaker mind fleeing. But he did not have that luxury. Something had to be done. "Can you see anyone in charge down there? Or anywhere someone might be?"

His guide, one of the changed dragons, whose eyes were keener than his own, scanned the area. "There appears to be no one, but there might be an alarm if you go closer."

"Can we go down there and look?"

The other of his escorts, said, "We are at the border between Thulor and Vatarik. If we go beyond, we could be seen."

"I think we need to see if we can do something to stop those men being used," Rhovert said carefully.

"Then wait, I will go higher and see what I might."

The tall tan skinned guide, moved to one side, and changed to his dragon form, trotted to where the land fell sharply from the ridge, spread his wings and plummeted. Moments later he reappeared in their sight, rising up and heading for the static army.

"He is still young enough to think himself immortal," the other guide muttered. "Yet he has grand-whelps that are already full grown."

"Are your females also in the guise of humans?" Rhovert asked, as he watched the dragon circling the army.

"Yes, most of us choose that shape, for we do not require as much food that way. But our women are few, many of the human looking women you saw are merely dragon friends. It is the hope of all of us that the new dragon mage will lay many eggs, both male and female, to revive our numbers."

Rhovert was spared the need to comment by the return of the dragon.

"The plain reeks of demon. Nothing moves, not even the normal mountain and plain creatures. The humans are mixed, many are of Thulor, most of Vatarik, and some from the lands beyond."

"Can you tell anything of the magic holding them?"

"Only that it is not dragon magic."

"How close do you think I can get to the men?"

"The magic extends for a dragon-length from the nearest humans."

Rhovert was thinking of the Serpent's reaction if he came back here and this army had dispersed. He pummelled his mind for the slightest idea of how.

"Can you fly over again, but carry something small as you do?"

"What do you have in mind?" the dragon mind voice came to him.

"Just a minute."

Rhovert went to his saddle pack and reached into the one where he had shoved the glass orb Roman Gold Dreamer had made. "This – it will need to be held so at least one side of it faces down, and has a clear view."

"I can hold it so," the dragon agreed after trying it in his front talon. "Shall I go now?"

"In a minute – I want to get onto the King's wizard. I am hoping he will be able to see what is there, and hopefully has an idea of something to upset the stasis spell."

Rhovert took the orb back and shook it, seeing that both his escorts, the dragon and the man-dragon, were eyeing the device with interest.

He looked into the glass, and finally saw Roman's face come into view.

"Oh, you've decided to speak to us again, have you? A certain monarch is threatening to shove you in his dungeon."

"Roman, I have something important –"

"All your sire wants to hear is that you are moving your tail back here."

"Tell him, I am of no use in a dungeon. Now, shut up and listen. I want you to keep looking into the orb, okay? I want to show you the army that is just across the border in Vatarik. It is a company of statues right now, and I want to see if you can see the magic and suggest a way to disrupt it so these men can scatter."

"You are serious? Yes, show me."

Rhovert gave the orb back to the dragon, who held it carefully, and didn't seem to hear the squawk that came from it when he dropped again to take flight. He repeated his aerial foray, and returned to the ridge.

"Well?" Rhovert demanded when he held the orb again.

"A real mess of a spell," Roman told him. "Nothing like I have seen before."

"Demon magic I suspect," Rhovert added.

"Why do you say that?"

"Because my friend here who flew the orb over that army, said it reeked of demon."

"What friend?"

Rhovert turned so the little image of Roman in the ball, could see the dragon.

"That is not Petulor," Roman gulped. "Are there many more of them?"

"Yes. There will be a delegation from here coming to the palace – they are probably already underway, traveling in human guise. One has one of your little gadgets – so you may be able to track them with it. They say they can travel unnoticed."

"But Dragons..."

"Roman, you can ask all your questions of the dragon scholars when they get there. I need your thoughts on that magic."

"Yes, right. Let me think."

While the voice from the orb was silent, Rhovert asked, "How far does your protection come?"

The human-seeming dragon said, "Only to the border."

"Can it be extended, say to the far side of the plain?"

His two escorts looked at each other, and after a while, one said, "It may be possible, more of us are coming here. If we do it, it cannot be for long. What do you think you might do?"

"Well, if Roman has an idea to disrupt that magic, I want to try it. But I don't want the Serpent to sense it and come at me."

"At least my son is not actively suicidal," a different voice came from the orb.

"Father! We can't leave that army there, just waiting to come at us."

"No, with that I agree. I just do not want you in the line of the fighting. Roman tells me you want the men to disperse. Has it occurred to you that the Vatarins may try to stop you, once they are mobile? They may believe the tales their king is giving them."

"Perhaps they will be less patriotic when they realise how their king has had them treated," Rhovert suggested.

"And what if all of our people have those little controlling demons?"

That was an idea that Rhovert had not considered. However, his escort said, "No, I do not think that would be so. The little demons need the host to thrive. As these men are, they are not eating or drinking, so the little demons would die."

"Well, that's an interesting idea," King Westron's voice came clearly. "Who will guide our people back to Thulor?"

The reply came from the dragon. "We will fly over, once the men are free. Those who believe the enemies of Thulor, will want to run from us. Those who remember that dragons were once friends, will allow us to lead them."

"Dragon, I have no wish to insult you, but you have been hiding up there a long time. The memories of the common humans have you as mythical beings, or only remember how hard it was for all of you to stay fed."

"Father, we have to try it. The men back in Ackbridge, were a bit sluggish when first released from stasis. If I can get one of our people healed quickly, I can give him directions. Once he gets all who want to serve you, up to the ridge that marks the border, they will have an escort. The dragons will try to stretch the protections, like I think you heard. I don't intend to stay any longer than I can help."

"You have certainly stirred up a fire ants nest up there," Westron sighed. "It needed doing, and at least, that corner of my realm is no longer a nest of the enemy."

"You have no premonitions of when they will decide to attack?" Rhovert asked his father.

"No, nothing is clear, but I feel it in my bones that it will not be delayed much longer. I don't know why they have been delaying."

"The serpent has a reason, but who can guess what it is?" Rhovert agreed. He saw his father's face move from the orb, and Roman came back.

"There may be a way. I have been speaking to my old master. He has read of something like what you have there. He said to look for one of the six or eight anchor points. They will likely be marked in some way – maybe just a pile of rocks, or a stake in the ground. Those points hold the stasis field together. But he said, with the area being so large, a lot of stress is on those points. That is where you should try to break it. You may have to break two or three, anchors, to get the field to vanish."

"Did he suggest how to break it?"

"Well, yes, but his idea uses magic, and you would need to be a strong mage."

"So what use is that?"

"Well, you may not need that. His majesty reminded me that even though we still haven't found the eighth talisman, all of the others have a touch of anti-magic."

"Yess!" Rhovert hissed. His face creased into a malicious grin. "My thanks, Roman, and to your former mentor. If I can get some of our people back, I will finally feel I have done something worthwhile."

"Just don't start fighting any Vatarins!"

"I have no intention of that. I will aim to be just one of a very confused, suddenly awake, bunch of fighters."

"Then you will be coming back here?"

"Not on your life. I am going after my wife! Petulor took her off somewhere."

Rhovert shook the orb to end the communication, and shoved it back in his pack. He didn't want Roman or his father, to command him differently.

His escort spoke as he took the reins of his horse in one hand. "We will try to extend the protection, for as long as we can. You will be on your own once you reach the plain. When you leave from there, you will need to head to the north east."

"I appreciate your help. Hopefully, we can meet again," Rhovert said sincerely.

"Go with the wind in your wings, King's son. I will speak to your mind when we have moved the protection."

Rhovert began the steep descent to the plain, on a narrow zigzagging trail. He had to move carefully, for the footing was loose, and there were jagged rocks from earlier rock falls. The message from his dragon escort came as he was just reaching the flat ground. He found a large rock to tether his horse, then checked his weapons, and walked towards the rigid statues of men.

He couldn't see the magic field, but he felt the effect when he was close to it. He was still a dragon length from the nearest statue. He began to walk east around the perimeter of the field, scanning the ground for signs of one of the anchor points. He was walking through shin high grass, which was still except for where he moved, when he saw a slight movement ahead. His talisman was heating up and instinctively, he drew his sword – then jabbed it down where the grass was starting to move. Something began to thrash wildly, and after a moment became still. He lifted his sword and saw the carcass of a tiny serpent hanging from the tip. He tossed it far away into the grass.

"Nasty little guardian," Rhovert said softly, to ease the fright. "Does that mean the anchor point is just about where I am?"

Using his sword point to investigate, he came to a low flat rock with a smaller one sitting atop it. It was placed just outside the line where Rhovert sensed the field to be. Now, prudence suggested that he did not want to be too close to the rock, when he touched it with his talisman. So after taking it from around his neck, he tied it to the tip of his sword, and held that at arm's length. He did not forget to invoke the protection spell Roman had taught him, and held his free arm between the talisman and his eyes.

It was well that he did. The breaking of the anchor point, resulted in a brilliant flash of light, and heat.

After waiting several heatbeats, he reached out to feel for the shield. The feeling of buzzing on his hand was still there, but it seemed to be at a faster tempo.

"One down," he told himself, as he moved on to where he guessed the next anchor point might be. He used his memory for how it looked from above, to guess at landmarks to help him.

His approach to the next point was slow and cautious. He guessed there would be another snake guardian, and wanted to kill it quickly, before it knew what was happening. He didn't know if the creatures had a way to let Ciabolo know someone was interfering here. He just had an increasing feeling of needing to hurry.

As soon as he saw the movement in the grass, he acted again.

Like before, his lunge was instinctively accurate. The second snake guardian was tossed away, and he again had his talisman tied to his sword. This time, the reaction to the breaking of the anchor was even more violent. Even with his eyes covered, what light still reached them was enough to momentarily blind him with the glare.

The buzzing had become audible, like a swarm of angry stingers. He moved back, and waited. Silence descended after a loud thunder like clap.

As his eyes began to see again, the men that had been within the field, began to move around – unsteady on their feet. One of the nearest ones, midway within one rank, began to turn. He was Thulan, judging by the clothing he wore, but no farmer or trader.

"Therry!" Rhovert called, recognising the son of one of his father's lords.

The man looked up. "Wha...t?"

Rhovert went closer. "Wake up man! Do you know where you are?"

The man looked around. "No...this isn't Orchardvale."

"Listen, Therry. You were taken by the Vatarins. You have been in stasis here, they were going to make you fight your fellow Thulans."

Therry didn't seem to be comprehending yet, and Rhovert recalled his talisman and how he had intended to heal one of the men. He took it in his hand, and held it to Therry's cheek.

After a minute, his eyes widened, and he spun around, seeing where he was. Then he finally saw Rhovert. "Who are you? You are not one of those bastards that grabbed me?"

"No, I'm Berto, and I am giving you the chance to get back across the border. You need to move fast, get all the other Thulans to go with you, before the enemy realises what I did and comes to rectify it."

"Help me shake sense into them," Therry said.

Rhovert saw the sense in that, and hoped he had enough time to touch all the Thulans with his talisman. As more men became aware, they obeyed Rhovert's direction to run to the spot where his horse was tethered, and to begin to go up the trail that led from there. They even began dragging some of the still partly stupefied men.

It turned out that all the Thulans were together, perhaps so they were sent to fight first. As the ranks frayed with the deserters, some of the further rank began to notice what was happening. As luck would have it, they were still groggy. Rhovert knew he had to leave, and raced with Therry and the last few Thulans.

He pointed out the trail to Therry, and swung himself into his horse's saddle. In his mind, he heard, "Keep close to the rise for as long as you can. You will be hidden there. We sense some of the enemy racing this way."

Rhovert kicked his horse's side to make him take off, and the animal was not loathe to do so. Using his hands to guide his horse, Rhovert risked a look back. He could see the last of the Thulans moving up the trail, and over to the north, dust rising from where mounted horsemen were racing to see what had happened. He would have to keep going east, to keep within the protection of the dragons, however far that extended. He had no longer had any intention of crossing that plain. He would have to skirt it before heading any further into Vatarik. He would keep going until it was too dark to see, or until he found somewhere with water and cover.

As night fell, he found a suitable place – a copse of straggly trees, and scrubby bushes. There was a trickle of water from a tiny spring in the towering rock face. He led his horse into cover, tethering it so it could graze on the scant grasses. He activated the spell for a ring of protection, and curled up in his travel blanket behind the low bushes. Food was some of the travel rations, and water from his flask. The horse would be happy lapping from the spring.

He intended to continue on as soon as the sky began to get lighter. He did miss the company of Atlantis, but he was no longer a tyro at travelling on his own in the wild country.

He believed he had got away clean, for there had been no sign of followers the previous day, or of any other travellers. He hoped his luck would hold. However, when he rolled over on waking and carefully raised his head top see over the bushes, he saw a grinning figure, sitting cross legged just outside the boundary of his spell. He grimaced before removing the protection and demanding, "Do my sisters know where you are?"

"Not exactly," the unrepentant Nelsi admitted. "But they went off with your lady, because the dragon insisted."

Rhovert decided that he should not have been surprised. It was logical for them to be the 'help' Petulor had mentioned.

"What about Prosper's troop?"

"The Captain promoted Anders, and told me where they were going. They have a really good map. Your lady predicted you would be coming after her as fast as you could. With me though, you will be faster still. I can guide you, and keep you out of the way of those you need to avoid."

"Well, I am all for that. You have local contacts, I presume?"

Nelsi grinned even wider.

CHAPTER 44 - Atlantis, Leanne and Finora

"Are you sure we are going the right way," Leanne grunted as she scrambled up the steep path, and leading her reluctant horse in the dark. The only light around them was from the nearly full moon and a low floating witch light.

"We are going in the right direction," Finora assured her twin. She was also on foot, and maintaining the pace her stockier sister had set. "I can sense the energy of the next stone. We should see it soon."

Finora was proved right. Just around a slight bend in the trail, a second glow, vaguely reddish in tone compared to the blue witch light, could be seen. On coming right up to it, they discovered it was set just past where another track went off to one side of the trail. Finora recalled her blue witch light so she could check the map provided by Nelsi. It was marked by symbols rather than words.

"There is a place to camp, just up that path." Finora pointed. "We should stop here until morning."

Leanne disagreed. "I think we should keep going, while it is too dark for anyone to spot us."

"We are almost to the ridge top," Atlantis pointed out. "It will be downhill from there. In daylight, the horses can find their own footing."

"In the morning, we will be noticeable," Leanne persisted.

"None of us have seen the country at this point. Last time, we came up through Thul Run. Yes, we have the map, but it doesn't really tell us about the terrain. If we wait for daylight, we can scout ahead and see what's below."

Leanne felt a yawn coming on and decided to agree with the others.

They were all awake at first light and having a hasty breakfast of dried travel food and water.

"However did that damn spy find this trail?" Leanne commented as she looked around the little clearing where they had camped.

"From what Nelsi said," Finora recalled, "the spy said he was a trader. They probably know all the trails."

"Smuggler, more likely," Leanne said. "Since we turned onto this trail, we've seen no sign of habitation whatsoever."

"We need to tell father that he needs to put some kind of watch here," Finora said. "I could set a passive watcher, but it would alert anyone that came this way that was sensitive to magic."

"It might make them consider turning back," Leanne said with more hope than realistic belief. "It is bad enough trying to block the main trails, and the ones the locals use. This is more like a goat track. Looking at that map, this whole border is porous. El Rasho could send troops through at a hundred places and we'd have no way to stop them."

Sensing that Leanne was discouraged at the thought, Atlantis said, "We only need to cut off the serpent's head, neutralise Ciabolo and El Rasho, and the Vatarin army will be leaderless and easy to overcome."

"That sounds easy when you say it fast," Leanne growled, thinking of all the lowly peasants who would suffer in the process.

"Our people are already putting food supplies away in safe places," Finora reminded her. "El Rasho won't be able to get as much as he might hope from the farmers to support his army. That won't sit well with his regulars. And if our people don't fight, they'll probably be let alone."

"How do you figure that?" Leanne challenged. "Why would he leave people alive who could attack when his back is turned?"

"If he wants conquest," Finora considered, "he'd want control of the land. But to sustain his victories, he'll need people to grow food and so on."

"Have you forgotten how he conscripts for his army?" Atlantis asked her. "He doesn't care about Thulor's people. If he wins, he can let those who are farmers go back to their proper work – but I would bet he would still control them. We still need to kill the two leaders."

"Are you thinking we should try to kill them when we get to the citadel?" Leanne asked.

"No! That's not why we are going." Atlantis had felt a really strong shiver travel down her spine. As much as she liked the idea, something told her it wouldn't be safe to try. "No, we need to rescue a mage gifted child, and Maeven too, if we can."

They removed all traces of their camp and returned to the trail, all alert for watchers, or trouble. At the top of the ridge, they had a long look at the land below. Low growth on the slopes gave way to sparse grasses and bushes on the sandy plain. They spotted a group of spindly trees, and made that their first waypoint.

"It is not hard to tell we are in Vatarik," Atlantis commented when they were scanning the way ahead from that scant cover. The land was dry and arid, unlike the lusher greenery of Thulor.

"Ciabolo must be draining the life from the land," Finora guessed.

"Well, we can't stay here," Leanne directed. "However, we will need a story to explain why we are here, where we have come from and are going to, and why."

"And we don't want to look too weak, or as if we have anything of value," Atlantis added.

"Nelsi's friends in that town we can just see, said that the king's recruiters for the army usually leave farmers alone, particularly if they farm the staple crops. He has to feed his soldiers, and supply the brigands," Finora told the others.

"More likely if they farm a luxury crop," Leanne guessed. She held her hand out for the map. "Last time, we came through a town that grew java bushes. We could say we are going there to get seeds to grow on our farm."

"And what do we grow now," Atlantis grinned.

Leanne considered. "Smoke weed. You know, the stuff father outlawed."

"And what are we using to pay for it?" Finora asked.

"Seeds!" Leanne said, after looking around for inspiration.

Atlantis looked for what had prompted the idea. "Yes! These trees have hard shell pods that won't open until there is rain."

The idea didn't spark any shivers of premonition, so she was happy to knock seed pods down from the tree, while the others collected the pods from the ground.

Finora studied the pods, looking for a way to open them. "These pods are distinctive. It would be bad luck if someone asked about them and recognised them. If we can get the seeds out, it will be harder to dispute our claim."

"Okay, we do it. Then can you make all three of us look like farmers?" Leanne asked. "Brawny, stupid looking, except when talking crops? Fi, you could be an overworked farm wife, and Atlantis, what about you?"

"A farm hand with a scowl and a limp," she decided. "The horses need to look like the next place for them is the knackery, or they might get appropriated."

"Is that too much, Fi?" Leanne thought to ask.

"Not if we each pull power through the talismans. It is a lot harder to do it here."

The three riders that emerged from the trees, looked nothing like those who had entered them. All felt better for having the illusion on them, because there was the possibility of meeting soldiers that had seen them before.

Once they left the trees, there was no cover for miles. They had located themselves on the map and were headed for the next town, which had a well, according to the map's glyphs. Their recent stopping place should have had a spring, and had once, but the symbol was now crossed out. As a result, they were carefully rationing their remaining water between themselves and the horses. Atlantis had also collected some of the greenest branches and leaves from the trees, and this was bundled behind her. Most people would assume it was for firewood, but she had explained that there might be a way to use it if they were really stuck for water.

By necessity, needing to find water soon, they merged onto a more travelled road, but even then, they had only met two lots of travellers, both going the opposite way. The first had been an old, wizened farmer, with white hair and sun bronzed skin. He was encouraging an equally old donkey to pull a small cart full of manure. He had eyed them warily, and kept going.

The others were a pair of riders, who slowed to look them over, and then continued on.

"If I didn't know how good you were, Fi, I would think they could see through your illusion," Leanne muttered.

"I had that feeling too," Atlantis confirmed. "We had best watch our backs. Likely they will come back."

When those riders were out of sight, they gave their horses the signal to increase speed, maintaining that until they came to a rocky outcrop. The rocks looked to have been eroded by water in some distant past.

"Let's rest here," Atlantis urged. "I want to see if there is any sign that there might still be water under the sediment. This looks like an old river."

She dropped from her horse and let the reins drop. Her horse stayed where it was. Then she dropped the arm's length into the old river bed. She spent time carefully scanning the rocky sides of the old river bed, determining that she would not stay if she saw no signs, but her luck was in.

"Here," she called, just loud enough to reach the others, and they walked the horses closer.

Finora joined her. "How can you tell?" she asked, looking everywhere.

"Something I read in my great grand sire's journals. He would have used magic to draw water back up to the surface. Let's try our talismans."

Leanne looked down from the bank behind them, and said, "Well, I'll be...It isn't much, but, here, put my hat under it."

It was only a trickle, emerging from a crack in the rock, and dribbling down the rock face to the sand, where it was immediately absorbed. Yet, when Leanne's leather hat was pressed against the rock, water began to fill it. It enabled them to give each of the horses a drink, and to refill their water skins. When they had enough, Atlantis removed her talisman and the trickle stopped. The rock soon dried in the oppressive heat.

As they were remounting, Atlantis noticed a cloud of dust coming up the road along their back trail.

"Is that the old man coming back?" Leanne asked.

"Looks like the same wagon," Atlantis said. "But there are two people on the driver's seat, not one."

"How much further to the town, Fi?"

"Several miles. Maybe half a sunmark."

"Let's pick up the pace," Leanne directed. She was thinking that being in the town would be safer, but when they began to see the rows of java bush, off to the side of the road, and the scattered huts, they also saw other riders heading into the town from the other direction. Figures doing what was needed to tend the bushes, suddenly dropped tools and raced for the hovels grouped in the centre of the town.

The graceful gait of the distant horses was a giveaway to the quality of the creatures. They reached the little village, well before the disguised Thulans. Their intent was clear, for after they tethered the horses in the open village square, they began to enter the hovels, and carry stuff out. Screams of outrage carried in the still hot air.

"I don't think they are traders," Leanne murmured, as one of the figures dragged out two boys, barely old enough to be in their teens.

"I would say, from their matching outfits, that they are some of El Rasho's bully boys," Atlantis guessed.

"Just what we don't need," Leanne said in disgust. "Let's wait a bit, and pull up behind those bushes. The land rises a bit there and it might be enough to give us cover."

Her eye for ground proved accurate, but their passage had been noticed by the riders coming up behind them. Soon after they had stopped and Leanne was watching the town, Finora whistled softly. She recognised their warning cadence and growled when the cart with the two men pulled up near them. She joined her twin, letting Atlantis keep watching the town. She recognised both the men and the cart, but of the cart's original driver, there was no sign. She shaded her eyes, as if from the sun's glare, and feigned recognition of neither.

"You be acting mighty suspicious," one of the new arrivals challenged. Leanne saw that he was now wearing the old clothes the old farmer had been wearing not too long ago.

"Huh!" Leanne grunted. "You gone and been pulled off too, like ye has summon to hide."

The man laughed, as if it was a good retort, but Leanne felt it like a ghost had touched her spine.

"Right we did," the man agreed, slapping Leanne on the back in mock friendship. "Them fancy gents up ahead be no friends of us."

"Best to avoid a face meet, huh?" Leanne suggested, having the idea that was the truth.

She tested out a theory. "Yes, saw then drag out two boys, not even old enough to fight. Reckon they's for the king's army."

The men tensed ever so slightly, then the second one said, "Them fancy pants look to be laying out the rules." He pointed, and nudged Leanne to look. He began a tale of a time when they had thwarted other of the bully boys who worked for the king.

Atlantis had already decided the same thing, and while she seemed to be watching the distant events, actually had more than half her attention nearby. The comradely boasting, was meant to keep the dull witted farmer distracted while they stole the horses or the saddle bags. They were likely brigands, working on their own, and who would not want to meet the enforcers close up either. Or maybe, they were deserters?

Finora had been keeping very still, holding the horses, and so far neither man had been aware of her. The first man, with eyes still on Leanne and Atlantis, began inching closer to the horses, and then began fingering the buckles on the bags. Finora smiled, and with an unnoticed movement, eased her grip on the horses' reins. The nearest, sensing a stranger, turned its head and snapped at the man's face.

"Best ye move away a bit, Laddie," Finora said, her voice sounding like that of a crone. "He be a right ornery cuss now."

The man, who had stepped back in a hurry, jumped at the sound of the voice.

Finora went on with a cackle. "Probably thinks you have there a treat and ye be keeping it from him. He don't know that treats be as scarce as his dead dam's teeth."

Atlantis appeared to limp back from her watching position. "The geezers be gone into inn now. Reckon we be safe to go on now."

"We'll ride down there with ye," the two men said, after a quick exchange of whispers. "Maybe them bullies won't trouble any of us then."

Leanne shrugged. "Please ye selves." She went to her horse and climbed awkwardly up. When Atlantis urged her mount closer, she whispered, "They be like a rash." The direction of her gaze, at the two men, indicated who she meant. They had just been 'helping the old woman onto her horse'.

"Yeah, we'll need to lose them," Leanne agreed. "I reckon they do suspect us of having valuables. Felt that shorter one fingering my pockets. We certainly don't need them following us to our destination. They might just turn us in for money."

Once back on the road, they moved at the pace suited to the old creatures their horses looked to be. The wagon followed, able to maintain the pace. The men who had stolen it, didn't see that the three farmer types in front of them were talking quietly. 'I seem to recall this place," Leanne said as they drew closer. Until then, it might have been any of a dozen similar towns that grew java bushes. "The inn has a one eared barman."

"Good food, but lousy beds," Atlantis added. "So that puts the main trade road three to four miles to the west."

"How does that help us scrape these guys off?" Finora asked.

"I have an idea," Leanne revealed. "Fi, is there a way to make some of the dried tree stuff that Tis collected look like fine grade smoke weed?"

"Easy. Do you want it to give the same effect if they try it?"

Leanne's grin was answer enough.

In the town's communal stable, Leanne paid a few coppers to have their horses kept together in a loose box. They also arranged for a light feed and water for them. To give them a rest, they unsaddled the animals and gave them a rubdown. The other two men seemed to be dawdling around their horse and wagon, without even giving the poor creature a drink. They didn't notice what their intended victims were doing until Leanne hefted a leather pouch and announced, "I be off to be doing me some trading, Yousef. See the nags get their feed. And you, woman, sees to getting us some feed."

Atlantis immediately picked up a fork and began poking it into a pile of dry java bush, or rather, what remained after the leaves had all been stripped. It was what the few other horses in the stable had in their feed boxes.

The two men decided to follow Leanne, and Atlantis made sure they stayed interested in her by calling out, "Ye best be takin' your other sample, oldster!" she tossed a second pouch, this one full of the prickly spiky leaves of the bush she had carried from near the border. She saw the glance the two men gave each other, then quickly returned her eyes to the prongs of her fork. They were hooked.

Leanne ambled into the inn and looked around. There were one or two people she decided were locals, the three bully boys and the couple who ran the inn. The latter were trying to look busy, while still eyeing the unwelcome enforcers. She stopped on the threshold, and felt the two men from the wagon run into her. Her face stayed neutral as she felt the pouch of smoke weed lifted from her pocket. The one of seeds was in her hand.

"Hey! Farmer!" a voice called out.

Leanne didn't react until she had reached the bar and asked for an ale. She shrugged roughly when the man grabbed her shoulder. "What's your problem," Leanne growled, while she watched the clay mug being filled with her drink. "Can't a man wash the road dust from his throat?"

"I asked you a question," the same man insisted.

Leanne twisted her little finger in her ear, as if trying to clear it. She heard a faint sound of disgust from behind her.

"Did ye? Sorry. Me throat and ears be right dusty. What can ye want of me?"

"You live here, farmer?"

"Just visitin', Sirs."

"What for?"

Leanne glanced around, as if checking for listeners. "Me's after some seeds for the java bush. Want to try growing it on me farm, down south a ways."

"And how will you pay for them, farmer?"

"Gotta try. Maybe I can work here for a bit. Don't got any spare copper bits."

The enforcer continued to study Leanne when she turned to her drink and took a long swallow, then belched loudly. The enforcer decided to return to his fellows.

The barman with the one ear asked, "Do I know you?"

Leanne asked him a question, the prelude to a lewd joke she had told him on her previous visit, when she had been on her way to rescue Maeven and Petulor's egg.

He chuckled softly and grinned faintly. "You be friends with those others that followed you in?"

"No, but they are like a rash."

"They were here last night, but better dressed. Caught them trying to rob my coin pouch. They reckoned they were traders, looking for trade goods. I say they be much like yon gentlemen, but out for them selves. And I recognise old Unc Hazers clothes. Did they have a wagon?"

"Yup. Smelt of manure. They caught us up a few miles out of town, but they'd been the other way on horses not that long before. Think me too dumb to realise it."

"Bastards," the barman swore. "I'll send someone out to look for Unc, but he's probably too late."

Leanne winked and said, "I've a mind to give them trouble." She hefted her drink and ambled over to the two men in the dark corner.

With her voice low, but not so low that the sharp ears of the enforcers would not hear her, she said, "Barman say you be traders. Didn't look it, and ye never said it, but is that true?"

"We trade when we can," one of the men said cautiously.

Leanne nodded. "Ye fit what me mate told me. Says you deal in weed."

"You have us wrong, farmer," was the instant denial, and the man fidgeted in his seat. His eyes flicked to where the enforcers sat. His mate was doing something with his hand, under the table.

The men would have denied it even had it been true. The tavern, even when it was nearly empty, was still too public to discuss weed.

"We trade when we can get goods that are needed elsewhere."

"Well, I be wanting to –"

"Quiet fool!" the other man hissed. "We don't have weed! It's illegal."

"Only to the likes of us," Leanne persisted, unruffled. "but it be real good for ridding crops of pests. We use it for that."

Leanne sensed the enforcers coming closer. Her talisman was warming, though not becoming hot.

"Traders!" One of the enforcers greeted the two men. Another gripped Leanne's shoulder and gave a yank. Leanne grumbled, "We be talking trade."

"Begone, farmer. You can talk later."

Leanne shrugged again and returned to the bar, still listening to the confrontation. "Where you be from, traders? Where are you going? Where are your trade goods? What do you usually trade in? Where are your travel passes?"

The barman's wife sidled up to her husband, whispered something as she slipped something into his hand, glanced at Leanne and disappeared back into her kitchen.

The conversation in the corner wasn't going as the two men wanted. They didn't have satisfactory answers, and the enforcers, who were indeed corrupt, were also not fools. They sensed the men were hiding something. Next they had dragged the two men out from behind the table and were checking their pockets. One leant over and recovered a pouch from the floor. He looked inside, took out a pinch of the stringy dried vegetation and sniffed it. Their whole attitude grew more intent. Finora had crushed some of the spiky bush Atlantis had collected, then and spelled it to resemble, and smell like, smoke weed.

"Psst!" the barman hissed to get Leanne's attention. "You be allied to the southern brotherhood now?"

He flipped a stone token so that she could see the carving on it. It was one of the tokens Nelsi had given them as a means to get help from the Vatarin thieves' league.

"Had you as more of a noble kind, last time you was this way."

"The southern brotherhood has members with extra skills," Leanne admitted. The barman nodded.

"How can I help?"

"We will be coming back this way," Leanne said.

"Coming fast, I reckon, like last time."

"Or faster," Leanne agreed. "My sister will have told your wife our needs."

"Aye, she did. Food and water for you and the horses, a safe place to sleep, and a nursing woman?"

Leanne just smiled and didn't explain. Instead she said, "And if it is needed, a distraction."

The barman nodded, wise enough to refrain from asking for further explanation. "Done. We don't have much to spare, but your friend is generous." He nodded then, at the corner. "One of them bastards took your pouch."

Leanne grinned briefly. The men were now claiming they found it in the stable. It might have been the truth that they didn't know what was in it. However the enforcers believed it was smokeweed from what their eyes and noses told them.

"Must be the farmer's pouch," one of the men tried.

At the bar, Leanne said quickly, "I told them I wanted to trade smokeweed seeds for java bush seeds. They didn't get the other pouch." Leanne drew that one out. "These are sage bush seeds out of their hard shell. Just pretend they aren't."

Once again, the barman nodded. "The stuff might be illegal, but I reckon that's so's nobles like our new king, can have it all. Filthy stuff, but smokes off pests you say?"

"Birds have a feast," Leanne agreed. "But theys eat too many and they flies off funny like."

Leanne had to go over her story again when the enforcer asked about the pouch. "Yeah, thought I'd dropped it. They must've thought to sell it. I was going to show a demonstration...oh, I don't smoke it. That's illegal. But ain't no law says I can't kill pests with it."

By the time she'd finished her rambling story, she had given the enforcer hints about the two men who were able bodied, but not doing their bit for the king's army - likely stealing army supplies and selling them, that she judged they were about to be conscripted.

"I'll just confiscate the seeds, farmer. You don't want to be in trouble for selling illegal plants. Stick to java bush."

"Don't have nothing else to offer for trade," Leanne said, allowing a hint of disappointment to creep into her stolid farmer's voice.

"Stick to java bush," the enforcer repeated, then to her surprise, he put a silver bit on the bar. "Then when you have a harvest, send word to Nickel Astralis. You'll be well paid, and helping the king to defeat his enemies."

"Wrong time of season for seeds," the barman opined. "You'd have to come back when the days start to cool. But our farmers don't want competition."

"Enough for all," Leanne contested. "Stuff's in high demand in the south. We can share profits."

The enforcer moved away, and Leanne pushed the silver bit towards the barman.

"That was all hokus," Leanne assured the barman. "But with these thieving types around, it might actually be wise to collect seeds. In case something happens to the established bushes."

He was quick to nod, as he watched the two men being hustled out. "Your gear be safe?"

"Yes. We will be back this way within a ten day."

The detour they took, heading south, was uneventful. Once they were out of eye shot of the town, they rode east to the trade road, and headed north.

CHAPTER 45 – Atlantis, Leanne and Finora

Atlantis signalled for them to stop when they caught their first glimpse of the citadel. It stood atop a hill, and had the late evening sun glowing off its western façade.

"Looks so deceptively picturesque," Leanne growled. "Except that we know he type of creatures that live there."

"We should be outside the range of the foot and horse patrols," Atlantis told them. "The citadel faces east, so this side has the labyrinth. Arlen said that they don't worry too much about this area, because if anyone finds a way down, the dark creatures will get them before they can go very far."

"Didn't stop us," Leanne remarked. "Will you have to get past the area where the roof collapsed?"

"No. That's closer to the citadel, around to the north a bit. I am not intending to go near the Wives' garden. Arlen told Roman that there was a way in and out somewhere around here – at the furthest point from the castle. He doesn't think his brother knows this part of the labyrinth, and as far as he can recall, his father never came out this far. That may mean Ciabolo hasn't explored this far either, but we can't be absolutely sure."

"So, how did he know about it?" Finora asked. "Did he go exploring by himself? With all the nasty creatures out to eat him?"

"He said he remembered it, and it was a secret."

Leanne grunted. "So what are we looking for?"

"A wooden trap door," Atlantis told her.

"Well, that's going to have us quartering this area in full view of any guards that look this way from the citadel walls."

"First, we need to set up our camp," Atlantis said. "If Finora can hide it, it gives us a refuge."

"I can do that, and if we set up just off that little rise near the trees, anyone walking this way can be easily deflected around it," Finora considered. "While I do that, shouldn't you start looking? We won't have much daylight left today before you'd have to stop."

"Camp first," Leanne decided. "What did Arlen say about where to look?"

Atlantis began to recite, "Stand facing the servant's gate. When the dip in the distant mountain is behind you move so that your left arm points to the river bridge and your right arm points to the traitors mound. When you make a perfect cross, the door will be under your feet."

"That gives us a better idea, but likely it will still be hard to find. We can go and see if we can pin point the landmarks today, and start searching at first light tomorrow."

Leanne and Atlantis were already trying to spot them, but stopped when Finora directed them to bring the horses.

The camp was basic - a fireplace, three bedrolls on the ground, the horses tethered where they could graze on the scanty dry grasses, and the packs where they could act as seats or pillows. When Atlantis slipped out via the single opening, and if there had been a watcher it would have seemed like she slipped from behind a slender tree, she moved to look around. Finora was good! The invisibility spell had totally hidden people, horses and the small tent and cook fire. The faint breeze was blowing from that direction and even the smoke smell was unnoticeable. Leanne came out a moment later and they began to circle the citadel, looking for the landmarks.

"The servant's gate?" Leanne mused. "Any idea?"

"I think it might be like a small back way in and out," Atlantis suggested.

Leanne pulled out a slender metal tube with a series of glass lenses within. She put it to her eye and scanned the line between the citadel's white stone and the reddish sandstone it was built on. "I think I see it. About a fingers width from the right turret."

She passed the tube to Atlantis, who looked and agreed. She turned to look at the distant mountain range, and thought there were three places that might be what the reference to a dip referred to. She gestured for them to keep going around. The river they knew, for they had crossed the bridge on their way to where they stopped. Using those two points, they looked to the mountains, but none of the three places that might have been the dip, suited the instructions. Finally, as the sun was setting, they headed back to their camp. They had been alert for King El Rasho's guards, and patrolling Enforcers, but all stayed as small moving dots in the distance.

What they did notice, as the light dimmed, was the hunting calls of the night creatures, and reinforced their personal protection spells. Some of the sounds had no relation to any creature either of them had encountered. This close to Cibolo's lair, they could well be night demons.

A breeze was rising as the light dimmed, making the air chilly. As they approached their hidden camp, it grew strong enough to be raising dust. Both sensed magic at work, but as their talismans stayed cool, they realised Finora was hiding their tracks. The subtle repulsion spell tried to move them from the opening, but as they knew it was there, they could force their way on.

Once inside, they felt the air was warmer, and they saw the tiny fire over which Finora was boiling water. Just enough for a hot drink and to make a thick stew of water and crumbled dry trail rations.

By unspoken agreement, they spoke quietly, when they were close together, and only if it was important. Atlantis was particularly quiet as she was concentrating on a mental vision of a crudely drawn map and rough estimates of distance in terms of Arlen sized strides.

"I think we need to be closer to the citadel and look in the other direction," she announced softly. "I think there is another bridge that way."

CHAPTER 46 - Maeven

The King and his wizard were away from the citadel again. The whole atmosphere was different. The servants walked a little straighter and her guards were more relaxed, though not less alert.

Maeven felt strong and full of energy, despite the weight of two babies.

She was purposefully acting like a dutiful expectant mother, by sitting quietly and sewing little gowns for a royal girl child. And when no one was around, making two little pouches for Petulor's scales. These would be placed around the neck of each baby so that they would have Petulor's protection. It might be arguable that they would need the protection more that she would, but they would be unable to defend themselves.

At least she did not have to worry about letting out the waist of her own gowns. If it wasn't for the ribbons at the sides of the light gowns worn by the Royal Wives, they would be like the bivouac tents of her father's army.

Maeven put down her sewing and closed her eyes. The babies were kicking now and she relaxed to enjoy the ticklish sensation. She must have dozed for a time because she woke to the sound of voices.

Her guards, believing her asleep were chatting to pass the time; something they would never do if the King was in residence.

Maeven had come to be reasonably fluent in Vatarin, or at least understood more than she spoke. From the conversation outside her door, the guards were not very alert. It was an opportunity Maeven decided to make the most of.

Very quietly, she placed the scales in the pouches and made both pouches disappear and follow her as if they were in a pocket. She already knew that there was enough power in the scales to power her spells. Now it was time to practice another.

She chanted the spell that would make her disappear, and she did – all but her hands.

"Darn, that's the wrong spell," she chided herself, removing it and saying the newer version of the spell. This time, she totally vanished.

Rising from the chair quietly took some effort but she did so without alerting the guards. They were apt to look in when they heard unexpected noises. She used her natural stealth to walk to the door, unlock it and open it just a crack.

In Vatarin, she said in a faint whisper, "In the space of forty heartbeats you will stand and be asleep until I tell you to wake."

Half a minute later, the guard stopped talking mid-sentence.

Maeven wasted no time, she intended to go to El Rasho's suite and search it. There had been no opportunity since the wizard had caught her.

As she left her quarters, her instincts switched to 'thief' as she made her way quickly and quietly along the stone passages to the Kings suite. With him away, there were no guards and few servants. The latter would not question her actions.

The King's suite had only an ordinary lock, simple to one of her skills. Inside, she quickly glanced around, confirming it was empty. There were thick fur rugs covering the floor but she chose to step around them.

She took extreme care when searching through El Rasho's closet of expensive robes and through the scented wooden chest. Her scalp itched as she searched the latter and felt hard objects amongst the silky items. She let her fingers examine some of them, some she drew out, like the clear vial of tiny white pebbles that gave her a really bad feeling or the casket of tiny crystal vials containing coloured liquids.

In the chest, pushed to the back against the wood was something that felt like parchment folded over. This gave her a different kind of tingle and she carefully pulled it out and opened it up.

At first look it was blank, but as she wondered about it, faint marks began to appear.

The writing, if that was it was, made no sense to her but the rest of it seemed to be a map with little pictographs providing information. It might have no value, but she folded it over into half and half again, and made it so it would follow her invisibly.

An inner sense, valuable to thieves, warned her that she should leave. She looked around to ensure that all was as she found it and to memorise the room. Only then did she notice the small half door, partly hidden by a drape. She was positive that door had not been visible when she had first entered.

Two instincts flared in her mind. One was the itch that warned her of magic, the second was the urge to flee. Maeven fled, pausing only to relock the door.

Her bare feet made no sound on the stone floors and though she watched where she was going, her mind was picturing herself in her chair by the window in her quarters. By mere moments, did she arrive there, awaken the guards and reach her chair.

The Captain of the Royal Guards, or Chief Enforcer, strode into her room unannounced, and found her blinking in confusion and her sewing looking as if it had slipped off her lap.

"Your pardon," he said, bowing only slightly and not giving her an honorific title. "The wards on his majesty's apartments were breached. I had orders to check on you."

"I am sure your men at my door will have told you I have been sleeping. I get so tired these days," Maeven said politely. "Besides, my Lord has made it clear to me that I am not to come seeking him in his apartments."

Her tone was demurely innocent as the Guard Captain stared at her. He knew the King didn't trust this woman, but she seemed so retiring.

"The rooms are warded against those of dragon blood," he said, startling her.

"As you may know Captain," Maeven continued in a genteel tone, "my current condition keeps me here most of the time. I do not have the chance to leave and I miss the chance to speak to the other women, even to Jilli, who used to be a maid at the palace of my father, King Westron of Thulor."

From the way the Guard Captain's face twitched, she had startled him again. It seemed that he had not known the rank of this Royal Wife.

"My apologies, Princess." He bowed a little lower this time.

"I am grateful for your concern, Captain," Maeven lied politely.

"I am glad you are safe. There are those in the Kingdom who do not wish our King to have dealings with our enemies."

The words were carefully neutral in meaning, and having uttered them, the Captain departed. Maeven quickly ran to the door after he had left.

"Be doubly alert. There may be an agent of the enemy in the palace; one that seeks to find the Princess."

The door was closed properly and Maeven returned to her chair, still wondering if they thought she had triggered the alarm. She was sure she hadn't, or the alarm would have happened when she entered the room. Therefore, she would also need to be alert for an agent from Thulor. It had been a long time since the two thieves had contacted her and too long since Petulor had promised help.

CHAPTER 47 - Atlantis, Leanne and Finora

In the morning, when the sun was just cresting the horizon, Atlantis shrugged on a small fabric backpack as well as the one she had packed for travelling. Finora and Leanne had already ensured that when they left their protected camp, no trace of their presence remained. They all knew where they would be looking that day and headed directly across the open ground to where the terrain became uneven. They reached the first of many dips in the ground, just as yells and shouts and battle cries rang out. They threw themselves to the ground, Finora and Atlantis crawling fast along the gully, while Leanne carefully looked for the source of the noise. A troop of mounted soldiers had arrived, from out of nowhere – probably via some type of demon portal, and were going through a series of battle exercises. It did not seem that they had been noticed, and Leanne was torn between watching how the horsemen were being trained and helping to find the entrance to the underground labyrinth.

Finora looked concerned, but Atlantis said, "Tell her to keep watching. We can keep looking for the door." She knew the twins had their own way to communicate, and her mind was comparing the details from Arlen's crude map with the details of the terrain.

The landmarks – gate bridge and dip – fell into place, but the reference to 'Traitor's Hill' was obscure. It was the cawing of three crows that drew her attention to a spot on what she thought was a small rock outcrop. On it was what looked to be a cairn of rocks, but when she moved along a winding gully to get closer to it, she discovered it was made from sun-bleached bones. A few had fallen from it and were lying loose, she carefully reached for one and saw signs that they had been gnawed on. She recognised the tooth marks from the deadly cave hounds that lived in dark places like the labyrinth. She shivered, and quickly returned to where Finora was watching. Now that she had the last location, she backtracked to where all four lined up. Even then, the door was not obvious, but she realised that the state of the bones of the cairn suggested that this area had not been frequented for many years. Now she looked for a suggestion of an unnaturally flat area. Finora used some magical spell to help look and she pointed at an area on the slope of one side of the gully. Together, they felt the ground give slightly at that point and began to scrape dried dirt from the wooden door.

Finora must have alerted her twin, for Leanne arrived just as she was lifting the door. The sorceress had already squirted a special oil on the hinges to make them move without sound or sticking. The rest of the oil was now in a stoppered vial in Atlantis's pocket.

"Put up a shield, Fi. In case those horses come this way."

While her twin began the quiet incantation, Leanne asked, "You going in?"

Atlantis nodded.

"We will set up another camp – in the trees near the bridge. We will mark the entrance here, and the entrance to the camp. Do you have any or your brother's little orbs with you?"

"In my main pack, there is one of the smaller ones. I have some fingertip sized ones. They work the same, but not with actually visions. Just colours. Red means trouble, green means all's okay, white will be when I'm on the way out."

"Do you want us to come if there is trouble?"

"No. You won't know what you will be coming into. If you know there is trouble outside, think that at the orb and I will know to be extra careful on the way out."

"Dragon's luck, then," Leanne said, gripping her sister in law on the shoulder for a moment. "We will be ready to go as soon as you come out."

Atlantis shrugged off her travel pack, keeping only the small fabric one, and slipped into the entrance. The wooden trap door had shown signs of long neglect. That more than anything else was reassuring. The cave hounds would not be hanging around a place where no food was likely to be found. There was some light reaching into the narrow passage, and before she left there, she inverted her fabric pack and put the few loose items into the pockets of her dark travel clothes, and shook the fabric out to become a black hooded robe. This had been obtained in the last town they had gone through, thanks to one of Nelsi's 'northern brothers'. It was a close copy of the normal servants garb worn in the Citadel of the King of Vatarik. She still had her leather breeches and jerkin underneath but they would not be seen. Under the black robe, her arms were bare to the shoulder. Her outer jacket, she left near the doorway. She also had one knife in a hidden sheath.

Once before she had merged in amongst the servants in the citadel. She had discovered that they were trained not to be curious and not to draw attention to themselves or to their fellows. If they thought she was strange, they would still say nothing in case it was their superiors testing them. On her previous visit, Atlantis had mastered the art of appearing to be busily employed while searching the citadel. She was sure she would be able to find Maeven and attach herself to the servants in that area.

She gave a low whistle and the trap door was closed behind her. Before moving on, she checked what she had in her pockets. The barest minimum – lock picks, hinge oil, presents from his majesty's spy master, Nayfor. The small colour changing orbs, which were about the size of children's marbles only of glass, not wood. There was a small pouch of crushed dragon shells, well charged with magic she could draw on for minor spells or healing. She had a few flat smooth stones she could use to make a glow light, some charcoal sticks and a few squares of bleached cloth. She would have felt better to have her sword, but that would be the utmost folly. Even the one knife she had, in a padded sheath strapped to the inside of her leg, would be enough to have her killed if anyone in the citadel learned of it.

Little enough, but also dangerous if she was searched. Servants owned nothing but what their masters gave them. The rest of her protections were stored in her memory. Spells Roman had taught her to focus her mind's intention. Protection spells that could be powered by her talisman, or if that was unable to receive Petulor's power, by the dragon shells. She invoked two of them before she moved. One was a repulsion spell that she knew worked on the cave hounds. It should keep any of the nasty creatures from being interested in her. The other was a protection spell, that would make any person who saw her think that there was nothing strange about her, and she had every right to be where she was.

As a last thought, she recalled a spell her brother had used to make walls of natural earth or stone, glow faintly. Just enough to see by in otherwise pitch dark. She had not expected it to work in the heart of Vatarik, but it did.

CHAPTER 48 - Atlantis

Atlantis had the feeling that some power was indeed directing her. Maybe it was Petulor, but in any case, she followed the vaguely lit passages and ignored the dark openings. Her mind instinctively remembered each turning, distances between them and the feel of the caverns she passed through.

Initially, the passage had been little more than a tunnel dug through the ground and roughly sealed by a thin layer of cement. She put the question of why it was made out of her mind. That passage had given way to a rough chasm in the rock, where the ground had cracked and moved apart. She had to edge through and was glad she did not have her pack with her. Then, when she reached the point where she estimated the walls of the citadel were, she came out into caverns like she recalled from her previous foray into this labyrinth. Here she started to hear the quiet snuffling sounds of the creatures that lived in the darkness. She strengthened the repulsion spell, and increased her pace – a dark shape in near total darkness.

She moved silently until she came to another passage, where she felt a movement of air. It carried a rank musty smell. It reminded her of her last visit, when King Westron's three daughters and herself had outwitted El Rasho and Ciabolo, and brought down the ceiling of a large cavern. In doing so, they'd emptied the lake above to flood the cavern. It meant she was nearing her destination, for the lake had been at the end of the Garden of the Wives. She allowed herself a moment of mirth. The flooded cavern had been where Ciabolo had stored a vast amount of valuables – gems, coins, metals and other things he coveted. Had he recovered them? Part of her doubted it. That was the deepest part of the cavern system, and Ciabolo, even in his serpent form, did not like water.

She compared her mental map of where she was to her memory of the citadel above, and decided the glowing walls were directing her around the collapsed section.

Arlen had told her brother that there had been an entrance to the labyrinth from the suite he had once occupied. Atlantis knew that suite from her previous visit. It was where he, when he was still El Haba, had kept Maeven after bringing her from Thulor. Once in there, she would know her way around. Arlen had insisted that Roman tell her not to assume that suite was unoccupied, but also that he believed that way would not be guarded. He had never used it, and no one had ever hinted to him that they knew of it. As far as he knew, the only time that way out had been used, was when his mother had fled the citadel when he was ten.

The suite had been the one assigned to the king's chief wife, and he had stayed there after his mother had gone. He had not been forced to move out, since his father had not taken another chief wife.

If for some reason she could not enter that way, her fall back plan was to enter via the former king's suite, although she expected that El Rasho, or Ciabolo would have appropriated that space.

The glow stopped just beyond the section of wall that felt like wood, not stone. She risked making one of her stones into a brighter light, only so she could locate the opening mechanism, and put oil on the hinges. Once the positions were in her mind, she dulled the stone and returned it to her pocket. Then her hand turned the catch upwards and she pushed on the door, just enough to open it a crack. Light came into the tunnel, daylight from the glass sections of the roof, she recalled. She stayed still and listened carefully for five minutes, before opening the door enough to see through. In front of her was a rack of clothes, all seemed black – the colour El Rasho preferred, not the lighter shades his brother had worn. It was incentive to be even more careful. She edged out of the passage, sliding the wood panel back into place, but having it so the catch on the passage side did not drop back into place. She looked until she found the way to move the catch from the inside.

It was well hidden. The wall there was covered with a layer of colour, or rather colour applied to a layer of cloth that was in turn glued to the wood. She ran her fingers over it, where she guessed the catch to be, and felt the fabric give slightly there. It had been deliberately hidden.

Only then did she crawl to look out from under the hanging clothes. Her view was limited to floor level, below a curtain that hid the clothes rack. She still saw no movement and heard nothing. She carefully stood up, and moved to peer around one end of the curtain. She saw the huge bed, which had all the curtains drawn open, and was neatly made. She saw a low table and two chairs, and shelves with all sorts of…trophy's she guessed… and spare weapons on a rack.

She risked stepping out, and looking around. The side room, a smaller bedroom, was empty – but the bed was not as neatly made as the one in the main chamber. She wondered if it was a servant's room. That might be a complication. She checked also, the bathing room. That showed signs of having been used recently, and had not yet been cleaned. Servants would be on the way there any time. She needed to get out of the suite.

She opened the door a crack and listened. She heard no sound, and when she opened the door further, saw there were no guards at the door. Without wasting any more time, she moved into the passage and strode away from the new king's chosen suite.

Some subtle warning caused her to slow and adopt the shuffle walk of the citadel servants. Moments later, two guards came hurrying around a corner. She immediately moved against one wall, keeping her head looking down, the hood hiding her features. The men ran past, not even glancing her way – she may as well not have existed.

When they were past, she resumed the servants shuffle, but at a faster rate, heading for the nearest stairs down to the servants level.

Just before she reached the stairs, she sensed a presence beside her and felt her arm gripped. "Quickly," a low voice urged.

Atlantis was hearing loud voices, and as her talisman was cool, decided not to ignore the urging. From the voice, she could not decide if the voice was from a male or female, but either way, the person was not an enemy. She was hurried past the stairs, into part of the upper servant's wing.

"In here! Get those boots off!"

Atlantis obeyed, taking the flat sandals the person gave her, and putting them on as the figure took her boots from view.

When she returned, Atlantis asked, "Why are you helping me."

"Are you from Thulor?"

"Declanor and Thulor," Atlantis admitted, feeling it was safe to be honest. There was a faint sigh of relief.

"I have prayed to the dragon that someone would come," the person said, and now Atlantis was sure it was a female, and possibly not originally from Vatarik.

"When I saw you, I knew!" the woman went on. "The servants here do not wear boots. The guards are roused, you would soon be caught."

"I thank you, and yes, the new dragon mage, Petulor, insisted I come to help Ven. Maeven I mean, she is the one Petulor calls Dragon Mother."

"To get her away?" the woman asked, hopefully.

"If she will come," Atlantis hedged.

"She is very near to her time, although the king does not expect it to be for a while yet. However, as there are two babies, it is not unusual for them to come early."

"A boy and a girl," Atlantis confirmed.

"The dragon told you?"

"Yes."

"What is your name?"

"Atlantis Gold Dreamer."

"Are you a sorceress?"

"No. My brother is the wizard."

"You have magic things?"

"Some..."

"Maybe that's what did it?"

"Something broke the wards around the king's suite. The guards were not on duty there because he is away. Now, they are in a right state. They have to find the intruder before his majesty returns, or some will be given to that wizard of his."

"So, it's me they are looking for."

"I expect they will be looking for a male intruder. Women here are not thought to be strong enough or smart enough to be a threat."

"Can you help me get to Ven?"

"Aye, I can. But not right away. They will be watching her, thinking either that she has been up to mischief, or that someone is out to prevent the birth of the king's heir. But don't you worry, your friend has all her wits about her. She seems to know just how far to provoke those who consider themselves her betters. Though some of her immunity will vanish once the boy is born."

"How are you known here?" Atlantis asked the woman.

"Most call me Doty, when I am not being called Old Woman. I am the midwife, and was once the nurse to Malokin's lads. My true name is Hendra Woolweaver."

Hearing the name, Atlantis blurted softly, "I have met Kellthea, her mother was..."

"My sister. The girl would be a woman now, and better off for not being here. Her father lost interest in her mother when the girl was born, and the new king would have had her killed. And he would do the same to his brother, now he is king, to prevent rival claims."

"Dragon's breath! I knew he was a bastard. But Ven and I got the better of him before. Him and the Serpent, and we have their measure."

"Don't under estimate the Serpent, he is still dangerous, even though he currently only inhabits the body of a hedge wizard. It was he who ensured Malokin's rule, by having all his kin, but for a lucky few, killed. And when he is here, that wizard seems to have ears everywhere. So it is well they are away. Now, I will tell the Chief Servant why you are here and have him assign you to me. For now, just follow me and do what I say. Don't speak to anyone else. The other servants will think you are new, and I am training you. As for the chief servant, if you are no friend of the king, he will be on your side, but he will not be able to show it."

CHAPTER 49 - Maeven

Jilli flounced into her room without any pretence of politeness.

"What have you done now, bitch? You've got the guards acting like the place has been invaded, and they think I caused it."

Maeven had only just awoken from sleep, but she was instantly alert. "I've been asleep. What are you on about?"

"Don't give me that! I know you told the guards you were a princess, no one else knew that."

"Oh, that," Maeven said, so casually it further infuriated Jilli. "I was giving them reasons why I hadn't been prancing around near dear Rashi's private rooms. As if being huge with his bastards is not obvious enough."

"That hasn't stopped you yet," Jilli spat. "I told them that!"

"Well you can't blame me if they have fire-ants in their fancy uniforms. I've got guards at my door, all day and all night. I know it is so I can't go walking around, not that I have the energy anymore. They might imply it is to protect me, but I know what Rashi thinks of me. Anyway, I thought you liked getting the guards' attention."

"Not when they seriously think I am a traitor. What exactly did you tell them?"

"Nothing they didn't already know, or should have known. I told them I was in no condition to be interested in poking my nose out of my room, and I wished I did because I even missed the pleasure of your company since you at least spoke Thulan."

"You told them you were a king's whelp. That means nothing here."

"So? I was bored. I like startling that officious Chief Guard. Anyway, what's going on? I heard something about wards on the king's room being breached. That is probably why they thought of you. They know I am not allowed there."

Jilli snorted. "Like I said, that didn't stop you. Anyway, I know I haven't been there, and if it wasn't you, it was probably another of your father's spies. They will find him you know. And torture him until he tells them everything he knows. Rashi has learnt a lot about the defences your puny father is relying on. He'll be able to destroy them all, take over his kingdom and trample all the people to dust.”

“He thinks he can,” Maeven retorted. “He’s never told us his plans, so why would he tell a mere spy such things?”

Jilli tried a different attack. “Do you know that his wizard has a way to turn Thulan farmboys into fighters for his army? Isn’t that delicious? They will be fighting their friends and family.”

“So?” Maeven kept an even tone, with difficulty.

“Don’t you care that a chunk of his army is made up of Thulans?”

“Nothing I can do about it,” Maeven said with a shrug. “But I bet that wizard my father found has some nasty ideas.”

“Your ineffective father doesn’t even know that some of his Lords have already pledged to Rashi. They will fight against him.”

“If you really think I care all that much, you’re deluded,” Maeven lied. “Do you think my father wants me back? That I will be seen as anything other than a traitor if I went back? I’m pregnant! With the brats of a son of Vatarik, and I haven’t even tried to escape, or kill myself.”

“You couldn’t anyway,” Jilli smirked.

“How’s he to know that? Anyway, he’s never given me any reason to care what happens to him.”

With a snarl of frustration, Jilli flounced from the room. She had failed to get the reaction she had wanted from her rival.

When the door had slammed shut, she heard a sigh as if someone had been holding their breath. With her attention on JIlli, she hadn’t been aware of the servants who had come to work in her room. She glanced their way, then appeared to ignore them.

Then she said aloud, but as if to herself, “Well, she’s in a mood, isn’t she?”

She pretended not to hear the muffled giggle.

“You might as well make the bed. I doubt if I will be getting anymore sleep this morning.”

“Are you ready for your breakfast, my lady?”

“After I get dressed, and have a light wash,” Maeven said. The servants knew she didn’t need help for that, and changing one oversized sheer dress for another took only a few seconds. However, it was a chance to give the two women a brief respite, and they appreciated even that little consideration.

The fact that she had made a point of thanking her servants, when no one else was around, had led to an unstated arrangement. They would talk softly, as if to each other, just loud enough for her to hear. It gave her word of what was going on in the citadel, and sometimes beyond.

This time, she heard, "His majesty is off checking on his infiltrators, isn't he?"

"Apparently. Didn't I hear that he sneaks across the border all the time?"

"He goes there, but he uses some kind of magic – his wizard gets him there and back quickly."

"Is that how your Freddie gets to and from where the army is?"

"Probably. Himself wants the farm boy conscripts trained up, but he don't what them in his back fields. That's for his loyal regulars."

"I heard Freddie boasting that himself has troops ready to cross the border in two dozen different places."

It went on as they made her bed, cleaned her fireplace and made it ready for when it grew cool again in the evening, laid out what she needed for her wash, and found a clean dress for her.

The servants left, and she was alone until others came with her breakfast.

The hints about El Rasho's army had unsettled her. She knew she could do nothing about that situation, but did wish she had a way to pass on such useful snippets of news. She had to believe that her father's troops, his spies, and his lords were finding out about such things. All she could do, when the opportunity arose, was to feed El Rasho and the Serpent misleading information and blatant lies. Sometimes they forgot she was only a woman, hadn't been near her father much in years, or that she should have no idea how to go about protecting a kingdom, and demanded answers to questions. She remembered the questions, for she thought they were subjects that worried them.

CHAPTER 50 – Maeven and Atlantis

Events conspired to keep Atlantis from her friend. First because the guards somehow suspected Ven, and were watching her closely. They also questioned the king's chief concubine, Jilli, and when they let her go, she had gone straight to see Maeven. Going in when that one was around was a bad idea. The former maid from King Westron's palace, might just recognise her. Even when the old woman went to check on the mother to be, she told Atlantis to stay hidden.

When the old woman was not working, and her work load was light these days, she coached Atlantis on being an unnoticed servant and what she would need to do if Maeven went into labour. Her pupil was a fast learner, and grateful to the woman for protecting her friend as much as she had.

Then, during a session two days later, a kind of shiver went through her, and she saw the old woman had also felt something.

"They are back," the old woman explained. "The king and the wizard."

It didn't take long for word to pass around that El Rasho was in a foul mood, and anyone who even looked the wrong way at him was likely to become a toy of the wizard. Atlantis shivered. Yes, she had been like one of the servants before, and escaped. This time, though, the stakes were higher. It would not be enough to behave like one of the servants, her body language hadn't been instinctive. The old woman had seen right through her pretence.

When word came some hours later that Maeven was in labour, she hoped the old woman's lessons were enough.

Maeven wanted to scream at the babbling women and tell them to go away.

Except for Jilli, who was stalking the King, all seven of the King's other wives had converged on Ven's chamber within an hour of her labour starting. Each had advice for her; ignorant advice, for none of them had ever been pregnant. They were all more of a nuisance than a help, finally one had the wits to go get the old woman.

Her one desire at the moment was for the babies to be born well before El Rasho stopped giving his guards a hard time. He would not be expecting her to be giving birth for another month at least, but would probably come and hassle her when he'd finished venting his anger elsewhere.

The old woman came into the room with several black robed servants. Two carried a pot of steaming water and the third a pile of linens and a bag slung over one shoulder.

The old woman had taken her satchel of herbs and started a brew in a kettle on the hearth. Now she proceeded to tyrannise the wives so either they chose to leave or to become moderately useful. Maeven's two guards quickly returned to their post at the door and watched uncomfortably from there.

The old woman poured a goblet of warm, herb infused water. She handed it to one of the black robed servers.

"Drink this, my lady," a very soft voice spoke in Maeven's ear. A blessedly familiar voice.

Maeven looked at the half-hidden face under the hood and reached for the cup. For a brief moment, as if fumbling, she let her hands cover those of the servant. Only her eyes betrayed the recognition and relief of knowing that her friend was near.

The drink eased the intensity of the pain without making her mind fuzzy. It gave her the strength to walk around when urged by the old woman. The same servant stayed with her providing support.

Maeven listened to Atlantis talking softly to her, responding only by increasing the grip on her hand. As time progressed, the cooling water in the pot was replaced by fresh hot water.

To distract Maeven from the contractions, Atlantis mentioned how she had found Wystan and that he was safe with her sister in law. Then she told how she had come to be there and how Maeven's own sisters were near to the citadel, waiting to help her and the children escape.

"No," Maeven whispered as if it were a grimace of pain. "Just the girl."

Atlantis exclaimed softly and wanted to argue but Maeven said nothing else.

"Did Petulor's three scales arrive?" Atlantis asked.

"Two," Maeven answered just as a powerful contraction took hold of her.

As she helped Maeven back to her couch, Atlantis saw El Rasho enter the chamber followed by a non-descript man in grey robes.

"Snakes breath! It's his foulness and his wizard!" Maeven managed to say.

Atlantis glanced at the Vatarin King who was staying by the door. The avid expression on his face showed he was enjoying the obvious pain the mother of his heirs was experiencing. The wizard stood beside him watching everything, no doubt for reasons of his own.

Maeven had no energy to spare for wondering how they knew to come there, her contractions were coming closer together and she knew, without the old woman telling her that the first baby was about to be born. She followed the woman's advice, and squatted over a cushioning pile of furs.

With another powerful contraction the baby arrived, deftly caught by the old woman who allowed Maeven to be helped to a lying position. She placed the child on Maeven, above her still bulging belly while the birth cord was cut. Maeven raised her head to see the new life she had created, saw it was a boy and touched his head, his dark hair still slicked with birth moisture and drawing his first breath with a bellow of outrage.

El Rasho appeared beside her and appeared about to lift his son and heir, but the old woman picked the child up first and passed him to a servant.

"He must be cleaned as befits a Prince of Vatarik," she said crisply.

Her glare caused her former charge to move back, just as a gush of blood and membrane was delivered.

With a look of disgust, the King moved back further but his eyes watched as the baby was cleaned.

The wizard had not moved but his gaze was still taking in everything.

When the baby had been dressed in the traditional Princes' robes, he was for a short time given to Maeven to hold. With Atlantis standing between her and El Rasho, Maeven spoke the words to recall one of the pouches containing Petulor's scales. As soon as it appeared in Maeven's hand, Atlantis took it, tied it around the baby's neck, and tucked it inside the clothes. Maeven then spoke the words to make the pouch invisible again.

The old woman made no comment; she simply took the new prince from Maeven and walked him over to the King.

While El Rasho was totally awed by the child he held in his hands, the wizard took his gaze from the mother and briefly touched the baby's face.

"The child hass no magic!" the wizard growled to the king. "But in sspite of the lingering ssmell of dragon, it bears the blood of Vatarik."

"You doubted this child's paternity, wizard? His hair is dark; his skin is olive, not pale like its mother."

"Where that wench iss consserned, I trussst nothing. I ssmelt a whiff of magic, just for a moment."

El Rasho frowned. "If she tried to harm my son, I will kill her."

"You will leave her to me!"

"I have no further use for her, she's yours."

The wizard only nodded and turned his attention back to the group of women. He sensed another whiff of magic.

The women were agitated. A second baby cried. The sound was like a weak mew – nothing like the hearty bellow of the first-born.

Maeven saw and heard through the illusion she had just cast, repeating words that Atlantis had told her. The baby, placed on her now collapsed stomach, drew a deep breath and to Maeven's ears roared a challenge that rivalled her brother's. The pouch with Petulor's scale was already around her neck.

"The second child – what is it?" the wizard asked sharply.

"A girl, my lord wizard," the old woman replied with equal sharpness. "It is weak and sickly, much smaller than the other."

Atlantis took the baby girl and began to wash her. She was positioned so she could glance between her task and El Rasho.

The old woman was attending to Maeven, and Atlantis knew she would be a formidable protector for her friend, at least until the wet nurse that had been arranged could be summoned. She had admitted, when she had been summoned, "I am an old woman. I have no authority beyond the care of the Royal Babies."

Atlantis had nodded in turn, accepting the limitations of her new ally.

When Maeven was cleaned up and lying on clean bedding, the old woman brought the boy back to her. The girl was lying on a small bed, watched only casually, it seemed, by a servant. But the servant was Atlantis.

The few remaining Royal wives had gathered to admire the new

Prince and even they were ignoring the girl child.

"I don't want it!" Maeven said clearly as the old woman approached.

The other wives became rigid with shock.

"I never wanted to have his bastards. Well he's got his heir – let him feed it!"

The old woman ignored the outburst and continued to approach.

"You will feed my son, woman!" El Rasho roared at her. "You do not need to feed the other. I have no use for a girl."

"I have no use for either!" Maeven snapped, eying El Rasho and his wizard and deliberately keeping their attention on her. She was aware of Atlantis taking the quiet baby girl out of the room.

"You pledged to obey me woman," El Rasho snarled a reminder with equal force but less volume. "To obey the rightful King of Vatarik."

"May the dragon take you!" Maeven swore at him. She acted then as if the coercion was too strong to resist, but in reality, it was too weak to stop her if she chose to ignore it.

Therefore, with a show of reluctance, Maeven obeyed and begun to do the thing she really wanted to do, feed her child.

The nearness of Petulor's scale was giving her back her strength and healing her, even as the suckling of her son was helping her body to recover naturally.

It was hard to treat her son casually. She wished with all her will that he would know she loved him and how sorry she was to be leaving him in the control of the man who thought he was his father.

Atlantis slipped quickly away, and found the corridor that led to the King's apartment. There were no guards in her way – they were all concentrating their attention on the women's' quarters.

None of them had even questioned her as she left with what looked to be a dead baby dressed in a poorly made silk gown.

She intended to leave through the same tunnel she had entered from, even though she must have tripped some sort of magical protection on her arrival. She hoped that the wizard had not yet reset it.

That was the quickest way out. If there turned out to be a guard at the King's chamber, she would continue onto the old altar room and claim to be taking the dead baby there to be in the care of the gods. The tunnel from that chamber was, according to Arlen, partially blocked. She hoped it still had room for her to get through.

The most important thing, was getting the child away. Almost equally so, in her own mind, was to get Maeven out of there. She had time, for Maeven would not be left alone for a while. All the wives would be fussing over the boy. The idea of leaving him, left a sour taste in her mouth.

She found the passage to the king's chamber deserted. His guards had been outside the birthing chamber. She felt it was safe to go in, confirmed it with a quick look around, including his bathing room. Noises came from a smaller side room, and she hurried for the hidden door. Whoever was in the throes of lust, was living dangerously. She was just closing it behind her when she heard, "Where are you?" and then, "Damn servants, they disappear just when you want them."

Atlantis hurried to shut the door and move the catch. The voice had been female, and had spoken in Thulan. It had to have been Jilli, and if she had needed any more proof that she considered herself queen, then her going into El Rasho's private chamber settled it. But it had not been the king with her – probably one of his guards.

Back in the dark, Atlantis quickly retraced the way she had come, pausing only to activate the little orb that would warn her sisters-in-law she was coming out. She wanted to hand the baby over to them, and head back in to Maeven.

They met her just inside the passage, the door was slightly ajar, and so a little light came in.

"Did you have any trouble?" Leanne asked in a whisper as she passed the baby to her twin and began to help her position the front sling that was hidden by an over tunic.

"No guards – except that Jilli came out of a side room just as I had got out into the passage. I'm surprised his Foulness lets her get away with fornicating in his rooms. She was probably with his guard."

"I've heard he uses her as a reward for his guards when he doesn't want her around," Leanne commented. "She has no taste at all and since she is as persistent as a rash, he probably gets tired of her too."

Atlantis grunted agreement, as she settled her own clothes and an extra knife into place under her robe.

"How's the little one," Leanne asked Finora.

"She's a fighter, Lee, and she has a touch of magic," Finora said. "Why didn't Maeven come?"

"Everyone is cooing over the boy. She said only to take the girl. I am going back, to try to convince her to come away. She may want to stay near the boy," Atlantis guessed. "She was distracting His Foulness and the wizard when I left. The boy is probably safe enough, but His foulness would have had this one killed."

The three women heard an abrupt roar of protest in their minds.

"NO! Dragon Mother, No!"

"Petulor, what's happened?" Leanne asked in her mind, holding her talisman.

Finora had turned her attention towards the citadel and tried to probe it with her magic. She shook her head in frustration.

"I can't see past the barrier."

Atlantis began to trot, to get back to her friend.

"I'll go back in and find out what's happened," she called over her shoulder. "I'll follow you later. Get the baby away and take my horse, you'll need it for the nurse."

"Did Maeven name her?" Finora asked and Atlantis slowed. The baby was snugly slung in a cocoon in front of the sorceress.

"No," Atlantis realised. "Though, I think if you named her after your mother, Maeven won't object."

Leanne and Finora nodded at the same instant.

"Rheanna, then," Leanne agreed as she turned to help her sister and the precious bundle back to their camp and their horses.

CHAPTER 51 – Atlantis

Atlantis did not wait to watch her companions leave; a sense of urgency was driving her back into the dangerous citadel.

Travelling through the tunnel for the third time, Atlantis kept her hand through a slit in the black robe and on the hilt of her very sharp knife. At the low door leading into the King's chamber, she stopped to put her ear on the door, trying to determine if Jilli was still in there. She could hear nothing, so she opened the door by a very small amount.

"...You will name thiss wench as queen."

Atlantis heard the hissing voice and recognised it as the voice of Ciabolo, the Serpent.

"Ssince you would break your promiss to merge with me."

"But Master..." El Rasho seemed to grovel.

"You will give the wench powerss equal to yourss!"

"But..."

"Or am I to kill you and asssume the title of regent for your sson?"

"No Master."

"Bastard," a female voice screamed. "You promised to make me your queen!"

Atlantis pushed the door open a little further, and through a gap in the hanging clothes, was in time to see the former maid, Jilli, launch herself at another woman. She gasped, Jilli's intended victim, was Maeven. As she watched, Maeven grabbed the maid by the throat and, with strength Atlantis did not believe her friend capable of – lifted her a few inches off the ground.

"You will obey me!"

Atlantis tried to see the speaker. The voice was Ciabolo's, but where was he?

"Never, bitch," Jilli said with difficulty.

In a flash, Maeven's other hand joined the first and she squeezed until Jilli was a dead weight.

Atlantis saw something fly madly around the room and settle on the guard standing by the door. The man gave a shrill scream and slumped unconscious.

"Was there a need to kill it?" El Rasho sounded sulky.

"Take it ass a warning," Ciabolo told the king. "Obey me and it won't happen to you. If you make another effort to kill me, I will feed you to my little demonss."

"Very well," El Rasho agreed with ill grace. "I will name it Queen – but I will withhold granting it power until you are in complete control."

"Perhapss that iss wisse," Ciabolo agreed. "Even weakened, the wench iss sstubborn and fightss me. But in thiss body I am protected from dragonss magic. In fact I can pull power from plasces that your weak wizard could not."

"You can use dragon magic?" El Rasho asked, suddenly fascinated.

"Yess!" Ciabolo hissed.

"An unexpected advantage," El Rasho's voice grew silkier. "One worth the inconvenience of having to use a female body."

"I have not forgiven you, King. If you think I am weaker in thiss body, you are wrong. It makess me feel young again. My kind all sstart ass femaless and then become neuter or male at the change."

"Well it's leaking blood all over the rugs on the floor," El Rasho spoke with contempt.

A long hiss was the answer to his observation.

"I will go to the old woman!"

Atlantis closed the door and backed off down the tunnel, her mind was reviewing her mental map of the underground passages. Arlen had mentioned one from the chapel and there was a way into it from here but it was narrow. Rather than make her polished stone glow, she drew out the small wizard light her brother, Roman, had made for her. He had assured her that it was not magic, so no wizard would sense it. She needed it now to find the other tunnel, though she was also counting her steps from the King's room and trying to allow for Arlen's longer stride.

There! A shadow on the wall.

Atlantis felt along the wall and then shone the dull light down to see where her feet needed to go.

Yes, it was the passage, but over time, parts had collapsed. If she was able to get through, she would emerge in an abandoned room, well away from El Rasho's attention.

Picking her way with care, Atlantis managed to avoid hitting her head on the low sections, but could not avoid cuts and scrapes, as she had to crawl over some sections of rubble or risk trapping her feet. When she had estimated the distance again, she stopped to search for the door.

The passage had grown worse as she had proceeded along it, and if she could continue further, it would eventually join into the labyrinth beneath the lake behind the citadel. She could not control a shudder at the thought of the frightful creatures that had lived there when Ciabolo and his servants had also occupied parts of it.

The door was not hard to find; a large chunk of rock had smashed it open. There was a hole that she could crawl through without tearing her robe.

The room fit Arlen's description and the thick dust everywhere proved it had not been visited in a long time. Merely walking through the room, past the stone table and benches, raised dust that tickled her nose. The presence of such a room in the citadel was a puzzle. It made her think of the little hill community where Maeven had lived, but there was no time now for that puzzle.

Perhaps there might be something in her Great Grand Sire's journals about Vatarik. He had travelled widely.

Atlantis shook off as much dust from her robes as she could before leaving that room, then walked as quickly as she dared towards the rooms where Maeven had been.

Only when she was close to her destination did she slow and adopt the cowed stance peculiar to the servants here.

The door to the room was open and two male servants were carrying out the unconscious body of El Rasho's wizard. Only his mouth betrayed that he was still alive; he seemed to be babbling noiselessly. Then she noticed the red stain spreading from a knife wound in his side. She slipped into the room, keeping to the walls while she watched.

A big-breasted peasant woman was nursing the new boy prince. The old woman was scrubbing at a red stain on the stones near the door.

"Let me do that, old mother," Atlantis offered, helping the woman to her feet.

"Why did you come back?"

"To help my friend," Atlantis replied quietly.

"It is too late, the Evil One has her."

"Ciabolo?"

"Shh, yes. Rashka refused to let him merge with him and tried to kill him. It didn't work; all he did was force the Evil One out of the wizard's body. He took over your friend when she was still too weak to resist."

The scene, overheard in the King's chamber, now made dreadful sense.

"You should go," the old woman warned.

"I know," Atlantis admitted. "Will the boy be safe?"

The old woman glanced at the baby. "Yes, I swear it. I will let no harm come to him. He is the future of Vatarik."

Atlantis decided to risk a dangerous question. "When Ciabolo merged with the former King, how much freedom did he have?"

The old woman looked shocked, almost afraid. "How did you know about that?"

"I saw him die, but please, answer my question."

"There were times when Malokin was himself – well, human at least, but mostly he was not around. The other was dominant."

"He can't bear bright light, unless he is merged with a human, can he?"

"Yes, again, how did you know?"

"I've had dealings with him before..."

"And lived...?"

"I had help, but he underestimated us. He never thought a woman could best him and he didn't expect a servant to either."

Atlantis felt her talisman grow very hot. Danger! She quickly dropped to her knees and began scrubbing; keeping her head down and her face covered by her hood.

Maeven, or at least her body, strode into the room but it was not her voice that Atlantis heard.

"Woman, what iss wrong with thiss body? It bleedss!"

Atlantis had a very strong desire to laugh.

The old woman answered decisively.

"My Lady, you have just birthed twins. The bleeding is natural. It will ease in a day or two, just like it does for your monthly cycles."

"I want it sstopped. Now!"

"That is not possible. I will ask a servant to bring some rag clouts!"

A roar of annoyance almost deafened Atlantis.

"Woman! I am not the weakling female you sseem to ssee. You know what I am!"

Atlantis risked a look at the old woman – she was standing firm.

"My... Lord, I had not realised... but I can still do nothing. It is a problem with the body you have taken. The inconvenience will be fleeting."

The second roar was more of frustration.

"I want thiss body cleaned up!"

Ciabolo strode towards Atlantis, who had her head down, scrubbing again.

Before she knew what was happening, what felt like a huge burning hand lifted her by her neck until she was off the ground? She was forced to see what held her. At first glance, it looked like Maeven, yet it was not.

Where Maeven was short and slight, the body before her gave the effect of taller, broader creature. It was still dressed in the filmy gown, but the skin under it glowed faintly with purple marks. The eyes were not the blue of her friend, but orange. She needed no more proof of what creature had taken her friend.

Atlantis took the old woman's example; she showed no fear and let her body hang limply. Finally, Ciabolo lowered her back down.

"Lord, lie down. We will tend to your needs," the old woman directed.

Ciabolo scowled but strode across the room. The old woman spoke quietly to Atlantis.

"Come and get some water, soap and cloths."

When they were out of the room, she continued.

"Show no fear, say nothing, and just do as he asks."

Atlantis nodded, still shocked by what had happened to her friend.

When she returned with the water, she tried to avoid looking at the body on the couch, but she was directed to wash it.

The purple marks had faded, and it was almost possible to believe that it was Maeven she was bathing. That was until she glanced across the orange eyes that were watching her with smouldering intensity.

Atlantis felt her hands burn when she touched the skin of the one that she bathed. Then she became aware of the cool breeze blowing through her, cooling her hands and healing the burn on her neck. Her talisman still felt hot against her skin.

In spite of the discomfort of touching the hot skin, Atlantis made sure she was being very gentle. It was partly out of respect for her friend's body but more because she did not wish to anger the creature now dominating it.

It was necessary to remove the blood soaked dress, but as the body cooperated and sat up it was almost as if the controlling mind had gone elsewhere. A voice she recognised spoke to her.

"Go away, 'Lantis, please!"

Atlantis looked at the face she had been avoiding. Light blue eyes, full of anguish looked back at her.

"How can I help you," Atlantis asked quickly.

"You can't, he's too strong" was the tortured reply. "He's lulled just now, by the nearness of your talisman but..."

The blueness of the eyes changed to orange and Atlantis quickly looked away.

"The babe sleeps, old woman!" the peasant nurse spoke in a thick dialect. She had no interest in the one she thought to be the baby's mother.

"The nursery is prepared – take Solokin there."

As the woman carried the baby past, Atlantis heard faintly, "The eighth piece – you have to find it."

Atlantis flicked her eyes across the face of the body beside her. The orange fire was back.

"I wissh for clothes."

The old woman bustled forward with her arms full of richly coloured satin garments and placed them beside Ciabolo. "I have them here, My Lord. Clothes more suited to your importance."

"You there," she ordered, turning to Atlantis. "Take that stuff away and come back with clean water to finish cleaning in here."

Atlantis wasted no time collecting the dirty clothes and linen. She left the room with them and the dirty water. It felt like the orange eyes were watching her every move until she left the room.

She was shaking as she went back towards the servant's area. There was no way she was going to stay any longer. She could do nothing to help her friend at the moment and had plenty of reasons to get back to Thulor as fast as possible.

CHAPTER 52 – Atlantis and Rhovert

Atlantis retraced her steps to the room with the stone table. There she drained the bowl of water into the hidden way and stuffed the linens under rocks. The bowl, being made of clay, was easy to shatter. The pieces were the same colour as the rocks and were soon hidden amongst the rubble.

She drew her knife now and shook the wizard light to make it brighter. As she crawled back over the rubble, she tried to keep her knife in front of her and to listen for sounds other that the ones she was making. Her talisman was still warm about her neck and that, she knew, meant danger was still around her.

A low growl was the only warning she had, and in the low and narrow passage, there was no way to avoid the creature that made it. Instinctively, she drew her knife arm back and lunged.

A shrill scream replaced the growl but her second lunge silenced it.

Atlantis forced herself to crawl past the dead cave hound, in death, its lips had retracted, baring its long, needle-sharp teeth; the tips of which were discoloured by a dark stain. She shuddered, hoping that she would not meet any more of the magic created creatures. She had neither food nor fire to distract them if more scented her out.

Once she was back in the main tunnel, Atlantis wanted to run, but that would make too much noise. Instead, she stifled her fear and walked purposefully towards the tunnel's exit.

She was within a few lengths of the exit when she heard growling behind her. This time she did run – hoping to get out into the bright daylight. Her instincts suggested that the creatures would not want to follow her out there. She kept running until she was at the edge of the trees.

The creatures had stopped, just outside of the tunnel and were sniffing the air cautiously. When they found the scent of their quarry, they began to approach.

"Oh no you don't," Atlantis warned them, backing into the sunlight, though not too far.

The creatures suddenly charged her. She swung her knife, slashing the eyes of the nearest one and preparing to stab the second.

Suddenly, the second creature was flung backwards and the blood crazed one was fleeing back to the tunnels. It did not get there. An arrow flew past her ear and embedded in the hound's throat.

Atlantis swung around, realising that the other hound had an arrow in its neck and that there was a scruffy looking man putting down his bow. Beyond him, two of the king's enforcers were riding up on black horses.

Atlantis threw her knife into some bushes behind her and hoped it was hidden. A servant found to be carrying a weapon was punished with death. In that moment of distraction, the mercenary grabbed her roughly and pushed his mouth onto hers. She tried to struggle free.

"Hold there!" A strong voice called out the command as the two horsemen drew close and stopped.

"What you want?" the mercenary snarled. "This be mine!"

"The wench is a palace servant," the first horseman spoke again. He had not dismounted, though the second one did.

"A runaway," the second added, walking over to the mercenary and his captive. He picked up something from the ground. "And a thief as well. This belongs to no servant. Stand aside, peasant. This servant must be punished and returned to the citadel."

The mercenary stood firm and maintained his grip on the struggling captive.

"How she be punished?" he demanded.

The mounted guard eyed the mercenary.

"With five lashes for being away from its post. With death for carrying a weapon."

"Aw, the knife be mine. I dropped it catching the wench. She don't appreciate a real man. How about you or I give it the five lashes and I take it away to punish further?"

Both guards smiled unpleasantly. The one that was on foot took something from his belt. Before either servant or mercenary could react, he had lashed out with it.

"That get me, ye fools!" the mercenary roared, covering the slight sound that Atlantis could not stifle.

Atlantis was glad for the thick leather vest she had under the black robe. Her back hurt but the lash had not cut her back, though it had cut her arm.

"Too bad, scum! If ye want the wench, ye'll stand firm."

After that, the mercenary watched the lash and moved them both subtly so that only the wench's back was touched. When the fifth lash had been delivered, the wench seemed to faint.

The guard rolled up his whip and remounted his horse.

"The wench be yours! Best take it far away. If we find it with you, we will have to kill you both!"

The two guards watched as the mercenary collected the knife the guard had dropped again and stuck it in his belt. Then they laughed as he tossed the wench on his shoulder and strode off.

"Have fun, she-man!" they laughingly called after him.

"Rhovert, you great lout! You can put me down now," Atlantis ordered her husband. "Thanks for killing those creatures, but no thanks for the rest."

Prince Rhovert of Thulor grinned as he obeyed but sobered before his consort saw his amusement.

"I didn't think you recognised me," he said quickly.

"I didn't at first," she admitted. "I have never seen you look so filthy, but I have also never been so glad to see you."

"Ah, well, the dirt served as a disguise once I had finished a bit of business at the border, and ran into that cheeky Nelsi. It has been a week's hard ride to get here. I'm sorry about back there – I had to trust Leanne was right and you still had your leather vest on. She warned me that those types were out to prove they were better than anyone else."

"I'll forgive you, Prince. Help me out of this robe before those creeps return."

"Dump the robe here. My horse is just up ahead and I grabbed your spare clothes from Leanne. How's your back?"

"Hurting like I'd been trampled by a horse and my sword arm is killing me! I had to leave my boots behind too."

"Can you run?" Rhovert asked, thinking that the guards' advice was of value.

"Try me!" Atlantis challenged, thinking that far from there was an excellent idea.

Atlantis felt better once she was dressed in her usual leather breeches and added the long sleeved jerkin and her spare boots. From a distance, with her hair cut short, she could be mistaken for a boy riding behind an older brother.

What was even better was the little trick Rhovert reminded her of. He told her to hold her talisman, put the other hand over the cut on her arm, and imagine the cut healing. She felt the cool breeze of dragon magic flowing through her and the pain in her arm and in her back faded.

"You met your sisters, then," Atlantis commented.

"Yes, they were heading for the town with the java bushes. Said they had a wet nurse organised."

"Yes," Atlantis agreed. "We'd better get going."

"How did things go? Why didn't Maeven come out with you?" He mounted first, and helped Atlantis up behind him. He saw how her face had gone pale. "What's wrong?"

"Just go."

Rhovert gave the command to his horse to gallop, and hoped the black clad bullies did not change their minds and follow him. After a while, he realised that his consort was shaking, as she clung to his back.

"'Tis? Are you alright?"

"I feel like a traitor, leaving her there!" Atlantis admitted to her soul mate. Her voice was unsteady, but he heard it clearly.

"Tell me about it," Rhovert urged, sure in his mind that he was not going to like what he heard.

Atlantis told him everything that she had seen and heard. From the growing tension in her husband, it was obvious that he was upset. She was clinging to him to stay on the horse, but the contact was bringing her comfort. She who had always prided herself on being self-reliant...

"You could do nothing else," Rhovert sighed. "We'll have to tell Father about this. He won't like it either. That damned Serpent is right – Petulor won't harm him as long as he is in Maeven's body. If he can draw on dragon power through her..."

"He thinks he is doing that – I hope it is just the little amount that Petulor gives her to power the little spells she can do. I'm not sure if he is aware of dragon magic being used around him. His touch burnt me, but at the same time, I felt that healing breeze. At that time, the serpent seemed somewhere else and Maeven was there for a moment. She said being near my talisman lulled him, but it wouldn't last. She also said we had to find the eighth piece."

"Eighth piece of what?" Rhovert asked, thinking aloud.

"The eighth talisman!" Atlantis said impatiently. "Remember when we were trying to build the shield to protect Petulor when she hatched? We had seven pieces and we needed eight."

Rhovert did recall.

"For most of my life and Father's too, we only knew of six pieces. Now we know where that murdering wizard, Tormore found the seventh piece, but where is the one Gamman Mogray's wife had? That must be the one we have to find."

"What do the other pieces do?" Atlantis asked, hoping to distract her mind by the puzzle.

"Leanne and I have the ones for defending, for swordsmanship. Finora and your brother have the ones for magic. Father sees – into the future, I think. Mother's, the one you now have, gave her visions – warned her of dangers that were imminent. Maeven – well, you know what she's good at. Stealth, sneakiness and being as annoying as that dragon!"

"This one didn't give me enough warning to help Maeven."

"You couldn't have done anything at the time," Rhovert reiterated. "And you haven't had it all that long – not like my mother and grandmother. You aren't like them, you don't expect others to act on what you see."

Atlantis snorted with wry amusement. She had never been that sort of female.

"That's not what I meant, wife! Father gave Maeven's to Arlen. He said it had found something of value in him. His nature is nothing like hers. For years, Father tried to find a new bearer for that one of yours – someone like my mother – yet it chose you. It found something of value in you. Maybe it is because you are good at puzzles, or because of your excellent memory, or because you are descended from some ancient wizard or because you are the only woman smart enough to have me."

"Some of that may be true, but none of it helps me to find a way to help Maeven."

"With the dragon's help – we'll find a way," Rhovert said quietly, but he did not feel that confident.

"Let's catch up to your sisters."

"Yes. I told them we'd meet in that town. Then they will travel with us to the border and we will take little Rheanna to Gisella in Declanor."

"Then what?" Atlantis asked. "Then how do we stop all of El Rasho's army pouring into Thulor. Was that business at the border related to part of El Rasho's army?"

Rhovert chuckled. "You heard about that did you?"

"Yes, while I was at the citadel. The servants hear everything, and about that – El Rasho was livid. But you got rid of one, but he has over a dozen more. Surely he will invade soon."

"Let's hope my sister can distract Ciabolo for a while. It seems she isn't going to give up, since she tried to talk to you. We need to get the little one to safety, and report to father. He can see the future, maybe with what we can tell him he will see one where we do prevail. He has called in scholars of history and with the dragon scholars coming to help him he may find the key to winning. Until then, we do what we can do to delay the invasion."

It wasn't the assurance she wanted, but he was right. And if they could get Maeven rid of the Serpent, maybe she would know his weaknesses.

They could not let Ciabolo win.

End of Maeven – Dragon Agent

The story continues in Part 3
Maeven – Dragon Champion

Other Novels by Margaret Gregory

WANDA: FROM BAD TO WORSE

If she was going to die young, like her mother, Gwen Willard was determined to die rich and she had very few years to do it. Her first step was to leave home. She met Hooch, who taught her some exciting and illegal skills. She was the Draco's lucky mascot until she came to the attention of the police. Then her uncanny knack for predicting trouble, warned her to flee to the city and change her name.

Life wasn't easy. She was 15, had little money and no regular job, but her new skills came in handy. Then she crossed the path of an evil and unscrupulous man and she didn't want him to have his way.

WANDA: CHOOSING CRIME

Wanda was free. She was never going back to jail. But she was homeless, almost penniless and Harrison Franklin had a long and vengeful memory.

Jim Phillips had a long memory too, and Wanda had saved his life. Could he save her from Franklin?

WANDA: RISKING LIFE TO LIVE

The euphoria of successful heists were what kept Wanda Dean alive. At 23, she was crime boss Harrison Franklin's top agent – well paid for absolute obedience. That's all that mattered. Until she met Mike Johnston and her boss ordered him killed. For that, the Franklins were going to pay. In Risking Life to Live, justice conflicts with loyalty and the penalty for betrayal is death.

WANDA: A NEW LIFE - HIDDEN SECRETS

Even before beginning as a covert agent for the US Government, Wanda is abducted by a foreign operative. After being rescued, there are signs that she had been subjected to hypnosis. With an important government gathering imminent, her handler must ensure she is not a security risk.

Can Wanda's psychic extra senses help her recognize and resist the implanted commands and clear her for secret work?

WANDA: A NEW LIFE - FIRST MISSION
On her first covert mission for the US Government, Wanda calls on the skills that made her a skilled thief to convince a revolutionary general that she's an ideal recruit. When her team mates' covers are blown, it is up to her to ensure that two missing scientists and confidential Government documents are not smuggled out of the US.

WANDA: FULL CIRCLE
Three generations after the alien Kumatan left Earth, their own world is suffering from alien invaders. In desperate hope, one returns to Earth seeking help - little knowing they had left one of their own behind. Wanda, a child of the third generation, answers the call.

ERIN: THE FORCING OF WISDOM
For years, Erin has used the intricacies of cyberspace to banish unwanted emotions. Others call what she does hacking, and her manipulations criminal, but now her skill was exceptional - in, out, traceless. She was wrong. Someone betrayed her.
Travis has dangerous plans. He needs an electronics expert – one he can coerce through fear. Erin was perfect.
With the inescapable threat of prison looming, Erin accepts his offer of sanctuary. When she realises his intentions, she is in too deep. But the terrifying of innocents is unforgivable. She cannot walk away. She is an empath and shares their distress. She has to help them, even if it means prison, and insanity...

ERIN: THE CALL
(including ELISABETH AND TANYA: BLOOD CALLS TO BLOOD.
Elisabeth's sister, Wanda, had been missing for half a year. Multiple authorities had found no trace of her, or her two colleagues. Yet she knew her sister was still alive and had answered a call for help from an alien who had once lived on Earth. Along with her newly found cousin Tanya, she has started to sense things from her missing sister. Enough to know that she is in dire trouble, but not enough to help her.
While looking for traces of the aliens, Elisabeth makes some unexpected discoveries about her family. Yet even with the help of a second newly discovered cousin, she fears she is not strong enough to help her sister and the others to return.

ERIN: THE CALL
Convicted cyber-criminal, Erin Mason, is startled into awareness
in an unfamiliar place, with no memory of escaping and only vague
memories of getting there. Voices in her head were urging her to go
west, and they were getting more urgent.
After a chance meeting with covert agent, Jim Phillips, when she helped
save his mission, he realised that she might be the key to another, more
personal quest – to find three missing state department agents.
All he must do is keep Erin safe, and hide her from an intense police
search, until he can introduce her to cousins she was unaware of.
However her uncontrolled psychic gifts conflict with a logical mind
that prefers the ordered intricacies of computers and electronics.
She only wants to shut out the voices and the madness she sees
looming. Can Phillips convince her to help him, before the forces of
the law find her?

THE SERPENT'S SHADOW - Three books in one.
Janna consorts with terrorists to protect her friend Prince Ali from
assassins.
Former cyber-criminal, Erin, becomes part of the merchandise of
stolen tech secrets.
Jim Phillip's team is sent to neutralise the leader of the terrorist
Cobra Sect.

ROYAL FAVOUR
A quick in-out investigation by US State Department agent, Wanda
Martin, is compromised when she is caught after an illicit survey of
an ultra-private club. When she should have been gone, team leader
Jim Phillips, must organise medical help for her serious wounds as
well as adapting his plans to thwart a traitor wishing to turn a tiny
European Kingdom into a haven for international crooks.

FOREIGN AGENT - THIEF
When US Trade Consul, Allan Wexford, and his daughter go missing,
Wanda Martin flies to Austria to find them. Operating on her own,
using old and new skills, she begins to unobtrusively unravel Wexford's
movements. In spite of all her skill, she becomes a person of interest
to both the police and a group of violent criminals, and she is set up
to take the fall for a heinous crime.

PRISONER - SPY
On remand for murders she didn't commit and a robbery she never intended to do, Wanda Martin tries to keep from thinking of the inevitable outcome. Yet it is soon apparent that the Russian crime family, whose plans she wrecked, want revenge, and even in prison she isn't safe.

KORVU: THE BEGINNING
The prequel to The Wild One
Jai Ansuni was the first female Atapi sorcerer for thousands of years, but she dare not reveal it. However, when tribal sorcerer, Stacion Ansuni escalates the enmity between Atapi and Kumatan to an ominous level. Jai and her womb mate, Con, try to mitigate his atrocities but can two young Atapi, not even a score of years old, win against the powerful sorcerer?

THE WILD ONE
Sixteen year old Jai Cassidy thought she was finally free of her family until she is discovered by her other relatives...the ones that aren't human. Jai uses her natural perversity and cunning to escape their control, but catapults herself into the middle of a deadly feud between two alien races.

ATAPI SORCERESS - The sequel to The Wild One
Jai Cassidy is beginning her mission of reversing the decline of the non-humanoid Atapi. As a sorceress and an Atapi-Human hybrid, she is vehemently disliked by the male Atapi sorcerers and the humanoid rulers of Korvu. Her task is complicated by the treachery of a group of alien engineers, who are inciting insurrection and harsh reprisals.

THE TYMOREAN TRUST BOOK 1 - POWER RISING
The Tymorean Trust - When peace rules Tymorea - Peace reigns in the universe.
Chosen to be the Advocates of the mystical and incorporeal Guardians of Peace, twins Tymos and Kryslie must first learn to control and use the power rising in them - or it will destroy them.
On Tymorea, only the ruling Triumvirate Governors are powerful enough to guide the strong-willed alien-bred twins until they have mastered their power.

THE TYMOREAN TRUST BOOK 2 - GREAT ONES
The peace of the Guardian Planet, Tymorea, is in deadly peril. War there will create ripples of unrest and destruction throughout the settled universe. Tymos and Kryslie, still adolescents, have barely mastered their power and Llaimos is still less than a year old, but they are the three chosen to be Advocates of the mystical Guardians of Peace, to safeguard the Tymorean Trust.

THE TYMOREAN TRUST BOOK 3 - RETURN TO EARTH
Even before the war on Tymorea, the Elders foresaw that Great Ones Tymos and Kryslie would have an imperative mission on Earth.
But as the Tymoreans prepare to build an Earthbase to support them, they discover that specifications for two vital protective shields are missing. Now, nearly a century later, Tymos and Kryslie must find his work and build the generator before the base is found.

THE TYMOREAN TRUST BOOK 4 - EARTH MISSION
Just before their graduation from the prestigious WSRA Washington University, Tymos and Kryslie Ward deliberately disappear.
The Great Ones have foreseen the capture and death of the new Tymorean missionaries and discovered that the leader of the Eastern Imperium plans to undermine the United World Nations.
Tymos and Kryslie must protect their kin and prevent a potentially devastating world war.

THE TYMOREAN TRUST BOOK 5 – ALIEN CONTACT
Tymos and Kryslie Ward, hide their Tymorean intelligence and abilities while working as low ranked technicians at the WSRA's lunar base. When an alien ship arrives at Lunar One, pursued by a powerful enemy who will stop at nothing to get what he wants, only the two Tymorean Great Ones have the knowledge and abilities to overcome him, but to do so they must risk their sanity, and their souls.

THE TYMOREAN TRUST BOOK 6 – INVASION
Great Ones Tymos and Kryslie go to rescue the crew of Earth's first deep space mission – and discover that Ciriot space pirates have discovered Earth's location. When the Ciriot invade in force, the Great Ones reveal themselves so that Earth can gain vital help. However, Kryslie becomes the victim of Ciriot, who want to control her mind and make her betray the people of Earth.

TRICKS
Tom and Jo Dwyer had a reputation for playing tricks – and getting detention. They didn't seem to care about that, so long as they made their class laugh. That was until someone began to turn their tricks against them, and it was no longer funny.

THE MAGPIE'S DAUGHTER
Andy is almost 18 and free of her brother. Outwardly honest, Martin was really a crook, but she didn't dare prove it. When she runs away, Martin comes after her. Owing money, he wants her inheritance. What can Andy do when his enemies find her?

THE CHANCE TO BE ME
Abandoned by her relatives on the brink of the summer holidays, orphan Brenda Jacobs finds herself travelling to a strange town to stay with strangers. The thought that it might prove to be a more enjoyable time than she expected, is confused by finding the last person she wanted to see, travelling on the same train. And again when he offers to let her join with his friends for the summer. But people she's never met start to cause her trouble, and the machinations of her relatives make her future seem bleak. Just when her spirits are lowest, an unexpected discovery changes her future completely.

www.ingramcontent.com/pod-product-compliance
Lightning Source LLC
Chambersburg PA
CBHW072007180726
48291CB00001BA/166